THE BLACK BOY

by

Michael Dixon Whitehead Balls

Illustrated by John Durham

Edited by Lucie Young

ISBN 978-1-5272119-3-3

DEDICATION

This book is dedicated to the Memory of
It's Author

Michael D W Balls
(the BRAVEST OF MEN!)

written whilst suffering from a terminal illness in 2005

ALSO

To Sue his beloved wife

With love from all of his family xx

Published 2017

CONTENTS

CONTENTS (continued)

THE BLACK BOY

CHAPTER ONE

In the first half of the eighteenth century, the red and black built house which was to become '*The Black Boy Alehouse*', was typical of the period. Constructed towards the reign of Queen Anne at the beginning of the Georgian era, it was built as a rectangular two-storey building with a hipped tiled roof, and although larger, it was very similar in appearance to the pair of cottages, built at the same time, which stood beside it. The two buildings were separated by a narrow cart-way between, which led to the stable area to the rear of the cottages. Behind the stables were the cottage gardens, where the occupants grew vegetables and kept a few chickens. Built, as they were on sloping, well-drained gravel soil, there were dry cellars beneath each of these buildings and these were used to store a variety of goods, foodstuffs and materials, which needed to be kept away from the damp. From the outside, the existence of these cellars was not apparent as it simply looked as though the extra depth below the wall of *The Black Boy* and that beneath the front doors of the cottages was simply there to accommodate the variance in ground levels. Few people therefore knew of their existence.

The Horne family had long resided in the area and the name was well known. John Horne had made both his name and his living from the manufacture of bricks and tiles, to the extent that within his lifetime, the tiny hamlet on the lower slopes of the hill upon which the larger village of Danbury stood, was to be named after him. When he started his business in the second quarter of the eighteenth century, he had lived in the first of the cottages beside *The Black Boy* and had then bought it and its neighbour before moving on to a larger house further down the common and two families of his workers now lived in what had originally been named *Horne Row*, albeit two cottages hardly constituted a row! A bit pretentious but perhaps he had intended to build more there. Instead of that he built a row of cottages on the eastern edge of the common to house his ever growing work force. These cottages originally took the name *Horne Row* and it was the connection of both sets of cottages which gave the hamlet its name of *Horne Row*. Later the row became known as *Kiln Cottages* for obvious reasons, being built, as they were immediately beside the kilns where John Horne's workers lived and worked.

John Horne was in the most a good employer and his workers' income of nearly seven shillings a week was marginally between that of the five, to six shillings of the local farm workers, and so they jealously guarded their jobs, particularly as while they worked for John Horne, they only paid six pence per week for their accommodation. Lose your job and you and your family would be turned out of your house and more likely end up as so many families did – destined for the workhouse. However good an employer John Horne might have been, it was a hard-cruel world with little room for sentimentality.

John had two sons, John Junior, the eldest, who ran the brick and tile business with his father and William the younger brother by some four years, who found, that whilst working for his father, he was little better than one of his labourers. There was no room for the two brothers in the business and John senior hardly seemed to notice his younger son, making it abundantly clear that it was his brother John who would, as the eldest, take over the business on his father's death. By the time William was in his early twenties he knew that he had to move on, so in 1775 he went to his father with a proposition.

He would not enter into a dispute with his brother over the owner-ship and the running of the business, if his father would lend him fifty guineas. This was a colossal sum of money, but William explained to his father what he wanted it for – he wanted to buy *The Black Boy Alehouse*, evicting the most recent string of previous leases, and buy the first of the stocks of drink and food needed to stock the place. William was no fool and knew that he would benefit from his father's generosity to his workers, as they would come to his – the only alehouse on that side of the hill and less than two hundred yards from their cottages. There they would spend their surplus money buying his beer. His father being a canny business man himself agreed and loaned him the money.

He moved in late summer of that year and shortly afterwards during a harsh winter that followed, his father died. On his death bed he released

William from his debt and so the alehouse was now his to run without fear of the future.

The following year William married Annie Rowlings, the daughter of an oyster-dredger from West Mersea. They had met during one of William's many trips to do business with her father and they had married in September 1776. Matthew Rowlings did not warn his future son-in-law of his daughter's sharp tongue and vile temper, so William went into marriage believing his red headed bride to be as sweet as he had always found her to be. It was not long before he discovered the true nature of his wife, by which time it was of course too late!

Matthew Rowlings ostensibly made his living as an oyster-dredger at West Mersea from where his boat plied across the estuary and up to the Blackwater at Maldon, from where the oysters were transported to the ready markets of Chelmsford, Brentwood and even as far as London. In order to supplement his income from this trade, Matthew, like so many of those who made a living from the sea, were not averse to a bit of smuggling on the side, which because of the huge taxes levied on up to two thousand separate items, ranging from tea to tallow candles, was a very lucrative business to be in. There was little defense against this trade by the Revenue enforcers as the shallow drafted boats, like Matthew's could negotiate the creeks and inlets on the Blackwater with ease. He would meet a smuggler's cutter on the mouth of the estuary, or, perhaps out in the Wallet, a deep-water channel there, and transferring the smuggled goods into his dredger, carry them ashore to one of the numerous creeks off of the main river, offload to a waiting pack of animals and carts and then resume his trip to Maldon with his legitimate cargo of oysters.

There was little danger of being apprehended though in these early days, as the Revenue yawl, "Queen" was the only anti-smuggling vessel on the river, she was kept mostly at anchor in Maldon for the exclusive use of the "Tide Surveyor" and was easily spotted as she slipped down the tide and the news of her departure would rapidly be broadcast amongst those who needed to know. From the Revenue Men's point of view, even if they had wind of a shipment, there were dozens of creeks and inlets off the Blackwater to which it might be landed, so it was an almost impossible task.

The Maldon Collector of Customs had a pretty thin time as hundreds of smugglers' boats slipped in and out of the Blackwater unmolested. In

William's early days at *The Black Boy* he and his customers benefited from what had become an accepted free trade. Landowners, the clergy, the gentry, and even the judiciary were happy to turn a blind eye and even participate in the trade and the Revenue riders, of which there were a handful only at a time, paid scant attention to an insignificant alehouse. Annie's father Matthew was the main source of this benefit and he and William carried on a brisk business with carts delivering in the early hours, shipments of Gin, brandy, tea, tobacco and snuff.

William and Annie had no children, which was hardly surprising, when after their first year of marriage, they had since rarely shared the same bed. This was the cause of even more sourness in Annie and resentment of all around her. From William's part, as he often pointed out to her during their frequent quarrels, he was the one who made the decisions and she was merely his wife and a servant to the alehouse. If he ever wanted to throw her out (if indeed he were to find the courage!) he would do so without hesitation. She believed this event was unlikely to occur, not just because William was in the main a kind man, or in her opinion, a soft one, but also because of the friendship he had with her father. She knew that he was unlikely to wish to sour this and so she made no attempt to mend her ways.

Helping Annie was little Jane, who had been just thirteen years old when she first came to work at *The Black Boy*. She was from one of the largest and poorest farm worker's families from Home Farm towards Sandon village. She had two older sisters who worked as scullery maids at the big house, Woodhill, a mile down the road towards Sandon and Jane had been waiting her turn, in the hope at the age of fourteen, she might also get a similar job to her sisters, either at Woodhill, or perhaps one of the other larger houses locally. In the meantime, she washed tankards and trenchers, served at the tables and suffered the mostly good natured banter from the customers and the constant nagging tongue and heavy hand of her employer's wife; all of this for one shilling a week! Jane too had red hair like her mistress, but her temper was far less fiery. She was a thoughtful gentle girl, one who knew her place, but was tough enough to accept and endure what life threw at her. Three years had passed and she was still washing tankards and trenchers at *The Black Boy*. Her sisters were still at Woodhill and there were no vacancies, either there, or elsewhere.

Jane was now a comely girl of seventeen and the banter from the tables which she served had now become of a more serious nature.

Most nights, *The Black Boy's* front room, which served to accommodate his customers, was well filled with not only his brother's workers, but also farm labourers from the nearby farms. *Paternoster Farm* and *Ludgores Farm*, the two nearest, were on the south facing slopes of the hill and extended from the common to the brook at the foot of the hill. Their names had been derived from their earlier association with the Priory, which stood on the other side of the valley at *Bicknacre*, where they grew the vines, which produced the grapes to manufacture sacramental wines for the church and of course whatever surplus there was went to the priory cellars for the monks themselves! For almost ten years, the situation at the alehouse remained unchanged, Will now thirty-two years old, had grown bored and found less in life to either excite, or, please him. The only excitement, and perhaps purpose in his life had been the association with "Free Trading", in which he had been dabbling, but with recent moves by the Prime Minister, William Pitt, in an attempt to halt smuggling by reducing the duty on tea from a staggering 127% to 12.5%, William felt that it was only a matter of time before duty on many other commodities would likewise be reduced. Annie, of course, had become even more bad tempered and bitter than she had been before, although the change had been gradual over the years and Will had hardly noticed it.

That Saturday evening *The Black Boy's* parlour was full as usual for the last and the busiest day of the working week. Although, many of its patrons had to work on the Sabbath, tending flocks and cows, which had to be milked, most including the clay workers, rested on a Sunday, going to church for the matins and evensong. Beyond this, the rest of the day was theirs, so on a Saturday night there was no hurry to go home to sleep before another early start and hard day's labour. By 9.00pm that evening the alehouse was in full swing, beer sold by the pint, or, quart tankard at a penny a pint, was flowing and the drinkers had got to that stage which was the fine line between singing and brawling. Usually at this point of the evening, William Horne would serve his better customers, that is the clay workers to whom he owed family loyalty and a recognition that they were the ones with the most money to spend; tuppence worth of Geneva, however, this evening was different.

"I don't know what it is that's made you forget our gin Will, you old miser!" called a good-humoured voice from one of the rough hewn trestle tables around which sat seven or eight of the clay workers on long benches.

"Yes, Will, when are we going to get our penneth of Gin as always on a Saturday night?"

Those around the table took up the cry and began banging their tankards on the table. A few of the other tile and brick makers scattered about the room joined in, but noticeably the farm workers together with the few itinerant tinkers and gypsies who were currently camped on the common, started to grumble and the grumbling turned to angry exchanges between the two sets of drinkers. Those of John Horne's men, which had been seated elsewhere around the room, now rose and joined their fellowes around the first table. Will, seeing how the mood was changing, stood with his back to the door to the pot-room; ready to make a swift escape through it, should things become more serious, because although he was a large man and not one to avoid a fight when necessary, he was aware that it was always better to come in from the side rather than stand between two warring sides! He then did the only thing possible to allay a certain fight between the two factions. "Alright," he called above the noise, which eventually abated sufficiently for him to he heard "Alright, I'll give you all, every man here, whether clay digger, puggler, kilnman, cartman or farmer, even you damn tinkers to who I owe nothing as you ain't never been regular customers here, two penneth of gin."

He waited for the grumbled applause to die down before he walked to the table at which sat the man who had first spoken out for the remainder of his colleagues. Leaning low so that no-one at any of the other tables could hear him, he said in a quiet angry voice, "you Sam Rowe should know better than to shout out for something that I have always given as a gift from me as a bond between you, John Horne's men and myself at this alehouse, particularly as you also are my neighbour. You work for John, live in one of his houses and in the old days you and me worked together." Turning to the second man who had spoken out - "and the same goes for you John Laytham." Standing up again he said more loudly for the rest of the room to hear, "Now listen up to what I have to say to you all." Moving back to the door of the pot-room he directed Annie and Jane to serve everyone present with a quarter of Gin.

Jane scuttled away immediately to do as she was bid, while Annie stood her ground, scowling at her husband.

"What did you have to do that for," she spat at Will, "fair enough for Sam Rowe and his lot, but not for the likes of tinkers and the like."

"What do you think might have happened if I had refused them? You are not blessed with much sense are you woman? A few penneth of gin is better than me getting my head and house broken by this lot. Now you follow young Jane and do as I tell you, or I'll take a stick to you."

Annie glared at him and looked for a moment as if she was about to argue further, however, with a shrug she grudgingly went into the pot-room and re-appeared with hands full of tankards of gin. When every man had been served and had settled down to drink his portion, Will turned to the assembled and now relatively quiet company.

THE BLACK BOY

CHAPTER TWO

"Enjoy your free gin boys, because it's likely to be your last, and before you start ranting and raving you had best hear why." Silence had momentarily descended on the room and Will took advantage of it. "To keep *The Black Boy* running as a legitimate alehouse, I have now got to abide by the law. Up until now everyone I know, even those up at the big house have had his little extra and nobody seemed to mind, but now things are different. Two years ago in '83 a man called Pitt in London took off most of the duty on tea, I know that this don't mean much to you all here, but it does to the smugglers."

"We don't know about that, but I do know about this man Pitt, got the same first name as you Will?" It was John Laytham speaking; he went on, "but why do smugglers lay so much store by it? there's more than just tea being smuggled isn't there? Tell us that Will, and why does it affect you and the rest of us!"

"I'll tell you why John, because suddenly much of their profits have been lost, what do all the gentry….. and the gin and tea shops want? Tea!…. and there was more profit in tea than anything else. Now there isn't any money to be made in that particular commodity, the smugglers have got to look for something else. There's fewer boats coming in now and until they find a profitable alternative to tea, then getting the goods to make it pay will be more difficult….Oh, they'll find an answer, that's certain but the penalties get heavier day by day and the money that they can make on other goods isn't like what it was before on tea, top that, fifty years ago the worst a man caught for smuggling could suffer was to be pressed for a spell in Farmer George's navy, not a bad life really for a seafaring man who's spent his life braving the worst that the sea and storm can throw at him; and then it was transportation to the colonies, on the other side of the world, with no chance of ever seeing your family again. Now, not only do these brave men who bring the goods over the seas, risk their lives daily in the normal pursuit if their trade, but now with this war with France, they've run the gauntlet of both English and French ships-o-war, on top of that they risk being giblet-bait if caught by the Revenue Men. What you should know too is that anybody caught six miles off the coast and suspected as a smuggler, can also end up with a stretched neck … if he gets as far as the magistrate that is. So now you know why there isn't going to be anymore grog and anyone who wants it, has to pay the going price as laid down by the law of this land. I got Revenue riders calling here on a regular basis now, sometimes once a fortnight, the first for many a month and they always have a good nose round, so I can't have spirits and the like that don't have the king's stamp on it.

Will looked around the room, now thick with the tobacco smoke from twenty or so clay pipes.

"Does that mean that you won't be selling bacca no more?" asked one of the labourers from Parternoster Farm.

"No, it don't, I've never sold tobacco at anything but the proper price and so you'll still get it here at your usual rate Old Wilf, don't you worry your old head about that, you'll not see no difference in the price."

Old Wilf, who had carried that name since being comparatively young, was a man in indeterminate age with his weather-beaten face, his pure white beard cut like a biblical prophet and his broad, but hunched shoulders, he could have still been in his fifties, but was more likely to have been passed sixty. When he stood up, he could be seen to be stooped like so many of his fellow agricultural workers from ditching and hedging in all weathers, with little more protection from wind, rain, sleet and snow than an old sack over his head with one bottom corner turned in to form a hood, another across his back, perhaps yet another around his waist as an apron.

He winced from sitting too long as he dragged himself to his feet and with a wave of gnarled hand, swollen from many winters of chopping ice covered turnips and mangols, went out of the parlour door, down the steps, unhitched the reins of the horse, which had stood patiently outside awaiting his return, and climbed onto the tumbril, which he had brought with him along with his eighteen-year-old mate, James Towns, up the lane from Paternoster. The horse looked round enquiringly at the cart's occupant.

"You wait horse, I'll tell you when", one of the perks of the job was the use of the horse and cart, which as the senior horseman at the farm, was Wilf's responsibility whenever the men went to *The Black Boy*. The farmer worked on the principle that at least the horse would find its way home even if its passengers were incapable of doing so after an evening's drinking. There were very few other perks, the only one which old Wilf could, or, would ever recall was the beer, which Farmer Jennings laid on both at ploughing and at harvest time. A gallon of beer a day was allowed per ploughman. The flagon was placed in the center of the field to be ploughed and each time the ploughman and his horse came level with it he would take a draught from it. Ploughing started at first light and ended when it was too dark to see the furrow. Long before this, the daily flagon would be empty! The beer at harvest time was given to all of the workers, including milkmaids and the domestics, who worked in the farmhouse and also to the casual workers who camped on the common and for payments per-acre cut and sheaved the corn. The men worked in line scything rhythmically and moving gradually through the field. Behind then their women folk and older children, bundled the cut corn and tied it in sheaves with loosely twisted strands of straw.

The alehouse door opened, sending a yellow light from the room behind flooding down the steps and then closed behind James Towns, who climbed up on to the tumbril beside Wilf. "What do you reckon of that then old Wilf?" "What do I reckon of what?"

"This here smuggling lark."

"If you was to listen to what Will had to say, young Jim, you wouldn't ask that. As far as I can see, it's dead and gone. The way I looks at it, if like Will say that the rich folk what to drink all this tea, don't have to buy from smugglers no more, then the best part of this business be finished, and so they'll give it up." Old Wilf shook the horse's reins and clicked his tongue. The horse moved off in the direction of the lane leading to Paternoster Farm.

There was silence in the cart, broken only by the crunching of the horse's hooves and the iron rimmed wheels on the gravel road. Every so often one of the wheels dropped with a crash into an unfilled pothole and the cart lurched. Whenever this happened, Wilf growled at his horse.

"You silly old bugger, you could see it coming and you never even tried to miss it."

"You don't really think that do you? I mean, as they'll give up smuggling?" Without waiting for a reply James went on. "Have you ever given thought to smuggling yourself Old Wilf?" Jim peered at his older companion in the dark, unable to clearly see his face. The reply was a long time coming and they were nearing the farm entrance before Wilf spoke.

"Near on forty years ago, between '45 and '51, I drove a cart from *Mayland* to *Baddow* every second night when the tide was full at *Mayland Creek*. I was a young man then Jim, just twenty years old, about your age, when I first did it. I was with seven, or, eight other carts and a dozen or more pack horses. We loaded with the goods off the board, and drove for all to see, never caring who did see, all the way to Baddow, time after time. I always carried a load of grog, brandy and gin in harf-anker tubs. I could get upwards of sixty such on my old cart, that's close on two hundred and seventy gallons boy and weighed close to a ton and a quarter, and that old horse of mine pulled the load all the way, even up the great hill at *Purleigh*." Wilf paused as he stared into that space from the past and at the cottages in which the workers lived were beyond the farmhouse and the stables were opposite. They drew up in front of the stables and backed the tumbril under cover of the cart lodge beside them. Unhitching the horse, Old Wilf led her to his stable making sure that she had both hay and water for the night and closed the door. Outside, waited an eager young James. "So, you were a smuggler then?" he grinned at Wilf in the dark.

"So, if I was to say that I want to do smuggling in my spare time, you wouldn't have anything to say against it?"

"All I'd say boy is there's lots more risk in it now as there was when I were a lad, there's more revenue officers than before, there is folks that would tell on you and you would never know his name, even when you were swinging from the gallows. No, I do not give you my blessing, but I know what I did and why I did it and I don't suppose it'll make no mind to you anyway. If you are set on it you'll do it whatever I say, but I never want a word from you about it and if I ever hear from another I'll tell him he's a fool an then I'll tell you boy, you is also a fool for letting it be known." Wilf turned on his heel and without another word walked slightly unsteadily over to his cottage and without a backward glance through the door closing it behind him.

For a few moments, Jim Towns stood and watched his friend disappear into his cottage, before going to his own, where he shared a room and a bed with his three younger brothers. Tomorrow at sunup, which on an early November morning as tomorrow, would be in a little under six hours away, he'd ask Wilf how come he gave up the smuggling, which he had obviously enjoyed and profited from. The other thing he would do would be to go the *The Black Boy* and have a quiet word with Will. As silently as he could he slipped through the door of the cottage and crept up the ladder, which led to the loft, the sleeping quarters for the four boys. In bed he remembered that the next day was Sunday and unless he was able to get Wilf on his own he would not be able to speak to him, neither would he see Will, as *The Black Boy* was closed for the Sabbath.

Back at the alehouse, the landlord, at the table now occupied by five of his brother's workers - Samuel Rowe and John Laytham were there with three younger men in their early twenties, Joshua Roote and his younger brother Daniel and David Archer. The rest of the room was now empty, the remainder of the company having departed soon after finishing their free gin.

"We will have to talk some more about this." Sam was saying, "but, you keep it well under your hat, as I am not into idle talk and what I say is the truth." Around him his fellow workers nodded in agreement.

"So, do you all agree with Sam then?" Will asked unnecessarily. Again, the five nodded. "Any road, we will talk again when it's a quiet night here, but I want your sworn oaths that you won't gab to another soul about this, now, or, ever."

"You have it Will, no mistake" answered Sam.

Will got up from the table and disappeared through to the taproom door on the far side of the room. Moments later he returned holding in his hand a leather bound, well thumbed book, which he placed on the table before them.

"You'll understand me wanting it a bit more certain, I want you all to swear it on this here Good Book, saying "I swear by Almighty God that what we have talked of this night, I won't tell another living soul." He looked around the table and was about to push the bible towards Sam, he reached across the table and taking it in his hand he repeated Will's words. "Alright Will? It is best this way, of course you will be swearing your oath as well, won't you?" he passed the book to his neighbour John Laytham without waiting for Will's answer. John, who after swearing passed it to the three younger men who eagerly swore in turn. The last to swear was the younger Roote brother and he had to do it twice before everyone was satisfied. He then passed the bible across the table to Will who had not yet answered Sam's question.

"This here oath is a bit difficult for me to swear boys…" he started looking carefully at the puzzled faces around him before he went on. "You see, if we do what we have been planning, then I have got to find out a bit from a man who, in the past had a lot to do with my supplies. I am not mentioning any names, but this man will be our help getting on the right path. The one what we are choosing to follow if we do follow it that is!" His audience were listening keenly to his words, but there were scowls amongst them, which suggested disagreement.

"If we have sworn to the oath, then so must you Will," said John, "I don't know, nor, much care about this man who'll aid us, but I am sure that we can make out on our own, why do we need another?"

"You have not done a lot of thinking yet John Laytham?" replied Will. "Do you think that we can just go and find a boat coming in by just waiting on the edge of the creek down on the marshes? Oh, yes it is right enough that we can put the word about as to us seeking supplies of this nature, but how long before the word gets round to the Riding Officers and they fall on us one night as soon as we get going on our plans, or maybe a gang of ruffians over *Tiptree* lie in wait and slit your throats!?" He glared at John.

"Do you know that you can't trust every man you speak to? Course you don't and remember this, there is few born that don't want a reward from the revenue men, maybe they also want revenge for some past folly…. Well the man I'm talking of I know as I can trust with my life and no mistake, and he's the only one that I trust to make a delivery on a regular basis. So, I'll give you my oath, but only after I've spoken to this man. I want you to remember another thing all of you, that it is I who will be doing the trading and dealing and any losses will be on my shoulders! Also the first door the excise men will come knocking on will be mine!, So I call the tune alright?"

John started to say something, but then thought better of it, and it was Sam who spoke instead.

"Alright Will counting for the fact as you know more about this here business than the rest of us, I reckon that you will go along with you." Turning his head to look at each man at the table, he asked, "what say you boys?" They all nodded in agreement. It was time to be going, it was long past midnight and there was little more to discuss.

"By all that is holy it has been a long night and I'm ready for my bed," said Joshua clambering to his feet. "Come on Dan, let's be going due to us still being here after sun up."

His brother and David Archer rose to their feet and the three made their way to the door followed close behind by Sam and John. As the five of them appeared in the light, which the lantern inside threw through the open doorway, a dim figure that had until then been crouched listening on the top step outside the door, dropped down beside the steps concealed itself in the gloom there, melted deeper into the shadows thrown by the ivy which clung to the wall of the building.

Will watched them all go down the steps, closed the door behind him and walking over to the fireplace, stood for a moment before the fire, which still smouldered in the hearth. He kicked the end of a half-burnt log, pushing it back into the fire where after a few moments, it crackled into a weak flame throwing a flickering light around the parlour. He sighed and turning made his way to the back of the building where he had a bed, the one he chose to occupy in preference to sharing the one with his wife. On the morrow he would arrange to contact his father-in-law, Matthew Rowlings at *West Mersea* and find out the lie of the land.

Outside *The Black Boy*, the gypsy Reuben Belbin, who had been in the bar earlier, had heard all that Will had to say, through the cracks in the bar door, he had eavesdropped on all that had since passed between Will and his five companions. Earlier he had followed the other customers out, but he had seen that whilst everyone else had left the alehouse, these five men remained behind and appeared to be special friends with the landlord. His natural inquisitiveness therefore had been aroused and he had remained outside the door when all the others had gone. What he had now heard had further raised his interest.

He watched Sam Rowe say goodnight to his companions and make his way round the corner of the alehouse, passing close to where he was hidden, cross the space to the house next door and disappeared inside. The other four walked across the common towards the kilns, passing close by Reuben's own caravan. Once out of sight, he left his concealment and stealthily moved away, returning to his van by a round-about route, coming up to it from down the hill to the south as though he had been on other business that night. On the morn, he would set off early for *Tiptree Heath*, where he had been heading the day before when he had stopped for the night on *Horne Row Common*. There were those there who would be interested in and could profit from what he had learned that evening at *The Black Boy* and he, Reuben Belbin, would make sure that some of that profit would come his way.

THE BLACK BOY

CHAPTER THREE

The following Monday morning James rose early before first light. He had been in bed but a few short hours and then had not slept well. Although, he should be used to it, as he had spent most of his life sharing a bed, the kicking feet of his brothers at the other end of the bed where they top-to-tail, had disturbed and irritated him and he had spent the night angrily pushing those feet away, to the sleepily grumbled annoyance of the other three boys, James slept at one end and the other end was occupied by Simon, sixteen and Matthew 10.

When they had been small they never had a problem as their feet reached only the middle of the bed, but now that they had grown and both James and Simon were strapping young men, things were different.

"Do keep your feet to yourself, Simon. I know it's you that is kicking me, I'd know those hoofs anywhere, even without the smell. Now lie still, or devil knows I'll throw you down the stairs!"

"And what about you boy, your feet also are in my face," Simon pushed his brother's feet away after a few more grumble comments all became quiet again. James still could not sleep and lay awake in the dark with his thoughts of what he had heard Old Wilf say two nights before.

If only he could find an entry into the smuggling business, then he too might soon be driving a cart full of contraband from the Blackwater marshes, through the villages and hamlets on the way to maybe *Chelmsford*, with folk peering from behind darkened windows, not daring to show a light as the smuggler's carts and horses went by.

He had all of the Sunday to think about it and during the vicar's sermon, which seemed to dwell on the commandment 'thou shalt not steal', he couldn't take his mind away from smuggling. Who should he approach to make the start? He had made a promise to his old friend that he would not mention the subject of his becoming a smuggler again, so he could not ask Wilf. Although, there was a question, which from his own curiosity he would definitely ask Wilf in the morning. It was not quite the same nature as the promise, he had to know why the old man had given up the game as abruptly as he obviously had.

The only other person who might be able to help him was William Horne; not today certainly, *The Black Boy* is closed on the Sabbath. No, he would have to wait until tomorrow, but only after he had spoken with Old Wilf. Surely from what Will had said the previous night, he must have been very much involved with the free traders and surely would know who to contact.

James finally drifted off to sleep for an hour before dawn, but as always was then wide awake, his natural body-clock telling him that it was time to go to work.

He dragged himself from the bed and fumbled in the dark for the post at the top of the ladder and having found it, went down the ladder and into the living room below. In the dim light of the embers of the previous night's fire, which still smouldered in the open hearth in the centre of the room, he made his way to the table and took the tallow candle, which stood upon it to the fire he blew life into the smouldering embers, which eventually crackled into life as the few twigs which he threw on, caught light and lit up the room. Smoke from the fire swirled in the roof before finding its way through a hole in the reed thatching above. Paternoster's labourers cottages had been built a century earlier, before the advent of fireplaces and chimneys and before John Horne's kilns were producing bricks for such a modern innovation.

James lit the candle from the fire and returned to the table. There he drank a pitcher of milk which stood there, with the bread-crock beside it. He then poured more milk into an earthenware bowl and took a half loaf of bread from the crock and tore off a chunk which he dipped in the bowl of milk. Whilst he was eating, his mother came into the room from her sleeping quarters, which she shared with her two daughters, Jame's sisters and which was partitioned off from the rest of the room by a blanket hung from the ceiling. She was a woman in her forties with a care and weather worn face and grey hair plaited in a single plait, which would normally have been tied into a bun at the nape of her neck. Just from her bed, it hung down her back almost to her waist.

Her husband Jacob Towns had died two winters before from the ague,that fever common amongst marsh folk at the time and it had then looked as though the family would be turned out of their accommodation. However, James then sixteen years old was big for his age and Farmer Jennings agreed that they should stay on and that James would take his father's place as now head of the family. Not that young James was offered the same wage as his father, he was given five shillings a week, a shilling less than his father had been paid, but now brother Simon, was now two years older and of a similar age to that which young Jimmy had been when his father died, so he had started to receive a wage and there were two bread-winners in the family. The younger children earned a few pennies by scaring crows and rooks from seedling crops and sparrows and pidgeons from ripening corn. Or picking stones from fields after they had been ploughed. Compared with many families in a similar position, the Towns family was comparatively well off, but the children were growing up and were eating more. Also, it was unlikely that any of Jame's, or, Simon's siblings were likely to get a job on the farm.

"Still," thought old mother Towns, as she watched her second eldest Simon come stumbling down the ladder; "we have not done too bad after losing Jake, things could be a whole lot worse!"

"We got to go Ma, Old Wilf will beat us to it and that won't do, we have to spread muck on Brook field today, and after all this rain it's not going to be easy, nor, quick." He closed the door behind him, but almost immediately opened it again.

"Simon, you lazy beggar, what in Hades do you think you are doing sitting at the table – you are with me today spreading muck, so you get out here quick, if not you'll be wearing the print of my boot on your backend for ever and a day." Simon jumped to his feet took a last gulp at the milk pitcher, grabbed a piece of bread and ran out to follow his brother to the door.

Together they splashed through the puddles as they made their way across the yard towards the stables. It was now raining steadily and the ground had become muddy and slippery. It did not bode well for a day down on the upper water meadows spreading manure, a difficult and back breaking job at the best of times, but one which would now be made worse by the extra weight of rain-soaked muck. Arriving at the stables, they leaned over the door which closed off the lower half of the stable doorway, where, inside a lantern shed a pale yellow light and they watched Old Wilf for a moment. He was harnessing his favourite horse, a large Suffolk Punch mare and talking softly to her as he did so.

"There you are old gal, us'll soon have you ready and then we will get going with that old muck spreading across that ten acre field in no time flat."

"You two gonna do it on your own then?" asked a grinning Simon over the door through a mouthful of bread." Old Wilf looked up, "you mind your manners boy, you ain't to talk to your elders and betters like that."

"Don't you pay no attention to my brother Wilf, he don't mean nothing. I can see as you are ready to go, so we will set too...but, you take young Simon with you and he can help you load up … and you can box his ears if you are so minded." He grinned, opened the stable door and Wilf led the horse out. "Come on then Boy," he said to Simon, "you heard what your brother said, get your fork and look lively, us ain't got all day, and don't think that I'll be troubling to box your ears, you are a big lad now and I might come off the worse."

The two of them made their way to the cart shed where they hitched the horse between the shafts of a two-wheel tumbril cart and then, as they made their way to the midden behind the cowshed, they disappeared from Jim's view into the gloom of the early morning mist and the rain, which was now coming down even harder.

"Rain before seven, as clear before 11!" the saying ran through Jim's mind as he took down the lantern which Will had left hanging beside the door and went into the adjoining stable to set about harnessing his own horse. He only hoped the saying to be true; he didn't relish the idea of a day getting thoroughly wet and cold and then going home to try to dry out as he had so many times before, beside the inadequate hearth in his hovel. When the horse was ready, he led it to the cart shed, backed it between the shafts of his tumbril and hitched it up. He checked that his fork was in the cart before following in the direction of Wilf and Simon had taken and stepped into the rail filled morning of the open yard.

At the midden heap, Jim helped the other two finish loading their cart with the heavy stinking muck. Once completed, Wilf climbed up behind his horse and without further word, started moving off in the direction of the lade which led to the lower fields by the brook.

"Aren't you going to help Jim, then Old Wilf! He has no-one to help him load like I helped you!" Simon looked up at the old man perched on one shaft with his back leaning against the front board of the tumbril. "Oh yes he has," said Wilf without so much as turning his head…

"He's got you boy. It won't hurt a youngan like you to fork two loads!" Indignantly Simon turned to his brother who was grinning at him.

"That ain't fair Jim," he scowled, "I am going to be helping you both all today if I ain't careful, why hasn't Old Wilf got a boy with him like I am with you?"

"Because not, so you quit your moaning and get on helping me to load this here cart." Jim was struggling to detach a forkful of muck from the surrounding heap. He finally managed to tear it free and threw it onto the cart. It was going to be a hard-long day and sometime during that day he had got to speak to Wilf about the conversation the night before.

Half an hour later, with the cart full and Jim standing on the shafts he clicked his tongue, slapped the horses back with the reins, causing a fine spray of moisture to erupt from the wet back and off they moved towards the lane, with Simon walking slightly dejectedly beside the cart. They turned into brook field and could see the old man at the far end, unloading his cart in heaps in readiness for spreading. The two carts would each bring several loads before they would be ready to do this. Jim drove across the stubble left from the summer's harvest, to start a new line of heaps parallel with that of the old man. The cart's wheels sank into the wet ground and the horse laboured against its collar and harness. At the headland of the field, Jim jumped down to the ground and said to Simon, "You start heaping along the line Wilf's made brother, I have got to say something to the old man which is not for your ears boy; and don't get yourself in another of your moods, us ain't got time for that," he looked sternly at his younger brother. "Believe me Simon, this is important and one day I'll tell you of it."

He left Simon at the start of the row, where without a further word about justice, he had started to drag the manure off the cart into the first heap. Jim walked down the line heaps left by Wilf. The rain had now eased off and there was a brightness in the sky, which promised as the saying went 'clear by eleven'. Coming up to the old man he couldn't wait to blurt out the question which had been troubling him.

"You ain't walked up here just to pass the time of day have you James?" the old man leaned on his fork and looked shrewdly at the younger one. "I suppose not, so I'll come straight to the matter in hand."

"Before you open your mouth, you'll recall as what I said last night, I don't want to hear about what you are going to do, from you or anybody else."

"I know what you said Wilf, but this is not anything about that!"

"So, what is it then?" asked Wilf. Jim looked back to where his younger brother was working, well out of earshot of their conversation. "What I have got to know is why you give up the smuggling all them years ago and never gone back to it." Wilf looked at his companion and shrugged his shoulders.

"I don't see no harm in telling you since you have heard the rest, but now isn't the time, and this is only for your ears not your brothers. "You'll have to wait until lunchtime when we are back at the farm, after we have eaten, you send young Simon back down here with a load, and we will load another cart and while he's gone I'll tell you a tale about Old Wilf."

Jim thanked him and returned to his brother to help him finish unloading the cart.

"Are you going to tell me what you said to Old Wilf?" Simon asked.

"Like I said brother it is between him and me, so don't ask again."

During the morning the two carts each carried another two loads of manure to the field and deposited them in lines of mounds along the length of it. The three of them had helped each other to load each cart and on the occasions when Jim and his brother were ahead of the old man with the unloading, they helped him with that also. By mid-morning the rain had completely stopped and the sky showed signs that the sun was soon to break through. They returned to Paternoster and ate their midday meal in the cart shed. The meal was bread dripped in a broth and mostly vegetables, but also a small amount of meat, in this instance Rabbit. Each worker has his meal supplied by his family and of course the content did vary a bit, although, not noticeably, when food was for ever in short supply and anything edible found its way into the cooking pot. The three men shared their scant meal, dipping their bread into the communal pot. When they had finished, Wilf lit up his pipe and leant back against the posts beside which he had sat to eat his meal. Jim did the same, leaning against the wheel of a four-wheeled wagon which stood in the next bay of the cart shed. Simon, sitting on the earth floor, with his back to another wheel of the same cart appeared to be dozing off. A rat, bolder than the rest which scurried around the shadows at the back of the shed, ventured closer to the pot which stood on the floor between the three men. It ran past Simon's outstretched legs and Jim picked up a stone from the floor and threw it at the rat, which he missed, instead hitting Simon on the shin. The rat fled back to it's fellows and Simon let out a roar.

"What did you do that for?" he proclaimed violently, "you woke me up and you could have broken my leg!"

"Don't be daft brother, it was no more than a pebble!" Jim sneered laughingly climbing to his feet. "Do you ever stop griping? Any road, it is time to go."

Wilf clambered up and started towards the open yard. Jim kicked his brother, who still hadn't moved, hard in the leg. "Get up you idle begger, you ain't done a days work yet, do you want to see the master come out here and see that you are not working?" At this last threat Simon dragged himself upright grumbling about the unfairness of it all and followed the other two who had started to walk towards the midden. There they began loading Jim's cart.

"There you are boy, you have no need for grumbling now do you?" enquired Old Wilf of Simon, "us is all loading this here cart."

"Rightly said, Wilf," said Jim, "but I daresay he will, when I tell him he's to take the cart to the field, unload it and then start spreading what's there!" As he said these words, he looked at Simon who was looking both sullen and perplexed. "Don't you fret brother, we are just laughing at you. We'll catch you up before you've done a heap or two, we will load Wilf's cart and be there before you can recite the Lord's Prayer and add Amen!"

When the cart was fully loaded, Simon climbed up took the reins and drove out of the farmyard. In fact, although he wasn't going to show it, he was pleased to have given him the responsibility of driving his brother's cart on his own. It didn't often happen that way, but perhaps, he thought, now he might be given a horse and cart of his own. Oh, how he longed to be in Jim's position, after all he was of the same age as Jim had been when their father had died. He ignored the fact that for the first year after his death, his brother had worked alongside Wilf and hadn't had a horse and cart of his own until the July the following year. Proudly, Simon leaned back against the front of the tumbril and let the horse plod down the track to Brook field. He'd show the other two how well he could be left on his own.

Jim and Wilf stood by the midden and Wilf's cart and watched the boy drive off. Immediately, Jim prompted the old man and as promised Wilf began to tell his story.

For six years between 1745 and 1751 he had been, as he said the previous night, a member of one of the many gangs of smugglers which thrived along the Essex coast. For that time, he had enjoyed the benefits that the extra income from this trade brought, together with the accolade of being one of the brave "free-traders" who brought unreachable goods to the general public. Night after night, when the winds and tides were favourable and he received word of a landing of smuggled goods, he drove his cart to most of the Blackwater creeks south of *Maldon* and in company with a convoy of other carts and pack animals, he carried away merchandise to the towns and villages further inland. Occasionally, he would also get word that there were goods to be transported from landings at other creeks, also on the *Blackwater*, and north of *Maldon*.

Landings at these creeks were few, although, these places were the domain of the armed gangs who worked the area around *Tiptree Heath*, they didn't generally interest themselves in these landing places which, being on the Blackwater were closer to the revenue office in *Maldon* and so better patrolled by the Revenue's riding officers and the Dragoon's based there. They instead carried out their business in the multitude of inlets around *Tollesbury, Salcot* and *Virley*. There were however, times when their cargoes were diverted because of either the weather, or the presence of the Revenue cutters off the coast. On these occasions the boats were met by the heavily armed smugglers from the Heath whose strong presence was usually enough to intimidate those whose job it was to apprehend them. Or, they would be bought off to turn a blind eye.

One night Wilf had word that a boat, a lugger named 'Sprightly' would be landing a cargo of tea one hundred and fifty half-ankers of cognac brandy, one hundred half-ankers of Geneva and bales of tobacco at Goldhanger creek the following night. Wilf was to collect twenty five tubs of brandy and the same of gin on his cart and take them to Baddow as usual. Goldhanger, being North of the Blackwater, should have meant taking the cart through Beeleigh and Langford to avoid Maldon, where it might be noticed at night, but Wilf decided to go straight through the town, planning to return by the back road.

"By that time," Wilf reminisced, "I didn't worry about the revenue men, I had not ever seen them in all the years as I was driving my old cart all over the marshes. So, what I did that night was drive right through town and straight to Goldhanger. There was many folk that saw me go through and afterwards they told the magistrate so. What I didn't know was that those I was to travel with and work with were waiting for me at Beeleigh Road, so by going through the town I missed them. "When I got to Goldhanger, there was half a dozen carts and upwards of two score of pack horses. It was dark as pitch, and to start with I reckoned as they was my folk, but then when I spoke to a few I didn't recognise any of them. Riff-raff the lot I reckons. "Where have this lot come from," I asked myself, "I don't know any of them." And then this weedy runt of a man with a face like a weasel come up to my cart and said, "What do you want boy, this ain't none of your business! The "Sprightly" be our boat and what she's carrying be ours, so if you know what is good for you, you'll take your cart and go back the way you came."

"You hold on!" I said to weedy, "I have got instructions to collect both brandy and gin and I ain't going back without it." Before I knew it five or six of the weedy gang appeared from the shadows and jumped on me, dragged me off my cart and beat me really bad with their sticks, they then chucked me back on the cart and took me to Maldon. I didn't wake up until I was being dragged off the cart outside the Revenue Office in Fullbridge. The weedy one, whose name I heard was Jerimiah Spalding, telling Master Sherman, the Tides Man, who had been dragged from his bed and wasn't best pleased, that I am a well known smuggler and he and his fellows at great risk to themselves, caught me and delivered me to the law. I didn't see no scars on weedy, so I didn't see how he'd been at such risk, but, old Sherman didn't seem to notice that. Like I said, he wasn't in best humour anyway, so he ordered me to be put into gaol.

"Weedy then went on to ask how much I was worth?" Since he expected a reward for my capture. Sherman was too fly for that and he said only if Spalding could bring him two more like me who'd be fit for navy service, would he think about a reward.

"The next day after a night in the gaol at the warf, I was taken in chains to Chelmsford assizes and sent to the old County gaol by the river for six months." Wilf paused in his narrative. Jim who had in is short life heard of so many injustices, didn't question his tale, he simply asked;

"Was gaol as bad as they say it is?"

"Aye, Jim, just as bad, down by the river it was damp and cold and we worked from dawn until dusk at one thing and another. How long have you known me young Jim? All your life that's for sure and how long has I been known as Old Wilf?" Jim shrugged his shoulders as he leaned on his fork and waited for Wilf to go on.

"All my life as I remember, you have always been known as 'Old Wilf'."

"The day I came out of Chelmsford gaol, folk started calling me that, you know why boy? Because, though I was only twenty six years old, I looked sixty. Six months of hard labour in gaol, after the beating that I got off Jerimiah's gang, my hair were white and I looked like a scarecrow. I had the ague in gaol and I didn't think I was going to live long after that, but I did, and I have been known as Old Wilf for nigh on thirty-five years now and I will be Old Wilf till I die, I thank the Lord for that because I never suspected to get old."

There was a silence between the two of them for several minutes, Wilf living his memories and Jim trying to imagine the hardships that his friend had suffered during his time in Chelmsford gaol. This was an age of hardships and harsh laws, but for those who only heard of them, but didn't necessarily witness them, they were hard to imagine, after all life at its best was hard for most people, particularly farm labourers, so how much worse were the hardships suffered by those in prison.

"Come on now Jim, let us finish loading this here cart before your brother comes looking for you."

"Wilf, I know that I made a promise last night, about never speaking again of that what we talked, but I have to know, if you were me would you do it again?"

"As I said last night, you will do what you have set your mind to and nothing will change that, but, if your answer is yes and you ever come across a weedy little runt by the name of Jerimiah Spalding – he would be the same age as I am now - I'd ask you to crack his head like he cracked mine all them years ago, only have a care that he does not use his knife on you first!"

"Maybe he isn't alive anymore if he's that old!" Wilf looked at his young friend with a wry smile. "Yes, that is how I looked on the older folk when I was your age, but I'm still alive aren't I? And that evil little marsh-rat Jerimiah Spalding is still alive, I guarantee it, his name comes up too frequent to be that of a dead man."

THE BLACK BOY

CHAPTER FOUR

Will Horne woke on his cot in the back room of *The Black Boy* a little after sunrise on the Monday morning. He rose and pulling back the sacking, which curtained the only window overlooking the cart way between the alehouse and his neighbour Sam's cottage, he looked out. It was raining hard and as he watched, he saw Sam leave his house with his head bent against the rain and hurry towards the kilns on the far side of the common. This room was useful to Will, not just because it gave refuge from his nagging wife, but it also gave him a view of what went on outside. Neither upstairs, nor down was there another window overlooking the cartway.

It wasn't the best of days to be making a five or six hour journey to West Mersea, but perhaps it would clear up later. As long as he wasn't held up by the tide on the causeway and with his recollection of the tides he felt sure that he would arrive mid-tide on an ebb which meant that on his return he would have between four and six hours leeway.

There was no movement from the room above where he had slept which meant that Annie wasn't awake yet. He poured water from the jug into a bowl and sluiced his face, drying it on the tail of his shirt. Pulling on the britches, which he had discarded beside the bed the night before, and thrusting his pocket pistol, known as a 'barker', into the pocket of his tail coat, he went through to the pot room, where he found Jane pretending to be busy when it was evident that she had only just woken and vacated her bed beneath the pot room table.

Seeing her nervous little face, which he didn't first notice, became less wary when she saw that it was him and not his wife who had come into the room. He said in a kindly voice as he shrugged on his coat, "Alright Jane, don't fret, I'm going out now and your mistress Horne isn't awake yet, so you get yourself something to eat quick and if the food is missed, you say to her that I had it before I left." He smiled at her and went through into the parlour where he crossed the room to the outside door, beside which from a peg hung his old tricorn hat. Placing it on his head and pulling an oiled cloak around his shoulders, he went out into the rainswept morning.

The stables were behind *The Black Boy* and Will turned right of the door and made his way towards them. His roan mare whickered over the stable door as she saw him approaching. He took an armful of hay from the feed shed beside the table and a handful of oats and placed them both in the horse's manger. Returning to the feed store he took down the saddle and bridle from their rack and carried them to the table. He let her eat for a few minutes before saddling up and then taking the reins in his hand led her outside, where he mounted and set off towards Maldon.

As he crossed the common, he saw through the curtain of rain that most of the gypsy caravans had gone; when?, he did not know, but he had noticed that many had gone on their way yesterday morning, when he and his wife had walked past the common on their way to church at the top of the hill. He assumed that they had done so either during the night, or first thing that morning, but had paid not more attention to it. He turned his horse's head in the direction of the track that led towards Runsell Green, where he joined the Maldon Road.

He rode steadily through the morning and towards mid-morning the sky began to clear and the rain eased to a gentle drizzle. Beyond Maldon he had taken the road to the east, which skirted the marshes through Tolleshunt D'Arcy, thus avoiding the notorious area of Tiptree Heath. There was a constant danger there of being waylaid by footpads and other ruffians and Will saw no need to tempt providence in this area. By midday he had arrived at Peldon at the end of the causeway to the Island of Mersea. Here he stopped at the inn and over a quart of ale and a half shoulder of cold mutton he enquired after the tides. He learnt from the landlord, that the tide had reached the bottom of the ebb half an hour before and would be full at four that afternoon. He then asked after his father-in-law.

"And who might be asking about Matthew?", asked the landlord who until then had been friendly and informative was now on his guard with this stranger.

"His son by marriage, that's who."

"You will have to ask him yourself then won't you?"

"I was intending to do just that, all I want to know is, is he likely to be on the island today? with the tide coming in, I have only got three hours to find him."

"Well, you don't need to worry about that no more Young Will, because I am here!" came a voice from the dim recess of the tavern, a figure rose from where he had been sitting in the farthest corner and Matthew Rowlings strode forward. He was a large man, almost as large as Will himself. In his fifties, he had a grey beard, which was shaven around the mouth, the corners of his eyes were creased into deep crow's feet from an obvious good humour and from shielding them from a thousand suns and storms and his weather beaten appearance clearly indicated his living, he was a seaman through and through.

"Well my son, what are you doing here? How's that cummugin of a daughter of mine? I hope that you are keeping her in her place," he grinned as he grasped Will's great fist in his own and pumped his arm vigorously.

"Father Matt, I trust you are as well as you look, so good to see you after all these months," said Will, truly pleased to see the older man.

"I have come here to speak of times past and maybe times to come." Will winked at his father-in-law, "and here ain't the place to speak of it!"

"Alright Will, I take your meaning, but I see you're dining on meat and I wouldn't mind a bit of that myself."

Will sat down again at the table pushing the trencher with its half-eaten contents towards Matthew. "You finish that Mutton and then we'll go outside and talk of what I have come here to say."

There was no hurry now for Will to leave, he hadn't got to cross the causeway to the island and therefore there was no danger here at Peldon of being cut off by the tide. Matthew seemed totally unperturbed by the advancing hours and so Will asked him, "Why are you not fretting over the tide over the causeway?"

"Because my boat is tied up this end as I have got business tonight." He in turn winked at his son-in-law.

"That's what I've come to talk to you about father Matt. We'll have another ale while you eat your mutton and then we'll go out where we can speak without being heard." Matthew nodded and picked up the remains of the mutton joint and Will called for more beer. When it came Will pulled out his purse and threw a few coins on the table. "That should be more than enough and I should know as I have my own ale-house." The landlord made his way back across the room and sat at his high desk where he could see the whole room. Matthew and Will downed their beer and Matthew picked up what was left of the mutton joint and started towards the door, followed by his son-in-law.

"Oi, you big man!" the landlord shouted across the room, "you only paid me for food for one, and there was two of you!" "Aye," replied Will, "I paid for one and you served food for one."

"But two of you ate it! And Matthew's still eating and if I'm not mistaken he's got the evidence in his hand so help me God!"

"Don't you try it on Crocky boy," Matthew growled at the landlord from the doorway, "I was only eating Will's left overs, what he'd paid for, and don't you forget who takes care of you in these hard taxed times!"

"Alright, seeing as it's your boy Matthew, I'll let it go." Crocky Crockford said begrudgingly, deflated by Matthew's last statement. "But don't you forget too, in this inn, two folk eating off a platter be two folks fed, and by my reckoning that's two lots of vitals to be paid for!"

"Ah, stop your moaning boy, if I feel pekish and cares to eat a bit of what my boy's good enough to share with me, then I'll do it again, so we'll wait on the next time won't we?"

Father and son-in-law went out of the door and round the stable yard where Will's mare was being cared for by the inn's ostler. She had been rubbed down and fed and Will paid the man a groat for his trouble. He and Matthew then walked leading the horse down the road towards the causeway. Although, the road was solid, built up of stone and gravel, the surface of it was muddy and green with weed from countless tides, which twice a day swept across the causeway, which was exposed only at low tide. They paddled through the mud until they came to the creek, which ran in from the seaward side of the road. Lying in the creek was the oyster drifter 'MOLLY', the pride and joy of its owner, Matthew Rowlings. At the moment she was settled on the bottom and it would be an hour or so before the tide filled sufficiently for her to float and sail down the creek towards the open sea beyond.

"Tether your horse here boy and come aboard." Matthew jumped nimbly across the three foot gap which separated the drifter from the creek's bank and after Will tied the horse to a bush of broom, he followed him over. A boy of thirteen or so years, lifted his head off of the pile of rope on which he had been sleeping, while waiting for his master to re-appear. He'd been there since the full tide that morning when they had crept up the creek, moored and Matthew had left him to watch the boat while he went to do business at Peldon Inn.

"Get yourself ashore boy and stay on the road to watch for anyone coming, and don't come back until I call you – and Silas, you better keep a weather eye out, better than you was doing here; sleeping on watch in his majesty's navy you'll have been keelhauled for that, I might even think of doing that myself." Matthew watched the lad leap ashore and run back to the road and he chuckled to Will.

"He's a good lad and has been with me for twelve months now, keeps himself to himself and knows how to hold his tongue. Don't say much at the best of times, but he does his job."

They sat down on the boat's hatch and Matthew turned to Will. "So what is burning your britches so badly as you want to ride all this way to talk to me? I would wager a shilling that you are wanting to profit from a bit of 'free trading' again." He raised his bushy eyebrows and looked quizzical. "Am I right, is that the truth?"

"Yes, you are right. We had many a good thing going before this last two years and now I want to set off again on the same track.... Only this time we need a lot more caution. The difference now be that not a soul apart from you and I know the source and the companions of mine who will be in this with me will not know who is involved, they'll be doing the work.... and getting paid well for it... but, it will be me who will be doing the trading!" Will wasn't about to waste his words on this mission.

"What I want is to start up again, but not like before, when we had a load in every three months or so, this time I want to set up all the ale-houses, taverns and inns from Latchingdon to Chelmsford, and I would be looking at a load a fortnight!."

"You have got to be mindful that the Revenue's Riding Officers are getting everywhere now. There's more of them, and they don't try so hard to catch boats landing now, they are after carts leaving the shore and carrying away the merchandise." Matthew chewed on his pipe stem and spat over the gunnale of the boat. "I don't mind helping you my boy and at the same time helping myself, but I only have the one boat and I can only go to Maldon so many times with oysters. I'll have to make arrangements with others to carry their oysters for them so that I always have a cargo for Maldon."

"Alright father Matt, you make whatever arrangements as you have to get word to me as soon as you can." William rose from his seat on the hatch and held out his hand to his father-in-law. "You got business tonight and I have a long way to go, so now I'll be taking my leave of you. I'll wait for word when you can deliver the first cargo and where you'll be landing it."

Matthew shook his son-in-law's hand warmly. "Don't you fret boy we will soon have this going. I'll come myself one day when I have delivered a load of oysters to Fullbridge or Hythe Quay and tell you what you want to know. I'll hire a horse from the hostler up Market Hill, it is time I saw that daughter of mine in any case." He stood up and watched as Will jumped to the back. The boat was now floating again and the tide was rushing in muddy swirls around it and the distance to the bank had increased.

"Oh, one thing Father Matt," Will turned towards the board and spoke slightly sheepishly to the older man standing on the deck of the oyster board, "I think it might be aswell if you don't speak of our business to Annie, I don't want to rile her up like last time if you remember."

Matthew Rowlings remembered very well the tantrum that his daughter had flown into, firstly when she learned that he husband had started to do business with smugglers, and then more latterly when he had stopped doing business with them. To start she feared Will being caught, jailed or transported, how would that leave her she asked, but when that didn't happen and Will stopped his trade, she was angry that a lucrative income had stopped. As they both knew, there was little that pleased Annie Horne very much.

"I think that is a wise notion, Will, so you can be certain as she'll learn nothing from me…. Off you go and send the boy back here when you find him on the causeway!"

Will nodded his thanks and that he would. Mounted his horse and rode back to the roadway. The boy was there sitting on the stone which marked the end of causeway and Will sent him back to the boat. Then kicking the mare into a trot and then a canter, he set off back towards Peldon Inn from where he took the road to Maldon. Through Salcot, he saw a line of packhorses picketed outside the alehouse, and the two or three ruffians who were tending them looked suspiciously at Will as he rode by.

"I'll wager that they're from the Heath," he thought, but made a point of not looking too closely at them. "They have got business tonight here at Salcott Creek, or maybe Virle." He didn't see the fourth man who stood in the doorway of the inn and who was looking closely at him as he rode by.

He rode on through Tolleshunt D'Arcy and Goldhanger, coming into Maldon as dusk was falling, as was a light rain which had held off for the best part of the day. He arrived back at *The Black Boy* before many of his customers had appeared. He stabled the mare, unsaddled her and then rubbed her down with whisps of straw before filling her hay rack and her water trough at the door. He then went into the alehouse.

The one customer sitting in the parlour bar was James Towns, who leapt to his feet as soon as Will entered. "You are here early Young Jim?" he observed as he took off his hat and hung it with his dripping cloak on the peg by the door.

"I've come to speak with you Will about what you were saying on Saturday night. I reckon that I can get into this here smuggling game and can help you in supplies of the things you want!." He blurted out in one breath. "I can get a cart and all I need is to find a smuggling gang and get them to let me cart for them and I can get what you want at the best price." He looked brightly at the landlord.

"And what makes you think that I am interested in that game?" Will looked around the room to make sure that there was no-one else in there to have overheard what James had just said and he asked quietly, "I thought that I'd made it plain as a pikestaff that I am not having anything to do with such a carry on - surely you haven't forgotten that?"

"Yes, but I know how you once was in the business and might want to get in it again... on the quiet like."

"Well, you had best forget it young Jim, it isn't for me and it ain't for you and not something you want to talk too loudly about, so no more mention of it, alright." Will turned on his heel and strode across the room towards the pot-room, calling his wife Annie as he went. Young Jane appeared at the pot-room door and smiled shyly at her employer. She was followed by Annie, who barged the girl out of the way and confronted her husband.

"And where have you been all day husband?" she demanded, "I've been left on my own all day with no word of where you were and what you are doing! "You saw this here young Slut before you went," pointing at Jane, who now cringed behind the door, "and she says you didn't tell her where you were going either."

"Like she says, I didn't say where I was going because it isn't any business but my own." Will glared at his wife, "I hope you weren't harsh on the girl – were you?" Annie ignored the question and started to return to the pot-room. Will demanded his supper and sat at a table by the fire, on the opposite side of the room to Jim. He needed to sit quietly and to think about the day's events, not least of which featured James Towns. His best time for thinking was always when he ate. Wherever had Jim got the notion that he was about to go back into smuggling again? He hadn't been in *The Black Boy* when he and Sam had their discussion. He began to go back over in his mind all that he had said that night.

THE BLACK BOY

CHAPTER FIVE

Reuben Belbin arrived back at his caravan on the common after making a detour to approach it from the opposite direction to that which he would have taken from *The Black Boy* and upon arrival, after making quite sure that he hadn't been followed, or observed, he went inside. He need not have worried, it was late and the other occupants of the common were sound asleep. His wife Rachel and the three children too were asleep and Reuben decided against waking them immediately. He would get a few hours sleep before they left.

Rachel woke as he climbed into the bunk beside her. Sleepily she turned over and mumbled " It isn't time to rise is it Rube? I ain't been abed more'n hour or so."

"No woman, not time yet, but we will be gone before first light so no-none sees which way we are going. It is the Sabbath, so there'll be fewer folk abroad at that time – we've got business to do with Jerimiah at the Heath and I need to speak to him real quick. You sleep now until I wake you."

"What you got to speak to that old villain for Rube? He's only ever given you trouble and you knows it."

"You mind your tongue woman it isn't any business of yours." With that, Reuben turned on his side and dismissed his wife from his thoughts. He lay there thinking as to how he would best appraise Jerimiah Spalding of the opportunity which he was to offer him. It was a double-barrelled offer which he knew that the smuggler would recognise immediately and jump at. How though, was he Reuben going to benefit the most from it?

A short while later he was asleep. He had always had the ability to sleep and wake like a cat, a habit which stood him in good stead over the years and had saved him from gaol or worse on many occasions. He woke an hour before dawn and kicked his wife awake.

"Get the children awake and tell them do be quiet or they'll get my belt, then give me a hand with the horse."

Quietly they harnessed the horse and set him between the shafts, the children needed no warning on the subject as they knew from experience not to make any noise on occasions such as this and so the family's going was silent and unobserved by others on the common.

Reuben kept to the short sheep grazed grass on the common until he judges himself to be far enough away from neighbouring caravans for his iron rimmed wheels to be heard on the gravel of the road and then he joined the track leading to Runsell Green. From there through Beeleigh and Maldon and then Reuben turned north on the Totham and Tiptree road.

Tiptree Heath was a permanent camping ground for gypsies and being close to the villages of Salcott and Virley, which with their multitude of creeks, were two of the chief landing places on this part of the Essex coast for contraband goods, acted as a distribution centre for Maldon, Colchester and Chelmsford. Indeed, the Heath was the venue for almost continuous fair where contraband was bought and sold. With its large number of horses and donkeys which could readily be grazed upon the heath, it was ideally situated for the movement of contraband goods brought in from the sea. Many of the Heath's squatters now had permanent resident there in rude hovels and the place had a reputation for harbouring the worst riff-raff and most murderous of the gangs of cut-throats associated with smuggling in Essex. For this reason, the place was never visited by the Revenue riding officers whose lives would have been in immediate danger had they done so and even the Dragoons whose job it was to enforce the King's law and protect the revenue officers, were loathed to visit as their number were considerably fewer than the heavily armed gangs there and they too would have been in fear of their lives.

This encampment was led by one man who controlled all the separate gangs. A more unlikely leader for such a rabble would be difficult to imagine, with his small stature, his pinched and pock-marked face and in particular, his seeming lack of brawn, which would no more usually have been the mark of the leader of such a rough band of men. But, what Jerimiah Spalding lacked in brawn, he made up for with a sharp brain, a remarkable memory and an unbeatable agility with a knife. In his younger days, the latter was what had created both fear and admiration in those who followed him. Even now in his late fifties, he was as agile as a cat and had lost none of his ability when it came to using his knife. He had yet to be beaten in a knife fight even when up against swords or cutlasses. He never forgot a face, or name and had an iron in every fire from the banks of the River Colne to the Blackwater. He knew every shipment, every revenue rider's movements, every revenue cutter's position and the deployment of each company of Dragoons. His spies were everywhere and Reuben Belbin was but one of them.

Reuben's caravan pulled onto the Heath around midday on Sunday and he drove it to a vacant spot amongst the other caravans, carts and shanties which littered the place. Jumping down, he left Rachel to set up camp and to tether and feed the horse. Over his shoulder he called back to her as he set off towards the far end of the shire, where he expected to find Jerimiah. "You have vitals ready when I get back, I'm hungry now and going to be more so when I return." She was too wise and used to her husband's heavy hand to question how long that might be, so without a word, she too jumped down and sent the children off to collect firewood and water, while she unhitched the horse and tethered it beside the van. She then prepared the tripod and cooking pot within which she would prepare a midday meal for all of them - with what, she was as yet unsure, but as always she'd find something.

It was the best part of a quarter of a mile to Jerimiah's shack at the far end of the heath and it was lucky for Reuben that he had arrived when he did because Jerimiah was about to leave. His horse stood saddled and bridled outside and a string of pack animals, horses and donkeys, were congregated in an open area beyond the shack. As Reuben approached the door of the shack, its owner emerged dressed for the road. From his belt hung only the knife for which he was infamous, but also stuck in it were a pair of pistols. Another knife protruded from the top of his boot.

"I can't believe this here's a social call Reuben Belbin, this isn't your way is it? So what have you got to tell me? And make it quick as you can see I have business tonight." Jerimiah looked shrewdly at his visitor, narrowing his small eyes as he spoke and Reuben started to tell him of the conversation overheard at *The Black Boy*.

"Looks to me Reuben as if you and I have got to sit down and talk of this some more and now isn't the time when I'm busy - you come here tomorrow at first light, I'll be back by then and we will talk." Turning his back on Reuben, Jerimiah called to the men leading the pack of animals to get ready to move and mounted his horse.

Reuben had to step back out of the way of the horses and watch the man who he hoped might become his partner in this new venture ride away at the head of the column of pack animals. He realised at this moment that such a dream was more than just that, he would have to think very carefully about how much information he gave to Jerimiah and how much he would keep to himself for his own benefit. All he knew was that he must remember all that he has just said, because it was absolutely certain that Jerimiah would remember word for word.

Deep in thought he walked slowly back to where he had left his family, as far as he recalled, all that he had said in the few brief words he had with Jerimiah was that he had overheard a conversation between a group of men in *The Black Boy* discussing the possibility of setting up a smuggling gang and that because he had been outside the door, he had no idea who they were. He had not mentioned either the Landlord's name, or his involvement. He had thought even before he spoke to the smuggler's leader, that it would be wise to keep that piece of information to himself.

Rachel had the pot boiling over a good fire and was putting into it the pieces of a skinned, gutted and jointed rabbit. She added salt and a handful of herbs and gave the pot a stir. The children, as soon as they saw their father approaching, scuttled off to collect more firewood.

"Your back quick Rube, this here rabbit is going to a couple of hours cooking!" Rachel offered slightly nervously. "Be there anything else I can get you?"

"Where did you get the rabbit? That wasn't in the van yesterday."

"The children found it in a snare down by the brook when they fetched water and your boy put it under his coat so no-one could see it and he brought it back here. He doesn't know whose snare it was, so he skinned and gutted the rabbit as quick as he could and we put it in the pot as you can see!"

"Good Boy!" said Reuben proudly.

"Where is he now?" "Off getting more wood with his sisters I expect. The boy be pleased as punch if you would say that to him you know."

"Alright, I'll tell him when he comes back and I'll wait for my supper as I am not in a hurry anymore. I can't do my business until tomorrow first thing." Reuben sat on one of the caravan's shafts and took from his pocket a short clay pipe blackened by extensive use. He filled it with the cheap tobacco made from the stalks of leaves after the leaves themselves had been stripped off. These stalks normally ended up by being ground down for snuff, but were readily available in their underground form as a cheaper form of tobacco. Most smuggling boats brought in a consignment of stalks with tobacco, so it was readily available on the heath. He lit his pipe from a flaming brand, which he pulled from the fire and sat back to think his strategy for the morrow.

Perhaps he would let Jerimiah think that all he had heard was a vague undertaking by a group of workers at the alehouse from a smuggling band in Horne Row and that he would attempt to join it himself and at that stage inform Jerimiah to enable him to either take over supplying the goods to the band, or more simply, to waylay them with their first consignment and to take over the whole business. Yes, he decided, the least said the better and he was now glad that he had been given the space within which to think more clearly ahead. He certainly would not mention that it looked like it was the Landlord of *The Black Boy* who intended to run everything there. Reuben knew that he had to be careful though, he was dealing with a very dangerous man, one with a viciously cruel streak who was notorious for never forgetting, or, forgiving a grudge. Inevitably the person who had crossed him ended up with at best a good beating or some disfiguration such as the removal of an ear, or a slit nose, or even worse, a knife between his ribs or his throat.

Over their meal, at which he gave a grudging recognition of his son's contribution to it, "I hear as you put this here rabbit in that pot boy, good for you, I only hope that no-one saw you take it from the snare!" His son visibly glowed with pride, it wasn't often that his father ever did anything other than to grumble and to readily take his belt to him.

"No Pa, I made sure of that, and I hid it under my coat so nobody could ask where I got it from," he grinned sheepishly at his father. His mother Rachel gave a knowing look to Reuben who studiously ignored it. He had said all that he was going to say on the subject. "One day," the boy Robert thought, "Pa'll call me by my name, he never does, perhaps he doesn't remember it? Come to think of it, Ma doesn't often use it either, maybe she's forgotten it too?"

Jerimiah and his string of pack animals reached the creek at Virley and set up a temporary camp to await the midnight tide and the incoming lugger. By first light with the tide ebbed yet again and no sign of the lugger, Jerimiah left the two men there on watch for the boat and took the remainder of his gang and most of the pack animals back to Salcott, where the owner of the alehouse there was well know to him. Leaving two men outside to attend to the animals, he went in with the rest of the men. He'd now wait for that night's tide and so he might as well do it in comfort. In the mid afternoon, there was a cry from the outside "Rider Coming!" Jerimiah stepped into the doorway and as he watched the solitary horseman trot by, he caught of glimpse of the man's face. He wasn't a Riding Officer, of that he was certain, with his now old fashioned tricorn hat, he looked more like a farmer or a merchant, and as such no threat to Jerimiah and his men. He'd remember that face though and tucked it away into his prodigious memory for recognition one day.

The following morning, before daybreak, Reuben left the caravan and went to Jerimiah's shack. He learned that no-one had yet returned from wherever they had gone the day before, so he left word to contact him as soon as they returned.

It was not until the following day, the Tuesday, that he was summoned to Jerimiah's shack. He found the smuggler's leader there, sitting outside waiting for him.

"You look surprised to see me Rube. There's good reason as to why I wasn't here yesterday, our lugger was chased by a revenue cutter what came close to catching it off of Mersea. And not only did this make it late as he had to hide up amongst the oyster drifters and dredgers there, while the revenue men searched for his boat, the lugger's captain tells me as he dumped the cargo overboard fearing he was about to be caught. I wasn't best pleased, as we have lost half the cargo and a whole days waiting for it. He says he'll try to creep for some of it with a grapnel, but since he isn't to certain where he sunk it, I don't hold out much hope on him finding much. I was back here before dawn, not that is much compensation. So since it was half the cargo as us was expecting the unloading were quicker, even if a day late!"

Reuben looked suitably sympathetic, but Jerimiah went on. "And whose money was lost, not the captain's – no mine. All that cowardly verminous swab's lost is part of his share of the profit. Well, I say to him, he may have to sing for the rest of it, until his next cargo! Less of course he is lucky with his creeping'." He looked fiercely at Reuben. "But enough of bad news, I live in hopes as you are going to bring us good news Rube. You had best finish what you were saying two nights ago."

"I don't remember much of what I told you Jerimiah. You had best remind me so that I don't repeat myself."

If Reuben had hoped to confirm his memory of what he had already said, he was to be disappointed.

"That's alright Rube, I don't mind hearing it twice, so you start at the beginning and let's hear it all. Sit here while we talk." When Jerimiah smiled, he was at his most guileful and most dangerous; he grinned now as he moved a heap of harness off the only other chair outside the shack and invited Reuben to take it. So Reuben sat down and started by telling him how he had been in *The Black Boy* two evenings before and when he had left he had noticed that a group of men, he didn't know whether they were farm labourers or clay workers or what, were still sitting in the alehouse after all of the others had left. He said how he had listened at the door and overheard them talking about the fact that now smuggling was becoming more difficult and less profitable because of the removal of the tax on tea, they wanted to start up themselves in the business, but only in a minor way for the import of a few tankers of spirits and a bale of tobacco. He emphasized that this group was unlikely to cause much of a threat to Tiptree Heath's trade. He suggested to Jerimiah that perhaps he and Reuben should try to join the gang and so learn more about their intended activity. He went on to make his suggestion that Jerimiah, should he so wish with such a tiny operation such as this, could take it over at any time he liked, or if he so desired, possibly waylay the first consignment.

Jerimiah listened closely to what Reuben said. He noted with interest the playing down of what two days before had Reuben full of excitement. What had changed Reuben's mind since then he wondered? It seemed plain that he now intended greater things for himself and was going to keep Jerimiah largely in the dark. He would require close watching. He had never trusted Reuben, but then he didn't trust anyone!. When Reuben had finished, Jerimiah was silent for a few minutes.

"Is that all you have got tell me Rube?" he smiled as benevolently as a hungry wolf.

"I reckon so Jerimiah." Replied Reuben nervously. "I hope that it is of use to you, what do you think?" should I try to join them?"

"Yes I'd say you should and first thing I would like to know is their names, and how much the Landlord Will Horne knows?"

"You know him then?" Reuben was aghast, one of his trump cards had just vanished!

"Oh yes, I have never met him, but I know of him. He is the son-in-law to Matthew Rowlings from Mersea. It is my business to know men such as he. It would be no surprise that he's in on this here with the others." He leered at Reuben, enjoying the gypsy's discomfort at his intentional use of Will Horne's name. "You get the names of these folk and you join their gang. Then you let me know whats going on between them and the Landlord."

Reuben rose from his seat and with a servile nod to the smuggler he turned and started to walk away. "Remember Rube I look after those that look after me, but I'm awful nasty to those that don't!" Jerimiah threw this parting shot at him as he left.

Reuben turned briefly and winced when he saw the wicked smile on Jerimiah's face, but he turned again and kept walking. Back at the caravan, he bade Rachel and the children to harness the horse and prepare to move on.

"Where to Rube?" asked Rachel.

"Back to the common at Horne Row, we have got things to do there."

It was still early in the morning and they left the Heath before ten o'clock, taking the Totham Road to Maldon. They arrived back at the common below Danbury Hill, which they had left three days before, and set up camp once again, but this time well down the common away from *The Black Boy*. Reuben and his boy set off immediately to set rabbit snares in the multitude of runs amongst the gorse and heather of the common. This being common land, although, owned by the local Lord of the Manor, was free of a warrener and could therefore be quite safely snared without fear of prosecution for poaching.

Their snares were made from plaited horse hair and the boy whose job it was to make and set them had a large number, which he and his father now placed for quite a distance around the area within which they had parked their van. They needed both food for themselves and something which they could sell.

Later that evening, when it was fully dark, Reuben left his family and went up to *The Black Boy*. It was midweek and the front parlour was almost empty. Apart from one old farm laborer who sat beside the fire, hunched over a tankard, which he would make last all evening as he puffed on his almost empty clay pipe, there were no other occupants. Reuben took a seat at a table on the far side of the room, Jane came over to him to ask what he would like to drink.

"A quart of ale girl," he said. "Where's your master tonight?"

"He's in the back room," Jane replied, "talking to his friends."

Reuben immediately pricked up his ears. "And who are they?" he enquired. "Would I know them?"

"I have no notion of that Sir, I don't know you, except you were in here last Saturday night, but I don't know your name." Jane was, as instructed by her employer, wary of strangers and even more of those that asked questions.

"When you see him to talk to girl, you tell him as there's somebody here that wants to talk business with him - so you get me my ale and I'll just sit here until he's finished talking with his friends." Reuben gave the girl a friendly smile and sat back while she fetched his beer. Who was Will talking with in the back room, he wondered? Was it the group that he'd been with on Saturday night? He'd wait until they appeared and then he'd know. He'd seen clearly through the cracks in the door.

Half an hour passed before Will came through from the scullery. He has, soon as Jane told him of a Stranger's presence in the parlour broken up the meeting which he had been having with two of his fellow would-be smugglers, Sam Rowe and Joshua Roote, sending them off out through the back door of the premises, which gave access to the rear of Sam's house next door. He then had watched Reuben through the spyhole and recognised him as one of the gypsies who had come in that Saturday night from where they were camped on the common and he remembered this man as one of those who had free gin.

"A good evening to you, I hear that you want to talk to me, but I don't even know your name, all I know is that you were here the other night and drunk my grog." Will smiled at the gypsy as he approached the table at which he was sat.

"My name's Reuben Belbin and me and mine are camped up on the common, a short step from here. I surely do want to talk to you landlord, but what I got to say is not for prying ears and is private to you and me only."

"You had best speak your mind then. There's none to hear in here. Don't mind him by the fire." Will jerked his head towards the old man at the other end of the room. "He's deaf and daft aswell!"

"Alright then," Reuben began, lowering his voice. "I hear that you are looking to find a supply of grog and bacca and looking at someone with a boat to bring it in." Reuben wasn't yet about to tell Will that he had eavesdropped on the conversation on the Saturday night. "Am I right?"

"And where might you have heard that from? This is the first I've heard of it, you was here on Saturday night, I remember you as one of the gypsies in here and you'll recall what I said then about no more free Geneva, because I don't have it here no longer and nor will I have anything more to do with smuggling or such." Will didn't like the way the conversation was going. First of all James and now this from a complete stranger! Who has been talking? he wondered.

"So you heard wrong Reuben Belbin," Will said straightening up from where he had been leaning against the table about to go back to the pot-room.

"Oh, I don't think that I got it wrong landlord, I understand why you perhaps don't want to talk now, so when the time's right, you can find me in my van on the common. I'll be waiting for you Will." Reuben grinned slyly and winked at Will as he spoke. It was a mistake. Will was incensed by the conspiratorial familiarity of the man. He shot forward with surprising speed for such a big man, and leaning over the table, knocking the gypsy's quart pot of ale on the floor, he propelled him to the door, opened it and pushed him through it.

"I don't want to see you hereabouts again tinker. If I do I'll give you something to think about for many a day to come."

As he shut the door behind Reuben, some sixth sense made Will turn back towards it. He was just in time to meet the gypsy, who sent the door crashing open and leaped inside *The Black Boy* with a wicked looking knife in his right hand. Will parried with his left hand the thrusting lunge that the gypsy made and then with his right felled him with a fist like ham, which lifted Reuben off his feet and laid him flat in the doorway.

The old labourer by the fire seemed to come aware at this point and from the toothless grin amongst his whiskers, was enjoying the spectacle.

Will picked up the knife from the floor and then with the toe of his boot propelled the body of the gypsy down the steps. He stood on the top of the step and watched Reuben come round and groaning, drag himself to his feet.

"If you think that is all that I have got in store for you if you comes round here again," Will barked at him "You would be wrong, now go and don't come back." Reuben said nothing and limped away in the darkness towards the common. What was he to tell Jerimiah Spalding? Not only had his approach to the landlord been a failure, but he also failed to discover the names of the smugglers. If it had been them that Will was talking to in the back room, they must have left by another door. He stumbled on towards the common wondering how he could find out what he needed to know, now that he could not enter *The Black Boy* again. That Landlord William Horne was something to be reckoned with and definitely not to be taken lightly! The one thing he knew was that he, Reuben Belbin would get even one dark night, for if he didn't do the deed himself, he knew of enough people on the Heath who, for a small sum, even a favour, or for the fun of it would do it for him!

That Tuesday night, James Towns had decided to make a second attempt to speak to Will, but he had been hovering outside *The Black Boy* trying to pluck up the courage, but also trying to think of perhaps a different approach, like perhaps seeking his advice instead of point blank offering his services. He was still pondering when he arrived on top of the step and saw through the cracks in the door, the gypsy at the table opposite. He too, like Reuben on the Saturday night, overheard the conversation there. He also saw the gypsy being propelled across the parlour floor, but before the door opened and the gypsy was ejected, James had beaten a hasty retreat around the corner to where Reuben had hid before. Jim saw Reuben pull out the knife even before the door was shut again, but he had no chance to shout a warning before Reuben went crashing through it and lunged at Will, who then knocked him down and sent him tumbling down the steps. He had heard what he passed between the gypsy and Will, and from what he had heard not only did it confirm what Will had said to him the previous night, but it didn't look like a good moment to speak to Will! He waited therefore until he'd seen the gypsy limp away into the night, before turning away and returning to Paternoster Farm.

Maybe, he thought as he walked down the lane, it might be a good idea to speak to the gypsy and find out where his source of supply was and indeed find out what he was offering Will, he'd try that tomorrow night.

THE BLACK BOY

CHAPTER SIX

Will realised that he had made an enemy of the gypsy the moment he closed the door having watched him limp off, but this was only one of the two things that irritated and worried him. The first was the gypsy's certainty that Will was contemplating consorting with smugglers and that he would do so at the gypsy's convenience. How had this Reuben come to this conclusion, coincidentally within such a short while since the idea had first been discussed that in the parlour of *The Black Boy*? He must have been either told something by someone or had overhead someone discussing it. It was this that particularly concerned him. If the enterprise was to get going at all, absolute trust was required. He thought that with the oaths that were sworn that night, all would be well….and now this! But not only the gypsy, but young James as well! Oh, he didn't worry about Jim, he was a Horne Row boy born and bred and would be loyal to his own, of that Will was certain, but this Reuben was a different matter entirely. He had appeared from nowhere, had certainly vanished from the common for two days and now was back with this suggestion. He would have to get to the bottom of this.

For a long time after he ejected Reuben through the door and down the steps, Will sat at the table vacated by the gypsy and contemplated what should be done. The first thing had to be a meeting with the other five and as soon as possible. He'd speak to Samuel and get word to the rest to meet early the following evening. The second thing was to speak with Matthew and find out if he knew anything about the gypsy. His father-in-law had promised to visit as soon as he had a cargo of oysters for Maldon and that should be any day now and then the first cargo of contraband would be arranged.

Will rose and went through to the pot-room. The parlour now had half a dozen customers, but none of them was one of the five. Jane was serving them and Annie was sitting at the pot-room table mending a leather tankard with waxed twine.

She looked at Will as he entered. "Why don't we throw away the old pots like this here and get pewter, or, even pottery what they are all using nowadays. I'm forever mending and making good." She grumbled, glaring at her husband. "This is only because you are so tight and mean!"

"Don't you do anything but complain woman? I aint mean, but I know the money I make and it isn't enough to throw away on fancy pots. Now I'm going to see Sam Rowe next door, so you look after the customers while I'm out."

"Don't I always?"

"No, you don't, you leave young Jane to do all that and then you scold her if she gets it wrong. So now do it!"

Will left the room without another word leaving his scowling wife glaring at his back and went through the back door to the rear of the building. He crossed the cart way and knocked on Sam's house. Ever since the old man, William's father had lived there, there had been a sign over the door, "Horne Row" in once bold, but now somewhat faded letters. Will knew it by heart having been born and raised in the house and he looked up to peer at it in the gloom; it was almost invisible and disappeared into the shadows when the door opened at the lantern light spilled out through it.

Sam peered out at his visitor and recognizing him he greeted him. "Good evening Will, what's on your mind? Nothing urgent I hope, please come in." He stood aside for Will to enter but Will shook his head. "I think we had best talk out here Sam, you got a house full of family and they don't want to hear what I have got to say."

Sam said not a word and carrying the lantern, came out and closed the door behind him. The two of them walked towards the stables at the rear and when Will was sure that they were out of earshot he stopped and turning toward his companion told him of both James Town's visit and that of the gypsy Reuben Belbin.

"So what do you think on that Sam?" he enquired when he had finished.

Sam thought about it for a few moments. "You can be sure of one thing Will, and don't say it hasn't crossed your mind to wonder, but none of us have spoken of it to anybody, we will not even talk amongst ourselves." He looked at Will, who though he tried to hide it, looked relieved. "You remember as we all swore a holy oath on the bible and we are God fearing folk who would never break such an oath!"

"Of course I know that Sam, but I did worry for a little while. So if none of you have spoken of it, how come both young Jim and the gypsy was leading the same way?"

Sam cast his mind back to that meeting in *The Black Boy's* parlour four nights ago. He then remembered that as he had gone round the corner at the front of the alehouse that night to return to his house, he had thought he'd detected a movement and a slight rustling in the ivy which festooned the building beside the steps. At the time he'd paid little attention to it and it was only now that he recalled it. It had been a dark night and there were always stray cats about and the ivy was home to hundreds of sparrows; anything could have disturbed that ivy. He told Will what he remembered seeing and hearing. "Course at the time Will I never gave it a thought, but it is possible as one of the two of them were skulking in there, perhaps they heard all as us was saying before we left. I know as that door of yours is full of holes anybody could probably hear talk inside."

"Yes, I can see the tinker doing that, but not young Jim, anyway he'd left earlier with Old Wilf, so we can count him out. He wouldn't have gone all the way back to Parternoster and then up again to listen at the door. No, it's the gypsy that listened, but somehow Jim got hold of it. We must find out."

"The first thing to do Will, is to go and listen at your door and see if what you are thinking is possible."

Will nodded and they made their way back to the parlour entrance, via Sam's cart way and thence to the front of the alehouse where Sam extinguished the lantern. They inspected the corner where Sam thought he'd seen movement and they quietly mounted the steps and stood at the threshold. Will hadn't noticed just how full of cracks the doors was. He put his eye to one and was able to see most of the room's interior. He noted that the table at which the six of them had been sitting on the Saturday night was clearly visible. He then put his ear to the same crack and listening carefully, could clearly hear the conversation within the room. Beckoning Sam, Will retreated down the steps. "It is clear to me as the gypsy stayed outside after the rest of the folk had gone and he pried on us." He said, "he won't be back here again, because like I told you, I tipped him out – at any rate he won't be back inside, but he might try again for information likes he got before, so we'll have to watch that door very carefully and what we say inside. From now on we'll only meet in the back room or the stable."

"When do you expect to see this man who is going to help us like you said? You said earlier this night, as you'd been to see him and that he's coming here soon. When?" Sam asked.

At the brief meeting, which he and Joshua had met with Will earlier that evening, Will had told them of his trip to see a boat owner, without saying who, or where, and that arrangements for the first shipment would soon be finalized. "Sam, I'll let you know all in good time, but first, we have all got to meet and make sure that we all know what we are doing. Get word to the rest and we'll meet tomorrow night in the stables behind here. You arrange the time Sam and let me know of it, and tell them not to let their going to the stables and not into the parlour be seen by anyone. Now I'm returning inside and I'll let you get back to your supper." Will climbed the steps again, after a quick glimpse through the door, entered the parlour while Sam returned to his family next door.

Inside Will greeted the few who sat in the bar. They were mostly John Horne's workers and amongst them were the brothers Joshua and Daniel Roote. To those two Will nodded and beckoned them over to a table on the far side of the room. There he simply told them to make a point of seeing Sam the next day as he would tell them what was going to happen next. Daniel tried to press Will for more information, but his brother stopped him from saying more, "hold your tongue Dan, we'll see Sam tomorrow like Will said." They then got up and returned to their friends at the far table and Will went through to the pot-room.

There he found a weeping Jane sat at the table struggling to mend a leather tankard which Annie had been repairing when he left. On both cheeks she carried the imprints of a palm and fingers where she had been violently slapped. On the far side of the table stood Annie, her face red from exertion and fury. On Will's entry Jane bent her head lower and tried to stifle her sobs, whilst his wife turned offensively towards him.

"You have been slapping the girl around again haven't you, you wicked woman, why? you was mending the pots, because you know how to do it, while she poor lass doesnt, that's plain to see!" Will increased by his wife cruel viciousness, which seemed to increase daily. "Do you think you will teach her by beating her? How would you like it yourself?"

With that Will began to move around the table towards his wife. To start with she didn't move, believing as like so many times in the past her husband would back down, but when he kept coming and seeing the look of angry disgust and plain dislike on his face, she began to back away. He caught her at the other end of the table and raising his hand struck her across her left cheek with his open hand, then quickly reversing the blow, backhanded her across the other cheek before she had a chance to fall to the floor from the first blow. Now she fell and Will stood over her waiting for her head to clear before he spoke. "You have had that coming for a long time woman, and so perhaps you will now mend your ways and start doing as I say. There'll be no more slapping the girl around and no more arguing with me. Now get upstairs, mend the cut you have got on your cheek from my ring and then get out there and serve my customers."

Annie, almost meekly climbed to her feet holding her hand to the cut in her cheek caused by Will's ring, which his father had given him at the age on twenty one, and hurried out of the room toward the stairway which led to her room above. Outside the door she sent back through it such a look of venom that it might have burned through the elm door.

Will now turned to Jane who sat at the table and gazed at her savior through tear stained eyes with such a look of love and devotion that would have been more fitting on a puppy.

"Come on girl, dry your eyes and leave that pot, you have got folk to serve out there," pointing to the parlour door, "and I am coming in here too, to put anybody in his place that needs it! There's a few thirsty folk there I'll wager, and the drier they get the louder they moan!" He smiled at the girl and gently pushed her, still wiping her eyes on her soiled apron, towards the door.

On the following day, Wednesday, a middle aged man walked into the parlour bar. He was from his dress obviously a seafaring man and walked with that rolling gait, which told of rolling seas and decks. He saw the old laborer in his usual place by the fire and sat down opposite him. The old man didn't even look up, but kept staring, as he did most nights into his tankard of ale.

"Be the landlord here tonight?" the seaman asked his companion and when he got no reply he nudged his arm across the table. The old man slowly looked up

"Yes," he said.

More loudly the seaman asked "Did you hear what I asked you old man!, be the landlord here?"

"Yes."

"Is that all you have to say?" and when there was no reply the seaman said "I was going to ask you if you want an ale in that empty pot of yours, but perhaps I won't bother myself after all."

"Yes, I'll have one and thank you. I don't get many that want to talk to an old fool like me, who is deaf and daft as they all say. I am deaf, but I am not daft and I remember who you are, I have seen you in here when you used to come and see your girl, Annie. You're her Pa, Matthew aren't you?" This was probably the longest speech the old man had made for a long time and hearing him talk, all of the others in the room stopped to listen in amazement. Like all deaf people he spoke loudly even across the table to Matthew, in consequence all there could hear him.

"Yes, I am that and I reckon as it was time I see her again and of course my son-in-law Will."

"So you Will's Pa-in-law? Do you still trade oysters to Maldon from Mersea Island, I heard that was what you did a year or two back?" One of the tile makers wanted to know.

"Yes, on and off now I am an old man and can't lug them heavy crates any more." Answered Matthew, his brawny stature and muscled shoulders giving the Statement of a lie.

At that moment Jane came through the pot-room door followed by Will.

"What do you have to do to get an ale in this here alehouse?" called Matthew when he saw Will. "Come on there's two thirsty folk here both wanting a quart, so you get that girl there to bring them over here quickly. Oh, and I 'suppose you best have one yourself!" He beamed at his son-in-law. If only he'd been his flesh and blood son, he thought, the son he'd always wanted instead of the daughter that he disliked. Still he'd got him as the next best thing and he was good friend to boot.

Will grinned and strode across the room, greeting Matthew warmly.

"Right glad to see you Father Matt, I see that you have made a friend here, "nodding toward the old man, "you will find he doesn't talk much."

"Oh yes he does, when you say the right thing to him." Matthew replied loudly so that the old man could hear him, and the laborer looked up from his now empty tankard, which he pushed away toward to Will and grinned.

Jane brought three quarts of ale to the table and placed them before the three sitting there. As she left with the empty tankard she looked shyly and Will with the same adoration that she had shown before.

"You had best watch that girl young Will, she's got her eye on you and no mistake, even if she isn't much more than a child – what be she, fifteen, sixteen years old?" Matthew spoke is a low voice so that none could hear.

"Jane is seventeen now Father Matt, and a sweet girl she is too!"

"Then, who's been slapping her face, it wasn't you I'll be bound?"
"Was it Annie?"

"Yes it was, she'll be down in a trice and you can see that she didn't get away with it. Believe me though Father Matt, it is the first time I've lifted a hand to her in all the nine years of marriage!"

"You have done well then boy, I couldn't have lasted so long before I'd had done so. I look forward to seeing the result on my Annie!"

He didn't have to wait long before the lady herself came through the pot-room door. She looked around the room and noted all who were in there. Lastly, she looked towards the fireplace and saw the three sitting by it. There was no look of joy in seeing her father, who she'd not seen for almost two years, and certainly none for the other two either, but she walked over towards their table and greeted Matthew coolly.

"Good evening father, I wonder why you have taken two years to come and see me, and why we are so honoured now?"

Annie had applied a heavy application of rouge to her cheeks to hide the marks beneath and over this she had applied a lavish coating of powder. The cut made by Will's ring she had treated with vinegar and it now showed as a darker mark beneath the rouge and powder. She might have done better to have done nothing, because any form of make-up was alien to her nature. Her father looked hard at her before replying to her greeting.

"Looks to me girl! that you have either been kicked by a horse and you are trying to hide the bruise, or you are going to a ball, and I doubt that! anyway daughter, I have come to see you at last and to see Will here, who I haven't seen for just as long. "He glanced at his son-in-law to make sure that he had picked up the message, saw that he had and continued, "so how's life, apart from kicking horses! treating you my girl?"

Annie's face, as she stood there with hands on hips glaring at the seated men, said it all, "As if I care! It is much the same as always father, and I don't hold out much hope for much better times ahead!"

"Don't you ever have a good word to say about anything? I've never known such a misery as you. Perhaps that's why I haven't been for two years hoping you would have picked up a mite of joy somewhere. Well I've seen you now so I'll say farewell until next time. I want to talk to Will now before I go, so give your Pa a kiss on his cheek to take back as a memory." Matthew leaned towards his daughter who condescendingly leaned forward and gave his offered whiskered cheek a brief peck. Annie then with a "Good night father" turned back towards the pot-room.

Over her shoulder she threw a few suitably sharp replies at the other occupants of the bar who were also interested in her make-up. "Is that right a horse kicked you Annie?! And "You ain't going to no ball are you, less you goes with me my lady!?" and finally "I reckon as your husband put you in your place didn't he?" This last comment seemed to hit home because Annie didn't have a reply for it and went through the door without further comment, slamming it behind her. This raised a few eyebrows and knowing looks were directed at Will's back over by the fire.

Will was saying to Matt ,"I think we'd best go to the back room where we won't be disturbed, so bring your ale with you." Turning to the old laborer he almost apologetically,

"We'll be leaving you now friend, so you drink up your ale as you always do and enjoy it!"

"You be alright you two, not like that shrew what Will wed, and I won't say nothing different before your face Matthew, seeing as that's how you sees her yourself!" the old man looked sympathetically at both men. "I thank you for the ale Matthew and both of you for your company, good night." With that he looked back into his tankard again and the two got up and went through into the pot-room.

There they found Jane washing pots on her own. She looked up expectantly when they entered and her face lit with a smile at seeing Will. There was no sign on Annie.

"Where's your mistress?" Will asked looking closely at the girl and noticing for the first time how pretty she was under the dirty face and uncombed hair. "You had best leave them pots Jane and go out there again, there's no-one there again to serve."

"She went up the stairs I think Sir, anyway she never stopped here nor spoke to me." The girl answered almost smugly. She did as she was bid went into the parlour.

THE BLACK BOY

CHAPTER SEVEN

Will led Matthew into the back room and they sat at the small table there placing their tankards on it. "So, I hope you have got good news Father Matt." He said. " I am right glad to see you so soon again." He grinned expectantly at his father-in-law.

"Yes, it is news indeed, you recall that I was off to do business that night, well the cutter what was delivering to me will be pleased to do so again as often as you like. His next run is in a fortnight's time and he reckons to be off the Wallet at full tide on Wednesday night, that'll be about eight o'clock. Captain's name be William Dowsett, out of Paglesham and the Cutter's names the "Neptune." No one other than you and me need know of that Will." Matt looked across at Will, who nodded fully understanding the need for caution. "I've told the captain as you'll be taking a small load this time, but you expect trade to increase with each shipment, 'half ankers of Geneva, the same of Cognac brandy and five bales of Tobacco - what'll weigh about forty pounds each. I'll settle with Dowsett and we'll call this your first loan my boy. You pay me when you can and when you have sold on. Alright?" he smiled at the man opposite.

Will was at a loss for words. He had wondered how he was going to pay for this first shipment, but now that worry was behind him and he looked with affection at his father-in-law. "I won't try to thank you father Matt, but as you have put your trust in me, I swear I won't let you down!"

"I know that, if I didn't I would not be offering it."

"You had best tell me the total sum to be paid, so I can work out a selling price and what I've got to pay my men."

"The gin is 15/- a tub and the cognac brandy £1.7/6. The tobacco, all rolling leaf, cost you £3.1/- a bale. The lot be £121/- and before you ask it, I have taken my cut already! Now I know as it is a lot of money, but if I know you Will, you'll soon be showing a profit, you might even double your money with the first load!" Matt grinned and then went on.

"That night, today fortnight, you be waiting for me on Lawling Creek. Before it reaches Mundon Creek, down by the little farm with a brick house, there's a deep cut right up to the road. You be there Will and you take with you a spout lantern and from ten o'clock till I get there, you keep flashing it every few minutes. Tides full out at two in the morning and not flooded again till eight next morning, and I'll want to be away as soon as I can float my "MOLLY" again, so as I'm in Fullbridge first light as always with my load of oysters. I'll be a coming up the river and It'll be dark, hull down against Osea Island. You should be seeing me as I come round the Mundon Stone. At that point I'll have water abeam and aft of me and clear of land!"

Matt rose to his feet, having said all that he had come to do and started to move towards the back door.

"Are you not going to stop the night?" asked Will.

"No boy, I don't want to see her again just yet!" he grinned. "I stabled my hired horse with you and fed it your hay. I'll go out this way and none will be the wiser. I'll see you at Mundon Creek next Wednesday." He held out his hand and Will grasped it clapping his left hand on Matt's shoulder.

"You be a good man Matthew Rowlings and I'm proud to have you as my father-in-law and friend. I'll be there as agreed and I'll look out the old spout lantern what is hidden in the stable. I'll be meeting with my men tomorrow and to fix up the carts and like. Now take this light with you and leave it in the stable when you go."

Matthew took the lantern and cleared his throat grunting something like "you is a good boy too son." He went out with barely a glance behind him. At the stable he saddled and mounted his horse and set off immediately back to Maldon. It was dark, but he knew his way well. He took care, as he well knew full well that there were places along the way which were favoured by the few footpads and highwayman who frequented the grassed edges of the road in order to deaden the sound of its hooves. However, he arrived back at the Ostler's yard on Market Hill. He was stiff and sore from the ride, being unused to this mode of transport very often, he banged on his door demanding attention. The Ostler woke and came to the door in his nightgown, took the horse and the money from Matthew and bade him good night and went off to stable the horse, still in his night attire.

Matthew left the stable yard and went down the hill to its foot where his boat "'MOLLY'" lay at the wharf of Fullbridge. He went on board where he found young Silas dozing between crates of oysters. As soon as he heard his Captain's heavy footfalls on the deck, he leapt to his feet clasping the marlin spike which he had sat all night with in case of thieves.

"Good boy Silas, not sleeping this time I'll wager, you don't like the notion of being keel-hauled then?" Matt grinned at the boy in the dark and ruffled his hair, "You can sleep now as I'm aboard, but we will have to unload this lot," pointing to the crates of oysters," soon as the carts moore up, so you had best get your head down now."

The following morning Will roused to a tap on the window of his room. Getting from his bed, he pulled back the sacking curtain, pushed open the shutter and in the dim light of dawn he saw Sam outside.

"Good morning Sam. What brings you to knock so early?" he said.

"I'm seeing the boys today and less you hear otherwise, we'll be in your stable at seven o'clock tomorrow night. We'll come separately and round the back of mine so we are note seen passing your parlour door. It'll be safe that way since old Tom Wright next door to me died, and his widow went into the workhouse and the place has been empty ever since. I hear as John Laytham's going to ask your brother if he and his can move up here. Might be better don't you think Will?"

"We'll talk on it tonight Sam, like you say seven o'clock." Will pulled the curtain back again and while Sam walked off towards the kilns, he turned to pull on his boots. He had to decide on the profit he wanted to make and how he was going to pay his gang. He sat for a moment recalling the prices, which he knew were being asked by smugglers and realized that he would have to undercut these rates in order to build his market, but at the same time he couldn't afford to be mean with those who were going to do the work for him. No, he'd start at a rate which all would very much appreciate, five shillings per man for this small first shipment and thereafter he'd gradually increase to six shillings each. For a night's work and based on their income of seven shillings for six days work at his brother's works, this was a handsome extra income. He realized that he didn't need all five men for the first load, but considered the question and came up with the answer that to avoid any ill feeling he would employ them all, but the youngest Roote boy and young Archer he'd pay 4/- each.

With regard to his own profit, he would expect to be almost able to pay Matthew's loan off on this first load alone and at that rate he would be paying his way certainly by the third shipment.

He got up, rinsed his face in the bowl and went through to the pot-room. Annie was up and about before him for once and young Jane was sweeping the boarded floor. Both looked up as he entered.

"Have you eaten yet?" he enquired to neither in particular and receiving no reply from his wife and simply a shaken head from Jane he said, "well I have got to eat, so one of you get me some bread and a bit of cheese and bring it into the parlour…..Oh, and I'll have a jug of ale along with it." He went through to the parlour and sat at the table by the fire that he'd occupied the previous evening. The great logs fed into it last night were still smoldering in the hearth and the brickwork gave a wonderful warmth. He sat and reveled in both the warmth and the feeling of excitement, which the start of the new venture had given him. How much better to have an aim than to drift day by day as he'd done for the past few years.

After the initial enjoyment and the full occupation of getting his business at *The Black Boy* started in his first year there, and then the anticipation of a wonderful marriage the following year, when that latter proved very soon to be a disaster he had been left feeling unfulfilled. It had been then that he had drifted into a bit of smuggling with the help of his father-in-law, and for a short while this had given him a purpose, but for the past couple of years since ceasing to be a 'free-trader' he had slipped back into his listless ways until now!

He watched Jane as she went through to the tap room and returned with a pint of ale, which she placed in front of him with a shy smile. Shortly afterwards, as she turned back towards the pot-room, its door crashed open and out came Annie carrying a trencher of bread and cheese.

"Your face is looking better today woman. Better that is without all that paint and powder, looks better where you have washed it off!"

Annie put the trencher in front of him. "If you hadn't welted me there wouldn't have been any need for any of that" she growled.

"Take care woman, I've done it once now and any more of your miserable ways and I'll do it again, so start smiling instead of glaring and look like you enjoy life!"

"Will, I haven't enjoyed life yet, so I don't expect to start now." She spun on her heel and marched out through the pot-room door where Jane had just gone.

Will shrugged his great shoulders and fell upon his bread and cheese which he washed down with his beer. He wasn't going to let that woman sour his day, not when he had started it feeling so good.

Later that morning, he went out onto the common to see if he could see Reuben Belbin's caravan, but it wasn't where it had been the previous time, so he didn't look further assuming that the gypsy had taken his advice and left the area. Had he done so he would have found it tucked away in the gorse and scrub lower down the hill, well hidden from view.

That evening a little before seven, he was waiting in the feed store of the stables. A dark lantern stood on the oats-feed chest and William leaned against the wall beside it waiting for his men. On time, they arrived. He greeted each in turn and waited until they had formed a semi-circle around him, before coming to the point of their meeting.

"I've got good news for you, I've met the man who is going to supply us with our first shipment. A small one, as a trial, is coming next Wednesday. We have to be at Lawling Creek at ten o'clock and maybe have to wait an hour or so 'til the boat comes. We'll need two carts only this time, so I expect you to bring two of my brothers. I'll talk to him tomorrow to make it right with him… now with a small load like this one, we don't need five of us…." Will paused and seeing the disappoint-ment on the faces of the three younger men, he went on, "but so's we all know what's what for the next time, we'll all go." There was an audible sigh of relief from his listeners.

"For this first trip, Sam, Joshua and John, I'll pay each of you five shillings and you two, Daniel and David it'll be four shillings. Next time with a bigger load you will each get five shillings." He looked round at the men. "Alright with you all?" Seeing the nodded and happy agreement, he continued. "So, I'll tell you in good time where and what time we'll meet that night, but you make sure that the carts are clean and ready. We don't want tubs going to customers all covered in tile clay!"

He then said good night to each in turn as the five left to return to either their houses or to the alehouse door by the way of the rear of the next door cottages. Giving them a few moments to get on their way, he picked up a lantern and walking back slowly before entering the parlour bar.

THE BLACK BOY

CHAPTER EIGHT

Will spent the remaining time before the shipment was due in visiting prospective customers, but the first call he had to make was to his brother John, and the following day after the meeting in the stable, he mounted his horse and rode over to the tile works to find him.

He found John where he expected to find him, checking the fire temperature beneath the kiln into which he had placed the stacks of tiles to be fired. They were carefully laid in layers with thin laths between them to prevent them from sticking together. The temperature was critical in order that they were properly fired. In serious cases if under-firing this could mean that the finished tile could, within a few years, revert to clay from which it had come. John Horne, like his father before him was a stickler for a good product.

"G'day to you young William, what brings you here so early in the morning?" John straightened up and closed the iron door of the kiln's fire pit before turning to his brother. "You are very welcome brother, come on over to the side here and we'll have some tea." He held Will's bridle while he dismounted and led him to a small shelter beside the kiln.

Will hitched the horse outside and followed him in. There was a small fire in the back against the kiln wall and suspended over it was a cauldron of boiling water. From a chest beside the fire, John lifted the lid and removed a canister of tea, which together with a jug and two earthenware mugs he placed on the tope of the chest after closing the lid.

"It is the first tea I've had since last I came calling here John. I don't have anymore since I stopped the smuggling two years ago, so I'll relish it even the more."

"Oh, I still have it, but of course it is cheap now as the duty was dropped two years ago, so if that's when you stopped buying it, you best start again brother."

Will watched as John made the tea, strong and dark as he liked it and he took the proferred mug in both hands, warming them on it as he did so. "My customers don't often ask for tea, so I don't bother with it myself, anyway, it is on the matter of free trading that I have come to see you John," he said. "I'm going back into it again."

"And it is my guess then as you will be wanting my help, like before, right?" John asked quickly.

"Yes John, this first time I'll need just a brace of carts, but then later on maybe two more. I'm hoping that we can come to the same agreement as we had before. Two carts for a half-anker of spirit of your own choice. What do you say brother?"

"What men have you got to drive them Will? Or would they maybe my workers?" Seeing his brother's wry grin, he chuckled and said "I knew it, alright I won't ask you who, they know the risks and what they do after dark is not any concern of mine. If they get taken by the revenue, I'll replace them but I'm never happy to lose good workers, so they best take care. Yes, you can have the carts with pleasure, but lose them brother, and you'll be in my debt, make no mistake, I can't afford the loss of just one cart."

"Of course I understand and if we lose one to the riders, I'll return what's due, you know that John."

Despite their earlier rivalry and Will's discomfort with regard to his brother's right to own and control the tile business, once the agreement had been made with their father and *The Black Boy* was William's they were once again the best of friends and either would do what they could to help each other. The four years difference in their ages gave John a protective feeling towards Will and he was prepared to do what he was asked of him – within reason that was. He wouldn't, on the other hand, go out of his way to offer assistance if unasked; it was an arrangement, which suited them both.

John nodded his acceptance and they drank their tea sitting on the piles of bricks placed in the lean-to-shelter for that purpose, in comfortable and companionable silence. Will at last rose and shaking his brother's hand went out, re-mounted his mare and rode off up the hill in the direction of Danbury village. He had planned which establishments he would call on and the next one was the parsonage beside Danbury Church. Previously he had done similar business with the parson, who enjoyed both tea and brandy, Will was hoping that he hadn't lose his taste for the latter.

He rode up the hill, along the track which skirted the graveyard and approached the back entrance to the Parsonage. There he met the Parson's housekeeper who knew William from earlier days and without consulting the parson, agreed to take a tub of geneve and one of cognac brandy on his behalf. Had Will been offering port-wine, she would have taken a 'bottle or two' of that too because she well knew her employer's particular preferences! Will promised that the next time he would add port wine to his order. From there Will went to the Griffin Inn which stood on the top of the hill on the turnpike from Maldon to Chelmsford. After a little persuasion, and a substantial discount in price, Will managed to secure an on-going supply of spirits and tobacco, undercutting that which the tavern were currently paying its smuggling supplier. From there he called at two other alehouses in the village and by the same means, that is undercutting the prices being paid, he secured immediate orders for the goods coming in on Matthew's '"MOLLY"'.

The following day he travelled to Great Baddow where he had various acquaintances and agreed to supply them as he had previously done. Within a week, Will had placed all that was due in on '"MOLLY"'s' first cargo and he was well pleased. He had decided on this occasion to avoid the Latchingdon, Stowe Maries and Cold Norton areas as these would mean travelling a different road to that which led to Danbury and Baddow.

On the Saturday night following the meeting in the stable, *The Black Boy's* parlour was as usual busy. Old Wilf was there, James Towns, who was looking and feeling unhappy. He had attempted to see the gypsy during the past few days, but it appeared that he had moved on. James, like Will, had assumed this to be so when first he'd looked for his caravan and hadn't seen it, so he hadn't searched the common. He'd asked the other occupants of the common but, either they genuinely didn't know the whereabouts of Reuben Belbin and his family, or they had closed ranks, as their kind was used to doing. Reuben was in fact still there, hidden away in the gorse and venturing out only at night when he was unlikely to be seen.

Jim couldn't speak to Wilf about it, so he kept up a morose silence answering his old companion in mono-syllables. Wilf for his part ignored him and spoke only to the others who shared their table that night. Across the room Sam Rowe, John Laytham, Joshua and Daniel Roote and David Archer seemed in good spirits, anticipating the extra income which they would receive from the first smuggling venture. No thought was given to the possibility that they might be apprehended on the night by the Riding Officers, gaoled, transported or even hung.

"The tile workers seem wholly happy tonight don't they Jim?" observed Old Wilf, leaning across to his friend, "what do you think has made them so riotously happy?"

"Don't know Wilf, but they must be blessed of fortune aren't they, not like me, who never gets a thing right." Jim sunk lower in his seat and peered into his ale tankard. "Them Horne men always get the best of everything, whatever it is and us landmen get nothing . I gotta change that Wilf and you knows what I am talking about!"

"Whatever you got scheming you had best get on with it boy, or you'll be the death of me. I can't abide a misery, I've seen enough of it in one lifetime."

"Yes I will, but my first plan went amiss and I ain't started on my next."

Wilf looked sharply at James.

"Like I said before, what you do is your own affair and don't include me, but I reckon if you believed it to be easy and after no more than a week, you are going to pitch it away without trying. If your set on it, then don't let it go!"

Jim looked up and grinned at him. "Course, you are right old friend, I'll look into the matter in the morning, but now, lets have another ale."

For the rest of evening James perked up and was noticeably more like himself and it was much like old times again. He had made a decision to somehow find that gypsy, even if it meant going to Tiptree Heath, where Jim knew the man must have friends amongst the many gypsies who frequented the area. Tomorrow, he would start by searching the common properly, particularly the scrub and thicket area to the south by the brook.

On the way back to Paternoster that evening, Wilf said, "I know that I have told you in the past not to mention it again, but seeing that your are having trouble getting started, all I say is perhaps you ought to talk to Will, he might have a bit of advice for you."

"I have done that Old Wilf, and he denied any thought of going back into the smuggling trade again and told me to forget any such-like notion."

Wilf fell silent for a moment and then said, "perhaps he truly meant it then Jim, and without someone who is going to arrange the loads, and no-one to drive the loads for you? maybe you should take heed of Will and forget your notions."

Jim grunted but didn't reply. He'd already made up his mind and tomorrow after matins at Danbury Church, he'd look for the gypsy.

The next week was a long one for the tile workers, who were to carry the contraband. On the following Saturday, although the five of them were in *The Black Boy*, they were less exuberant than they had been the week before. They had yet to be told by William, where and at what time to meet the following Wednesday, and apart from knowing that it was to be at Lawling Creek, near Mundon, that the boat would land her cargo, they knew of no other arrangement. They were keen to have it all finalised for them.

It was difficult for them, because sworn to secrecy as they were, they couldn't discuss it in the alehouse and only amongst themselves with certain privacy. If Will didn't speak to them on Sunday, Sam agreed to ask him on their behalf. In the meantime, they would make sure that the carts which they were to use, would be cleaned of clay by Tuesday and not used on Wednesday.

At about eleven o'clock, the alehouse was almost clear of customers, most having left an hour before. Apart from the old laborer in his usual position by the fire, only two others remained, Sam and John. As they rose to go, the pot-room door opened and William emerged. He beckoned to the two and walked quickly over to toward the door. Reaching it, he tore it open and satisfied that no-one lurked there eavesdropping, he said quietly to Sam, "Meet me at your stable Sam. Wait until I get there and I'll tell you about what is happening on Wednesday night. Don't you wait John, Sam'll tell you tomorrow, so you leave like always, just say good night and head off home."

Without a word, John nodded and the two went down the steps. Will returned and helping the old labourer to his feet, bade him goodnight before watching him stumble off down the steps. He watched Jane as she picked up the empty tankards and he then followed her into the pot-room. Again, he was almost surprised to notice how pretty she really was, one day she would be some man's dream he thought!

Annie was at the pot-room table, this time mending a birch broom, whipping the birch twigs to the handle with reeds. She was very skillful at such things, being the daughter of a fisherman, who had taught her to repair nets and baskets since she was small. For once she looked almost happy in what she was doing. She would become engrossed in such chores and lose herself in them until something occurred to annoy her. That had happened when she had become bored with trying to mend the old tankards and had taken it out that day on the girl!

"You've not lost your touch with mending, have you Annie." Will remarked in a friendly way. "You have always been good haven't you?"

Immediately, his mood changed and Annie glowered at both the broom and her husband. "What do you mean by that?" she snapped suspicious as always of some criticism or other."

"Not a thing wife… I mean it."

In the background, Jane bent over the pots she was washing looking almost disappointed.

"I'm going out the back to see the horse be bedded down for the night, then I'll be back."

Will went through to the back room and then out of the rear door. There by stable and pigsty Sam was waiting for him.

"We've got to be at Lawling Creek before ten o'clock and it will take us best part of four hours to get there and be ready for the boat. We'll leave here come five o'clock and take the Purleigh road to the Wash and Blind Lane to Mundon wash. We'll then go down by New Hall Creek, I'll go ahead to look out for any trouble and you two carts will keep together." Will stopped for a moment "And one more thing that we have got to do. You'll find plenty of sacks what we can tie to the horses's hooves and around the cart wheels. We won't need them until after Mundon Wash, but the road from there will be gravel and the carts make a whole lot of noise! I know from times before. Alright Sam you got that?"

"Yes, Will I'll pass it on to the rest tomorrow. You have spoken to John, your brother about this haven't you?" Sam asked and in the dim light he saw Will's nodded reply.

"Til Wednesday then", they shook hands and parted.

THE BLACK BOY

CHAPTER NINE

On the Sunday morning following his decision in *The Black Boy* the night before, Jim for once was not amongst the congregation, when most of the community of Horne Row was trailing up the hill to St John's Church at Danbury; he had left the house early that morning having decided in the night not to lose time by spending an hour and a half at the Church over Matins. The Good Lord wouldn't mind this once and he'd ask for forgiveness the following Sunday.

First, he went to the stable to turn his horse out to the field behind, only to find that Wilf had been there before him and had done so when he turned his own mare out to grass. Finding this chore done, he filled the water butt and put hay in the manger, so that evening he would have little to do. Then he set off for the common.

He though he'd systematically work his way from Woodhill to the west across to Horne Row cottages in the east and back again and so on until he came to the foot of the hill where amongst the thick scrub progress would become slower and more difficult. If he hadn't found him by then, then the gypsy wasn't there. Was it possible to hide something as large as a caravan down there? He asked himself. Well he'd soon find out.

Jim watched his neighbours making their way up the hill from the seclusion of a patch of gorse. He saw his family in a group in the centre of the column and noticed that Simon kept looking around, obviously for him, but Jim had come to the conclusion that to confide in his brother was risky. He knew what a mischief he could be and the last thing he wanted was to have it known what he was hoping to do. When the church-goers had disappeared from view, Jim continued his search. By the time the service was over and the congregation had retuned, he was two thirds of the way down the slope, had left the sheep grazed open common and was amongst the thicket.

When he found the caravan, it took him by surprise, it was so well hidden and it was in fact the smell of Reuben's horse and Rachel's cooking pot that alerted him to its presence. He was about to step out into the open area beside the van, when a vice-like grip on his elbow from behind and a knife which appeared before his face stopped him in his tracks.

"And what are you doing here? Come on boy, tell me your business right now or I'll slit your neck!" Reuben's grip on Jim's elbow and his hold on the knife at his throat, were rigid. "You seem to me to be looking for somebody or something;" now it wouldn't be me by any chance would it boy?"

Jim swallowed hard, he had seen how the gypsy was unafraid to use a knife when he attempted to stab William, and now he was here with his knife at Jim's throat, far enough away from others to commit a murder without fear of being apprehended.

"I'll be right straight with you Mister Belbin, I was looking for you, but not for malicious design, only because I need your help!"

The gypsy hadn't been called mister many times in his life and he now revelled in the term. He was also intrigued that someone should know his name and should seek his help; did he know this lad? He was perhaps slightly familiar, but he looked like so many of his age that he couldn't be sure. He relaxed his grip a little. "Alright boy you seem to know my name, now I want to know what's yours, and how can I help you?"

"My name is James Towns, I am a worker…..a horseman on Paternoster Farm." He added horseman as he felt that for what he was about to suggest, Reuben might be less interested in a simple worker, than one who could have access to a cart. "You going to let go now? And I haven't got more than a clasp knife in my smock, so I aint no threat to you."

"Yes, I know that!" the gypsy chuckled, "I already felt you over for a pistol. I know how to be careful!" He carefully released Jim, but kept the knife in full view. "Come on boy and talk to me about what you're asking."

From nowhere there now appeared Rachel and the three children, but they kept a safe distance from the two men who now sat on two seats each made from forked branches dug into the ground and with a cross bar which acted as a bench seat. Reuben waited for Jim to begin. He'd learnt from Jerimiah that the best answers always came without a question being put.

James took a deep breath, "I heard what you said to Will at *The Black Boy* on Tuesday last, and I heard what he said to you. It is also the way I learnt your name; you told Will who you were. It doesn't matter how I came to hear, but from what was said, Will don't look to be interested, and you seem to be in the know." He looked at Reuben to see his reaction....there was none! Reuben realized that the young man had overheard in the same way that he had done on the previous Saturday, so he waited to hear more. "Well," went on Jim, "I have the use of a horse and cart and if you are wanting it for carrying a load at any time, I'm your man. I need the money, it'll pay and I'm willing to go anywhere so long as it is no more than a half night's travel at a time. My cart has to be back by first light of a morning."

"Alright James Towns, maybe we can do business together. At the same time, we can pull a stroke on that Landlord, William Horne, God rot his soul!" Reuben added viciously.

"I knows that you are not on exactly friendly terms with Will, but I don't mean him no harm." Jim interjected quickly, "he hasn't done anything wrong to me and that isn't why I have come to talk to you."

The gypsy quickly realizing his mistake reassured Jim. "Oh, don't you worry about that, young James, I am not about to do more than sell some goods." He said, and then in a friendly voice with a smile, went on, "call me Reuben if you are so minded. Now before we go any further together, I wonder if you would give me the names of the other gang members what is all set on this business of smuggling."

"What do you mean, Reuben, there isn't any other gang as I know of!"

"Where are they from? Here in Horne Row, or from roundabouts?" Reuben continued.

Jim genuinely had no idea what Reuben was talking about.

"Yes, Horne Row, in truth they're from the alehouse. There's five of them. Now you must know their names because I reckon as they drink in there regularly." The gypsy looked shyly at Jim, encouraging him to think hard as to who the five might be. He watched Jim's face as he thought about it, but from it he couldn't learn more than the fact that Jim was non-plussed.

"I'll think on it Reuben, but why do you want to know their names, I thought you could supply the goods yourself, why do you need other folk?"

"Yes, youre right Jim, we don't need anyone else, it was my inquisitive side which likes to know these things, simple as that. So, you forget it Jim, but of-course if you do find out, you can tell me then, alright?" Reuben stood up, gently knocked out his pipe to avoid breaking the delicate clay stem and gestured Jim to follow him. They walked via the labyrinth of paths through the scrub until Reuben stopped and turned and said to Jim. "Next time you come calling you hang a bit of old rag on this here bit of broom and I'll know to meet you here a day hence. Don't come barging in like today, if you do you will not be welcome. If you see a bit of rag on this bush, you come straight to my van, I'll have news for you."

Jim set off up the hill and behind him the gypsy watched him go, satisfied that at last he was getting somewhere and would soon have something to report to Jerimiah. At the same time, he now had to plan as to how he could get even with Will without bringing in help from the Heath and more importantly, how he was going to profit financially from it. He turned and made his way back to his family.

THE BLACK BOY

CHAPTER TEN

On the following Sunday during the walk to church, Sam told the others to plan for next Wednesday. It was difficult to contain young Daniel Roote's excitement, but his brother Josh's warning punch in the ribs and Sam's scowl brought him down to earth. They would meet after church at the cart sheds at the kilns, Sam would tell them more.

The sermon that day was interminable and although it was known by the whole congregation that the parson was not only a man well known for his prodigious consumption of alcohol, but as previously shown was a good customer to the smugglers, the sermon's theme was the avoidance of strong dink and abiding by the law. What was the Reverend Snaith trying to say?

By Tuesday night the two carts required were clean and awaiting the use to which they were to be put to. Two strong horses had been chosen, one was the one which Josh regularly drove and the other as used by David Archer. A collection of sacks and sacking had been put together and was lying in the carts ready for use.

Will went to see his bother John on Wednesday afternoon at four o'clock, to make certain that there would be no delay to their departure, and he was assured that all was as he would have wanted it.

"Good fortune brother Will, I hope all goes well and I look forward to my tub of Cognac.!" He grinned at his brother, "so now you know!"

They clasped hands and Will walked off towards the cart sheds. Dusk was approaching and with it a light mist was rolling up the hill. Will sniffed the air and knew that at midnight, that the mists will have become thick November fog. A perfect night for the job in hand.

The five smugglers were waiting for Will's arrival at that cart shed. Within half an hour it was likely to be dark. Eager to be on their way, Josh and David were already at the reins ready to go. When Will appeared the five heaved a sigh of relief and Sam climbed into Josh's cart while Daniel and John mounted David's.

"You all know the way we're going and I'll be ahead of you watching the road. We've five hours to get there, but I'd be happier to be there early rather than late. I'll come back to you every mile so don't stop for any reason." With that William mounted his horse and led his small column out from the tile works into the mist and onto the road to Purleigh.

As Will had foreseen, the fog began to come down thickly and he began to worry that it might not be easy for Matthew to find the landing point. If Will's light couldn't be seen through the fog, then he might miss Mundon Stone and the night would be wasted. They arrived at Purleigh Wash at around half past seven. Now, he had less than two miles to go. At the junction with the Maldon Road and Mundon Wash, they stopped and bound the horse's hooves and the wheel rims with sacking. Along Blind Lane from Purleigh to Mundon Wash there had been very few houses and their presence advertised by the horse's hooves and wagon wheels was unlikely to have been heard, but beyond that, there were houses owned by well-to-do people who might question carts moving at night! They were particularly wary of the White House, which was known to be the residence of a wealthy land owner and Justice of the Peace, whose position, with regard to smuggling, was unknown. At Mundon Wash, Will was there to meet the carts, and after their precautions and with the muffling effect of the fog, they made their way almost silently down New Hall Lane to the end, where they turned toward the brick-built farmhouse and arrived at the cut which Matthew has described.

There, Will took the spout lantern from his saddle bag and prepared it for use. It was shaped like a water can with a very long spout. In the body of the lantern was a candle, behind which was a mirror. The light from this lantern would be seen only at the open end of the spout. By moving his hand over this end, the user could flash the light towards a point ahead, sure in the knowledge that no-one else could see it. Will now took the lantern and standing below the saxifrage banks, which lined the cut, he began to signal towards the estuary. It was early yet, he knew, but the fog becoming thicker by the minute, there was a serious risk that Matthew could miss his light. He could see less than fifty yards now and the stone was almost a mile beyond! He began to despair, but kept flashing the light in hope.

Half an hour later he saw a dark shadow creep into his vision in the open water before him. It was the ""MOLLY"" in whose bow he could see young Silas with a long punting pole directing his skipper by hand signals at the same time fending the boat off of the mud banks. Ten minutes later she slid into the cut and a rope was thrown to those on shore. Once tied to the bank by means of mud spikes and a gang plank was laid from the boat's gunnale to the bank, the five men from Horne Row swiftly began unloading. Unlike many landing places where pack horses had to transport tubs of spirit two at a time by means of rope cradle over their backs to carts waiting off the mud some distance away, this was easy. The carts were but twenty yards away and the tubs could easily be carried by hand from the boat to the carts for loading.

Whilst his men dealt with this unloading, Will went on board to see Matthew. Young Silas assisted with the unloading, instructing which tub contained which spirit so that there could be no mistake later on.

"Hello Will," his father-in-law greeted him. "Good light you showed saw it right away!" he laughed at his own joke. "With this fog I was worried that you wouldn't be here and then I went further up the creek and I spotted your light exactly where it should have been!"

"It is some time since I used one of these spout lanterns, but I haven't forgotten how, even if I didn't know whether or not you could see it. How do you find this cut? You couldn't see where it was until you were here."

"Remember this Will my boy, I've sailed these waters all of my life and knows every inch of marsh and mud, I'll always find my way."

"Glad I am to see you anyway Father Matt," Will replied, "with any luck we'll have you empty in time to get off before the bottom of the tide. What do you reckon?"

Matt looked over the side at the ebbing water "Yes, if you can do it in another half hour, it should do, but with this fog it don't matter greatly. There's no revenue men going to be on the marshes tonight."

Will nodded and called quietly to his men, telling them to hurry the few remaining tubs of spirit and bales of tobacco. By midnight, the boat was unloaded, the carts ready to leave the ""MOLLY"" with a little help from the punt poles which she carried and which the captain and his small mate Silas now used to great effect, she floated off into the main channel of Lawling Creek and disappeared into the fog to continue her voyage to the wharf at Maldon.

Will mounted and led the two carts back the way they had come. Again, he rode ahead to ensure that they were not driving into an ambush of Excise men, or, another smuggling gang. They didn't remove the sacking muffling from the horses or the cart wheels until they had reached the far end of Blind Lane at Purleigh Wash. The remainder of the journey back was uneventful and within four hours they had arrived back at *The Black Boy*.

Pulling up before Sam's cottage, Will gave his instructions, "David and Daniel pull your cart up to the back of Sam's house against his stable, sheet it over with sacking, un-hitch your horse and take it and the two of you go off home…. And be quiet in doing it so as no-one hears you and wakes to look at what your doing!"

"Will, if we unhitch the horse and drop the shafts, with all that weight of licker, we'll never pick them up again!" remarked David. "We will do our best to prop the tumbril's front and back to make certain before taking the horse away."

"You knows your own horse and cart boy, you do what's needed, but whatever you do don't make any noise!" Turning to Sam will said, "You bring John and Josh and follow me up the hill. We've got a few calls to make this night." He turned his horse and the other three followed in the cart, up the hill towards Danbury Village. The Parson's grog would be delivered to his back door that night as would the orders given by the other three alehouses in the village. A small consignment to each of the three great houses and the deliveries were complete. All that remained in the cart were five bales of tobacco which would, over time, be divided into manageable packages and sold either by Will to his customers at *The Black Boy*, or, to a similar establishment.

Satisfied with his night's work, Will returned with his men to Sam's house and there they unloaded the tobacco and carried it round to the stables. For the moment they stacked it in the stable and Josh and Daniel took the horse and cart home to their cottage by the kiln.

When they had gone, Will spoke to Sam. "We've got to find a store for these goods in the future. It isn't any good hoping that nobody will come a snooping. Now I can't use my cellar because of The Riding Officers know of it, and that is the first place they will look if they're a mite suspicious, and we can't use yours due to your family will learn of it. So we've gotta find another hiding place."

THE BLACK BOY

CHAPTER ELEVEN

"There might be a way to hide the goods and nobody will be the wiser." Sam said quietly in the darkness and the fog, which enveloped the two men as they stood together on the cart-way between *The Black Boy* and the rear of Sam's house. "Do you remember the cellar here when you was a little'un Will?"

"Yes, I remember it well, we weren't ever to go in there, my old pa didn't want us to see what was there, but of course we all knew it was a bit of smuggling like so many did then, long before he took up the making of bricks and tiles." Will cast his mind back to his childhood and the warnings he and his siblings had received about the cellar from their father, and what would happen to any of them if there were to enter it. By the time they left the cottage for the larger one down the lane by Ludgores Farm, the cellar had been forgotten and Old John Horne's smuggling days were far behind him. "Anyway, your cellar isn't any good to us, you can only get to it from inside your house - right away your family would know all about it and you know how your littl'ns will talk."

"You never disobeyed your Pa, did you," Sam said…"You never went down there did you?" Sam asked, ignoring Will's reply; and not receiving an answer, he said, "I thought as much, it seems like your old pa knew what he was about, because there's another cellar here under this here cart-way!" He stamped his boot quietly on the track between the houses.

Will looked incredulous, "What do you mean another one? It is first I have heard of it, why do you only mention it now Sam, if you have known about it all this time?"

"I didn't find it right away when I moved in here from the little house down on the common, the door in the end wall where it goes under the cart-way was hidden behind a pile of boxes and a stack of timber, what I never needed to move for years. When I did, I found this here door and when I looked in, I was amazed as to how big that cellar was. It is like a tunnel and I reckon it is close to meeting up with your own wall there." Sam pointed across to the side wall of *The Black Boy.*

"Sam, you might have the riddle's answer!" Will said enthusiastically and without realizing the time of day added, "tomorrow you can show me this cellar, perhaps there's a way of entering it from out here so's not to enter your house."

"You mean today, I expect don't you?"

"Oh, yes of course."

They bid each other goodbye and went into their respective home,s in which the occupants were in the course of rising. Will went through the rear door into his room. For a few minutes he sat on the bed and thought about the night's work. All had gone well and once the second cart-load had been delivered the following night, he could start planning the next cargo. Much of that delivery he would do himself, but he'd need some help. Sam was the first obvious choice, yes, the two of them would manage the Baddow deliveries in one night easily. At the same time, he'd get Sam to show him the cellar.

He rose from the edge of his cot where he had sat and went through to the pot-room where young Jane was sweeping the floor. The hatch which led to *The Black Boy's* cellar lay against the outside wall. There was a mat over it which hid the ring handles by which it was raised. There was little point in hiding once the Excise Men had seen it during a surprise visit a few years before when they found Will down there checking over his contraband stock. Matters had been settled then with a substantial bribe to the two officers concerned, but it had meant the end of the use of the cellar as a hiding place for such wares. Will now used it solely for legitimate stock and to store items which were unlikely to be wanted just at the moment. Each time the Riding Officers called, and it wasn't always the same ones as those who had received the bribe, clearly word had obviously gone around amongst them that this place was a source of income, the first place they searched was the cellar. If they were able to catch *The Black Boy* dealing in smuggled goods they had two choices, either, report and seize the goods in order to receive a percentage of the contraband's value, or, to persuade the Landlord to part with a bribe, which of course had to be and was likely to be considerably more than the payment that they would get from the seizure. After all, smuggling was now a capital offense! Even with the most lenient magistrate who might be sympathetic to smuggling, it would mean a gaol term at the very least.

Will stood for a moment in the doorway and then retraced his steps to the window in his room. Carefully he paced out the distance from this window to the pot-room door and then from there to the trap-door. Jane was watching him with interest. He pulled aside the mat, raised the trap-door and descended the wooden ladder. At the foot of it he looked up to position himself under the edge of the trap-door and found Jane peering down at him.

"Girl, you get on with your chores, pay no attention to what I'm doing I'll be back up after I've looked at what we've got down here." He waited until Jane had disappeared before carefully pacing the distance from the hatch to the end of the wall and confirmed that the cellar was the same size as the pot-room above.

Now that he was sure the cellar's position, he went back up the ladder, but before he did so, he carefully inspected the brickwork of the outside wall, beyond which his father's extra cellar apparently existed, according to Sam. He'd have to wait until that evening to find out just what lay beyond the wall.

Jane was still sweeping the floor and as soon as Will appeared, he got the impression that her sweeping had been as close to the open trap-door as she could safely go without Will seeing her from below. He realized that she could have seen little because he hadn't taken either a lantern, or a candle with him. Anyway, what was there to hide at present? and it wasn't the likes of Jane who were his biggest worry, it was his wife who posed the greatest threat. Later he'd have to address that particular problem, but not now.

"You can shut the latch now young Jane, and put the rug back where it was and then you can fetch me some food, I've a mind to have a bit of meat and some ale." William had a long night and needed proper sustenance. He hadn't yet slept and was unlikely to do so before that night.

"Be it not too early for breakfast with meat Sir, my Ma always told us that meat wasn't good first thing in the day." Jane showed genuine concern.

Gently Will replied, "I think as your Ma was probably saying that there was not any meat to be had anyway, and was making it better for you by saying that it was bad for you. It hasn't hurt me and it is better than cheese!" He smiled at Jane's worried face. "Now when you bring it to me, you have a little taste yourself. Now we've got an 'R' in the month, the pork be wholly good, so you bring me some of that and you try it yourself."

He went through into the parlour and sat himself down. After a few minutes, Jane entered and served him with his food and drink. She then pretended that she felt ill holding her stomach and groaning. When Will asked her what ailed her, she grinned and replied that it must be the pork. "I only had a bit of it and I reckon my Ma was right. It don't do a body no good first thing, but…." She hastened to add mischievously "perhaps I haven't given it a fair go yet!"

Will didn't reply, but simply nodded his head. The girl had spirit, of that there was no doubt but now was not the time for banter. Jane took the hint from the look he gave her and she returned to the pot-room to await the first customers of the day.

When Will had finished eating, he sat back and considered how he should spend his day. He was eager to see the cellar next door, and he also wanted to finish delivering the cargo to Baddow, but neither could he do until the evening. He'd get some sleep before then, otherwise he wouldn't be in the best of tempers later. What the others would do to catch up on sleep, he didn't know, didn't really care, as long as Sam was ready to go that evening and able to show him the cellar, that's all that mattered to him right at this moment.

He then thought of Annie and how he was to keep his resurrected activities from her. Come to think of it, where was she? He hadn't seen her that morning and it was unusual for her to be late rising. He called for Jane, who immediately appeared through the pot-room door.

"Have you seen your mistress today?" he asked.

"No Sir, she ain't been down yet - perhaps she is still sleeping." Jane didn't look too convinced by her own statement and looked at Will with raised eyebrows.

Will got up and walked across the bar. "I'll go up and found out where she is, and you take care that she doesn't come down in one of her moods and take it out on you Jane - so be about your duties and don't be slacking."

Jane was disappointed to hear Will still thought his wife to be a threat. She had felt secure in the protection which this man had given her when Annie had beaten her, but he obviously hadn't got her tamed yet. Oh, how Jane fantasised about herself and her employer becoming lovers. "So, what if she was half his age…. One of the girls at Woodhill had become pregnant by one of the family's sons, when but a few months older than myself" she would say to herself. That of course had ended unhappily, when the girl was thrown out of her employment and her family had to raise the resultant child as one of its own, which, of course they could ill afford. Two years later, the girl and her baby disappeared. They were said to have left for the girl to find work in London, but no-one really knew. In Jane's dreams, it was Annie who left, or even better died, and Will took her, Jane as his wife!

Will climbed the stairs and entered his wife's bedroom. He hadn't been in there for a long time and he was shocked by its squalor. The bed was covered in bedding, which had neither been washed nor aired for months. In the front of the window, which faced west, away from Sam's cottage was a table upon which were a collection of both cosmetics and medications. Prominent in the centre of this array was a bottle of Laudanum, more than half empty and beside the bed was an empty earthenware bottle of gin. On the bed itself lay Annie, in what appeared to be a drunken stupor, but, as Will entered she raised herself on one elbow and looked at him through bleary eyes.

"And what brings my dear husband to my boudoir I wonder? It isn't to lay with me I'll be bound. Anyway I am sick and don't want touching, so go away!"

"You ain't sick woman, your drunk with both gin and Laudanum. How long have you been taking that devil's brew?" Will looked at his wife in disgust. "You sober up and then you come down, there's work to do."

"You don't believe I'm sick, do you Will? Why do you think I'm taking Laudanum? Yes I have been drinking the gin too, but only to help the other to greater effect. What I have got to do, is to see the old wise woman at Mersea,"

"An Old Witch!" said Will.

"Maybe she is, but she really knows her herbs and medicines, though and' I believe this is my only hope."

Will was about to tell her not to be so dramatic and whatever the illness was which she was purporting to suffer from, it was likely to be cured by laying off of the gin and Laudanum, but then a revelation struck him. If she was to go away for even a few days to Mersea, he would have the freedom needed to do whatever was going to be necessary in the cellar. It was the answer to a prayer and silently he thanked the lord for it! He pretended to ponder the matter for a few moments and then said.

"If you are really ailing and this woman can truly cure you, then I think as you should go and see her – but how are we to get you there?"

Annie couldn't believe her ears and immediately smelled a rat! Will had in recent years been anything but sympathetic to her well-being. "Why are you so set on me going, you have never been accommodating to my wishes before?"

"Because dear wife I know when your truly sick and when you're just thinking you are. If this witch can cure you, then the sooner you go to see her the better. I'll have words with my brother John, perhaps I can borrow his trap to take you to Mersea. This afternoon I'll see him and we'll see what's to be done." Will gave his wife a look which he hoped was full of concern and not believing his good fortune, left the room. He went downstairs with the parting reminder to Annie, to take care of herself and await his instruction. On no account was she to leave her room and food would be brought to her by Jane. If there was anything else she wanted, Jane was the one who would supply it.

Downstairs, the look of satisfaction on his face was plain to see and Jane who was waiting in the pot-room, was quick to notice it.

"Be the mistress unwell?" she asked with a knowing look, "or be she drunk?" You don't look like she's too bad, so what's to be done?"

This girl is becoming a bit too familiar thought Will, I ought to put her in her place, but truly her allegiance to him and the companionship which it brought was something new and welcome. He decided to say nothing to mar this relationship.

"My wife be sick Jane and I've got to get her away to a healing woman in Mersea soon as possible. Now you go up and find out what your mistress wants to eat, while I go to my brother to get hold of a trap to take her there." Will hurriedly went out and started towards the stable, but then decided that to saddle up his mare for the short trip over the common was hardly worth the effort, so he turned and strode off over the rabbit eaten grass towards his brother's kilns. There had been a slight frost early that morning and the fog had frozen on to everything as a hoar frost. The grass rustled with ice as his boots brushed through it.

He found John as usual by the kiln, sitting under the lean-to shelter and shipping at a mug of tea. As soon as he saw Will, he rose to his feet and came out of the shelter to greet him.

"I see that I got one of my carts back then Will, and both horses, but I'm still waiting for the other one and more importantly my cognac!" he grinned at Will. "Now, I don't see it in your pocket, nor, on your back, so either it is waiting somewhere to be delivered, or, it ain't going to happen, I'd like to know which brother!"

"Don't fret brother, I'll be bringing it tonight when I deliver the second cart load. But that's not what I have come to see you about now." Will followed John into the shelter and they sat down on the brick seats as before. When they were comfortable, he continued. "You are the only one as I know apart from the parson, what's got a trap and I want to borrow it." He waited to see his brother's reaction before continuing. John simply raised his eyebrows and waited for him to go on. "Annie is not well John and I've got to get her to Mersea as quick as I can. There's a wise woman there, a crone that can cure her, she reckons, and who am I to stand in her way? I said as I'll get her there, but it isn't any good sending her in a cart what'll take most of the day to get there, I need something a mite quicker, like a trap."

John listened and nodded. "Only one thing to ask you Will, why the rush now? Annie's been sick before and you never did this much for her then." He looked shrewdly at his brother." "Either, she be truly ailing or you want her out of the way for a day or two! Which is it?"

Will could rarely hide much from his brother. "I don't think as we needs to discuss the matter John, I have my reasons and all I need to know is, will you let me borrow your horse and trap.?"

"Of course you can, I won't ask anymore, so when do you want it?"

"Tomorrow, but I need one other thing John, I want a man to drive it."

"Haven't you got no-one at your alehouse that can drive her?"

"You knows I don't John, I've only got one worker, young Jane and she isn't any good for that."

"Yes, perhaps I recall her, nice looking wench, been with you for a bit of time now hasn't she? Perhaps she be good for other things?" John grinned at his brother. "Alright Will you can have your horse and trap and a driver to go with it, but at a price! My fee be half anker of gin to go with cognac and I'll expect it here tonight when you deliver the other." John was not going to let his brother get away with it, after all it was business!

"That's alright John, but don't you let Annie know, or let your man let on neither, about any brandy or, Geneva – as I know nothing about."

"Fear not, brother, she won't know anything of our business, as she clearly knows nothing of your own!"

Will smiled, "And that's the way I like it brother. I'll see you at your house tonight with the goods and tomorrow you'll send your man with the trap. It'll be best if you get your man to come to my house to collect Annie, that way there's no danger of her knowing a thing."

"Right." John nodded, "he'll be there by eight o'clock tomorrow morning'."

Very happy with the arrangement, Will made his way back to *The Black Boy*. Upstairs he opened the door to his wife's bedroom. She still lay on the bed but from somewhere had found another bottle of gin, from which she had obviously been drinking. She was now semi-conscious but well aware of Will's presence and as he walked in she turned towards him.

"Well husband, are you going to let me go to Mersea?" and without waiting for the answer, "I'll get there myself if I have to. You can let me have your horse can't you?"

"If you were to wait for the answer, you would learn more of what I have to say… I've talked to my brother John and he'll get one of his men to drive you to Mersea in his horse and trap tomorrow morning. So, you get ready what you want to take with you and I'll see you off in the morning." Will left the room closing the door behind him. Downstairs he found Jane listening at the pot-room door.

"So she's going away then?" she asked with a knowing smile. "How long for?"

"It is none of your business young Jane, you'll find out soon enough."
Will frowned at her, "Now get about your work and look lively. It ain't
until tomorrow as your mistress be going and there's much to do here."

Will pushed her into the pot-room and closed the door. He went
into his room and lay in his cot closing his eyes. After a few minutes he
was asleep.

He woke in the late afternoon and sat up, trying to orientate himself.
Swiftly he remembered what had transpired during the course of the past
twenty-four hours and the need for him to rise and prepare for the
evening when he and Sam would deliver the remaining contraband to
Baddow! He couldn't wait to get the chore done and then to learn the
secrets of his father's old cellar.

THE BLACK BOY

CHAPTER TWELVE

Sluicing his face and hands in water from the bowl, he dried himself on his neckerchief and went through to the parlour. The pot-room was empty and he found both Jane and Annie in the bar, Annie seemed to have sobered up but still looked distinctly pallid and Will began to think that she really was unwell. How badly, or how seriously this was the case he couldn't be certain, but the drink apart, she was not a well woman. Jane was keeping a wary eye on his wife too and at the same time keeping her distance from her and the two of them sat at opposite ends of the tables, waiting to serve those who required it. At this time, late afternoon, early evening, there were a few customers.

Two travellers who could have been tinkers, or workers looking for work of any kind were huddled beside the fire, which on a cold damp November day such as this, was a welcoming attraction for their ilk. Those who might regularly come in, would do so only after their day's work, which would mean not before dark. Even the old labourer, whose seat by the fire was now occupied by one of the strangers, would not be in for another hour or so.

Will stopped by his wife and asked, "are you ready for tomorrow? I reckon the trap will be here about eight o'clock …. Now I've got to go out to see Sam Rowe and I'll not be back for a while." He turned towards the door, and nodding a welcome for the travellers, who looked up at him with what appeared to be more than a passing interest, he left the alehouse by the outside door. Instead of turning left to reach the cartway between *The Black Boy* and Sam's house, he turned right towards the stable.

It was now dusk and in the dim light he slipped in behind the end wall of the stable and watched the path by which he had come. A few minutes later, his wariness was rewarded when he saw two dark figures coming stealthily towards the stable. He allowed the first to pass by, heading for the stable entrance, but as the second came level with him,

Will raised the short blackthorn cudgel which he always carried in the tail of his frock coat alongside his barker, and brought it sharply down connecting with the intruder's scull just behind his left ear. With almost no sound the man dropped to the ground and Will stepped over him, coming up behind his companion before he reached the stable doorway. He grasped the man's collar and pulled him backwards off of his feet where he collapsed on the ground.

"If you know what's good for you boy, you'll not try to get up, nor to find your weapon, whatever it might be, but just stay there and answer my question." The man seeing the strength with which his adversary had so easily pulled him off his feet, decided that discretion was the better part of valour and so lay still. Behind him his companion lay unconscious and unmoving.

"Who are you? What do you want? And whose paying you to spy on me?" Will kicked the prone man with each question.

"Have you killed my mate? He looks awful still to me."

"I'll be dealing with him shortly, not as far as I know he ain't dead yet, but if you don't answer my questions, you could be dead before him! Be quick about it, or I'll fetch you the same crack on the head as I gave him."

Will stood menacingly over the unfortunate man with his cudgel in his right hand, ready for instant use. After a short silence the man spoke.

"We have been sent here from the Heath to find out what you are doing in the smuggling line, that's all, and we mean you no harm." The man blurted out cringing before the landlord who towered over him.

"What you mean from the Heath? What's it got to do with somewhere like that, what's so far away? Who sent you?"

The man realised that he had gone to far and if he wasn't careful he could end up by mentioning Jerimiah Spalding's name, so thinking quickly he replied. "Was a man called Reuben Belbin what's from the Heath and he camped round here someplace."

"Was it indeed?" Will replied. Perhaps it made sense after all. He knew that he had made an enemy of that man and that he would try to get revenge in anyway possible. These people didn't worry him and he was relieved to discover that they weren't excise men. "Right, you can get up now and before you go, I'll have the pistol what I can see sticking from your belt." He bent forward and reached out for the weapon and dragged it from the man's belt. "You can get your mate and either carry him off or drag him, I mind not which, but be gone off my land by the time I return from the stable."

He lifted the footpad to his feet and propelled him towards his companion who lay groaning where he had fallen.

"I'll take the weight of that pistol you are carrying," said Will "and don't think about returning here ever again, not if you want to wake up on in the morning that is. And' by the way, you tell that gypsy Belbin the same goes for him too, although I already told him that!" He dragged the groaning man to his feet and watched the two of them disappear into the gathering darkness. He stood for a few minutes to ensure that they didn't return and then walked round the back of the alehouse to where the cart had been left the night before. There he found that Sam had hitched up to a horse, which he had brought back from the tile works with him after his day's work and was now waiting for Will so that they could be off.

With Sam at the reins, they drove off toward Baddow and Will told him of his two visitors. He made light of it, because truly he felt unthreatened and had no fear of these two. Had he known their real employer, he might have been more concerned, especially if he had spoken to Old Wilf.

They made their deliveries quietly leaving the goods ordered in the pre-arranged places and moving on without word to the occupiers of the various houses, inns and taverns which they visited. Their last drop was at the alehouse at Sandon, on their way back to Horne Row. By the time they returned to *The Black Boy*, it was close to midnight and most in the neighbourhood were in bed. All that remained in the cart were the two half-ankers for John Horne.

"I'll return the horse and cart tomorrow when I go to the kiln and I'll drop of those two tubs at your brother's house," said Sam. "Now do you want to see this here cellar?"

"You know I do, your family will be in bed now, so we can go down there and no one will come looking."

After they had settled the horse for the night with hay, water and a scoop of oats, they then went into the house named Horne Row. Inside, Sam took a lantern from the wall and lit it. In that room, which served as living room, dining room and kitchen, there was also a bed in which slept the two elder of Sam's four children. The rest of the family slept upstairs. The children didn't wake even with the light which was shed from the lantern fell across their sleeping faces. They were used to their father returning late at night from the alehouse, or perhaps a bit of poaching, which would help to eke out the family's food supply and it would take more than a flash light to disturb them.

Sam led Will to the trap-door, which was beside the hearth towards the front of the room. He raised it and holding the light over the opening Will could see the wooden steps descending to a dry earth covered floor. Sam went down the steps and Will followed close behind him. At the bottom he could see that the cellar was of the same dimension as the room above and in the wall facing the cartway there was indeed a door. Large and made from planks of sawn elm, it was placed centrally in that wall. There was no sign of the pile of boxes that Sam had spoken of, only a few useful crates and lengths of planking, stacked against the back wall of the cellar. He had long since disposed of the majority of the pile and kept only that which was of future use. Sam unbolted the door and pulled it open. Holding the lamp aloft, he stepped aside to enable Will to see inside. The light didn't penetrate as far as the end of this second cellar and as Sam had said, it was more like a tunnel in appearance. Will was fascinated. When had his father built it? Looking at the arched brick roof he realized that brickwork of this construction could only have been done within a trench and then covered over. So, it was either done in is father's time there, when anyone around could have seen excavations such as that and if so why did no-one remember? Activities of this kind were always known about in communities such as this, where there were few secrets; or had it been built at the same time as the houses, one hundred years before?

Will mused on the idea. Horne Row did not exist then as a community, after all John Horne hadn't moved into that house until nearly fifty years later and began the tile works even later than that. He could no longer ask his father and he was certain that John had no more knowledge than him. He finally settled for the fact that the cellar did exist but that its existence and who had built it, had been forgotten.

He took the lantern from Sam and entered the vaulted space. It was perhaps six feet at its centre and eight feet wide and ran for the distance of seven yards to the wall at its end. Will put his ear to this wall half expecting to hear sounds from the alehouse, but then he realized that not only was everyone there asleep, but the cellar there was closed from above. He paced out the dimensions once more and then while Sam watched him, checked the dimension from the front wall of the house to the second cellar. Satisfied with this night's work, Will stood with the lantern and peered back into the tunnel before closing the door and bolting it.

"Does your family know of this?" He asked.

"Yes, they know that there is more cellar than there was before and that it is behind that door, I told my Mrs when I first found it, but thought it best if the rest of them understood as it were only a bit of extra storage space for apples and the like. They're happy with that and haven't shown any interest in it since. None of them are allowed down here anyway being only little."

"Best it stays that way Sam. I reckon we've found the best hiding place as there was. I have just got to measure where that tunnel comes and where it would enter my cellar and we're in business!" Will clapped Sam on the shoulder enthusiastically. "I already have a plan of how to hide the entrance from my end and when those Revenue Riders come looking, which they will before long, mark my words, they won't find anything changed from last time they were here!"

"How are you going to hide it then Will? You can't put a door on it due they'll ask what's behind it."

"Don't you fret yourself about that Sam boy, I'll show you soon enough."

Will fairly ran up the steps to the room above. Everything seemed to be falling into place. He now knew where and how his contraband would be hidden and the work that needed to be done in preparation, could now, with his wife out of the way for a while at Mersea, be carried out without anyone else's knowledge. He helped Sam lower and lock the trap-door and saying goodnight, left his house.

At the cartway, he paved out the distances he had measured in the cellar. As he had suspected the tunnel's length was the full width of the track, ending at the alehouse wall. It ran from virtually the centre of Sam's house to a point which Will calculated to be almost immediately beneath the steps from the pot-room. He needed to check in the daylight but that fact too made it simpler. He returned to his room via the back door and threw himself on his cot without bothering to remove his coat, or boots. He fell into a deep sleep and woke at his usual time around dawn.

Quickly rising, he made his way upstairs to Annie's room where he found her sitting on the edge of her bed combing her hair by the light of a single candle. How terrible she looked, thought Will, and for the hundredth time wondered how he had ever thought of her as beautiful, or how he had come to marry her!

"I see as you are getting ready, so do you want a bite before you go?" Annie shook her head at Will's question, "you just wrap up warm in your best coat girl, it is a cold morning and although it isn't raining yet, it is in the air and mist isn't good for no-one's health anyway, least of all yours." Was he overdoing the concerned husband act? He thought perhaps he was from the look that Annie gave him, so he changed tack. "Right woman, I'm going down now, so don't you be long following me cause that trap'll be there before you know it, and I went to a lot of trouble to borrow it off brother John, so don't be late!"

That's more like my old self, Will congratulated himself and saw that the sour look had returned to his wife's face to confirm that she thought so too!

At eight o'clock, as arranged, the horse and trap, driven by one of John Horne's clay diggers, a strapping young man in his early twenties, arrived at *The Black Boy*. Will went out to meet him and saw that he carried not only a handy looking knobbed stick, but also a large horse pistol.

"Expecting trouble boy?" Will asked.

"You never know when you travel through Salcott and Virley. There's plenty that will rob you that way, or so I am told, so I make certain that I can look after myself."

"Looking at you boy, you don't take kindly to trouble from others do you? And I reckon you know how to handle it when you find it. So, my wife is in good hands!" Will turned away as Annie came down the steps from the parlour bar followed by Jane dragging a large carpet bag. He turned back to the driver, "just one thing boy, when you come back, call here and I'll treat you to an ale or two."

"Thank you kindly, I'll do that."

Will helped Annie up onto the seat of the trap and with a wave and a word of farewell, he and Jane watched then disappear into the mist which lay unmoving over the common. He gave a sigh of relief. He had no idea of how long his wife would be away, but he felt certain that Matthew would send word somehow if she was likely to return unannounced. He would soon be in touch anyway with regard to the next shipment.

Jane appeared delighted. She positively skipped up the steps into the parlour and went straight through to the pot-room, there she took a broom, dusters and a bucket and mop and humming to herself, she returned to the parlour where she began cleaning the room from top to bottom.

Will had followed her up the steps and now stood and watched her working her way round the room. "What you up to girl?" He asked, mystified by her activity. "I never told you to do this, or did your mistress tell you before she left?"

Jane almost sneered. "She never told me to do nothing even if she had, I'd not have done it, not for her that is, no I'm doing it for you Sir, it is high time as this place was cleaned up. She'd never do it and I would never do anything that I wasn't told to do, so it never got cleaned." She looked demurely at Will who was temporarily overcome by her attitude and by her pretty face and full figure, which he had been noticing more and more over the past few days. Why hadn't he seen before that this young woman was no longer a child, he had always thought her as, but had now blossomed into ripe fruitfulness? He pulled himself out of this reverie and gruffly told Jane to carry on with the cleaning while he went down to the cellar. He did not want to be disturbed there he said and therefore she was to stay out of the pot-room until he returned.

She shrugged her shoulders as if she was totally disinterested and continued to wash and wipe the table she was working on. Her back towards Will and he couldn't take his eyes off the swaying of her hips as she bent to scrub the table top. After a moment or two he turned and went into the pot-room. Jane heard him go and stopped her attack on the table, there was no need for exhibiting her hips if he wasn't watching.

In the pot-room, Will raised the trap-door and taking a tinderbox with him, went down the steps into the cellar. He took the lantern from the wall and striking a flame from the tinderbox, lit the lantern's wick and also holding a candle which stood in an iron holder fixed to the wall. Holding the lantern in front of him he paced out the distance from the rear wall and discovered that it would place the tunnel's position at the opposite end immediately behind and beneath the steps from the room above. Perfect he thought. Once I've cut through the wall with a doorway to suit the space beneath the stair I know how to hide it.

THE BLACK BOY

CHAPTER THIRTEEN

"Jane when did you last see your Ma and Pa?" Will asked as he emerged from the cellar and went to find the girl in the parlour where she was still hard at work.

She stopped scrubbing and stood up with a quizzical expression on her face. "What do you want to ask that for Sir? You know I don't see them at all except them days as they come to church at Danbury. They mostly go to Sandon church and it is a long way for them to walk to come here, and then it is only when Pa hasn't got the cattle to feed."

"Yes, that's what I meant, you only go to see them for a few minutes at most every three or four months. I reckon now would be a fine opportunity for you to visit them for a day or two while your mistress Annie is away." Will not only needed her out of the place while he got on unhindered in cutting through the tunnel, but also, he was finding her a disturbing distraction which he didn't want filling his mind just for the moment.

"But I don't want to go, Sir." She looked at him beneath long eyelashes and gave a little pout.

"It isn't what you want girl, it is what your family wants and more to the point what I want!" Will looked at the girl sternly and saw a look of anguish pass across her face. "It is only for a night or two, today be Friday so supposing we say you stay Saturday and Sunday, that way you can see your family and go to the church with them on the Sabbath. After church you can come back here. How's that? Anyway I thought as you would be pleased as punch to be going home."

"I'm pleased alright, but you sound like you don't want me here anymore, you aint going to get rid of me yet, are you Sir? I'm minded of the fact as I have been here for more than three years now and I haven't any prospect of another position here abouts."

"Jane, you haven't got a thing to worry your head over on that score, I just want you to have a couple of days with your family and perhaps give them a little help before you return. So tomorrow morning, Saturday, you best set off on the road to Sandon at first light and come back on Sunday afternoon."

At that moment, how Will would have liked to take the girl in his arms and tell her what he really felt about her and that she had no need to worry about her future, he'd take care of that. Instead he said "I don't want any more arguments now Jane, so just get on with your cleaning and be ready to serve the customers when they come."

The morning was now well advanced, although there were as yet no customers in *The Black Boy*. Will left Jane to finish cleaning the parlour, which suddenly she didn't seem to have quite the same enthusiasm for and decided to walk over to the tile works to see Sam. He also wanted to thank John his brother for the loan of the trap. He set off and strode over the common to his brother's works.

In the mist he didn't see the figure which melted into the gorse below where he walked and who spat on the ground as he watched him go by. Reuben Belbin had a vengeful look on his face and had already decided that the time was right to speak to young James Towns, who he'd heard nothing from since their meeting over a week ago. He pulled a piece of rag from his pocket and after Will had safely disappeared beyond the bushes, he made his way back down the slope and tied the rag to a bush.

Will right away found John where he invariably was and having thanked him for the use of the trap and answered as best he could John's questions with regard to Annie's health, he asked if he might speak to Sam.

"You don't have to ask that Will, course you can, he is over with the pugglers, checking what they've got ready for the kiln."

"I ask because it is the polite thing to do brother, after all you are paying his wage while he's talking to me aren't you."

"Yes youre right enough, so go and talk to him." He laughed as Will turned to go, "But don't be too long!"

Will made his way to where the pugglers, the men who moulded the clay into tiles and bricks prior to firing, were working. He saw Sam and called him over out of earshot of the men there. "Sam I've checked the cellar and I reckon that we can cut through in one night. We can work from my side as I've sending the girl away for two days tomorrow and the next day, and the noise won't be heard by your family, and even if it is, it'll be heard coming from *The Black Boy*, so they won't ask questions. I intend to start as soon as Jane's out of the way tomorrow morning. What I don't get finished you and I can do at night. Tomorrow being Saturday, the alehouse will be busy, so I mean to throw everybody out as soon as I can. We'll then get to work. You have got to make sure that your friends don't know anything about it when they leave, you leave to and go round to the back door, I'll leave it open and I'll have all the tools what we need. The rubble and that, we'll dump with your heap of broken bricks and tiles down at the works and nobody'll know where they came from."

Sam agreed to be there the following evening and Will returned to *The Black Boy*. He was frustrated that he couldn't get on with the job in hand, so sat in the bar with a tankard off ale and a trencher of bread and meat, which Jane had obligingly prepared for him during his absence and had brought to him as soon as he returned. He had acknowledged her smile with his own and she had returned to the pot-room humming a little tune. He dismissed her from his mind and began to expand on the plan he had already formulated as to how he would hide the doorway into the tunnel from those who do not know it's existence, but who wouldn't be suspicious of whatever covered it; a door was no good, doors always lead somewhere; a curtain could easily be moved aside by a casual inquisitiveness; panelling in an obviously dry cellar was unlikely to be hiding a damp spot and was therefore suspicious. So what could he do? He had thought of blocking in the area under the steps, but then realized that nobody, least of all Will Horne who was not known for wasting money, would go to that trouble and expense of carrying out such an alteration to what was quite obviously a perfectly adequate stairway.

So, what could he put there which would meet the criteria? What did the cellar need that it hadn't already got.

Everything down there was heaped on the top of everything else. That was alright with the larger boxes, but things like utensils for cooking and eating or drinking were also thrown into heaps, or, loosely into crates. That was it! Will would build a set of shelves, with a closed back like a kitchen dresser, but fixed to the wall so that what was behind it could not be seen. Hinges and some sort of hidden catch would be required and he knew just the man to make them for him – his brother's blacksmith, Abel.

Will pushed aside the remains of his meal, drank the last of the beer and walked purposefully into the pot-room. He had both solved the puzzle of the doorway was to be hidden, but also what he was going to do that afternoon. He was so full of joy that he grabbed Jane's shoulders drew her to him and kissed her full on the lips. Though instantly taken back she immediately responded avidly.

"Hold you hard girl!" he chuckled "Don't you get the wrong notion, I didn't mean it like that, I'm just so pleased to have thought up a plan as to where we can stack away pots and that and never need to go a rummaging in the heaps in the cellar no more." He gently pushed her away and continued with a lie. "When I was in the cellar yesterday I saw all them mugs and jugs and I thought, there must be a better way of storing them. Now I know what to do and I'm going to start right away.

Jane was visibly disappointed, "I thought as you was pleased with me, how I got your food for you and that…. and after all that, it was only something in that old cellar of yours!"

"Oh, I am pleased alright about it Jane, but…. Oh, never mind girl!"

Will was lost for words and went over to the cellar trap-door, pulled the rug and raised it. He'd get on with what he had planned before something else he might later regret. He lit the lantern at the foot of the steps and looked closely at the space behind them. To enable the dresser, to swing it open, it would have to be hinged off the back wall and to make it look authentic in fully utilizing the available space, part of it would have to slope to match the stairs. He went up the stairs to find the yard-long measuring stick which he kept there.

He returned to the cellar where the lantern still burned and carefully measured where the shelves were to stand. Having done so, he extinguished the lantern and passing through the pot-room, he called Jane from the parlour where she was serving. Almost right away, she stuck her head through the door. "Do you want me Sir?" she asked hopefully.

"I'm going to the yard at the back to get boards to make these here shelves," he said in a voice loud enough for all in the bar to hear. Anyone inquisitive enough would now ask Jane, to be told that at last he was fitting storage space into the cellar.

Will went out the back door directly to the stable, collected his saw and a hammer and his box of precious nails, which he had collected when he had demolished the old shed behind the stable. All the planks from that had been carefully stacked for future use, and the nails, hand made by the blacksmith, had been hammered straight and saved in the box. There was a fair amount of rot to be cut out of the planks, but generally the wood, which he intended to use was sound. He worked through the afternoon and by the time dusk began to fall, he had cut all the necessary lengths to form the dresser. He carried them in armfuls back to the cellar, which he found to be still open, Jane had not bothered to close the hatch. Will was pleased as it was obvious with the parlour door open that there was nothing to be hidden, either in the pot-room or the cellar!

He looked through into the bar and noted that his 'barmaid' was getting a great deal more attention than she ever had in the past. Perhaps it could be something to do with her auburn hair which had obviously received fervent brushing to shine the way it did, or maybe the hint of rouge which she applied to her lips. Where had she got that he wondered, his wife possibly! From table to table she was in demand, Will's ale sales were obviously doing well for a Friday evening, which was usually never notable for being particularly good.

"Looks like you don't need me to help you girl; If you do, give me a call, I'll be in the cellar fixing these here shelves."

"Alright Will... Sir….. I mean to say. The girl blushed at her near mistake. What had made her say that? Now, all in the bar was looking at Will and drawing an obvious conclusion, particularly with Will's wife being away, as everyone by that time knew. There were both knowing and envious smiles around the room, but no-one dared say anything. Will's reputation with his fist was well known.

He chose to give a condescending smile to the room in general and to return without further word to the cellar. He could hear the hubbub of speculative voices from the room he'd left and he could hear Jane's voice occasionally telling people not be stupid, or to mind their own business. After a short while he forgot all about them and began to put the dresser together. It didn't take long as the design was very simple. Firstly, he fitted the shelves between the two sides, one of which was shorter than the other to enable it to fit the slope beneath the steps. He then nailed on the boarding to the back and stood it up to admire his work so far. At least it fitted as it should have done and all that remained was to fill the angled corner beneath the stair and to fit a substantial upright each side, one to take the hinges and one to take the holding back catch.

The overall height of the 'dresser' was 5'6" and its width was 6' at its widest part. It was 9" deep, the width of the boards which he had chosen for the shelves. Will moved it back against the rear wall as though it was on the hinges which would come later. It was heavy which would mean substantial hinges. He would have to explain to Abel that the hinges were needed for a heavy stable, or barn door, the catch he wasn't sure as to how he'd explain. Open like this, he could see that the doorway that he and Sam were to cut the following night could be no more than 5' high and 3' wide. Once cut through, Will would make an additional door to fit the opening.

At that point, Jane appeared at the hatch above. "There's a young fella here what took your wife to Mersea this morning, says you told him to tell you when he were back and you would give him some ale."

Will put down his tools. He'd finished for the moment anyway and he went up the steps to greet the driver of the trap.

"I hope all went well?" he asked. "No trouble on the way there or back?"

"No sir, I delivered your wife to your father-in-law's house, she told me where it was and I left her there and came straight back, I didn't want to be anywhere near Salcott after dark!"

"Jane," called Will to the girl where she stood near the tap-room, "fetch this boy a quart o' ale, he deserves a wetting after the service he's rendered me."

THE BLACK BOY

CHAPTER FOURTEEN

The trap and its' driver left after another quart of ale and being the last customer to go, Will bolted the door. Jane was wiping down the tables. She had stoked the fire for the night and the platters and tankards were stood to drain, having been washed some time before.

"What's the time young Jane?" Will asked.

"I don't know, sometime after eleven o'clock, and I ain't young no more you know."

"You are when I'm old enough to be your Pa." He said almost sadly.

"I certainly don't think of you like that Sir, I always had great regard for you even before you stood up for me against your wife that day and it isn't the sort of regard what you have for your Pa!" She looked knowingly at Will and moved closer to him.

He didn't attempt to back away, if anything he too moved toward her. Suddenly she was in his arms and returning his kisses. For some while they stood like that in the center of the parlour bar. Will felt the warmth of her young body pressed against his and felt stirrings he'd not had for a long time. He caressed her back and then her breasts. She made no attempt to stop him, not when he lifted her skirt and let his hand slide up her thighs did she do more than groan in ecstasy. He discovered that she wore nothing beneath her petticoat and his hand reached the top of her thights, she sighed and pressed herself to him.

He gently took her hand and led her through to his room at the rear of the building. There he took her in his arms again and unfastened her dress and let both it and her petticoat fall to the floor. She stood naked before him and he marveled at the beauty of her young body. Urgently he removed his boots and britches, tore the shirt over his head and pulled her to him. "This is your first time ain't it?" he asked quietly and when she nodded her eyes closed, he slowed his movements to become more gentle. They reached a climax together and clung to each other still locked together. Finally, Will rolled off and putting his arm under Jane's head lay beside her deep in his own thoughts. She for her part was reveling in her new found power and position!

"Oh Will, that were wonderful wasn't it?" and then after a short space of time as her thoughts raced ahead, "what are you going to do now with Annie?" she was completely at ease now with using her lover's name.

"Im not going to anything Jane, so don't get ideas beyond your place." He replied angrily. "Nothing has changed and you will still go to your family tomorrow liked we arranged."

Jane pulled away from his arm and sat up to look down at him. "Do you mean to say what just happened doesn't make any difference to how things are with your wife?"

"Exactly that Jane, it makes no difference whatsoever and you had best get used to the idea!" Will sat up on the edge of the cot. "Come on girl, get yourself to your own bed and be ready to leave first thing, I'll be there to see you off." Jane had now began to weep and Will picked up her clothes, so recently discarded on the floor handing them to her, helped her through to the pot-room where she had her bed beneath the table there. Crying she went out and Will went to climb into his cot. Firstly, he removed the linen cloth which lay on it now stained with Jane's blood. At least she'd told the truth about being a virgin and now he regretted his harsh response, but right now he was worried about Annie's receiving of the news that her husband was playing fast and loose in her absence.

In the other room, Jane crawled into her bed beneath the table and lay there quietly sobbing. How could this man, the one who had protected her from Annie, who has been so kind and gentle with her on so many occasions, now be so cruel. She loved him, she knew, and she had thought that he loved her equally, but his rejection after they had made love, was something which she couldn't comprehend. She thought back over what she had said, surely he didn't still love his wife, it had been obvious for a long while that the reverse was the case, clearly, he couldn't have taken umbrage over her question about Annie. So what was it? Poor Jane was totally naive to the ways of men, so could never have understood that suddenly she had become a threat, talking the way she had, in any event perhaps fantasised about, where he got rid of Annie and took her, Jane as his wife.

Perhaps, she thought, it was that William was feeling sad that things were as they were and that he was feeling guilty at how wonderful their love making had been…. yes that must be it, oh poor man, tomorrow she'd reassure him that her love was stronger than that and that he had nothing to feel any remorse about. She dried her eyes, turned on her side and fell asleep.

The following morning, Saturday, Will awoke at his usual time but, instead of going into the pot-room as he would normally have done, he went out of the back door. At the back of the alehouse he waited for Sam to appear from his house next door. When he did so a short while later, Will called quietly to him.

"Good morning Will" said Sam, "you are waiting for me?"

"I wanted to let you know that I am already to cut through the wall to your cellar and I've got the perfect door for it what'll never be noticed. Like I said yesterday, I'll start as soon as Jane's gone this morning, but I can't keep the door to the alehouse closed for too long, so I don't know how far I'll get. I'll be wanting to start again as soon as we've got rid of the last drinker tonight. It has to be finished by Sunday night."

"What's this here perfect door then Will?"

"You'll see it soon enough, I have a lot to do before it can be called finished. I'll see you tonight." He turned back to the back door of *The Black Boy* and went through to the pot-room, there he found a smiling Jane tidying up the tankards, which she had obviously been preparing before he came in.

He was pleased to see her in good spirits and thought, that like him, the previous night was now merely a delightful memory. How wrong he was. She came to him and threw her arms around him. "I do love you Will, with all my heart and whatever happens, I'll always be yours!"

Will disentangled himself from her arms and pushed her away, although not too roughly as he not only wanted her to leave for her family home without friction, this weekend being all important, but this morning he found her as attractive to him as she has always been. "Now come on Jane we talked on this last night it ain't right for you to talk that way, so you get your things together and get going, it is daylight and you want to get to your family before midday."

She looked sadly at him and picked up the bundle which she had prepared for journey, "I was ready to go before you came in Will and I'll be back here tomorrow night before dark."

William snapped at her, "You best stop calling me that girl, people are going to talk."

Jane was about to say "let them!" but thought better of it and carrying the bundle, she went out of the door, down the steps and set off on the road to Sandon.

Will watched until she was out of sight, then went inside, closing and bolting the door behind him. He went straight through to the pot-room and lifted the trap-door to the cellar below. The rug had not been replaced the evening before when he had left the cellar and closed the trap-door behind him and he told himself that in future he must remember that nothing should be out of its usual place.

Down the steps he lit the lantern and with a piece of chalk, he marked out the possible extent of the hole he was to cut. Starting at the centre of it he began to loosen the first of the bricks with a heavy hammer and chisel. The lime mortar with which the house had been constructed made his job easier and the first few bricks in the outer layer came away comparatively easily. He didn't want to cut away too much in case his calculation as to the exact position of the tunnel was in any way faulty, so he knew he had to cut through the full depth, but in a small area only. The one thing he did not know yet, was how thick the wall was! After less than half an hour, his chisel broke through to the other side and he was relieved to discover that it had been the thirteen and half inches which he had expected. Carefully he broke away more bricks until he was able to see with the aid of the lantern and held it up to the hole, that its position was precisely where he had calculated it to be.

Will now spent another hour breaking out sufficient brickwork to enable him to climb through. There was a heap of rubble, which if seen from *The Black Boy's* side, would have immediately raised suspicion. He, therefore, shoveled it through to the tunnel and having swept the tell-tale red brick dust into a heap and passed that through the hole as well, he dragged the 'dresser' into place. He stood back and viewed his work. Yes, he thought, that's enough to fool anyone. That night, Sam would finish it, but right now he had to go and see Abel the Blacksmith.

He left the cellar, replacing both the trap-door and the rug and went out through the back door, locking it behind him. He dropped the key into his pocket and set off for the blacksmith's forge which lay a little above the common. As he left, going behind and then round the side of the old widow Wright's empty cottage, he looked across to make sure that there were no early customers hoping for entry into his alehouse. There were none. It was as yet not ten o'clock and apart from the travellers passing through Horne Row and those camped on the common, all other residents of the area were in their place of work.

At Abel's forge, a working horse stood waiting to be shod, its owner having left it hitched to the post there for that purpose, outside the smithy. The Blacksmith was working a curved strip of red hot iron into the shape of a horse shoe. It was large and obviously for the carthorse, which stood patiently outside. Will stood in the doorway and watched Abel as he flattened, then shaped the shoe, then beat the toe flanges squeezing the thin uprights from the still soft metal. The holes to take the nails he had already punched through and the shoe was almost complete and ready to be fitted to the hoof.

Abel plunged the shoe into a tank of water where it hissed and bubbled furiously for a few seconds. He lifted it out and still attached to the spike which was driven into one of the nail holes, Abel laid it on top of the anvil.

"Good morning William," he said to his visitor "you don't often come to see me, what is it, your mare need shoeing again?"

"No Abel, it is a set of hinges that I want made and a special door catch."

"That's no matter then, I can get them made for you inside a week."

"I'm afraid as that ain't no good, Abel, I need them now, today, tomorrow's too late." Will looked suitably apologetic, but at the same time firm in his request.

"I am not going to ask you why it is so urgent William, so you best tell me what exactly you want."

Will explained how three hinges would be needed as the door was heavy and that because the hinges would be close to the wall, they would have to be made in a certain way, which he explained to Abel who understood immediately, after all, he'd been making ironwork to suit every possible situation since he was apprentice to his father. The door catch was a little more difficult to explain, because what Will needed was Abel's ingenuity, without his knowing the precise nature of the problem. In the end Will made up a little story that both the hinges and the catch were for his father-in-law at Mersea Island and he needed the secret catch to keep out those who were not welcome, whilst allowing access to those who were.

"Why the hurry for today then?" Abel asked.

"Because he's coming here tomorrow, Sunday and I promised him as I would get you to make them for him, but then I forgot!" Will lied.

"Alright, I'll get them made for you, but I may not get them to you until the morning. What time's the man coming? will he be going to church, it being Sunday?"

The question threw Will off balance for a moment. He needed the hinges that night and not later than when he closed the door at *The Black Boy*. "Abel, to make certain, I'll come here tonight after I've closed the alehouse and I'll collect them, that way, it'll save you coming round Sunday morning, and that way I'll have them whatever time my pa-in-law gets here. How's that?"

"Your pushing me hard William Horne, but yes, they'll be ready tonight for you to collect when you say. Now you had best let me get on with it!" Able grinned at Will.

Will left the blacksmith's shop and walked briskly back to *The Black Boy*. There were no customers waiting to enter and anyone who had tried in his absence had obviously given up and gone away. He went to the back door, let himself in and before opening the parlour door, took one last look down the cellar to make sure that there was nothing required there before tonight. There was nothing he could think of, so he went back up to the pot-room and closed the hatch again. He was at a loss to know how to spend the rest of the day. He couldn't just sit and wait for customers, so he decided that he could spend time in, if not constructing the inner door, which would be needed in the cellar, at least preparing the planks for it.

Behind the stable he hunted through the heap of planks and found sufficient strong thick boards to make a door. They were roughhewn and the edges uneven, but he would cover the cracks which would occur when two boards were placed together, by planting a smaller vertical board over them on the inside. Of course! He thought, that's what I should have done on the parlour door before the gypsy had eavesdropped. There's no time like the present so he took his measuring stick and went through to open the parlour door. There were still no customers waiting so he measured the height of the door and the lengths of the timber, which he'd need to cover the cracks. Back to the timber heap, he went and selected the five pieces he wanted, cut them to length and returned with hammer and nails and went to work on the door.

By the time the first customer arrived, he had finished and was well pleased with the result. Anyone outside the door could neither see, nor hear clearly through it, what might be happening within.

Will welcomed the new arrival, a gentleman from his appearance, who was travelling to Chelmsford. When Will asked him where he had come from he appeared evasive, saying in a general sort of way, that it was from the other side of Maldon. Will decided not to pry into the man's business and got for him the vitals and ale, which he asked for. When he returned to the table with the food and beer, the parlour was still empty apart from the stranger.

"Would you be the landlord here?" he asked Will, who nodded.

"Yes Sir, I'm that, my name is William Horne."

"Then you would know Master Matthew Rowlings wouldn't you."

"Yes, he is my father-in-law. I hope that there is nothing wrong with him, is there Sir?"

"No not at all, he sends you his warmest regards. Forgive me, but I had to make sure who you were before I could pass you a message from him, which I carry here in this letter. I had to help him write it because, as you may happen to know, the good man can neither read nor write well." The gentleman passed the sealed letter to William who took it hesitantly, but made no effort to break its seal.

"Arent you going to read it then?" the man asked curiously.

"Matthew ain't the only one, that cant read nor write. I can't do neither, except sign my name, but, my brother can, so I'll ask him to read it for me when I see him next."

"Since I wrote this for Master Rowlings, I know what the letter states, so would you like me to tell you the gist of it, Master Horne?"

"Just to be sure that I'm telling the truth?" began the gentleman with a wry smile and without waiting for Will's reply went on, "it says that a load of oysters will be shipped to Maldon on the morning of the next Spring tide and twelve hours afore that, another load of a different nature will be delivered to the same creek as before. This tide is in three weeks time on the Tuesday night and Wednesday morning, that'll be tenth and eleventh days of December. That's all it says, except that he would like the same arrangement as before to be in place and word from you that all is well. Oh, by-the-by, he says that his daughter, your wife is seeking aid from the local wise woman and he thanks you for sending her to visit whilst seeing the crone!" He chuckled, "I rather think that his last statement was in essence untrue; she appears to be plaguing his life – his daughter that is!"

It was Will's turn to laugh. "I suspect she is Sir, but Matthew's a man as that knows how to deal with plaguey women!" they both laughed.

"Now Sir, how's it that you are carrying messages for the likes of an oyster dredger and an alehouse keeper? You are a gentleman after all!" Will had to ask.

"Simple really Master Horne. Firstly, I may not be quite the gentleman that you so obviously take me for and secondly, we're all in the same trade in one way or another. I'll not tell you my name, but I'll tell you that they are my ships that bring in the goods to folk like Master Rowlings. I'm not from hereabouts but do business along this whole coast from Paglesham to Felixstowe."

Instantly, Will knew who sat there before him, it was William Dowsett, the man Matthew had told him of. He kept the knowledge to himself. Gentleman, as Dowsett may now appear, Will had discovered during earlier, discreet but casual enquiries about the man, that his reputation as a smuggler was well known as was it for violence in which he was notorious, having built up his smuggling fleet from simple beginnings, but ruthless determination. He had been in fire-fights with revenue cutters on several occasions and one of his own cutters "Big Jane" boasted seven six pounder brass cannon and two swivel guns, none of which he was afraid to use. He would not be best pleased to learn that William knew all about him.

A few other customers had begun to drift in and Will had to leave that table to serve each in turn. Dowsett, for indeed, Will had been right in that it was he, asked as he got up to leave. "Do you not have help in your tavern. I know your wife is away at Mersea, but surely you have servants?"

"I've got one only and I've given her this day to visit her Ma and Pa. She'll be here tomorrow." Will explained, "I'll have to manage until then!"

Dowsett nodded and quietly said, "It is possible that we shall meet again and I understand that the business in our line is likely to grow, from what your father-in-law has said. I wish you well and look forward to greater things!"

William saw him to the door and went back to serving. Knowing now when the next shipment was due in, gave him a little breathing space. If he and Sam could complete the breaking through tonight and if they could fit the 'dresser' and clear the rubble tomorrow, then apart from the inner door, all would be hidden by the time that firstly Jane, then Annie returned.

That evening, it was a typical Saturday night and Will realized how hard young Jane worked. Of course, Annie worked as well but never noticeably hard. In desperation seeing young James Towns in his usual place with Old Wilf, and two or three of the men from Ludgores Farm, he went to him and asked, "Jim how'd ye like to earn a few coppers this evenin'? Both Annie and Jane's away an' I need help servin', what de'ye say?"

"I'll say how many coppers, Will, and how long for?" Jim answered.

"Let's say six shall we? And only until the last drinker's left."

"Don't forget as I'll have to walk home, that has got to be worth another penny."

Will turned to Wilf who was listening to their negotiations. "You will wait won't you Old Wilf so as you can take Jim home?"

"I won't and neither will that old horse of mine, she knows when it is time to go and she'd probably go without us both if we were late. No Will you either pay the boy seven pence, or you let him go early."

"What did I have to ask you for you old villain, alright seven pence if you have to walk and sixpence if you don't."

"Alright Will, where do you want me to start?"

"Get over to the other side there and when a body wants a fill of ale, you fill them and take their money, what you then give to me. Easy as that! Now Old Wilf, when you are going to go, you tell me and I'll see if Jim can go with you!" William went out to the pot-room and began sluicing tankards in the bucket of water which stood in the stone sink. He stood them to drain on the grooved wooden draining board to the left of the sink, something he had watched both Annie and Jane do frequently in the past. He began to regret sending Jane away, not only because of the extra work which it was causing him, but because he was yearning for her young body again.

THE BLACK BOY

CHAPTER FIFTEEN

Old Wilf got up to leave *The Black Boy* soon after ten o'clock glancing with a shrug at Jim as he went out of the door. If the boy was going to earn his extra penny, then who was he, an old man who wanted to get to his bed, to stand in his way. He chuckled as he climbed into the cart and horse and began his journey back to Paternoster.

It was a cold night with a clear sky and frost in the air. Wilf sniffed the air and quietly predicted to his horse that snow was not far away, certainly before Christmas.

Other customers were leaving the alehouse and by eleven, with a little encouragement from Will, the bar was clear. Jim started to help him to clear away the tankards and platters from the tables, but for some reason, which he didn't understand, Will seemed anxious for him to leave as soon as possible and told him that he would - "see to that in the morning." Jim took his seven pence wages and left by the parlour door. He heard the bolt shot-to behind him and he stopped for a second. Looking at the door, he realised that the cracks in it, which he had peered and listened through before, had been filled in. Perhaps Will did have something to hide after all!

He had noticed another peculiarity during that evening in that Will had apparently slipped away somewhere for half and hour and had returned with what looked like iron hinges, he couldn't be sure as they were wrapped in sacking. He went down the steps and set off towards the farm.

Inside the pot-room, Will opened the cellar before making sure that the back door was open to allow Sam to enter. He found Sam waiting outside with his tools and a bag of lime mortar, ready to start work on the cellar wall. They locked the door taking an additional lantern with then, they went down into the cellar. Sam was astounded when he looked through the hole which Will had previously cut. What a perfect hiding place, unknown to any other than the two of them and perfect size for what they wanted.

"So it does come up to your wall then, that tunnel what he made? He must of had the notion about something like this, way back then." Sam looked at Will as he asked the question. "Was he in business with the alehouse at the time?"

"I don't know just like I didn't know about the tunnel, but maybe you're right, anyway, too late to ask your Pa now!"

They set to work enlarging the opening to the size, which Will had marked on the wall earlier. Then while Will shoveled the debris into sacks, Sam mixed up the lime mortar and repaired the brickwork to the edges of the opening, re-laying the bricks for this repair, and making good all round. The sacks full of brick-rubble were then carried up and out to the back of Sam's pigsty, where it was hidden from view and where it could stay until a cart was available to carry it to the rubble heap at the kilns.

They then returned and fitted the hinges to the 'dresser' and to the back wall, cutting the hinge pins into the brickwork and securing them with mortar. They swung it into place and propped it so that the mortar around the hinge bolts had a chance to set. It worked perfectly and well pleased with their work, they inspected it carefully to make sure that as it stood, it could not be seen to be anything but a rack of shelves.

"Clever idea that Will!" Sam said viewing their work, "those shelves can never be taken for a door, especially when they are full of pots and that."

"There's still work to be done on it, but we've got until Sunday afternoon, that's this afternoon to do it. What we don't get done today, we'll do later and we can work from either the cellar or mine!"

"I must go to church with my family today Will, as they will think it odd if I don't , so I'll work with you until then and be back again after. As it is they are going to wonder where I've been all night!"

"Fair enough Sam, let's do what we can. The first thing is to clean away all trace of red brick dust, due somebody'll wonder where it come from."

They spent the next hour or so cleaning the tell-tale dust from the cellar floor, the steps and the pot-room floor until they were satisfied that not a speck could be seen. By the time they had finished, the grey light of a late November dawn was over the horizon. The sky was clear and it promised to be a dry day. The moon had yet to wane still showed itself high in the sky now, a pale white disk against the blue of the sky.

Sam went home to collect his family for church and Will closed the cellar and went out to his wood store at the back of the stables to finish preparing the inner door which he had started yesterday. He was going to be tired tonight he thought, but until he'd finished in the cellar, he couldn't rest, Jane was due back that afternoon.

When Jim left *The Black Boy*, an hour after Wilf, it had become noticeably colder. The stars in the clear sky sparkled and the moon, which had now risen over the horizon cast a pale yellow glow over the common.

The lane at Paternoster stood out clearly in the moonlight and Jim welcomed it to show him the way. He didn't mind a walk like this for that extra penny, but it would have been a different matter in the pitch dark without the moon. To wander off the track could be so easy and the surface water which filled them, each would have constituted a trap. He saw that the thin layer of ice, which had covered each puddle had in placed been broken by the wheels of Old Wilf's cart, but was not freezing over again.

Deep in thought about what it might be that Will had got to hide, he at first didn't see the shadowy figure which stood motionless beneath one of the elms which edged the lane. Was Will already involved in smuggling, or, was it something else. He'd seen and heard that Will had sent both his wife away to Mersea and Jane to see her kin at Sandon, perhaps that was part of it?

As he drew level with the tree, the figure detached itself and stepped into the road. Jim leaped backwards thinking that he was about to be robbed by a footpad.

"I trust you fare well young James. I've been a hoping to see you these last couple of days. Did you not see my marker, the bit of old rag on the bush?"

Reuben Belbin, now clearly visible in the moonlight, stood before Jim.

"Oh, Reuben, you gave me a turn! I never saw you there." Jim realising who it was, quickly recovered from his fright. "No, I never saw it, but, I aint been down there because I aint got nothing to tell you…"

Reuben Belbin spoke quietly, thrusting his face close to Jim's.

"I told you to watch that bush, and when the rag's there you come to see me. What do I do? sit and wait for you to call? I put the marker up you would want to see. So what is it that you have got to tell me now?"

"Like I just said, I don't know anymore than I knew before…." Jim started, but when Reuben started to look truly threatening, he remembered the knife which the gypsy had tried to use on Will, so blurted out…. "I think as there's something going on at the alehouse, because Will was acting real strange tonight, but I don't know what it be."

"Do you think as he is dealing with smugglers then? Or be starting up with his own gang? And did you find out who they might be?" Reuben had calmed down a little now and tried a more friendly approach. "I didn't mean nothing by getting riled just then, but I have got to know… . for our best interests that is" he added to put the boy at ease.

"I think he's started into smuggling again like I know he did before, but whether it is with a new gang, or not I don't know. All I know is that there's four or five of his brother's tile workers that goes in the alehouse and they seem to have plenty of money to spend, and they are always in high spirits, i'll promise you Reuben as I'll find out one way or another by next Saturday night."

Reuben clapped Jim on the shoulder and grinned at him in the dim light. "You can't say fairer than that." He said. "I'll wait for you on Sunday, if I've not seen you on Saturday night, Just one thing, who are these tile workers?"

Jim forgetting that Reuben had asked the question before and that he had then not answered, said; "There's Sam Rowe and John Laytham, then there's Joshua Roote and maybe his brother and their friend David Archer; and you won't see me on Saturday night next week because I'm only here tonight, walking home because I don't suppose Will ask me again, I expect his wife and the girl will be back by then."

"So, Horne is alone in the alehouse now is he?"

"Yes, until tomorrow when Jane gets back. Why do you ask?"

"Oh, no matter, just interested that's all," but the look in the gypsy's face told another story.

They parted company and Jim walked on towards the farm, whilst Reuben started off in the opposite direction, back towards *The Black Boy.*

THE BLACK BOY

CHAPTER SIXTEEN

The gypsy Reuben Belbin walked stealthily round to the front of *The Black Boy*, heading for the stable and the back entrance. In his hand was a knife. "When this night's work is done, I'll have back the one as that William Horne took off me afore!" he thought to himself.

Through the window of the parlour he could make out the light of the fire which still burned in the hearth, flickering on the ceiling of the bar, but the sill of the window was too high to be seen through, so he couldn't make out whether Will had retired to bed as yet, or perhaps still sat before the fire. He noticed that the cracks in the parlour door through which he had been listening that evening three weeks before had been sealed. He thought that he could hear faint noises coming from within, but they could have been made by crackling logs or even rats, which every house had its share of. The floor of the parlour, he remembered, was a patchwork of thin strips nailed over rat-holes. Any food dropped on the floor would receive nightly attention from the rats, which would not only devour the food, but also the wooden floor upon which it had dropped.

He went on towards the stable. His plan was to enter by the back door of the alehouse, find the landlord hopefully asleep, and kill him. Oh, what sweet vengeance! But at the stable entrance, he hesitated, perhaps he had better wait until he was sure that the man was asleep. He stepped into the feed store and settled down on the stack of hay in there, to wait in comfort for an hour perhaps. As he sat down, he felt something hard beneath the hay and feeling with his hand discovered a large bale of something wrapped in cloth. Immediately he knew the aroma which he had smelt vaguely when he had entered the building, but had not then recognised. It was tobacco. Closer investigation of the pile of hay revealed four more bales of tobacco. So the landlord was smuggling then! Now Reuben had a dilemna. Murdering him simply for personal revenge, but gave the murderer no other benefit than that, whereas with the strength of the knowledge that Will was Involved and was almost certainly the ringleader of a smuggling gang, the benefits were obvious. Denunciation to the right authorities would ensure a hefty reward, together with the satisfaction of seeing the landlord swinging from the gallows. Where, though was the rest of the goods? Surely the shipment, which had contained the tobacco must be hidden somewhere. Reuben had to find it.

He spent the next hour hunting through the feed store and the stable and then around the back of the building amongst the heaps of timber and rubbish accumulated there. All he came up with was a spout lantern hidden in the feed store. At least that was proof enough of the activities of Will Horne. Reuben left it where it was. He had no intention of tipping off the landlord that someone had been here. He finally came to the conclusion, the right one as it happened, that whatever had been there before had been moved on, leaving the tobacco for future distribution.

As silently as he had come, he left to return to his caravan on the common. He would wait until next Sunday to see if James came up with a similar report. Meanwhile, he'd return to the Heath to report to Jerimiah Spalding.

He had gone long before Will and Sam emerged from the cellar. Sam had gone off home to his family and Will went out to the wood stack to complete the door.

He noticed that the planks which he had set aside for the job seemed to have been moved from where he had leaned them against the wall of the stable. They had been pulled aside as though someone had been looking for something which they expected to be hidden behind them, but he dismissed the thought and in his tired state assumed that he himself had moved them.

He carried them inside and down into the cellar and began to assemble them into the required door. The frame within which it would sit had yet to be made and the hinges, which it required were something else he would have to ask Abel for, but these would have to wait. The first thing he had to do was to bring the tobacco out of the stable and put it in the new hiding place.

Two at a time, Will carried the bales down to the cellar and stacked them against the wall in the tunnel. It had been risky to leave them in the feed store the way he had but no harm had been done, nobody had found them and they were now safely hidden!

After church, Sam returned to help, but, by then Will had decided that he had enough for the day and by mutual agreement they closed up the cellar and Will let Sam out of the back door, bolting it behind him. He then threw himself onto his cot in the back room and tried to sleep. He had thought that he was now so tired, not having slept for a day and a half, that he would drop off easily, but is wasn't to be.

He kept thinking of Friday night we he lay on his bed enjoying the delights of Jane's young body and he could not relax. Knowing that she'd be back there this evening, he kept the thought of her in the forefront of his mind and the more he did so, the more he lusted after her. Finally, around midday, he gave up all thought of sleep and went through to the tap-room where he poured himself a half tankard of gin. He realized then that he hadn't eaten properly for almost as long as he hadn't slept and so he found the remains of a loaf of bread in the crock and together with some meat and cheese he sat down in the parlour to eat it, but he seemed to have lost his appetite. It was then that he realised how cold it was in the alehouse. The fire from the night before had not been stoked as would normally have happened first thing in the morning in readiness for the first customers of the day. Even on a Sunday, when he didn't open the alehouse door, this chore would have been done, but of course with no Jane.... Everything seemed to remind him of her, he couldn't get the wretched girl out of his mind. He got up and grabbing an armful of tinder which lay in readiness beside the hearth, he pulled together the dead logs and raked it into the ashes. He laid the kindling on the hot coals now revived and almost immediately it burst into flame. For a few minutes Will stoked the fire and when he was certain that it was going thoroughly, he returned to his abandoned meal, which he proceeded to pick at.

The gin he emptied in a gulp and returned to the tap-room for more. It is probable that, had it not been for a persistent knocking on the parlour door, he might had sat drinking gin for the remainder of the day, or at least until he had passed out!

"Who the devil is that it is Sunday and I am not open." He shouted through the door.

It was the voice from outside which said "Sir, it is Jane and you have locked the door and I can't get in," which made him leap to his feet throw open the door. On the step stood Jane and she looked at him with such a pretty little smile with her head cocked on one side, he was overcome with desire for her.

"You were not to come back until this afternoon." Will said, "But make no mistake, I'm real pleased as you are here, I have missed you."

Jane's face glowed with pleasure, "Have you really, Will?"

Taking her arm and drawing her into the room, Will closed and locked the door. Taking her in his arms he kissed her upturned face, tasting the sweetness of her lips. The bundle which she carried dropped to the floor and her arms encircled Will's neck drawing him down to her. He picked her up and carried through to his room.

"If I come in here with you, you won't throw me out again like last time will you?" she asked.

Will looked deep into her eyes and said what he knew she wanted to hear and what he at that point believed to be true. "No my love, you'll share my bed tonight and maybe many nights after." He lowered her feet to the floor and began to remove her clothes, but she gently pushed his hands away and removed her dress herself. "It is the only one I got." She said "and you are in danger of tearing it!." She then helped him out of his britches and they sank onto the bed together. Their love making this time was less frantic than the last and finally they lay together contentedly in each other's arms.

Will was asleep almost immediately. It had been a strenuous thirty six hours and now he was exhausted. Jane was happy to lie there in silence, relishing the knowledge that her lover, whatever his attitude had been the first night, had now realised that he loved her and was hers now for ever. She wondered when she should bring the subject up about Annie again and decided that for the moment she wouldn't mention it. Eventually, she drifted off to sleep snuggled up to the man beside her.

THE BLACK BOY

CHAPTER SEVENTEEN

Later that Sunday morning after his discovery in the stable of *The Black Boy*, Reuben Belbin and his family once again left the common and headed for Tiptree Heath. They waited until the church goers of Horne Row had wound their way up the hill in answer to the bell being rung in the church tower, summoning worshippers and warning them not to be late. It was clear, cold, but sunny morning with a threat of rain from the clouds gathering over the hill to the north.

The gypsy, who had left his family and the van where they had been camped, while he watched from a hidden vantage point amongst the gorse bushes, noticed that the landlord of *The Black Boy* was noticeably absent from the throng. Reuben had watched the villagers before and the tall solid figure of William Horne had stood out amongst the others, but today he was missing and he wondered why. Young James Towns was there he noticed, with his three brothers, two sisters and his mother in a group towards the back of line.

When the procession disappeared from his view, he rose to his feet and returned quickly to the caravan, to which the horse was already hitched and the family was ready to go. Carefully, they pulled away from their hidden camp site, brushing the wheel tracks from the heather and lifting broken bracken fronds upright again. The bracken was dead and shriveled now and it wouldn't be long before the first snows flattened it completely, but in the meantime, Reuben was planning to return before the end of the week and the better the camp was concealed from inquisitive eyes the better. They slowly walked the horse back up the common to the open ground where two or three travelling tinker's caravans were parked. As they passed by, they exchanged greetings, although they did not know each other. The tinkers spoke with strange accents, which meant that they were not from this part of East Anglia. "Good" thought Reuben, "If they don't know who we are, then they can't tell that we have left!"

Once on the Maldon Road, they headed there en route for the Heath. Reuben sat on the driving seat, with Rachel beside him. She kept up a friendly chatter, which he was content to join in with to start with. She at last was away from hiding and silence, which she and the children had had to endure for the past three weeks whilst camped at Horne Row and she was reveling in the freedom of it. After an hour or so, Reuben started to worry what he was going to tell Jerimiah Spalding and he lapsed into a brooding silence.

"Come on Rube, what's the matter with you?" Rachel asked turning to look at his furrowed brow. "Don't you want to talk anymore?"

"No woman, I don't, I got some thinking to do, so until I have done that, you keep your mouth shut. I'll tell you when you can talk again!"

Rachel shrugged, she knew too well her husband's changing moods and knew that to talk when he'd told her not too would almost certainly result in a clout from him. Reuben for his part returned to his thoughts and tried to work out his best advantages.

Firstly, and above all else, he wanted revenge on the landlord. He now knew that he was smuggling but as yet, did not know to what extent. He also knew that piece of information alone would put him in Jerimiah's good books. The problem was that if he gave him that information, Jerimiah would certainly want to use it to his own advantage and if Reuben were to inform the Excise men in order to gain the reward and of course his revenge, he would be going against the Heath's leader, which would result in dire consequences for him, Reuben.

So, what was he do? Perhaps he had better say that whilst he was sure that the landlord was involved, he needed more time to prove it, but he at least had three names, given to him by Jim, who rightly or wrongly, he could point a finger at and say that they appeared to be the leaders of the gang. Yes, that was likely to keep Jerimiah happy and off of his back for a day or two. He could maybe embellish it a bit here and there with a bit of heresay.

By the time Reuben had decided in his mind on the approach which he would make to Jerimiah, the caravan was passing through Maldon and out toward Totham and Tiptree. By late afternoon they arrived on the Heath and found somewhere to set up camp. All around the site, fires burned, not just for cooking, but now for warmth as well. The weather had turned distinctly colder and the fine rain, which the clouds had promised earlier, was now falling with sleet within it. It was twenty-fourth of November and it looked as though winter was to come early that year.

"I'll go and see Jerimiah tomorrow morning, so while it is still light enough, you take the children and get off to gather firewood, 'it is going to be a cold night. I'll find a fagott seller and see if I can buy a few penneth of wood from him." Reuben set off amongst the vans and hovels, which formed the Heath Community, while Rachel and the three children went into the woods to collect what firewood they could. With so many fires to feed on the Heath, the woods around had been hard hit and so they had to travel further into them to find enough fallen branches to fuel their fire.

Of course, like every family in every living van, they carried a supply of firewood with them, but that was only ever used in an emergency.

Reuben meanwhile was passing one caravan when a voice called out, "You are back then Rube." A fellow gypsy recognised him as he passed by. "Where have you been? Last heard you were over Danbury way. Is that right? What were you doing there?"

"Just passing through really Jake, done a bit of rabbiting there abouts and made a shilling or two, but I missed all my old mates and so I came back here!" Reuben grinned at the other man and hunched down beside his fire. "I have two questions for you Jake; first, who sells firewood about here now? And second, have you seen Jerimiah of late? Is he here?"

"There's an old woman a step or two from here along the road to Birch what sells mostly faggots and the like but sometimes a few logs." Jake replied, "regarding Jerimiah, I don't know, I ain't seen him for several days. He may be here and then again he may not. You'll have to call on him Rube."

Reuben after warming his hands at the fire, got up, thanked him and walked off down the road to find the wood seller. It was now fully dark and the sleet which was still falling stung his face as he walked directly into it. He found the wood seller's shack and purchased a bundle of firewood which included a few small logs and he returned to his caravan, with it on his back and with cold sleet blowing now from behind. He arrived to find that Rachel and the children had already got a fire going with the wood which they had collected. The horse was watered and its hay net was full and hung from the side of the caravan.

Reuben was frozen and dropping his burden, crouched down before the fire to thaw himself out. His coat steamed and his hands, which he stretched out before the warmth of the blaze eventually returned to life as he rubbed them together before it.

"You have a swaller or two of this," Rachel said, appearing beside him with a tin mug. "You look frozen to the marrow, and this'll warm you up." She thrust the mug of brandy into her husband's hands and watched as he gratefully took it and began to sip it.

"Youre a good woman Rachel, thank you. You always know how to look after me." From Reuben this was a rare piece of verbal gratitude and Rachel smiled with delight.

"You just sit there husband and warm yourself and I'll have your food ready for you as quick as I can." She went off up the steps into the caravan and returned with the cooking pot, which she suspended over the fire. She then turned to the children who hovered in the background.

"Whilst I get our supper ready, you three can keep the fire stoked up. Robert, you are in charge being the eldest."

It was an evening for joy all round, "At last my Ma's called me by my name! I wonder if Pa'll remember it now and say it too?" the boy thought and went about the stoking of the fire with gusto. He was unfortunately to be disappointed as his father now said no more and stared continuously into the fire, lost in thought.

The subject of his reverie was at that moment returning from business up the road in Colchester. Jerimiah arrived back at his shack at the northern end of the Heath early that evening and after unsaddling his horse and stabling it behind the shack he went inside. A fire had been laid in the fireplace and he took his tinder-box and put flame to the kindling. Stripping off his wet outer clothing, he sank down on the padded chair before the fire and contemplated the day.

He had not long been sitting thus when a knock came at the door.

"Who be there?" he called and a voice replied, "Jake Alderwood, can I come in?"

"Doors open Jake, come in and close it quickly behind you, we don't want none of that northerly to come in here!"

Jake entered, closed the door and came over to the hearth where he accepted the chair offered by the smugglers' leader. He looked at Jerimiah who said nothing but simply raised his eyebrows in question.

"I thought you might want to know that Reuben Belbin is back on the Heath. He come back today and told me he'd been rabbiting and the like over Danbury way." If Jake thought he'd get some reaction out of the smuggler, he was wrong, so he continued. "He asked me if you were about and I told him I didn't know one way or the other. He never said as he was coming to see ye though."

"Here you are, Jake my old friend, a tanner for your trouble." And Jerimiah spun the coin towards Jake who deftly caught and pocketed the six penny piece. "Now you get about your business and I'll be about mine, Goodnight to you."

The meeting was over and Jake was summarily dismissed. He went to the door without further word and disappeared into the night. Jerimiah sat for a while considering the information. Had Reuben come back after a three week absence with news or was it simply a call to say that he was still out there trying? To start with, he was tempted to go and see Reuben immediately, but then the more patient and incidentally, suspicious, side of him thought that it might be better to see if Reuben paid him a visit tomorrow. Finally, he settled for that.

The following morning, Monday, Reuben rose, unwillingly vacating the bed in which Rachel his wife had been so overwhelmingly loving the night before. She moaned as he left it, trying to hold him back, but he angrily shook her embraces off.

"Woman, I have got much to do today and lying in bed with you, pleasant it may seem now, ain't part of it. So let go and get about whatever it is as that you got to do, so I can go and see Jerimiah."

"Oh Rube, not him again? Because of him we spent three weeks in hiding on that Horne Row common, and to no avail!"

"How do you know it was to no avail? Why do you think I am going to see the man now? Don't you worry Rachel, all will be well for us in no time!" He spoke with such conviction that his wife believed him utterly and kissed him fondly before he left. Life seemed to be taking a turn for the better all round.

Reuben's van was not quite so far away from Jerimiah's shack as it had been three weeks before and it took him a few minutes to cover the two hundred yards or so to it. He had plenty of time to rehearse what he was going to report and was full of confidence that it would be well received.

There was no sign of life outside the shack, but smoke rose from the chimney. Reuben knocked at the door. He saw a movement at the window beside it and almost immediately, the door was pulled open and Jerimiah stood before him smiling his welcoming wolf-grin. "Rube my friend, I'm so pleased to see you. After three weeks I was beginin' to wonder if you was able to find out anything at all, but now I see you, I know as you've got a great deal to tell!"

"It really isn't much Jerimiah, but I thought if I had stayed away much longer hoping for more, you might think I have deserted you!" Reuben had planned to start off this way, hoping to prove to the smuggler that his loyalty was in the right place.

"Would I ever think that of you Rube?" That un-nerving grin again on the smuggler's face. "So, tell me what you know."

"I have been three weeks trying to get information and all I found out is this. There's three workers in the village what seem to be in a gang of smugglers, their names be Same Rowe, John Laytham and Joshua Roote and they meet in *The Black Boy*. Now, whether the landlord William Horne has anything to do with it I am yet to find out, nor can I discover where the shipments are coming in and from what vessel, but I reckon, given another week or so I'll know all." Reuben spoke enthusiastically and had himself believing every word. Jerimiah was less so.

"So how do you know that these three are smuggling and how do you know that they are the only ones, and why do you think that Will Horne isn't involved? I'd have thought that it would take more than three to run smuggled goods, unless the boat be tiny, and if these three spent so much time in the alehouse, they must discuss it amongst themselves and the landlord, and maybe others around would hear." Jerimiah's piercing eyes locked with Reuben's. "Why ain't you been sitting close to them to hear what they say?"

Reuben began to squirm where he stood in the doorway. There had been no invitation to enter, although he could see the fire which burned in the hearth behind the smuggler and feel the warmth of it too both of them. He felt anything but welcome.

"I confess" he said, "that I had a set to with the landlord very early on and he beat me and told me not to go back again, that's what made it difficult to find out too much."

Jerimiah exploded in rage. "You devil's spawn, do you think that's the way to get into a man's confidence?! What did you do to make him beat you?" He had moved forward from the doorway and Reuben backed away a couple of paces. He watched for the man's knife hand to drop to his belt but, as yet it hadn't happened.

"I went for him with my knife."

"What, and he then he beat you? What with? A Stick?

"No his fists, he is a big man and quick with it, he knocked my knife away and laid me out cold on the doorstep."

"You fool Reuben Belbin, call yourself an agent of mine? Why I'd do better getting your horse to find something out for me, and you let a man with no weapon beat you, who had a knife. You are lucky that I know what a difficult man this landlord be. He beat up two of my men who went quite independent of you, to see what they could find out. It ain't no excuse though for any of you, and now the man will be on his guard. Go back Rube and see what you can uncover, but don't come back here until you know something useful." Jerimiah, his outburst of temper now under control, clapped Reuben on the shoulder and smiling that smile again, nodded farewell and retired to the inside of his shack.

Reuben, feeling now very relieved, walked off back towards his caravan. He had intended to tell the smuggler about James, but now was glad that he had another card up his sleeve. He was shocked to learn though that Jerimiah had sent two others to find out what he was supposed to learn. Obviously, he was right to be suspicious of the smuggler's trust in him.

The following afternoon he and his family drove off back in the direction of Danbury, but this time they would camp for a few days on the common at Woodham Walter. As long as he was back by Saturday night, the last day of November, he would be in time to see Jim who hopefully would have more information.

THE BLACK BOY

CHAPTER EIGHTEEN

MOLLY'S SECOND CARGO

According to William Dowsett, Matthew Rowlings had promised the next shipment for the tenth of December at Lawling Creek and Will, at *The Black Boy* was now fully prepared for it. The cellar door had been finished and fitted from Sam's side in order not to be seen working in the cellar by either Jane, or any of his customers. When privacy was needed, Will sent her off on errands, either in Horne Row, or up to Danbury, anywhere, which would ensure her absence for an hour or two.

No message had been received from Mersea to say what benefit, or otherwise, Annie had gained from her visit to the healing woman and there was nothing to say when or, as Will perhaps wished, IF she was coming home. Certainly, Jane couldn't be happier that she remained away and was now falling easily into the role of the innkeeper's wife.

In bed, she gave her all to Will and he was now becoming lulled into a belief that his comfortable and contented life would continue for ever. She did her utmost to please him and during the day worked non-stop at each and every chore which was to be done, and all the while did it all with such a happy and contented look on her pretty face that she installed the same feeling in Will.

December this year looked like being even colder than last and during the first week, snow fell, albeit thinly, most days. Frosts were, as yet mild, and created little hardship, but Will knew how bitterly cold weather affected his brother's business and so indirectly his own. When that clay was frozen, it had to be thawed out with fire. That was of course after it was dug, and so the clay pits were filled with straw each night to ward off the frost and then cleared each day with the clay being dug as quickly as possible to prevent it freezing by the time it reached the pugglers. It was long, hard work with production falling to less than fifty percent on a good day and to virtually nil on a bad one. When it snowed hard, it would be worse.

As a result, John Horne's workers, who were paid day by day, lost valuable income on the days when they couldn't work, or , could only produce part of what they normally would. This meant that they had less to spend and so Will's business as *The Black Boy* would suffer.

He went to see his brother John at the tile works, the day before the ""MOLLY"" was due to deliver her cargo.

"John, I've got another cargo coming in tomorrow night. Can we have the same arrangement as before?" He said when he found him huddled beside the small fire in his lean-to beside the kiln. "I know this is a bad time for you John and it is likely to get worse as this winter hardens, but if your carts are not doing anything then you won't miss them will you?"

"Are you going to pay my men a days wage as well then brother?" John asked.

"Why? I've got a separate agreement with them for working outside their normal day, I ain't going to use them in daylight hours!"

"I know that, but the way things look, they's all going to be looking for another wage when I have to stop paying them. I know what you pay them Will and I thank the Good Lord for it, but you ain't bringing in a load a week so they can't earn that every week, and when I stop paying them, how are they to feed their families?" John was truly sorry for his workers, but the hard fact was that whatever hardships which they would suffer, he was not about to put his hand in his own pocket to help them more than he did already, with cheap rent and a lenient attitude to what they did.

"The best I can say is that I'll give each of them another shilling, a day's wage, and on top of what I pay them now, but only if they haven't been able to work and you ain't paid them for that day. Alright brother?"

"Yes, now what payment for the carts? Last time you gave me a tub of gin and a tub of cognac. That seems fair enough, one tub per cart."

"Hold on a minute John, you had one tub for two carts and I gave you another for use of the trap and your man!" Will said indignantly.

John smiled, "I know that be true, then, but times being hard like you say, a tub per cart the going rate. Will, where else are you going to get them?"

"No wonder as our Pa gave you this business, you don't miss an opening do you?" Will laughed, "Alright I agree, two tubs of gin though. If we have three carts I'll add one of brandy. Agreed!"

They shook hands and Will stood up in readiness to return to the alehouse, when his brother spoke again.

"You talk about not missing an opening brother, from what I hear, you ain't been missing chances yourself!" He looked searchingly at Will. "You have no need to look as if you don't know what I'm talking about, you know full well! That young girl as you have seemingly taken to your bed while Annie's away."

"John, I can't deny it, the girl has given me a new joy in life and what I'm going to do about it I've yet to work out. As you know, Annie and me never lived together, even her father said as he couldn't understand how we'd stayed together so long. All I can do is live my life by the day and hope that the happiness I have now goes on forever." Will spoke sorrowfully with no real conviction that his hopes would be realised.

His brother put his hand on his shoulder. "Will, all I warn is that if…. no…. when your wife learns of it, she's going to have her vengeance on both you and the girl. The other thing that I don't suppose that you have given much thought to, is what if she should get with child? How would you cope with that? And more to the point, how would Annie react to it?" John looked fondly at his younger brother and shook his head. "No doubt you'll find a way brother and I pray as you do."

Will gave a wry smile to John and walked off into the cold December morning towards the other side of the common.

He had already made arrangements with the others and although two carts only again were needed, as it was to be a similar cargo to the first one, he told the two younger men that he expected them to be there and that the same rate of pay as before would apply. They were delighted as any income at present was welcome when they knew what might happen if the winter became truly hard. So on the Tuesday evening as darkness began to fall, the two carts left the tile works for the journey to Mundon.

As before they muffled the horse's hooves and the cart wheels, but this time they didn't have the added protection which the fog had given them before. Tonight, was overcast and dark, with sufficient light only to see the dim shapes of the hedges which lined the road either side. It was also bitterly cold with a north-easterly wind blowing into their faces. The only saving grace was that as yet it was neither raining nor snowing. Their journey was slower than before, but they arrived at the landing place in Lawling Creek in good time and Will lit the spout-lantern and began signalling towards the creek's mouth and the main river.

Even in this poor light, the water showed up lighter than the surrounding land and before long, he saw the darker shape of a boat entering the creek by Mundon Stone Point. With the wind behind it, ""MOLLY"" fairly raced up to the landing place and at precisely the right point, came about and slid into the cut and came to rest. The sail was lowered and a rope thrown ashore.

Matthew leapt ashore and greeted his son-in-law. "Am glad to see you Will. Since getting your reply through our mutual acquaintance, I've heard nothing from you and though it is only been three weeks, living close by that daughter of mine has made it seem like three months!" He laughed loudly, then went on more seriously. "Today, when we are off loading the goods from 'Neptune' one of the luggers of our mutual friend, we spied a Revenue cutter coming up on us from the South, we were in the Wallet and she was hull down somewhere near Foulness when we spied her, and we had to be quick with the last of your shipment. I then raised all sails and with the wind at our stern, we made short work of our run to here. The lugger made off out to sea, heading for the Dutch coast and I think as the cutter would have followed him. I couldn't see once I was inside St Peter's point, but she was empty of all smuggled goods so even if the Revenue men caught up with him, he'd be clean!"

"I'm glad to see you too, Father Matt and sorry that you have had such a time with both Annie and the Revenue! We'll talk about both later, but first let's get unloaded and the carts away." Will turned from Matthew and called to his men who ran a gang plank from the ""MOLLY"" to the bank and began loading the carts.

"You had best know what I have got this time, Will. Geneva and Cognac as before, fifty half-ankers of each, two cases of twelve quart bottles of port wine and two bales of tobacco. There's also two bundles of Dutch cigars wrapped in straw and sacking about four hundred in each bundle. I know that you said same as before, but I thought as I would vary it a bit! Alright Will?"

"Yes it is good. I've got customers for both the port wine and the cigars. Now take this as payment of the first load and if you'll be good enough to wait on the payment for this I'd be grateful." Will handed Matt a bag of coins, "there is one hundred and twenty-one and a half sovereigns in there. Now how much am I in debt with this lot?"

Matt weighed the bag in his hand and thanked him. He then told him how much this load would amount to and they shook hands on it. The ""MOLLY"" was unloaded and the carts were ready to leave.

"I'll be away now Will, we never spoke no more about that wife of yours!"

"How is she?" Will asked with little enthusiasm. "Has the witch cured her and is she likely to be coming back to *The Black Boy*?"

"I am sorry to say that it doesn't look too bright as they say, she doesn't seem any better and she doesn't look like she wants to leave her old home. More's the pity. I won't be standing her miserable face much longer Will, and love you as I do, I am sorry to say that it was you who married her and you who's got to keep her!" Matthew stepped onto the gunnale of his dredger and young Silas began to pole them away. "Come over and see me before long and we'll arrange both the next cargo and return with your wife!"

The ""MOLLY"" slid away, the mainsail was hoisted and she was lost in the darkness of the creek. Will led his men and the carts back to Horne Row without incident. By the time they went through to Runsell Green, a fine snow was falling and the ground was white.

Back at the alehouse, they drew the carts around the side and unloaded directly into the cellar beneath the pot-room. Will went ahead and warned Jane, who was asleep in the bed which they now shared in the back room, not to come out under any circumstances. She understood this to be because he didn't want others to know the situation between them. She smiled to herself. "Silly, lovely man," she thought, "as if the whole village doesn't know that already!" but she remained where she was and listened to the sounds of the goods being carried into the tunnel.

When all was secure, he told Joshua and David to take the two carts and John and Daniel back to the tile works. Sam and Will watched them go, the wheels and carts leaving their tracks in the snow, which was now lying all around and still falling.

"There won't be another cargo this side of Christmas Sam, and I think as this weather be here to stay. It is early yet, not the middle of December and snow like this be falling. We can only hope as it comes warmer for a spell as it often does."

"If this lays thick tomorrow, the works won't be doing anything and we'll all be out of work. If that happens, I'll come here and help you Will to carry that load through to the tunnel. We'll see what's what tomorrow." Then saying goodnight, although most of the night had gone, Sam returned to his house and Will returned to Jane in their bed.

THE BLACK BOY

CHAPTER NINETEEN

On the last day of November, Reuben Belbin and his family had come back to the common at Horne Row. After a few days camped at Woodham Walter, they had arrived back on the Friday evening and had made their original camp site, hidden in the scrub at the lower end of the common. On Saturday night, the gypsy had waited in the lane of Paternoster in the expectation that he might see Jim walking home. Although, the boy had told him that it was unlikely that Will would offer him more evening work, Reuben was not a man to believe very much of what he was told. He was therefore both surprised and disappointed to see Wilf's cart come down the lane with Jim aboard. He melted back into the shadows while they passed and returned to the caravan. On his way back he took a small piece of rag from his pocket and tied it to the broom bush, which he passed on his way. Heaven help the boy if he didn't come to see him tomorrow.

On Sunday morning, the gypsy was at his vantage point to watch the church-goers of Horne Row wind their way up the hill. Amongst them he could see James Towns. He obviously wasn't coming to see him at least until after church. Either he'd nothing to tell him or he didn't think the meeting important. In either event, Reuben was not amused and scowled to himself as he walked back to his camp.

The church service finished mid-morning and soon afterwards, Jim walked into the gypsy's camp. He had seen the rag tied on the bush, but remembering Reuben's words last time, he approached the caravan with extreme caution, making his presence known long before he arrived by calling the gypsy's name quietly as he went. Reuben, who was waiting for him, sat nonchalantly on one of the benches and warming himself beside a cheerful looking fire which crackled with dry logs.

"I have been waiting for you young James, I'd expected you before you went to church, but maybe I thought to myself, Jim hasn't got anything to tell me so that's why he hasn't bothered to come to see me." His look of cheerful indifference hid his true feelings, but poorly. "So, be I right, or be I wrong?"

"Both really Reuben. Right, in that I didn't expect to find you here, you weren't here on Friday when I came looking for you midday, your caravan and everything was gone, so when today came, I thought I might as well go to church before coming to see if you were back. But you were wrong in that I've nothing to tell you."

"Alright Jim, set yourself down and tell me all you know." The gypsy gestured to the other seat on the opposite side of the fire and Jim took it.

"This week I saw all five of the tile workers, John, Sam, Joshua and his brother Daniel and David Archer all sitting at the table in the alehouse, and like I said last Saturday, Will's been acting mighty strange, with all sorts of comings and goings...." Jim finished mid sentence as the gypsy interrupted him.

"You are not telling me anything new Jim. You've said it all before, so unless you've got anything new to add I think our association be over. I'll find out what I want to know my own way, and if you'll take my advice boy, you'll stick with the work you know and don't try to meddle in what you don't."

"You mean to tell me as you aren't going to arrange for no supplies nor work for my horse n'cart? And when I have told you who is doing the smuggling here." Jim was dismayed, he'd given away the names of men he knew well to this man, who now was telling him that it was to lead no-where. His dismay turned to anger and then to a rage, fanned by the sneering look on Reuben's face.

He leapt to his feet and in one bound had crossed the fire with his stick raised to strike the gypsy, but the gypsy was quicker. From nowhere a knife appeared in his right hand and as Jim swung at him with his cudgel, Reuben drove the knife into Jim's side, where by the grace of God and good fortune, it struck a rib and instead of inflicting a mortal wound, caused little more than a flesh wound across his ribs. The knife caught his smock and Jim like lightening brought his cudgel down on the gypsy's forearm, breaking it and causing him to release the knife from his grip with a cry of pain and surprise.

Both men now injured and Reuben was unarmed, but he was still dangerous. With his good left hand he grabbed a length of wood from the stack beside the fire and began to move towards Jim, who was by now feeling the pain of the wound and would soon notice the weakness, which would result from the loss of blood, which was running from his wound, but he was young and he was immensely strong, as were all those who made their living laboring on the land. "Come near me again Reuben Belbin and I'll brain you like a pig at slaughter, but first I'll break your other arm, then see how you get on." he said, and then feeling the knife break free from where it had caught in his smock having worked loose by his movements, he heard it fall to the ground. Without taking his eyes off his adversary, he picked it up in his left hand, which blood was now also streaming. "And on top of that, I'll slit your throat soon as look at you, so hear my words." With that Jim backed away from the camp, making sure that he was not about to be waylaid by any of the gypsy's family.

Once he had reached the other side of the common, he felt safer. The gypsy was in no fit state with his broken arm, to attack a man with both knife and a cudgel, albeit a wounded one as was Jim. He staggered on down the lane to the farm, where he went to not his own home, but to that of Old Wilf. If anyone knew about wounds of this nature, Wilf surely did.

Wilf's door was opened by his wife who took one look at James and said, "Jim boy, you look like you need attention, come on in and get by that fire."

Gratefully Jim entered and sat where he was directed on the stool vacated by Wilf's wife. Old Wilf sat opposite on the only other, more comfortable chair in the room. "So, what have you been up to now young Jim? Looks to me as you either got on the wrong side of that old bull of ours, or someone took a knife to you, which be it?"

"That old bull never hurt no-one yet as well you know Wilf. No it was a gypsy with a knife what tried to kill me." James lifted his smock to reveal the wound in his left side. "I think I need it cleaned up and sewn up and I know how good you are with the horses so I thought as you would do it for me Wilf. Will you?"

Old Wilf got up from his chair and came round to the fire to peer at the wound. "Yes, there isn't much to it really, not much more than a scratch!" He turned to his wife who was hanging a cauldron of water to boil over the fire. "Come on woman, needles, thread, Stockholm tar and bandages."

"Don't tell me the job Wilf, when I already put on the water to boil. Everything else will be there before you can finish talking" She good naturedly chided her husband.

They cleaned the wound with hot water, washing away the blood from around it. It still bled but it was clean. The needle was threaded and it and the twine were dropped into the boiling water, the withdrawn and Wilf started to stitch up the wound, pulling the edges together and punching then to allow the needles to pass through both side in one go. As he worked, his wife mopped away the blood until finally he placed the last stitch and knotted it. Then after a final clean, Wilf applied a generous coating of tar and bandaged around Jim's chest with a length of linen torn from an old petticoat.

"That's the best I can do for you James. I hope it doesn't interfere with your work tomorrow. We are ploughing again while the ground isn't frozen too bad, so you keep that arm moving today and tonight, if not you won't' be able to handle the plough shafts tomorrow morning."

Jim thanked Wilf and his wife for their help and kindness and went back to his house. There he sat beside his own hearth in the centre of the floor in a mood of self pity. Why had he ever believed that the gypsy would help him? And what had induced him to give the names of the tile workers? He knew of course that he had been clutching at straws in his keenness to become a smuggler. How stupid he'd been, now look what had happened to Old Wilf all that time ago. Funny, he thought, that Old Wilf hadn't asked about the gypsy, or, why he should have tried to stick a knife in him. Did he know, or, was he simply minding his own business?

Simon, who had been out on the common with his friends trying to make acquaintance with the two or three local girls who were the desire of every young man in the village, came in and threw himself down on a stool. At first he didn't notice Jim's apparent discomfort.

"Oh, that Eunice Wainwright, she's just lovely, you should see her the way she walks and the way she throws her shawl round her shoulders, why she be something to behold!" Seeing no reaction from his brother, he punched his shoulder to get the attention. Only when James recoiled with a groan did Simon see that all was not as it should be.

"What ails you brother? Be you hurt?"

"It's no matter Simon, think nothing of it, I'll be better by tomorrow, now tell me more about young Eunice, she isn't more than fifteen years old is she? You don't want to be messing with her yet brother!"

Simon, back on his currently favourite subject, forgot Jim's pain and launched into a glowing reference to the girl of his desire, until his two younger brothers declared him boring and his two sisters began to throw different light on the merits of Eunice, who they well knew, being in their own age group.

Ten days later outside of *The Black Boy*, the gypsy's diligence had been rewarded. Earlier in the evening he had seen the two carts leave the tile works with five men on board and immediately guessed their destination and their business for that night. He couldn't guess which creek they were likely to be heading for, but whichever it was, he knew that some time before dawn they would return, either loaded with smuggled goods or having already distributed them. This latter, he thought to be an unlikely option as there was little time to dispose of two cart loads, unless they had a store somewhere. He couldn't follow them all the way to the marshes and back simply to find this out, no he'd wait for the carts to come back and then he'd know.

Hidden near the top of the common where he could see both the tile works and the road leading to *The Black Boy*, Reuben had spent an uncomfortable night. By the time he saw the carts coming along the road and pull up beside the alehouse, he was frozen to the marrow, and the broken arm which he had suffered ten days before, which was wrapped in cloths around two wooden splints, was aching abominably. His coat was crusted with frozen snow and his camouflage was complete, enabling him to get close enough to see what was going on. Although the light was dim, and the smugglers used no lights outside, he could see that the contents of the carts were being carried up the steps and inside.

"So," he thought, "They're storing it in there are they, well that's right handy, cause the Revenue will know just where to look and his frozen face cracked into a malicious grin." Having seen all that he wanted to find out and now feeling that if he didn't soon get some warmth in his bones, he might never move again, he crept away back to his caravan which was now back where it had been before. His only thought now was of revenge on both the landlord and the man who had inflicted the injury to his right arm.

THE BLACK BOY

CHAPTER TWENTY

THE REVENUE RIDERS' CALL

Four days after the 'MOLLY's' cargo arrived and was stored away in the tunnel, two Revenue Riders called at *The Black Boy*. There had been no sign of one for weeks and in fact, since Will had told his gathered customers on that night back in early November, not one had made a visit. They would always appear unannounced, but for the past two years never more than one at a time. This time there were two and they came with apparent knowledge and a smugness which suggested that they expected to find contraband on the premises.

They came into the alehouse bar, four in the afternoon of Saturday the fourteenth of December, sat themselves down before the blazing fire, which Jane had built in the hearth and ordered two mugs of Geneva. Jane went through to the pot-room and spoke to Will who sat there at the table cleaning his 'barker' and the horse pistols which he had taken from the two footpads.

"There be two gentlemen in the parlour, who by the way are armed, look like trouble Will. I know not who, or what they are but few go riding with both cutlass and two pistols, unless they expect trouble to fall upon them, or they expect to be that trouble! Have a look through the spyhole and tell me what to do. They want gin and not ale, which, at this time of the day be odd ain't it?"

Thanking her, Will rose quietly from the table and went through to the tap-room where he observed the two men through his spyhole. Right away he knew what they were and right away he knew why they were there asking for gin. They, as soon as the gin was served, would dash into the tap-room and look at the container from which the gin was poured. If it didn't carry the King's stamp, it was contraband and they would search the alehouse to find the rest. It had happened to Will before, but not this time he thought to himself. Last time he'd avoided the magistrate but it had cost him dearly in the bribe, which he'd paid the excise men.

Back in the pot-room he told Jane to serve the gin from the legitimate container in the tap-room and expect the two to inspect immediately.

"Be they Revenue Men then Will? They look better dressed and armed than others who have been here from time to time, and there's two this time." Will nodded and she returned to the parlour and gave the two men the gin. As Will had predicted, they immediately told Jane who they were and demanded to see the Landlord. She led them out to the pot-room where Will sat with both of the horse pistols pointed at the door as they entered. The Riding Officers stopped in their tracks.

"We are officer's of the crown Landlord, and to avoid arrest by shooting us would be a foolish thing to do, you would hang for certain for that even if you didn't for smuggling." The leader of the two men said.

Will lowered the pistols and turning them aside pulled the triggers, which simply allowed the hammers to fall, the flints sparking in the pans. "They weren't loaded and what would I want to be falling foul of revenue officers like you good men in any case."

"We want to see the tub what that gin your wench served us with, come from. We believe it to be smuggled."

"Certainly, go with the wench through to the tap-room and see for yourselves, and I assure you that I run a legitimate alehouse here and don't have any truck with smugglers." Will smiled at the riders. One of them went with Jane whilst the other remained with Will. It was clear that they were confident in finding what they sought, whatever Will said.

A few moments later the first officer returned followed by Jane. "William Horne, we remember you from a while ago and you was smuggling then. You kept your goods in your cellar, so show us in there if you don't mind."

"Gladly, I'll show you, but you won't find anything in there, we don't ever go down there except for fresh tankards, pot, trenchers and the like, there's a few onions, apples and nuts what we store down there, but nothing else, be there Jane?" Will looked at Jane for confirmation and saw that, although she vehemently agreed with what he had said, there was a worried look which crossed her face. Whether the revenue men noticed it was unlikely as they were too intent on pulling aside the mat and raising the hatch.

"You will need a light down there," said Will, "let me go before you and light the candle on the wall at the foot of the steps." So saying he unhurriedly picked up the candle off of the table and walked over to the cellar opening. The two revenue officers hadn't waited for him and were already down the steps and peering into the gloom of the far reaches of the cellar. When Will arrived at the bottom he lit the candle on the wall and raising the one in his hand he held it so the full depth of the cellar could be seen. The men began pulling aside anything and everything which might conceal contraband, but they found nothing. The 'dresser' didn't warrant any attention, it was what it appeared to be, shelving for the spare utensils, with which it was crammed full. Disappointed the excise men went back up to the pot-room. "You won't mind if we look in your other rooms will you?" Their leader asked. "We still believe as you have got contraband hidden away somewhere here."

"Seems to me as someone's being particularly malicious and has told you to come here and make my life difficult. You won't find any contraband here I promise you, but if you want, you look wherever you like, and perhaps next time you'll pay less attention to wicked gossip." Will held open the door to the back room and invited the officers through.

They hesitated and then realising the futility of their search, returned to the bar where they finished their gin. The information which they had received from the gypsy with the broken arm, was either false, or, the Landlord had managed to clear the goods away in two or three days since they had been told they had been carried to *The Black Boy*. The informant, who was expecting payment for the information, was going to be unlucky and was to be disappointed that the landlord had not been arrested and taken in fretters to Chelmsford gaol. When he had given the information to the riders, the gypsy had given the impression that the cash reward was of less importance than the apprehension and the inevitable punishment of the landlord.

Outside *The Black Boy*, that informant watched the door in anticipation of the sort of activity he longed to see, Will Horne in chains being escorted down the steps and being dragged off to gaol. He had seen the Revenue men enter, as he had been closely watching the place since he had to them of the landlord's involvement and his delightful anticipation of the revenge which was to follow grew by the minute. When finally, the officers came out and mounted their horses, which were tethered beside the door, he couldn't believe what he was seeing, so much so that he rose from his hiding place and was on the point of calling out to ask what was going on. Then realization came to him. The riders had come to an agreement with Will and weren't going to either report him or arrest him.

Reuben sank back into hiding and fuming with rage began plotting his next course of action.

THE BLACK BOY

CHAPTER TWENTY ONE

Christmastide came and went and the New Year of 1784 came in under a blanket of snow. Since early December, it had snowed on and off almost daily and by the time Christmas arrived, most of the roads were impassible with deep drifts covering them in exposed places.

Will had tried on one occasion to ride to Mersea to see his father-in-law and to find out the situation with Annie, but he had to turn back when his horse fell with him into a ditch beside the road near Beeleigh. The animal suffered a strained ligament in its foreleg and Will had to return on foot, the way he had come, leading the limping mare. The snowfall after that became heavier and in early January it snowed for two days continuously and the cold, which gripped the land was unrelenting.

Everything stopped in Horne Row. The gypsies had left the common to camp in sheltered places in the woods around Woodham Walter, with some returning to Tiptree Heath, where although no less exposed than on the common, they were at least with many friends and acquaintances where group gatherings created some comfort.

The Tile Works had come to a standstill. With such a depth of snow the carts found it difficult to get to the clay pits and with the constant fall of snow, the pits needed clearing all the time. It was finally decided that it would be better to let them lie under a blanket of snow, which would keep the clay beneath a few degrees warmer than the surrounding frozen ground. The tile workers were now out of work and although John Horne had conceded that none of them should pay rent while the situation lasted, neither would they be paid for work which they couldn't do!

The Black Boy's door remained closed much of the day with few customers from the village and none from passers-by, because of the impassible roads, there were none. The villagers who were his regular customers, mainly worked at the tile works and with no income, they had nothing to spend. The few who did come in, had little to spend and came solely to sit and talk by the fire, sharing the hardships with their fellows. Will's small income now came solely from the sale of the contraband stored in his cellar and which he was able to deliver one tub at a time, sat on a frame specially made to fit over the horses withers.

Reverend Snaith's housekeeper was delighted that Will had remembered the port wine which her employer was so partial to and took another tub of cognac brandy, as well as four bottles of the wine. The local alehouses were, like Will, snowed in and had little or no passing trade, and like him fewer local customers with money to spend, so although they each managed to take a few half-ankers of spirits and some of the cigars, which in his county district were something of a novelty, it was far less than their first requirement. As yet, Will had not ventured into Baddow where his other customers lay, but the Woodhill Road and the main Maldon to Chelmsford turnpike both had huge drifts across them and it had been just such a drift that Will's mare had fallen into and could easily have broken a leg. How much more hazardous with heavy tub of spirit weighing the animal down. No, Will had decided to wait until some warmer weather came. Sometimes in January there was a brief thaw and he hope that this year would be no exception?

At home at *The Black Boy*, Jane was loving her new found life. She welcomed the snow with all roads closed to traffic of all sorts. It meant with so few customers, that she'd be alone with the man she loved, keep the fires burning for him, cook for him and keep him warm in bed at night. It meant too that there was no danger of Annie returning just yet. Whilst Will hoped for the thaw, Jane prayed for more snow!

It was Jane's prayers that were answered. During the second and third weeks of January the snow continued to fall and the temperatures plummeted to twelve degrees Fahrenheit, twenty below freezing. By the time February had come and gone, the people of Horne Row, like so many hamlets and villages around were desperate. There was no work, therefore no money and so no food, and families were starving. Those who could, made a few pence from cutting and selling firewood or trading their wood for scraps of food. Or, they poached the land for anything which ran or flew and which they could eat.

Many of the inhabitants died during this winter, particularly the old and the sick and many of the processions which wound their way up the hill through the snow to the churchyard at its top, carried a coffin in its midst for burial in the iron hard ground.

By the beginning of March it looked as though the worst of the winter was over. The weather had turned distinctly milder and despite the sceptics amongst the older generations who foretold that 'March comin' in like a lamb' was likely to bode ill for the end of the month when it ' went out like a lion', everyone began to look forward to the Spring and better days to follow. As the snow began to melt and roads again became passable, Horne Row dragged itself out of the despair into which it had sunk. The Tile Works began work again and the kilns which had been dormant for three months, now each carried a blossom of smoke above it denoting that the fires were again alight and the place was again in business.

With the coming of Spring, John Laytham got permission from his employer to move up into the house next to Sam Rowe. His family was still the same size, having grown by one child in the previous Autumn, but having lost that child's grandmother, John's mother, who had died during the terrible winter; it had been the birth of that child, which had prompted John to request larger accommodation offered by the old Wright house, before his mother had passed away. John Horne, his employer, had still agreed that he and his family should move there. The family's house by the kilns would now be vacant for another family, and as yet there was no one to fill it, John Horne had no doubts that he would fill it before another month was out. Spring was always a time when disillusioned farm workers sought better and perhaps more constant employment, although, this winter had shown that nothing was constant for a man who was confronted with the elements of the weather.

The old sceptics were right. The final week in March brought gales and heavy rain interspersed with snow flurries. Jane again thanked her maker for this further respite. She had yet to tell Will, but she had known for two months now that she was pregnant and she was unsure of his reaction. More to the point, what would be his wife's reaction when she found out? Will had obviously notice her gently swollen belly as he had remarked a few days before as he caressed it, that she was putting on weight even though she appeared to eat little.

Will have been unable throughout the winter to get to Mersea because of the road, but for the past two weeks, when it seemed that the roads were likely to be clear enough to travel, he had been putting off the journey and now with the weather turning inclement again, he once more postponed the visit. There was of course more to it than a dislike of bad weather and difficult roads. He did not relish the idea of seeing his wife again, and more so he thought he would have to return with her. Every day that he could find an excuse to put off the trip, was a blessing.

That night he and Jane lay together after they had closed the alehouse to the few customers who had been gradually returning over the past few days, he raised the subject. "Jane, a long time ago, and it seems like a lifetime, but, I know it was only last November, you asked me a question."

Jane turned her head towards him snuggling into his beard and neck. "Did I?"

"Yes, you asked me what about my wife, Annie, and I said that it made no difference because things were as things were." Will paused before continuing. "Well, that's how things were then, but it isn't how they are now. Now, I know I love you and I've never loved my wife even in the beginning the same way."

"Oh, Will, how I've yearned to hear you say those words. I know as you are old enough to be my Pa, as once you said, but I love you with all my heart, for the man you are, however old you may be."

"Wait a little, I ain't that old you know!" He said with a laugh and playfully punched her in the ribs.

"I don't think you should do that Will, you might hurt the child!"

Will sat up quickly and looked down at her. She wondered if she had been right in choosing this moment to tell him of her pregnancy.

"What child? What do you mean? Are you with child?" he blurted out.

"Yes, Will my dearest, I am with child now these four, nearly five months, are you pleased?" The look on Will's face told her that she need not have worried, he was delighted.

"Dear Jane, a child! My first! Be I pleased? Of course I'm pleased. Oh, Jane this is wonderful news!." He smiled lovingly at her pulling down the blanket which covered them to reveal her abdomen and gazed on it with awe. He was silent for a moment. "It does mean that I have got to go now to Mersea and see both my wife and her father and it isn't going to be easy." He lay back down beside her, relishing the warmth of her nearness. He ran his hand over her belly and felt the slight swelling.

"And to think that I said that you were getting fat!" he laughed. "Come now my love, let's sleep as we need to do some planning tomorrow and no mistake."

Contentedly they lay in each other's arms until they drifted off to sleep. "Was this going to be the way for him to get his release from Annie, or would she cause more trouble." Will thought as he sank into a satisfied, but nonetheless troubled slumber.

THE BLACK BOY

CHAPTER TWENTY TWO

The heavy rains and the thaw at the end of March had turned roads into quagmires and they remained almost impassable, as they had been under the drifts of snow. It was the second week of April before Will was able to travel to Mersea.

Young James Towns had started to drink again in *The Black Boy* on a Saturday night, accompanying Old Wilf as he had before the hardships, which they had all suffered that winter. Although, James was right handed, Will had noticed that he seemed to favour his left hand more than usual and he asked him what injury he had received to cause this. Jim was reticent to tell him and merely shrugged it off as - "bit of a kick from me horse!." Once when Will had asked Wilf the same question, the reply had been "he told me you were kicked by his horse didn't he?" So, what else do you want to know?" At this stage, Will had decided to leave the matter alone, although by the attitude of both horsemen, it quite clearly was something beyond a kick, it was something which neither wanted to discuss, or, explain.

Once Will had made the decision to travel to Mersea, he approached Jim on Saturday night before he left the alehouse with Wilf. "Jim, I know as you helped me out before Christmas when I was short-handed here, but would you be happy to do it again for a couple of nights while I be absent?"

"How do you mean Will? What do you want me to do?"

"I am going to Mersea for maybe two days and I can't leave Jane to run the place on her own without a man on the premises to both give aid and protection. Now, I know that how you are employed by old Jenkins in the daytime, but would you come in here when your work is done and help here until the door closes on the last customer? It'd be for two nights at the most, but it'd give me a great piece of mind that Jane and *The Black Boy* were in good hands." Will laid it on a bit thick, but he desperately needed assistance. He could have asked Sam, but Sam had a family to whom his first loyalty lay and he felt that James, given the right incentive, was likely to be thoroughly diligent.

"Yes, I'd be please to help you Will." James replied instantly. The guilt which he felt for having betrayed, both, the alehouse keeper and his patrons was acute and he wanted to do all that he could to make amends.

"Are you not going to ask how much it is worth?" Will asked, slightly surprised.

"Yes, of course I want to know that, but I know how you will be fair on the price."

"For each of the two nights I'll pay you a shilling and if all's well when I return, I'll pay you another, making three shillings in all."

Jim was delighted, three days pay for two nights' work and after the hard times, which had been the lot of all for the past three months, it was manna from heaven. He agreed and shook Will's outstretched hand.

"There's one more thing, young James," Will said, still gripping his hand, "the personal safety of Jane is in your hands. She is very dear to me and I trust you to look after her while you are here."

"Don't worry Will, all of the village know that she is your woman now and most are pleased about it, of course there'll always be those who aren't, but that's their look-out. I'll do what you ask and with pleasure." Jim at that point would have laid his life down to repair the damage that he had done with Reuben Belbin.

On the following Monday, seventh of April, Will hung one of the pistols, taken from the footpads, at the front of his saddle, put his barker in his tail-coat pocket together with this cosh and with provisions in case of a delay in his journey, said goodbye to Jane at the foot of *The Black Boy's* parlour steps. "You make sure as you keep the door closed against those who you don't know and maybe afraid of. James Towns will be here tonight soon after dark and will stay until closing, and then the same again tomorrow night. You look after yourself and our child, and I'll be back in two days at the most. Oh, and the pistol what I left is on the shelf in the pot-room is loaded and primed, all you need to do is to cock it and fire it at anybody as is danger to you." He kissed her goodbye and mounted his horse, turning towards the common and to the road to Maldon.

All day he rode without stopping, but it was late in the afternoon when he reached Peldon. The sate of the road was awful, with every low point flooded and the rest a sea of mud. The stage-coach which ran between Chelmsford and Maldon and then on to Colchester, had left deep ruts in the turnpike and it was obvious where it had bogged down completely and had to be hauled out by additional horses. A single horseman stood a better chance of getting through, but it still took Will many hours to complete a journey, which previously had taken less than four hours. "If Annie refuses to stay here and I've got to bring her back," he thought, "how am I going to do it?" A trap would never get through the worst places and unless Annie was fit, or even willing to ride, there was no chance of getting her back. He just hoped above hope that she would concede to Jane's position and decline a return to the alehouse, he was going to tell her that he no longer wanted her back, but he knew how stubborn his wife was and didn't believe that she'd stay without a fight.

The nearer he drew to Mersea, the more apprehensive he became, and at the Peldon Inn, he called in for a little 'Dutch Courage' as Geneva was termed for good reason. Crocky greeted him like a long lost friend and sat at the table with him while he drank his gin.

"I won't ask you for a platter of mutton Crocky, in case you try to charge me for two!" Will joked with the landlord.

"Oh, I'll not make that mistake again Sir, your father-in-law ain't dropped that subject since you were here last. Every time he comes in here for the past four months, when he's been able that is with the winter what we's had, he ain't let me forget it!" Crocky Crockford grinned at his guest and accepted the pint of ale which Will offered him. "Are you expecting to cross to Mersea this night?" he then asked.

"Yes, but I know not of the tides. When can I get over?" Will replied.

"It will be low enough on the causeway by seven this evening, so you've got a couple of hours to wait. You might as well have some mutton!"

"I'll do so with the promise as I pay for only one!"

Two hours later, with a full stomach and glowing with "Dutch Courage", Will left the Peldon Inn and rode across the causeway. The edges for the most part were marked with poles, but the centre section, where the boats passed over it at high tide, and which was still knee deep to his horse, was unmarked and Will had to pick his way cautiously, keeping the poles on the far side in view, which in the dim light of the stars was unreliable. He successfully made it through to the far side and rode off onto the island.

On the west side of the island lay the main harbor surrounded by a labyrinth of creeks between small part submerged islands called holms. It had been for a hundred years and still was, a smugglers paradise! The local people knew the creeks, inlets and waterways like the backs of their hands and for a Revenue boat to follow one of them into this maze would be foolhardy. Contraband goods, therefore, made their way ashore without interference from the excise men, partly because of their inability to catch the smuggler and in part because they were paid off to allow goods to land on the 'hard', that area of land on the edge of the water below the village, which had a solid stony surface and base on which carts could be drawn.

Will headed for the row of cottages on the high ground overlooking the harbor, which was a forest of the masts of luggers, drifters, dredgers, wherries and every type of fishing boat imaginable. At the last cottage in the row he stopped, dismounted and hitched the horse to a post with a tethering ring, which stood beside the wall which divided the house from the road. He went up the short path and knocked on the door, which after a short while opened to reveal Matthew's wife, Will's mother-in-law.

"Will, I ain't seen you since you married our daughter Annie. I know you have been here cause Matt tells me when he has seen you, but you never call to see me? Anyway, come in, 'tis good to see you, how are you?"

"I'm well mother-in-law, but I've come to see Annie. How is she?"

"Have you come to take her back with you? She ain't here you know, she lives with the wise woman, who she swears has cured her of the illness that ailed her. I think it is her mind what wants healing though, she don't seem right to me!" Leading Will inside the cottage, she said, "I've got to say that she was driving us both mad with her miserable ways and bad tempers, especially Matt, who has been spending more time at the alehouse round the corner than here at home when she was here to stay, simply to get away from her."

Will replied gently "Look mother, I think I'd best to talk to Matthew afore seeing Annie, to better find out the lie of the land you understand, so I'll be back here later."

"Alright Will, I understand, you go and see him, he'll be right pleased to see you, on that you can be sure." She opened the door and led him back to his horse, which he remounted and rode around the corner to the 'Sail and Anchor'. There in the bar, he found his father-in-law, sitting at a table with two other oystermen.

Matthew looked up, saw his son-in-law and a broad grin spread over his face. "Will," he said "I thought as you had deserted us, you haven't been near for four months and worst of all you left that wife of yours here with us!" Matthew rose and greeted Will warmly, introducing him to the two other men, as "this here's the boy, no, the man who I am proud to call son. It maybe only by marriage to my daughter, but a true son he be to me!" Matthew was well in his cups by this time and might not have been so forthright had he been sober, but Will was touched by this small speech.

"Father Matt, you know well why I haven't been able to get here before now, the roads be only just passable now and it took twice as long to get here than usual. Oh… and I did try before in December, but my horse fell in a snowdrift and lamed herself, so I had to walk both of us home!"

"Alright my boy, so what now? Be you on business, or to see your wife?"

"I don't think as business be best talked of here and in any case it's been slow with the weather being as it has. I hope it'll get better as Spring gets here. No, I'm here to talk about Annie, but again what I have got to say be for your ears only!"

The two companions of Matthew Rowlings got up in amiable fashion and moved to another table. In a smuggling community such as this, they were used to people wanting privacy to discuss their business.

"Now then young Will, what's on your mind regarding my daughter?"

"Your wife tells me as Annie's staying with the witch woman who cured of her ills. How long has she been there?"

"Near on a month now Will. I have to tell you that it's been a rest and a relief for both your ma-in-law and me. How much longer we could have suffered her wicked tongue and temper I don't know, but tell me Will, are you going to take her away with you?"

"When I came here, I didn't have no mention of what I was going to do. I had to find out how Annie was and then decide the best thing to be done. The trouble is that I have got something to tell you which is hard for me to say to you Father Matt, but say it to you I must, as you are the one man as I owe the truth to." Will took a deep breath and plunged in,

"I've found another love, a true love, what I never had with Annie, and I haven't shared the same bed in all but the first few weeks of the marriage, so that is why we ain't given you any grandchildren. I've had eight years of hell with your daughter and now it's time to end it. The girl I love is now with child and has been near on five months and I want that child, more than I've ever wanted anything in my life." Will looked up in anguish at his father-in-law across the table. "I know as I won't get your blessing Father Matt, but I just wanted you, above all people to understand."

Matthew was silent for a few minutes. "I ain't never said that you would not get my blessing son, and if life was more simple I'd be pleased for you, but I don't know how you go about such things as this. The church doesn't take kindly to their vows being broken and above all Annie won't either." He paused for a moment his brow furrowed in thought, "can you not take the girl as your mistress and keep her and the child as you would want?"

"Can you see Annie taking to that, I can't. No, I've got to speak with her and persuade her somehow to have our marriage cancelled, or annulled, or whatever the word is, and let me live my life to raise a family and be happy. What Annie will do then I don't know, but all I hope dear Father Matt, is that you and me remain friends as before."

"Will my boy, that'll never change whatever happens between you and my daughter, rest assured of that."

For ten minutes the two of them sat in silence. Finally, Matt said, "I think my advice to you Will is for you to say nothing to Annie now. Do I ask you who this love of yours is Will? Or can I guess? Be it the young girl that works for you, name of Jane I recall?"

Will nodded, "You are right it is her and before you say something about being young enough to be my daughter, we both know that, but it makes no matter to us."

"I may have thought it but seeing your face boy when you talk of her, I'd never say it." Matt sucked on his empty pipe, re-filled it, took a spill from beside the fire, lit it and then the pipe. "All I can do is wish you good luck my boy. Now are you going to see Annie and find out what she's going to do?"

"Yes, if you tell me where to find her I'll go in the morning. Thank you Father Matt for your support and your friendship, I find it hard to be talking to you like this about your own daughter and I am sorry as it never worked out the way that I had dreamed."

"Remember Will. I still sail every week to Maldon with my load of oysters, so I can always get a message to you from there, or, if you have a reason to speak to me, I am always there on a Wednesday tide." Quietly he added, "are you ready for another shipment yet? and when?" Will nodded, he said, "come on son, let's go and see your ma-in-law, and we can talk on the way back."

THE BLACK BOY

CHAPTER TWENTY THREE

William and Matthew began to walk back to the cottage, leading Will's mare. On the way, they spoke of the next shipment. "You asked me in the alehouse, if I was ready for another shipment, well I am, but I must tell you first that I've have got ready the full payment for the last, which I know is very late in coming, but I've not brought it with me because the chances of being robbed in these parts be high, so I didn't want to risk it. I can pay you when next you come to Maldon."

"Don't worry about payment Will, I knew that you would pay me next time. Now, about another cargo, I can't tell you right now, but I might know by Wednesday night, you can pay me then. You want the same as before, or more?"

"I'm hoping for more customers over the next two or three months, so, if I say another cart load of assorted goods, on top of two as before, that should do it. You'll need to let me know where you are planning to come ashore with it, but until then we'll reckon on it being Lawling as before, shall we?"

"Yes, unless I tell you different."

Arriving at Matthew's cottage, Will removed his horse's saddle and bridle, replacing the latter with a halter and a nose-bag of oats and leaving it tethered outside, then entered the house.

"There isn't much to tell you mother-in-law, things haven't been right between Annie and me, as I expect you know from her, but I am going to see her in the morning to see how she is and what she means to do." Will expected that Matthew would explain to his wife as much as he felt it sensible to do so and didn't say more on the subject. "Now, I ask you for two things, one be a bed for the night and two, directions to find the crone's house."

The woman went up the steps leading to the floor above to arrange a bed, which up until recently, Annie had been using, while her husband,

Matthew, with the aid of a piece of charcoal which he pulled from the fire, drew on the surface of the table, a map for Will to follow to find the house where Annie now was. Matthew's wife came back down to the living room. "Before you go to see Annie and the crone, you better to know a few things Will." She started, but Matthew interrupted her.

"The boy knows all there is to know woman, I have told him."

"Oh, no he don't, not less you know all I do." She looked sternly at her husband who shrugged his shoulders and let her continue. "Annie was always a strange child, what with her tantrums, her cruel nature with living things and the way she never played with the other children because they were afraid of her. Then you married her Will and while you was courting her she changed and were all sweetness and light and we thought as all was well. But, we knew before long that things had changed and we expected you to throw her out years ago, but you didn't Will, and for that we're grateful. Now when you see her, you keep back a step because her hate for you be vast, if all she's told me be right. Now the crone that she's been living with isn't a lot better, only she be much slyer and cleverer. She is a crone, wise woman, and one what knows all the cures for all the ailments using herbs and potions and the like, she be a witch. So, you take extra care with her. Now I have said all I have got to say by way of warning and if I be repeating what my dear husband said then so be it, but I doubt he's said as much!"

Will thanked her and gave her a hug. "I know how Annie can be, but I'm glad to be warned about the crone. Thank you mother."

The following morning Will rose and saying goodbye to Matthew and his wife, he set off towards the lane in which the crone lived. He found the house without much trouble as it was isolated at the end of the lane with a small patch of cultivated ground around it within which she grew a few herbs and medicinal plants of every description. The house itself was old and somewhat dilapidated, its thatched roof showing clearly the residency of numerous rats, their holes being everywhere. The reed thatch was still serving its original purpose but needed renewing in several places. Beneath the eaves hung bunches of strings of fresh and dried plants and several other things, of which William was not too sure of their origin! It was quite obviously the right house!

He dismounted and went to the door, he had to stoop low beneath the thatch in order to knock, he then stepped back to await an answer.

There was none. He knocked again but again there was no reply. The occupants were obviously not in, so he sat down on the bench set against the front wall of the cottage to wait. Beside him was a wooden box with air holes over it. Inside things stirred, but Will didn't feel inclined to be inquisitive!

An hour later he heard laughing voices approaching from behind the house. One he recognised as Annie, whilst the other was from an older woman, the laughter being more of a cackle. Around the corner came Annie and a woman of late middle age. They were laughing and chatting together in a way which William had not heard his wife do since before they married. The women were both carrying baskets of herbs and roots and appeared not to have a care in the world, happy in each other's company. Then they saw Will's horse and then Will, and their mood changed. The smile on Annie's face vanished, to be replaced by a snarl of anger.

"What you doing here William Horne?" She spat at him. "Don't tell me as you have come after all this time, four months to seek news of my welfare. Well I don't need you here, so you can go back and run that poor place as you call an alehouse and good riddance to you!"

Will couldn't believe his ears. Annie was actually saying what he'd hoped all along that she'd say, but in his wildest dreams he didn't expect it to be this simple. "Are you telling me as you ain't coming back to *The Black Boy*?"

"I don't think I could say it planner if I tried; could I Sarah?" she asked turning to her companion, who shook her head with its tangle of grey hair, vigorously, smiling a cunningly possessive partially toothless grin.

"Sarah here cured me of my ailment and be now teaching me the ways of the healers, so's I can be a wise woman like her. So until I am ready I ain't coming back to Horne Row." Annie spoke with perhaps more determination than she had shown before.

"What do you mean, until your ready, how long are we talking of?"

"I don't know, but you'll be the first to learn when it is." She narrowed her eyes and gave her husband a venomous glare. "Now, you go when I return, it'll be on my terms and don't forget it. Bye-the-bye, how you been managing without my help with only that slut Jane to assist you? Not too well I expect," she smiles a malicious smile and Will felt the same old anger as before begin to well up inside him. Carefully he forced it down and did not allow the look on his face to betray his emotions.

"Very well Annie, if that's how you want it to be, I'll say farewell until I have word from you and farewell to you Sarah and thank you for healing my wife. How she expects to learn all that you know from a lifetime of learning in just a few months, I don't know, but I am sure you both know what you are up to."

He mounted his horse and without a backward glance rode off towards the causeway. The time was now eleven in the morning and the ebb had reverted again to the flood and the water was again rising over the roadway. Will's mare splashed through it without effort and soon they were on the road home. The ride back to *The Black Boy* was uneventful except for the coincidence of seeing a string of pack animals outside the alehouse at Salcott and a group of men standing attending to them and drinking ale. One of these looked strangely familiar and Will was sure that even at this distance, he knew him, but for the moment couldn't place him.

Standing there with that man was Jerimiah Spalding. The two of them watched the rider pass by, "That be that landlord of the alehouse at Horne Row," said Reuben Belbin, "now I wonder what he be doing down here?"

"What's more interesting is what was doing here back here in November last. I saw him go by then from this very doorway. As I told you before Rube, I never forget a face, and now I have a name. I think you can be sure now that the man be smuggling as what else would he want over here. My guess is that he's been to see his pa-in-law, Matthew Rowlings at Mersea. We need to keep a close watch on both of them. Maybe it's time for you go back to Horne Row. I can find others here to do what you do for me."

Will dismissed from his mind where he thought he had seen the man before and continued his journey home.

At *The Black Boy*, he turned his horse into the stable yard at the back and was met by Jane who ran out and threw her arms about him as soon as he dismounted. "Oh Will my dearest, you are home in barely a day and half and I have been that worried about you." She paused, looking round quite expecting to see another horse, or, trap behind. "What happened with Annie? You've not brought her back with you?"

"Wait until I've fed and watered the horse, then we'll go in and you can hear my news and I'll hear yours." He hugged her to him and then released her and she followed him into the stable. While she filled the water trough from the outside, Will rubbed the mare down, filled her hay-rack and put in a spoonful of oats in the manger. When they had finished, they went arm in arm into the alehouse through the rear door.

It was late in the afternoon and as yet there were no customers in the parlour bar, so they sat beside the blazing fire, which Jane had built in the hearth. Will gently pointed out to her that firewood cost money and that at this time of the year with the weather getting warmer, it should no longer be necessary to have such a huge fire. She smiled back at him and said that she wanted to make sure that the warmth of its welcome should reflect the warmth of her own. He was lost for words in his overwhelming love for this gentle and feeling girl, who he wanted more than anything to become his wife. Even if they couldn't be 'churched' it wouldn't matter once Annie had finally left.

"So, tell me Will, what happened with Annie, why isn't she with you and when is she coming back?"

"My dearest Jane, the news is better than we could have hoped. I told Father Matt about us and about the child and he was as kind and as helpful as if he was my blood father. Though Annie's his daughter, he still gave us his blessing and wished us good fortune."

"Oh, Will I am sure that is wonderful news, but what about Annie? When's she coming here?" Jane's face had taken on an apprehensive and unhappy look.

"This be the best news of all, she ain't coming here for some time, maybe months, maybe a year or so. She wants to be a wise woman and so she's taking teaching from the wise woman that cured her."

"She's what?" Jane was dumfounded. "A witch you mean don't you Will dear?"

He laughed, "Yes, you're probably right, but whatever she be learning to be, it's going to take a little while, so we can get on living our lives together." He leaned across the table and kissed her lovingly. "I don't know what will happen when she does return, but you be sure my love that I shall be here to protect you all the time.....now how did young Jim get on helping you last evening?"

"Very well, he were here soon after leaving the farm and stayed until the last customer had gone. He's promised to be here at the same time tonight, that's very soon, but you won't need him now will you?"

"Whether we need him, or not, he can work the night and I'll still pay him the three shillings that I promised him. He's a good lad and we may well need his help again."

Jane fetched Will a tankard of ale and they sat together contentedly talking over the affairs of the day and yesterday. A quarter of an hour later, James Towns came in. He was somewhat surprised to see Will and looked crestfallen when he asked him, "I' suppose you won't be wanting me tonight now you are back Will?"

"Nonsense young Jim, we'll be glad of your help, Jane's been telling me what a great aid you have been to her yesterday and as I promised you three shillings, then three shillings it'll be." Will smiled at the bolly, who thanked him delightedly. "So now go on, earn your money and do whatever it is that Jane needs doing and serve our customers like you did yesterday." Will waved him off towards the pot-room and Jane got up and calling for him to follow her, led the way out to prepare tankards for the evening.

Will sat by himself staring into the fire. Whatever had made Annie decide on this course? The woman could be unpredictable at times, but most of the time…… What would happen when she eventually did return? Would it be before, or after the child was born? And what would her reaction be to either a heavily pregnant Jane, or, a newly born baby?. He couldn't contemplate the rage into which she would fly. Would she then go back to Mersea? It was clear that her parents no longer wanted her there. Her mother had indicated that she might be off her head, and Will had always been suspicious that she was a little mad. Not made enough to be sent to the made house, which he had heard tell of, but there were times during the past years when he had doubted her sanity when she flew into a temper which was on the very edge of madness. Oh well, he thought, who knows what the future holds in store for a person, only the Almighty knows that, and he continued to stare into the flames lost in his thoughts.

It was Tuesday night and trade was as usual on a day early in the week, slow. A few of his regular customers came in and each spoke to him in a friendly way. No-one seemed to be in the least way condemning of his relationship with Jane, although there were few in the village that did not know of it and he now made no attempt to hide it. Several people asked when Annie was coming back from Mersea, but none with much enthusiasm. Will didn't commit himself, simply saying, "I have been to see her and she'll come here when she's good and ready, maybe this week, maybe next, maybe a month or two…"

That night after the last customer had gone and Jim had left clutching his three shillings, with a promise of further similar work in the future, the doors were locked and Will and Jane went to bed. They were tonight in a more leisurely mood and certainly more carefree with their love-making than they had been previously, partly because of the joy they found in the fulfilment and warmth of their deepening love for one another. They lay in each others arms for a long time afterwards, each deep in their own thoughts. It was Jane who broke the silence.

"Whenever she comes back, what's she going to do when she finds us sleeping together? Even though you ain't shared the same bed for so long, it won't be natural for a wife to know her man is in bed with another woman in the same house."

"I don't know Jane dear what she'll do, or, say, but all I know is that it ain't going to happen yet, so neither me, nor you needs to worry. Now you sleep my love and fret about it when it happens and not before." Will kissed her and together they drifted off to sleep, locked in each other's arms.

The following day, Will went to see his brother John. He needed to arrange for the loan of three carts in the near future and so he needed to agree a rate with him.

"Yes, no trouble there Will," his brother said, "just tell me when you want them and they're yours. We agreed I think for the extra cart, another four and half gallon of cognac didn't we?"

"You old villain brother, you know as it was one of gin!" Will punched his brother's arm, "and that's what you get." He grinned at his brother.

John smiled, "thought as you might have forgot Will, but I should have known better! Did I hear that you went to Mersea to see Annie on Monday."

"I was there Monday and yesterday and come back yesterday evening. She's decided not to return to Horne Row as yet, she's learning to be a herbal woman, wise woman, witch – whatever you like to call it. Why, I don't know, but I am thankful of it that she ain't coming back here yet."

"You sound more than pleased as she's staying away Will, I know that you and Annie don't fit too well as man and wife, but then I look around and see that there's few what do. Surely it ain't that bad?"

"John, dear brother, you have no idea. The past eight years has been hell. We ain't shared a bed in most of that time and we avoid each other most other times."

"I didn't know it was as bad as you say, though some of us have wondered why you ain't had a child or two. I have to say that I've never liked Annie overmuch and I've always been a bit wary of her temper."

Will decided not to mention Jane to his brother yet, nor about her forthcoming child. He would find out about both in due course even if he didn't already. He thanked him for the loan of the carts and promised to let him know by the latest a week today.

On Wednesday morning, Will set off on horseback to Fullbridge wharf at Maldon. He arrived to see the "'MOLLY'" taking up the river towards the quay. Fifteen minutes later she moored alongside another boat already tied to the wharf and Will watched Matthew cross from one boat to the other and then step onto the quay.

"Your next cargo be arranged Will, for the twenty-ninth of April; again it is a Wednesday and in a fortnight's time. If there be a change to Lawling I'll get word to you."

"Thank you Father Matt, and here's what I promised you." And turning his back so that none could see, he handed over a bag of coins to his father-in-law, who nodded and secreted the money bag in his coat pocket. They shook hands and Matthew returned to the "'MOLLY'" to assisted young Silas in unloading his oysters to the waiting carts. Annie and what Mrs Rowlings had said about her was not mentioned, so Will decided that there would be another time for that and remounting his horse he rode up Market Hill to meet the high road to Chelmsford.

As he rode he hummed to himself. It was a bright sunny April day. The hedges and trees were all in bud and bursting with fresh green life. The grass beside the road had begun to grow up, pushing itself through the mud which had, but a few days ago, covered it. Soon the dust from the road would give another blanket; but for now it struggle upward to healthy green spears. Birds sang all around him, telling of their joy having found a mate, built a nest and now watching over that mate as she filled the nest with eggs.

At this moment in time, Will couldn't have been happier. He was in love with Jane who was expecting his son, he couldn't ever think that the child might be a girl; Annie was safely in Mersea and unlikely to return for some time and he was expecting the smuggling business to thrive.

Ahead of him on the road to Beeleigh he saw a caravan moving slowly behind a plodding horse. It too was going towards Danbury, but as he pulled alongside it and was about to call 'good-day' to the driver, he saw a flurry of movement on the driving seat, where it seemed that one of the two people there, hastily disappeared into the inside of the van, leaving a lone woman apparently taking over the reins.

They were obviously gypsies but Will didn't recognise the woman, who acknowledged his greeting with a nod. Had he known who it was that had vanished inside, he would have viewed things differently, but he was so full of joys of the world, it didn't occur to him to be suspicious or to speculate why the person had done so or who he might be.

THE BLACK BOY

CHAPTER TWENTY FOUR

Will met with his fellow smugglers on the Friday after this meeting with Matt. They met as before in the stable and he told them of the next shipment, which was arranged for the following Wednesday week and that this time they would require three carts. The drivers would be Sam, John and Josh and the other two would ride with the latter two. He told them that Lawling Creek was to be the landing point once again.

"Be that wise Will?" asked Sam, "to use the same place regularly seems to me to be a risk of somebody noticing and perhaps following us in there."

"It's been a long while since our last trip so it's not as if it has been at regular times. No, I don't think that there is a risk. Anyway, it's not our choice, its where the boat can get in, and we have to accept the skipper's choice as he's got a heavier load this time and he knows what his boat can do. He may change it to somewhere else, but I doubt it." Will glanced at the five of them, "Are you all happy with that?" they nodded in agreement.

"Right, until next week then, in between I have got to find us some more customers down Cock Clarks, Norton and Purleigh way. We may need to deliver some of these goods on our way back, but I'll tell ye about that if needs be." Will dismissed the men and returned to *The Black Boy* via the back door. Inside he found Jane busily running between the bar, the pot-room and the tap-room, serving customers, washing tankards and platters and all with a happy smile on her face and a cheerful word to say to everyone. For a few moments, Will stood in the doorway and watched her, brimming with emotion of his love for her. "This be what living and life be all about," he thought to himself. "For the past eight, or nine years I have not known what I have been missing. Now I have got it all; a woman who I love deeply and one who loves me; a woman who's filled with happiness and fun, and knows what it is to laugh; a woman who's going to give me a son and last but not least, I've got a business with a future!" He laughed happily aloud and strode into the room, catching Jane up in a bear-hug of emotion.

Jane squealed, "now look what you have done, you have made me spill good ale all over the floor!" She put the two tankards which she was carrying out to the parlour, onto the tap-room table and returned his hug. "Now are you going to let me serve your customers, or ain't you?" She smiled up at his face and he planted a kiss on her lips. She retrieved the tankards and went through to serve the two who'd asked for them.

When she returned to the pot-room, Will was sitting on the edge of the table, waiting for her. "I have been thinking Jane dearest, watching you working so hard, that we could do with some help here. I willingly help when I am here but there'll be many times when I am not, and an alehouse ain't the place for a woman to be running on her own. Now, you had Jim to help you for two nights and I don't know if you would have done as well without him. So I am going to ask him to help out perhaps twice a week. He could do all the heavy work, what you shouldn't be taking on much longer in your condition anyhow!"

"It is hard work and no mistake Will, but I am happy to do it, so long as it pleases you. Yes Jim were a great help, especially on the Monday that you went to Mersea, and it be a comfort that a strapping lad like Jim be here to take care of trouble; but why?, are you expecting to be away a lot? I know that it isn't any of my business, and I won't press you for an answer dear Will, but it might be as I can aid you if I knew why." She stood between his knees where he sat on the table and pressed her body against his, putting her arms about his neck and drawing him towards her.; gently he pushed her away.

"Oh my darling Jane, you talk about aiding me, well this ain't doing it! If you don't stop what you are doing, I'll have to take you to our bed and then what about the customers?.... And seeing the look in your eye, no we aren't going to do it on this table. There isn't no lock on that parlour door!" He chuckled and Jane giggled and they both reluctantly drew apart.

"If Jim comes in tonight, I'll ask him if he wants the work. If not, we'll find another." Will said and led the way through to the parlour. Just before he went through he said, "before too long my love, I'll tell you why I'll be away at times, but now isn't the time, so be patient."

"Will my dear, I told you that it wasn't my business and I meant it. If you want to tell me in good time then that's how it will be. But don't you fret about it…. It's no matter." Jane patted his arm and pushed him towards the door.

In the parlour there was a good gathering for a Friday night, it looked more like a Saturday. Most customers would leave earlier on this night than they might on a Saturday because of their work on the following day, but to Will, it was encouraging that so many were forgetting the dreadful winter which they had experienced and were now coming out to spend their odd surplus coppers. It had happened only in the past two or three weeks, but a new feeling of optimism was abroad!

James Towns say quietly by the fire, which after Will's comment, Jane had been less enthusiastic in making up and so whilst still welcoming on a cool evening, it was not the roaring blaze it had been. He sat at the table habitually frequented by the old deaf labourer. The old man sat opposite him and occasionally they spoke to one another. Both were content in their solitude.

Jim was speaking, "I ain't never heard no-one speak your name, I suppose you have got one?"

"No-one ever asks boy, they mostly think I am daft so they don't think I was given a name, but I was, it is Abraham, only those as use it call me Abe. Thank you for asking" the old man looked up. "Now, I saw you serving in here a couple of nights, nigh on a fortnight back wasn't it? Your name is Jim if I ain't mistaken?"

"Yes, Jim Towns, I am a horseman down Paternoster Farm, what are you and where from?"

"I'd be a gardener at the big house, Woodhill, been there for the past forty years, but I don't know how much longer. There used to be just three of us, but now there are twelve and they got another young man starting there this week, that's two in the past month, and I know as it'll not be long before they'll want my house. My missus can't work no more so it'll be the poor house for us soon." Abe reverted to staring into his beer as was his habit, not waiting for a reply, nor, expecting one from his young companion.

Jim turned this thought over in his mind, thinking of the inevitability of old age and what it brought with it. He was a young man and if he remained a farm worker for the rest of his life, at the end of it, all he could look forward to was what poor old Abe had coming to him. There was little sympathy for the old and infirmed anywhere in the land, most workers ended up in this situation, if they lived that long. It was perhaps the lucky ones who died, whilst still employed, although their wives and families were then the ones to suffer.

He had hoped to improve his situation by getting in with smugglers, but that hadn't worked out and although the guilt which he had felt for his betrayal of the tile men, had been lessened since his fight with the gypsy and the disappearance of the man, his family and caravan soon afterwards, it was still there and he felt that he had a debt to repay.

Unseen by Jim, Will had come into the parlour and now after walking across the room to where the boy sat, he brought him out his reverie with a clap on the shoulder. Jim jumped but then grinned when he saw who it was. "Hello, Will, you caught me deep in thinking'."

"I see that Jim. Now I have got business to talk about with you so would you come through to the pot-room so we can do that?" Will moved back to make room and Jim stood up and followed him as he asked. He was a little nervous as to what business Will was going to talk about. Had he heard about his meetings with Reuben Belbin?

Jane remained in the parlour, calling a cheerful greeting to Jim as he passed by, but going about serving customers in order that Will could speak to Jim in the comparative privacy of the pot-room.

"Jim, you did me a service the week before last, when you helped Jane those two days. "Will began as soon as the door was closed behind them.

"Yes, but you paid me right generous, and I am thankful."

"I'm glad you were happy with it, but now the fact is Jim, I need your help again but more regularly, like two days every week and they mostly be Fridays and Saturdays, but there'll be other odd days aswell. Do you want to take it on?"

Jim was delighted. What had he been dreaming about in the bar just now, it was an answer to a prayer. "Will, I'd be more than happy to do the work for you, so long as it's evening time after I finish at Paternoster." He beamed at the landlord.

"Yes, it will be. What I need Jim is help for Jane, particularly the heavy work like moving casks of ale and the like, chopping and bringing in the firewood, though we won't be wanting that much longer. Now, I'll pay you a shilling a day as before and on the days what I am not here, you will get another tanner for the extra vigil over Jane and to stay until she closes the door behind the last to leave."

"Like I say Will, I'll be glad. When do you want me to start?"

"Tomorrow would be a good time. Alright?"

They agreed and Jim went back to his seat beside the fire, filled with the joy at having increase his weekly income between two shillings and maybe three and sixpence per week. Not as much perhaps as one night's work with smugglers, but this was to be regular work. All the difference in the world!

On the following morning, Saturday, Will saddled and bridled his mare and rode to Purleigh, where he visited an old acquaintance at the Bell Inn which stood on top of the hill. There he renewed the business, which he had in the past and the inn-keeper agreed to take regular deliveries of merchandise. Two other alehouses also entered into agreements with Will and by the time he rode through Cock Clarks, the alehouse there took the last that he had to offer. Will was very satisfied with the way business was building and so when he rode back in the late afternoon over the common at Horne Row, his mind was far removed from the gypsy who he had thrown out all those months ago. He therefore didn't see the dim figure, standing watching *The Black Boy* from the shelter of the trees and bushes which lined the road opposite.

Soon after Will returned, the other target of Reuben Belbin's hatred and revenge appeared. James Towns walked by and up the steps into the alehouse bar. He noticed that the boy looked around him before entering and appeared to focus on where he was standing amongst the bushes. He edged a little further behind the tree which sheltered him. He knew from other surveillances that this man normally on a Saturday night rode up there on the cart with the old man. So, what was he doing arriving on foot? Did it mean that he would return to the farm on foot? If so what an opportunity for the revenge which he craved and for which his ever-aching arm cried out for. He would keep watch for a short while and then return later in the evening when he'd expect Jim to leave. If he walked home....!

Jim walked into the bar in readiness for his evening's work. He was greeted by both Will and Jane who sat at a table in the parlour eating their evening meal. "Have a sup of ale before you start Jim." Will offered and when Jim nodded thanks, Jane hastened away to the tap-room for it.

"Will, as I came in just now, I swear as I saw a body skulking in the bushes across the road. He was watching this house, that I am sure, but who it is I aint certain." He waited for Will to reply, but before he did he suddenly remembered; "It wouldn't be that gypsy that you threw out of here would it?"

"How did you know of that Jim? You weren't here that night." Will replied quickly.

Jim was caught with the need to lie, how could he say that he had watched it happen and then have I all come out what about what has happened since. "It is common knowledge as he tried to split you with a knife and you threw him out. I don't remember who told me!" he stammered.

Will looked at him, remembering the coincidence with both Jim and the gypsy approaching him about smuggling at almost the same time back in November, but he kept his council for another time. He like the boy and apart from this small discrepancy he trusted him also. "You could be right young Jim and it is strange you say that, because when I come back from Maldon on Wednesday I passed a caravan much like his heading this way and the driver acted a mite suspicious. I reckon it could be him back her now. We'll have to watch out."

Jane came with ale and Jim drank his hurriedly in order to carry out his work and avoid further conversation for the time being with Will. He was a little worried now about his journey home, he had come out that night without so much as a stick and undoubtedly he would be walking into an ambush set by Reuben Belbin, who would, he knew be seeking revenge for the broken arm. It was, therefore, with relief that Old Wilf overstayed his usual time and in order to get the ride home, Will allowed Jim to leave a little earlier than the leaving of the last drinker.

As the tumbril crunched over the gravel past the gypsy's hiding place, he saw the two figures in it, Reuben growled to himself. He has seen Old Wilf's cart standing outside of *The Black Boy* when he had returned to his watch on the place, but had hoped that like once before, Wilf would leave first and the boy would follow walking. This time it was not to be, but there would be others……

THE BLACK BOY

CHAPTER TWENTY FIVE

On the following Monday the Riding Officers re-appeared. This time they made no pretense as it was the same two and they knew precisely what they were looking for and where to look. It had been a Saturday when they were called before and early in the morning. This time they arrived in the afternoon and went straight through to the tap-room.

"Ere! What are you doing in here?" Jane spoke loudly from the doorway to the pot-room. "You get back to the parlour and I'll serve you there!"

One of the men continued his inspection of the ale casks and the gin tubs, while the other came towards Jane. "We be officers of His Majesty's Revenue and we've been here before so we know what we are looking for so the next place we look will be in your cellar, and we know where that is hidden, so you had best let us through there," at the same time running his hand down her cheek... With that they barged past Jane, pushing her out of the way, only to be confronted by the large figure of Will, who grabbed the man by his coat lapels and held him rigid in the doorway.

"I suspect you enjoy pushing about those that can't defend themselves, well here's one who can and if you so much as lay another finger on this lady again, I'll forget that you're an officer of the Crown, and you'll be sorry to have done it. Now if you'll tell your friend there to put away his pistol, what at present is more likely to be a danger to you than to me from our places in the doorway, I'll let you go about your work, not that you'll find any more than you did the last time. I told you then, there ain't no smuggled goods in this here alehouse."

The riders leader spoke to his companion and told him to do as Will bid him and then Will released him from his grip and allowed them both through to inspect the cellar, which they did, but even less thoroughly this time. It was obvious that it wasn't being used as a contraband store and they emerged and left *The Black Boy* with the words, "our informant is quite certain as your smuggling William Horne and one day we'll catch you and find where it is hidden. Plain it ain't here, so maybe we ain't looking in the right place. You be sure of one thing, we ain't giving up!"

The day before "'MOLLY'" was due with her next cargo and just over a week after the excise men had made that second visit to his alehouse, Will visited Paternoster Farm to ask Jim if he would work the following Wednesday night 29th April. He would, he told him, receive his first six-penny bonus, because Will would be away for the night. Jim happily accepted and assured him that he would be there soon after his work on the farm had finished.

Back at *The Black Boy*, Will explained to Jane that he would be away on business the following night and that James would be there to help until the last customer had left. She simply nodded but didn't ask where he would be all night. It was probable that she had a good idea already, what might keep a man away from his bed at night beyond that might be another woman, but this consideration never crossed her mind with the knowledge she had of their love for one another.

On Wednesday evening Will had left to meet the carts at the tile works before dark and before Jim had arrived. He guessed rightly that Jim's work had continued longer than anticipated, he was therefore not unduly worried and so he kissed Jane goodbye, saying that he would expect the boy to turn up soon and that he himself, would be home in the morning. He also explained that he would have goods with him, which would need to be carried down to the cellar as soon as they arrived. He would explain more in the morning, but if she heard it going on, which undoubtedly she would, she wasn't to concern herself and not investigate.

The three carts were ready with the five men already waiting to be off. It was yet not dark and Will was a little nervous of leaving in daylight when the chances of being seen were so much greater, but, he couldn't leave it any later, or they'd not arrive on time for Matthew, who had reckoned to be in the creek by eleven o'clock, so he led the way to Mundon by the usual route and left the tile works just before dark, the latest he dare leave it? Was the informer someone who had seen something on one of the two previous occasions. Was it one of his brother's workers? Will's fears were well founded and the small convoy was observed by several, not least of which a certain gypsy.

Reuben had been watching both the alehouse and the Tile Works every day since his return a fortnight earlier. His earlier assumption that Will had done a trade with the Revenue Officers has been proved false when he had visited the revenue office to ask for his reward for the information which he had given back in December. That had been a few days after he had witnessed the officers leaving empty handed and had thought they had a deal with Will. Reuben now wanted revenge on those two officers and so to that end he was going to report them to their superior in the hope that they would be suitably punished for aiding and abetting a smuggler. However, who should he meet at the door to the Excise House as he was about to enter, but the very two men, who immediately grabbed him and began verbally chastising him for telling lies before setting about him manually. When the gypsy vehemently argued that he knew what he had seen and that the merchandise was unloaded at the alehouse, and if they hadn't found it they either weren't looking in the right place or it had been moved before they got there, they finally believed him. "You'll get nothing this time gypsy, but you keep your eyes open and you tell us quick as you can if you know of another cargo coming in. Better still whether you have find out where it be landing'" Reuben promised them that he would in future try to do that. That had been before he had returned to the Heath where he had spent the winter. Now he was back on watch on Horne Row Common.

Standing watching the carts at the Tile Works, the gypsy was not in a position to see James Towns arrive for his evening work at *The Black Boy*. Nor, could he have seen that he carried with him a stout cudgel and an ancient flintlock pistol. Beneath his smock and tucked into his belt he also carried Reuben's own knife.

The journey to Mundon was uneventful and the carts arrived at Lawling Creek in time to guide Matthew's boat into the cut. It was very heavily loaded this time and had to come in on a fuller tide that previously. After mooring, Will directed his men to load one of the carts with goods for Purleigh and of the remaining two, one for Baddow goods and one for Danbury. The Purleigh load was to be delivered that night on the return to Horne Row and was to be driven by Samuel Rowe with David Archer to assist him.

All went well in unloading and Will drew his father-in-law aside out of earshot of the men. "You know what your Mrs said about Annie, she's right, Annie is ready for the mad-house I reckon, and that old crone's a witch if ever I saw one, and likely to turn Annie into one too. I don't want her coming back to *The Black Boy*, because I am afraid of what she'll do." Will didn't need to explain what he feared and Matthew understood.

"Did she say when she'd be expecting to come back?" he asked.

"No, and less it be out of spite, it won't be soon because she be wrapped up with the crone in learning the tricks of the witch's trade and that could be years!" Suddenly Will saw a ray of light in the darkness of his thoughts about Annie, perhaps it would be years by which time she may well have forgotten all about *The Black Boy* and William Horne, but Matthew's voice penetrated his thoughts.

"My Mrs told you that she is strange and cruel; that ain't changed and if that girl can be spiteful she will be, so don't you put your hopes too high, you take care of that girl and the child she be carrying for you." Matt looked into Will's face over the water. "You be assured that if I hear of Annie moving your way, or any plan to do so, I'll come over and get the news to you." He slapped Will on the shoulder and turned to supervise young Silas in the remaining few tubs to be landed and loaded onto the carts. "Same arrangement as before Will? You pay when you have sold and is ready for the next. Looks to me as your trade be building nicely!"

"Yes, it is that and I have got here the profit that I made on the past two cargoes, what'll nigh on pay for this lot. You'll tell me what I still owe you and you shall have it the next time we meet." Will handed Matt a bag of coins and Matt weighed it in his hand. "You are doing well like I said son, so let's hope as we can build on it some more!" He said looking at Will with a grin of what looked like pride.

The 'MOLLY' was re-floated and pushed out into Lawling Creek where she sailed, now clearly visible, into the main river and on towards Maldon where Matthew would deliver his load of oysters in the morning.

The carts with Will at their head, scouting the road ahead, set off back towards Danbury. At the turning to Purleigh, Sam and David left the others and set off up the hill to first the Bell Inn and then to the other alehouses, to deliver the goods, as always in pre-arranged dropping points, which weren't necessarily outside the destination's front door! At the Bell there was an outhouse at the rear, into which the two men stacked the tubs of Geneva and brandy, a bale of tobacco, some snuff and fifty cigars. Similar arrangements at the other alehouses had been made and ranged from a chicken house at one, to a hole in the ground covered by an old door at another. Sam and David finished their deliveries at Cock Clarks as dawn was breaking in the east and they hastened homeward. Sam left David to put the horse and cart away at the kiln, returned and would not be at work at the tile kiln for the rest of the day.

As he approached his house, he saw a figure, very like the gypsy, who Will had described as having overheard their conversation through the alehouse door and who had subsequently been thrown out by him. He crouched behind the bushes watching *The Black Boy*, probably invisible from there but easily seen from the direction from which Sam was approaching. He must have eyes in the back of his head thought Sam, because as soon as he himself saw the gypsy, the man spun round and hurried off, disappearing quickly into the scrub.

Sam continued home and having told his wife that he had returned, he went round to the rear of the alehouse. The door there was bolted on the inside so he went round to the parlour door.

John Laytham's cart stood empty outside and the door was open. Inside Sam found Will and John stacking the cart's contents in the cellar at the foot of the steps. They had all but finished when they say Sam looking down at them.

"You know that you have left the door open Will? Anybody could have walked in and seen what you are up to in there." Sam said, "I came round to warn you that gypsy was here watching your every move and I reckon maybe if I hadn't come in when I did, he could have paid you a visit."

"The gypsy you say? Where was he?" Will snapped as he emerged from the cellar.

"Over the road in the bushes, he were well hidden and you wouldn't have seen him."

"He's gone now? Jim warned me that he were about here on Saturday last. I'll have to find out where he is camped and give him another warning. But for now, John you go and get my brother's cart back to him. I hope that Josh and Daniel will be back there soon." Turning to Sam he said, "they went to deliver goods to Baddow before going back to the Tile Works, I just hope they remember to drop the three tubs into my brother's house! Now will you wait a bit before going back." To John he said "I'll come over later and make it right with my brother."

"Alright Will," John said, climbing onto the cart and urging the horse into a trot, which soon carried him round the corner and out of sight.

Will now spoke urgently to Sam. "We have got to get those goods into the other cellar now Sam, because I know what trade that gypsy might have done with the riders. It is certain as it were he what informed them before and he must think that we got the goods away quick so when the riders come, they couldn't find anything. This time we have got to be quicker!"

"That's right with me Will, let's do it now, it won't take the two of us long, but this time I think you should lock the door! Where's your Jane by-the-by? Does she know of what you are doing?"

"I think she's guessed, but she holds her tongue and until I tell her she'll stay in the back room. Of course, she doesn't know of the tunnel!"

Will winked at Sam. "And I think it is time to seal off your end and brick the door up, what do you say?"

"Yes, the sooner the better if those revenue riders start to get clever and look for another store close by. The first place what I'd look at if I was them, would be my house, especially as it be still named Horne Row."

Back inside with the door now firmly locked, they returned to the cellar and moved the contraband through to the tunnel. It took them under half an hour and they emerged hot and sweating. They sealed up the entrance with the 'dresser' checked all around for anything they had missed and left the cellar.

"I'll go and get Jane," Will said. "And she can get us a pint of ale each to wash down the dust!" He went to the back room where he found Jane sitting quietly on the bed waiting for him to come as he'd promised two hours before, when he arrived back and told her that he would be unloading goods into the cellar. He kissed her briefly and asked her to come through to get him and Sam an ale a piece. He then returned to where Sam sat at the pot-room table. "Now I know as I've held you from your work Sam again today, and I have promised my brother when you were all laid off work in the winter, to make your money up were ever necessary, I'll do the same again today. I'll come over to see him later this morning and tell him. I'll also ask him for enough bricks to seal up your door."

Behind them they heard Jane close the trap-door over the cellar steps and replace the mat. She said nothing although she had peered down and seen nothing that had not been there before, which she found surprising.

"When did young Jim leave you tonight Jane?" Will asked.

"After the last customers had gone, he helped them out the door in the end because they didn't want to go!" Jane chuckled. "Did it just like you do. He be a big strong boy now you know! And then he left, but before he did, he asked if you had powder and shot for an old pistol what he was carrying, I didn't think that you would mind so he loaded this old gun, stuffed it in his belt and left. I locked the door behind him. I noticed as he had a great knife in his belt as well and were carrying a cudgel. I asked him why he was so well armed for a walk to Paternoster and he said you never know, who, or what you are likely to meet on a dark night! And then I sat by the fire waiting for your return, and that's where I were when I heard the cart and unlocked the door."

"So, you don't know any more about Jim? I'll go see him later today."

Will got up. "I'll thank you Sam, to take this here wage for tonight and some extra like I said." He counted out seven shillings into Sam's open hand. "The two shilling extra be in case you have to square any time lost with my brother and for the extra work in the delivering and helping me just now. Thank you!"

Sam likewise stood up and with a word of thanks to Will and a wave to Jane, he left.

Soon after Sam had left, Will rode down to Paternoster Farm to see Jim. He found him in the field above the farm-yard, hoeing mangolds and turnips. They had been planted in the old manner of spreading by hand and raking in and a row needed thinning to allow each individual plant to grow. Seed drills were a thing of the future! The whole work force of Paternoster was there, not just the labourers, but also the horsemen, in order to get the job done as rapidly as possible, each having a pre-determined area of his own to thin. Even with the eight to nine men available, it would be several days before it was done.

Will rode to the edge of the field nearest to where he could see James Towns working beside his brother Simon, and beckoned him over. Jim put down his hoe and straightened his back before walking over to where he sat on his horse. "Good morning to you Will, what can I do for you?"

"I've come to enquire as to your welfare Jim. Jane tells me as you left *The Black Boy* last night armed with as much protection as might be carried by a Dragoon! I have come to ask you who it was against the gypsy or something else?" Will looked down at the young man, who now looked both guilty and embarrassed. Will felt a twinge of sympathy for him, he obviously had something that he hidden and Will knew that he was about to tell him. He was right and after taking a deep breath Jim confessed.

"Will, when I said that I heard from another about you throwing out the gypsy, it weren't the truth. I was there and I saw it all. I heard what he said to you about getting your smuggled goods and I heard what you says to him. I saw him draw his knife and try to stick you with it and I saw you throw him out. That's how I knew who he was when I saw him that time." Jim looked at the ground and then back at the man on the horse. "Will, I am so sorry for lying but there's more!"

Will waited and the rest came out. How Jim had sought out the gypsy to see if he could help him get into a smuggling gang and how the gypsy had shown his worst side ending finally in a fight in which he had been knifed and had given Reuben a broken arm.

"I never did think that you had been kicked by your horse Jim, who stitched you up? Now let me guess, Old Wilf weren't it? He's been stitching horses and cattle all of his life!" Will now smiled at Jim. "Don't you worry no more Jim, I never believed as you was anything but good. So, did you meet with Reuben Belbin last night? I don't think as you did due he wouldn't have been skulking outside the alehouse early this morning. The way you was armed, he'd more likely be lying in a ditch somewhere!" he chuckled.

"I expected him to waylay me all the way home so I took my time and was careful at every likely place, but he weren't there. Perhaps he never saw me get there, to the alehouse I mean."

"I am glad that you are unharmed, I'll expect to see you tomorrow night, Friday." With a nod, Will gathered up his reins and kicked his horse into a canter, riding off towards his brother's works. He was very tired now, not having slept since waking the day before and he was also anxious to get back to Jane, who he had seen but briefly in that time.

THE BLACK BOY

CHAPTER TWENTY SIX

The Riding Officers arrive on the following day early in the morning before *The Black Boy's* door had opened and before William had left his bed. The day before he had pushed aside his tiredness and again after the door had been closed behind the last customer. He had then slept until Jane roused him to the fact that someone was hammering on the parlour door.

He rose, pulled on his britches and shirt and thus attired staggered, still only half awake, to the door, which he unbolted and pulled open. He was confronted by the two now familiar faces of the excise men who pushed passed him with cutlasses, with the hilts of which they had been banging on the door. "Now, we'll see what you've got in your cellar shall we?" Their leader smiled in anticipation of what he now expected to find, and led the way through to the pot-room. There stood Jane with a cloak around her shoulders covering her dress which she had pulled on but not fastened beneath. "Be this another of your inspections to see what we sell?" she asked with a sweet smile, "or is it an early need for ale?"

"My, you are pretty and no mistake," leered the leader, "just from your bed and with your hair all down like that!"

Will swiftly leapt before him, risking the cutlass which threatened him. "you may be on the King's business but you'll keep a civil tongue in your head and all the same and speak to this lady as a lady and not one of your harlots!" He thrust his face into the man's, pushing aside the cutlass blade as though it were not more than a blunt stick. "Now I'd be much obliged if you would apologise to the lady!"

The officer grinned a slightly lopsided grin and turned to Jane. "I didn't mean to cause any offense madam, but I meant as I said, you are a pretty woman!" Jane smiled at him and tried to give a little curtsy, which revealed more of her then was intended, much to the delight of both revenue men and the irritation of Will!

Will raised the trap door and led the men down into the cellar lighting the lantern there and holding it aloft. The place looked much as it had done when they had seen the last time. The poked around, hunting for some sort of evidence and although they looked more closely at the'-dresser', they inspected only the larger tankards and pots on it to see if they hid anything. Of course, they found nothing.

"What's your informer had to tell you this time?" Will said scathingly. "Why does he reckon I am a smuggler and when does he reckon I have goods delivered? And more to the matter, if I did where are they? This spy of yours ain't up to much is he? So I wonder what he be after all." Will thought for a moment, "you don't think that he laughing at you in some way be he?"

The leader hesitated a moment before answering. "He tells us he is sure, so much so that he saddled up his old carthorse and rode down to Maldon to tell us as soon after he said as it were here. He ain't done that before." He again hesitated, realising that by that he might have said too much, his eyes searching Will's within, which he saw recognition of the informant. To cover up the gaffe, he hurried on….. "We don't know how you do it, but somewhere about here you have got a hiding place. The next time we'll bring with us a company of Dragoons and they'll find it if it be here abouts."

Will led them to the door and watched them ride off at a gallop back towards Maldon. He closed the door and turned to find Jane stood behind him. She had discarded the cloak and now stood there in nothing but an open-fronted dress. Will looked at her for a moment and then said. "He were right, you are pretty and no mistake!" and he laughed. "But I reckon your more beautiful than pretty and so is this." He leaned forward and ran his hand over the now very noticeable bump in her belly. "She is five months now you say, and I reckon as he'll be a good big boy, what do you think?"

"If it ain't a girl that is Will, you never know." Jane smiled fondly at him and hugged him to her. "I do hope for you dearest, it is a boy."

The smuggling trade, which Will was building up was doing extremely well and loads were now being arranged fortnightly. Some more of these had been to Lawling Creek again but because of Sam's earlier warning and the knowledge that the gypsy was all the more keen for the smugglers to be caught with the contraband in their procession, Will arranged with Matthew for the landings to be at different creeks.

The Black Boy was too doing well, as a direct result of the smuggling, with customers being attracted by the cheaper rates at which Will was selling his spirits and, Old Wilf's great delight, his tobacco to his regular customers.

Perhaps it was because of these factors, together with the approach of the child sometime in August, that allowed Will's defenses slacken. He had at one point half-heartedly searched the common for Belbin, but hadn't found and assumed that he had gone for good. Unbeknown to Will, the gypsy had moved half a mile away to the far side of the common which stretched across to Gay Bowers in the east. So it was in mid July when nights were at their shortest, being close to the summer solstice, that he and his men set off in broad daylight to Mayland Creek to meet Matthew's 'MOLLY'.

Their departure was as usual watched by the gypsy, but now from a discreet distance because of the daylight. From this new vantage point he couldn't hear what was being said, so he had no way of knowing where the carts where headed that night. He had known that a cargo was coming in tonight because he had received a message from Jerimiah Spalding at the Heath that Matthew Rowlings was expected to meet a lugger that evening to take on board a load of contraband. No-one knew where he was heading to off-load the cargo, but because the gypsy had overheard the mention of the creek at Lawling more than once, he had assumed that was where he would make his landing and this is what he had reported to Jerimiah. He and his gang would be there ahead of Will to intercept and to steal the cargo with a personal promise to Reuben that not only would he receive a good percentage of the value of the goods, but that William Horne would receive the sort of beating which he would not like to receive again, even if indeed he survived it.

Reuben had given up on the idea of any form of personal gain from the intervention of the excise men, either by way of cash reward for the recovered contraband or by way of revenge in seeing Will hung for smuggling. He had therefore decided that by getting Jerimiah to apprehend the three carts, he would see a cash return, although probably smaller than he might have received from the revenue's reward. This would depend upon the generosity of Jerimiah, who was not known for that virtue! He would at the same time however gain his revenge on the man who had humiliated him that night at the alehouse. It had been a long while ago, but Jerimiah Spalding had pointed out to him during the cold winter when he was still suffering dreadful pains in his arm and had talked about revenge on James Towns.

"Reuben my friend, revenge be a dish best ate cold. Be patient it'll come!"

This time when he had met Jerimiah on a visit to the Heath in May and told him of his plan, Jerimiah had reminded him of what he had said regarding Jim.

"Reuben, you remember what I said before, about revenge being a dish served cold, well now you can do the same with this here landlord, because I know how much you gripes inside against him taking your pig-sticker off you and throwing you out." The smuggler had then grinned his wolf-like grin, which always left the gypsy with an unpleasant feeling that he should watch his back. Was the smuggler also planning a cold dish?

This time, Reuben Belbin didn't return to watch *The Black Boy*. He knew the carts, even if they escaped Jerimiah's gang, which was extremely unlikely, wouldn't from his previous knowledge of their timing, be back before four o'clock the next morning, so until then he returned to his caravan on the east side of the farther common.

Meanwhile, Will led the three carts to Mayland. There as arranged they met the oyster dredger 'MOLLY' and unloaded her cargo onto the three carts in the now usual way. While this was going on, Matthew took Will to one side, but before transacting the financial part of the business there and then as they had become accustomed to doing over the past few loads, Matthew spoke urgently.

"Will, you should know as Annie came to see her ma and me two nights back to say that she is leaving Mersea soon to go back to you at *The Black Boy*."

"Did she say when Father Matt?" Will asked in alarm.

"No, but you be on your guard my son and keep her away from the Jane of yours. Best if you stay with her, all you can until you know as Annie be back. Who is with her now?"

"Young James Towns, what helps her when I am not there. He won't let anything befall her of that I am certain, but now you have made me want to hasten home to make sure, so here's the coin as before and I think as with the problem with Annie, I won't want another shipment until I let you know. I'll come to see you at Fullbridge when the time is right." Will shook his father-in-law's hand. "I'll say farewell until then Father Matt. Thank you for telling me of Annie, but I think as now I'll be away back home as quick as I can. I'll leave Sam to arrange the rest of the loading and delivery."

He called Sam to him and explained his hastiness to be away. "You know what goes where Sam. You take the one cart to Purleigh and John and Josh go back the way we come to *The Black Boy*. I'll meet them there and unload as before, and I ask you to get there just as quick as you can. The cart what Josh be driving can be taken to Baddow later so we'll pull it up behind your house until you return."

Sam nodded his agreement and returned to supervise the remainder of the loading. Will with a wave, rode off back towards Horne Row.

Jerimiah Spalding was becoming more and more irritated by the waiting which he was experiencing at Lawling Creek. He had look-outs posted all around the inlet to make sure that Matthew's dredger couldn't slip in unobserved, but by the time the sky in the east had begun to lighten, he realized that he was in the wrong place and that the "'MOLLY'" was not coming. He knew however from information received, not from the gypsy but from 'others in the know' that William had been trading with Inns and Alehouses in Purleigh. That would be where he would now try to catch Will and his carts.

Calling his gang of ruffians together, they mounted the pack animals which they had brought to transport the cargo in the event of anything should happen to make the carts, which they expected to capture, unusable, and rode off in the direction of Purleigh. One or two of Jerimiah's men knew all of the likely outlets for contraband goods in the village and so they started at the 'Bell Inn' and began to work their way back in the direction which Sam had taken a short while before.

They came across him, just after David had removed the door covering the pit behind the first of the alehouses and were now about to offload gin, brandy and tobacco and snuff consigned to this drop. Jerimiah rode up close to the cart and spoke in a threatening hiss to Sam who stood on it about to hand down the first half-anker to David, who stood beside the cart. "That there load looks to me like it's got me own name on it! That name be of Jerimiah Spalding, so I'd be obliged if ye'd step down a moment while I take it over."

"And who does he think he is this Jerimiah Spalding what thinks as he can just step in like that?" Sam replied. "You and your gang of cut-throats won't be doing anything of the sort in the face of this!" Sam reached down into the cart and straightened up holding a blunderbuss with its short bell shaped barrel pointing at the gang leader …….. Or, where Jerimiah had been the moment before Sam had looked down to pick up his weapon. In that wink of an eye, the gang leader, who had manoeuvered his horse against the side of the cart, had moved his body over the withers of his horse and now drove the long knife for which he was infamous into Sam's unprotected side. He twisted and then withdrew the blade, grinning over barred teeth as Sam slumped down amongst the cart's contents. Jerimiah raise himself from his horse's neck and turned to David who now stood in abject terror against the cart's side. "Must be your turn now boy, so what is it that you have got to raise against me then, eh? Another blunderbuss like your mate? A pistol? A blade?"

So much was this sadistic man enjoying himself that he didn't see the muzzle of the blunderbuss shakily rise in the cart until it was pointing directly at him, nor did he feel it's load of nails, shot and stones which blew his chest apart, spreading blood, flesh and bone over all those who had been watching the scene and who now surrounded his lifeless body.

Sam's final act was witnessed by not only the gang from the Heath but also the villagers, wakened by the ruckus outside their houses culminating in the explosive discharge of Sam's blunderbuss. Faces appeared at windows and doorways and from nowhere people began to gather.

Violence and even violent death was not uncommon event for the ruffians of the Heath. They watched with indifference when their leader had cold bloodily killed Sam with a knife, but now upon seeing Jerimiah killed in this way, the gang, who hadn't even dismounted at that point, lost their nerve and demoralised by the thought that they were now in danger of being hunted down for one or both of these deaths, they fled, galloping off back towards Maldon and Tiptree Heath, where they would be able to hide in amongst the protection offered by the community there.

David Archer, with blanched face and shaking knees, saw them go and in a daze dragged himself aboard the cart and whipped the horse into a canter. He drove the animal hard, not allowing it to slow until he had passed through Cock Clarks. He then allowed the snorting and heavily breathing creature to slow down to a trot. The horse which spent its days pulling carts, ploughs and harrows on the farm was unused to such demands being put upon it and so David had to finish the journey to *The Black Boy* in short spells of both trotting and cantering.

Will had arrived home well before the others and had been mightily relieved to find Jane safe and sound and no sign as yet of Annie. He was busy unloading the first cart and had sent the second to Baddow to deliver its cargo, rather than leave it behind at Sam's house as he had first planned on doing, when he heard the approaching sound of the hooves and wheels of a cart being driven fast over the gravel road and when it appeared around the corner, was alarmed to see that it was Sam's cart being driven by David with no sign of Sam.

David pulled the horse to a halt beside John's cart, most of the contents of which had been transferred to the cellar of *The Black Boy*. Tears streamed down his face and he was as white as a sheet, even after the exertion of driving the horse hard all the way from Purleigh. He seemed unable to speak and could only point into the bottom of the cart behind him. Will craned over the cart's edge and saw Sam's body lying there in a pool of blood. The blunderbuss had fallen back across his chest after he had discharged it in his last living moment and he now looked as though he was proudly showing it off, there was even a hint of a smile on his dead lips.

Will stared at him for a few moments, aghast at the thought that something of this nature should have happened. What was he to tell the poor man's wife and family? What was he to tell his brother who had now lost a key worker? He finally turned to David. "You had best tell me what happened and who did this to Samuel. Now get you down from the cart and come sit on the step here while I get you something to bring you back to life again." He helped David down and went through to the parlour and into the pot-room, where he spoke to John Laytham, who was transferring the goods to the cellar. "John, we's had an accident and Sam's dead. You had best come outside and hear it from David. I'll just go and get him a pot of cognac brandy to steady him up."

Back outside, they sat David on the step and he thankfully sipped at the brandy, the colour slowly coming back to his face. Gradually between bouts of coughing brought on by the spirit, but prompted by his listeners, he recounted the events of the night.

"You say that it was this Jerimiah Spalding what killed poor Sam? And it were Sam who killed him with the blunderbuss?" Will asked.

"Yes," nodded David, "And brave it was too with all them ruffians stood around. There were only the two of us, and Sam he stood there like he had a gang of his own behind him. There was only me and he knew I wasn't armed."

"Alright David," Will said matter-of-factly to try to remove the emotion from the scene, "We'll get your cart unloaded here and we'll carry poor Sam round to his house for them to mourn him. Then you take your cart back to the Tile Works and say nothing until I have spoken to your employer. Here's your five shillings for the night and an extra shilling for the extra trouble. Now drink up your brandy and help with the unloading."

Sam's death was felt by the whole community of Horne Row. He was a well known and well liked member of it, and his funeral when he was buried at Danbury Church, was attended by almost all. The killings had been reported to the Magistrate the following day, but because it was known that Jerimiah Spalding was a notorious smuggler, it was assumed that both men who had died were involved in smuggling, so the authorities took the view that no further investigation was needed as it was simply a case of two villains who killed each other. Nobody had apparently enquired after the goods which they were reputedly handling at the time, nor about the cart, although there had been plenty of witnesses at Purleigh.

One man who was pleased to hear of the death of Jerimiah Spalding was Old Wilf, who when Jim told him gave a wry chuckle. "Least you didn't have to break his head for me as I told you, Sam broke more than that and good for he. I am only sad as to poor Sam losing his life that way, especially at the hands of scum like that weedy runt Spalding."

Sam's wife was philosophical once she was over the initial shock of losing both her husband and the family's bread winner. "He knew the risk what he run, and he never were a man to back off a fight. He died perhaps as he would have wanted and when I first see his body, I know as there was a smile on his face, so that tells you doesn't it?" She looked at Will for his agreement, which he gave with an approving nod. "We have spoken about it enough times, so I know that the next stop will be the workhouse for me and the children. There are many who have gone before, so I know what to expect." She shrugged her shoulders resignedly and went to move to return inside the house, which she had shared with Sam. Will stopped her with his hand on her arm.

"Listen Mrs Rowe, I'll talk to my brother and ask if you can stay here as long as your rent is paid and so long as he doesn't want the house for another family. I know that John Laytham's old cottage is still empty, so until that's filled he won't be having need of this one."

"Oh, 'that is good of you Master Horne, but how am I to pay the rent, albeit but sixpence a month, when I haven't any work?"

"I'll pay it for you, and it won't be a debt what you'll owe me, it'll be a gift from a friend of your husbands. With harvest being just around the corner, you should find a bit of work, enough to keep body and soul together, and I'll talk to the housekeeper at the rectory, who is always putting washing and the like out to others. Maybe she'll find you some earnings."

"You are a kind man William Horne and me and mine thank you for it."

THE BLACK BOY

CHAPTER TWENTY SEVEN

So much had happened since William had left his men and Matthew at Mayland Creek on that fateful night. He had ridden 'hell for leather' back to Horne Row, desperately worried that Annie would arrive there before him and would in some way harm Jane, so when he got there to find that his fears were unfounded, he was not surprisingly very relieved.

Jane had opened the door to his frantic knocking and they had fallen into each other's arms, where after a short while, Will related what his father-in-law had told him. "I was so worried for you Jane, and I still am. That woman be a danger anyway and with her witches learning she now be a bigger one. I am not going to let you out of my sight until we be sure of what she'll do when she comes here…. And come she will of that I've no doubt."

"Dearest Will, I ain't afraid of Annie now, not with you to look after me, even if she is a witch. Do you believe that she can cast spells over folk? Does she have the evil eye?" Jane's look of innocence as she had peered up into William's face touched his heart and he squeezed her to him.

"Don't you fret on that count my dearest, witches ain't all they're said to be!" he said reassuringly, although he felt no confidence in the statement.

When the two carts of John and Joshua had arrived a couple of hours later at the alehouse, Will had sent Josh and his brother Daniel on to Baddow to deliver the contents of that cart, while he and John had unloaded the second cart into the cellar. At that point all was going well and apart from the warning with regard to Annie, there was little difference between this consignment and those of any previous one over the past few weeks. All changed however when, whilst they had been doing this, David had arrived with Sam's body and the remains of the load which should had been delivered to Purleigh. These goods had to be carried in and stacked in the cellar, which by now was becoming full.

After sending David back to the Tile Works and John home, Will awaited the return of Joshua and Daniel before attempting to move the contraband into the tunnel. Of course, he now didn't have Sam to help him in this task. There was nothing for it but to do it himself, alone. It had been a long and stressful night and he was tired. Jane watched him as he made the effort to go into the cellar again and to dismiss her to the back room. Gently she said to him, "Dear Will you don't need to hide things from me. I know that you have got another hiding place down there ever since the revenue men were here last time. I saw that the cellar was empty when it should have been full. So if there's anything I can do to aid you, I'll do it now with all my heart."

"I guessed as you knew Jane, and if there were a soul in this world that I'd trust with the secret, it would be you." Will looked tiredly, but adoringly at the girl. "Right, you can keep watch at the door whilst I put away as much of the goods as I can."

She had then gone to watch the approach to the door while he opened the 'dresser' and begun stacking the tubs, casks and bales away in the tunnel. By the time he had finished, it had been mid morning and the tunnel with the two cartloads plus goods from previous shipments was filled almost to capacity. Will had sealed off the tunnel by closing the dresser-door and had wearily climbed the steps to the pot-room. He had called Jane from her position on the parlour steps.

"Now Jane, before I have finished I have got to see my brother John and make things right with him. But I am not leaving you here while I'm over there at the Works, so you can come with me."

They had gone and Will settled with John, payment over the hours lost by his men and paid him his dues in spirits as agreed. With regard to Sam Rowe's family, it would be a day or two later, after the funeral, that William would broach the subject of rent for the house and help for the Rowe family. That would be shortly before Annie returned.

It was a week later that she arrived. It was Saturday morning and Jane was resting on the bed in the back room. She had risen with Will and had eaten some breakfast, but now was lying down again. She was now eight months pregnant and heavy with the baby, which she carried. He was going to be big like his father, she kept telling Will, who would joke that he'd make the little chap pay when he was born for having put his mother through having to carry such a burden for all these months! Most afternoons now she needed to lie down and take the weight off her feet and when walking about, she had to support the baby with her hands clasped beneath her abdomen. With but two, or three weeks to go, she was radiantly happy and was equally radiant in her appearance.

Will was in the tap-room, placing the wet sacking over the casks of ale to keep them cool in the summer heat, and at first didn't hear Annie enter as she moved so quietly up the steps and into the bar, that she caught him unawares. He was aware that she must have been stood there watching him for some minutes before, guided by his instinct, he spun round and saw her. She was standing in the doorway, carrying a large rush bag in her hand and dressed all in black, like a widow in her weeds he thought. On her face was a cold, but satisfied smile and dropping the bag to the floor, she spoke to her husband.

"So you're having to find work to do are you? Where's that little slut Jane, and why's she not here to help you? I suppose you have got rid of her just when we'll need her here!" Annie grinned maliciously at Will. "Oh you will recall what I said before about coming back on my terms? Well my terms is that you get that wench back here, and make her work."

Will sprang upright from his task and glaring his hatred at this woman who dared to come into his alehouse and dictate to him about the woman who was the love of his life and the centre of his universe. "You are an evil witch Annie…. You be the worse for your stay in Mersea with that crone and I don't know what you were hoping to gain by coming back here. I hope that you have not forgotten the beating that I give you that day when you were slapping Jane around. Now I'll have you know woman, that you are not welcome here any more and so I'll show you the door and to save you from my hand again, you had best pick up that bag of yours, filled no doubt with all manner of wickedness and leave!"

Will's voice was rising louder with his anger and in the back room, Jane was woken by the noise, pulled herself to her feet in alarm. Opening the door, she walked carefully through the pot-room supporting her child as she went and into the parlour, from where Will's raised voice was coming.

It is possible that had she not appeared as she did, Annie might well have left as requested. Will's outburst had not been exactly as she had anticipated and now it seemed that after all, Will was not the push-over which she had expected and undoubtedly, his right hand was formidable as it ever had been. However, it happened as it did and when Jane walked into the room time stood still for a measureable moment.

Annie spun to confront the woman who had just entered and fell back a pace when she saw her condition. For a moment, she could do nothing but stand and stare at Jane's belly, during which time her face went from one shade of red to another of purple. Finally, she raised her flintlike stare from Jane's belly to her face and then to Will.

"So, this be how you have been enjoying yourself with the cold winter months, is it?" She hissed quietly. "And this is why the slut doesn't work any more? Of-course she mustn't do too much in case of harm to the child!" She sneered. Her face had now taken on the look of the truly insane and her eyes blazed hot with fury and deadly cold with venom, and she began to advance slowly like a beast of prey stalking its victim, towards Jane who backed towards the pot-room door.

Will leapt forward to come between the two women and thrusting Jane behind him back through the door, he confronted Annie and stopped her resolute advance by holding her back with a hand pressed to her chest. He was astounded at the strength that the woman seemed to possess as she continued to press forward and he was mesmerised by the lunacy in her eyes as her gaze pierced his own. Over Will's shoulder, Annie saw the object of her hatred pass through into the pot-room and made an even greater effort to push past Will, to get to Jane. Will grabbed both her arms and held her back, at the same time calling an urgent warning to Jane. "Jane, shut that door right now and stay there until I say as it is safe to come out, and that won't be until this madwoman's out of the house." Will hoped that his wife might not remember that there was no lock or bolt on the pot-room door and would therefore abandon hope of access.

The expression of Annie's face gave nothing away beyond the malevolent grimace, which was transfixed there. Her eyes however took a sly look as she allowed her body to relax against the bear-like grip which Will had upon her arms. That small but insistent voice within, which had from childhood directed her to carry out the many small cruelties which she had performed throughout her life, now spoke urging cunning.

Beneath half closed lids, she looked up at her husband's face. Was that fear she could see there? Gleefully, she saw that she was right. Of course, the man was afraid, not perhaps for himself like many of her unfortunate victims had been during her youth, but for the slattern Jane who seemed to care for irrespective of his whelp, which she carried. "Now" she thought, "I'll make you pay. You couldn't give me a child, but you gave this creature one just as soon as I was out of the way. Oh, what antics you both must of had ….. what cavorting ……. what delight! Well, now you'll both see the reward of that coupling!"

Annie let her face soften and her shoulders drop resignedly. The tension went from her body and she stood there with her chin on her chest and her eyes now closed. Will, fooled by the change in her, relaxed his grip and finally released Annie's arms, which dropped to her sides where they remained unmoving. Will stepped back, still keeping himself between his mad wife and the pot-room door. Annie turned to retrieve the rush bag which she had dropped at the tap-room door. She walked across the bar, around the tables, picked up her bag and after peering inside it, apparently to satisfy herself that its contents were still in place, she began to walk towards the parlour's outside door.

Will relieved at seeing that the danger had appeared to have passed began also to move towards the door. To do so he had to pass beyond one of the tables, which placed him between it and the outside door and it and its benches between him and Annie. Seizing her opportunity, Annie leapt towards the pot-room door and with her shoulder barged through it, her hand diving into her bag as she did so, re-appearing clutching a long double edged dagger.

Leaning with her back against the other side of the door, had been Jane, who was now catapulted to sprawl on the floor beside the table in the centre of the room. She landed badly, on her face and on the child, which was so soon to have been born. With a shriek of pain, she tried to turn onto her back only to be violently aided by her assailant, who with a scream of fiendish pleasure, dragged her onto her back and plunged the dagger into her abdomen. Jane was unable to do more than to gasp and twice more, Annie thrust the knife into Jane's unborn baby. The last thrust also opening her womb and the now dead, unborn baby boy fell to the floor. In this final act, Annie was dragged off her by her hair by Will, who now was uncontrollable and inconsolable with terror and grief, felled with colossal blow from his fist.

The scene in the pot-room was Dante-like. Jane lay on her back with her belly torn open with her and her baby's blood pouring onto the floor around her. Kneeling over her bent Will, the tears streaming down his face and his voice raised in a cry of anguish as he rocked her back and forth while cradling her head in his hands.

Behind and to one side sprawled the unconscious Annie. The dagger, still in her hand, which lay motionless beside her, dripped Jane's blood on the wooden floor boards.

For a brief moment the scene remained unchanged, then Will felt a faint and weak movement from Jane. Her eyes fluttered open and she looked up at Will's distraught face. Gathering her strength she spoke. "Dearest William, you did your best to keep her off… but she was too cunning for both of us… I am so sorry that the son you wanted isn't going to be, and won't even have a name." Sadly, she looked up and there eyes closed for a moment and Will tried to speak, but his voice failed him and he was unable to clear his throat. "I'll ask you for one thing Dear Will… make sure that I am buried with your son, somewhere where you can come and see us both and mourn…" Jane's voice faded and her eyes closed for the last time leaving Will crouched there, now holding her lifeless body to his chest and weeping.

He lifted her body and carrying it across the room, laid it on the mat, which covered the cellar trap-door and having gently wrapped her and the baby in it, he turned his attention to Annie who still lay semi-conscious on the floor. With awful intent, he took a tankard full of water from the butt where Jane had once washed the pots and tankards, walked over to where his wife lay and removing the knife from her hand, threw the water in her face. He then stood over her waiting for her to come round completely. After a minute or so she opened her eyes and saw William's expressionless face looking down on her. To get her bearings, she looked around the room and saw the body of Jane rolled up in the carpet on the cellar hatch.

"Ah," she said with satisfaction, "You are going to get rid of the sluts body then Will?" You had best do that hadn't you, as you will be hung for her murder! You are the only one who could have done it ain't you? I haven't been here since before the winter. No-one saw me come, I made certain of that and no-one will see me go!" Annie was almost crowing with delight. "Now I am going back to Mersea and if I am asked about this I'll deny that I was ever here. Good-bye William Horne."

She rose to her feet and for the first time saw the dagger in Will's hand. Almost in slow-motion and unable to move as though in a dream she watched it make an arc upwards from below the level of Will's waist until the tip entered her lower abdomen. From there it continued to travel upward, slicing through her belly and her stomach until it came to rest beneath her rib-cage. Here, Will twisted the dagger and withdrew it, to watch the agonies which his wife was suffering. She staggered backward but remained on her feet clutching in horror at her entrails, which now began in their slippery fluidity to escape her retaining fingers. Will watched impassively and made no attempt to, either aid nor, to inflict further injury.

THE BLACK BOY

CHAPTER TWENTY EIGHT

When James Towns arrived at *The Black Boy* that Saturday afternoon, a shocking sight confronted him.

He had gone early to see if there were any chores that needed doing or errands needed to be run before he started work that evening, helping in the bar. He had been sure the night before when he had left that there was little to be done, but it was as well to be sure. With the debt that he felt he owed Will, he continually wanted to be of assistance and to prove his sincere loyalty. He also got pleasure from assisting Jane, who he admired enormously, in no small way.

The door to the parlour was open and as he ran up the steps he had no inkling that all was not well. From outside all looked normal. The July sun shone down warmly on the walls of the alehouse and a small breeze carried with it the scents of the wild honeysuckle, bracken and gorse from the common. It was only when he reached the top of the steps, and was about to enter the room, that he was aware of the familiar smell of butchered animal and of the loud buzzing of bluebottles. At first, he thought that the body that lay on the floor with its red hair spread over its face was that of Jane. A second glance, which took in the whole grisly scene told him that the hair was too red for Jane, whose lovely auburn locks Jim had so often admired. The coarse, unkempt bright red hair could only belong to Will's wife Annie.

Will sat at the table staring unmoving down at the woman's body, which lay with its entrails spread beside it on the floor. A swarm of flies rose as Jim entered the room, momentarily disturbed from their feast, only to settle again to continue with their banquet. Annie had been eviscerated, gutted like an animal, there on that spot. The only difference between her and a beast was that the animal would have been dead when it happened, whilst Annie, although, quite definitely so now, clearly hadn't been at the time. Her hands were still wrapped around her intestines, in a final mortal attempt to push them back inside her opened belly.

Young Jim had seen plenty of horrible sights in his young life, but none so horrendous as this. He walked over to Will, averting his gaze from the sight on the floor and placed a shaking, but comforting hand on his shoulder. "Oh Will, I am so sorry… how did this terrible thing happen and who did it?" He was lost for either words to describe his horror, or, to question the act itself and he stammered over the words. James then looked around in terror, realisation dawning on him and relieved as he was that the body was not Jane's, that she was missing!

"Where be Jane, Will? Is she alright?" he cried out.

Slowly Will lifted his tormented face to gaze at Jim's concerned one. "Yes Jim, she be alright now," he said in a surprisingly calm and gently voice. "There's no one that can harm her where she is now."

"Where is she? Can I help her? Oh, Will tell me she is safe from the fiend what did this to your poor wife."

For a moment Will's face showed deep anger, and then tears of hurt sprung in his eyes. "Jim, it was me alone that did this evil, evil witch in. It don't matter now why I did it, although, I'll tell you that there were good reason for which the Good Lord will, I know, forgive me, so don't ask James Towns - and Jane waits for me in a place where no further harm can befall us; soon I'll join her there." Will took hold of Jim's arm and using it to help himself up, rose to his feet. "Now Jim would you please go to the rectory and tell the parson that a Magistrate be needed here to clear this matter up."

"But Will, if a Magistrate come, you will be arrested and be taken to Chelmsford Gaol, and they'll very likely hang you there in very short shrift! No, we must think of another way to go." Jim's brow furrowed as he thought desperately what should be done next for Will to escape punishment.

Will patted Jim's arm. "Jim, dear boy I ain't going to run away and avoid justice. No If you don't do what I ask, then I'll do it myself. I want the matter over and done with and as quick as possible."

By the evening of that day, it was all over. With the coming of the magistrate together with four Dragoons from Maldon, thought necessary to apprehend the perpetrator of this brutal murder, a crowd had gathered outside *The Black Boy*. Villagers from Horne Row and Danbury and a few from outlying districts, crowded around the steps to the alehouse's entrance, craning to get a look at the murderer and his victim.

Local people could not believe that a man like William Horne could have committed such a callous murder. It was simply not in him to do so, they argued. Of-course, they all knew that he and his wife had never got on together, but this? And where was little Jane, who had become the murderer's woman, to whom he had apparently been devoted? Where had she gone? Had she run away?

When the victim's body was carried out wrapped in canvas sheets everyone surge forward to get a look. Gratuitously, those carrying the body allowed the canvas to fall aside in order that the crowd could see for themselves the damage that had been inflicted upon the body. There were gasps of horror and of amazement from the crowd as they peered with relish at the torn belly and overflowing guts. The bearers lifted the canvas bundle into a cart and then Will was led out.

His hands and feet were manacled, even though he had showed no signs of attempting to break away, or, to escape. His captors started to push him down the steps from the parlour door, but he paused, his bulk making it hard for them to propel him forward. He spoke quietly to the Dragoons, either side of him and as they in turn stood still, he lifted his head to look down at the audience before him. His face was impassive, almost tranquil in its calm. It showed neither remorse nor sorrow and when he spoke, his voice held the same resolute, quiet determination of a man who knows precisely how bad things have become and what the future holds in store.

"All of you that live here in Horne Row, have been my friends and friends know as to the man they's friend of. Don't judge me as one that you don't know, but as a friend what you do… I won't pretend that I didn't kill the thing as I called my wife.. I did, but you should know as she were the most wicked and evil woman that ever walked this land and the world is well rid of her." He nodded to his warders and started to continue down the steps. To one side he saw his brother John standing with a look of disbelief and anguish on his face. Will stopped again, "John," he said, "*The Black Boy* is yours now, but if you don't have a mind to keep it going, I'd ask you to give it to young James Towns here…." And he pointed to Jim who stood close by, "a fair chance of doing it for you. He'll not rob you and he'll keep it orderly and clean."

John nodded, unable to reply to Will, descended the last step and allowed the Dragoons to help him onto the cart, which would carry both him to Gaol and Annie's body for burial in Chelmsford, knowing that this would be his last moments in the place he called home.

The notice advertising the forthcoming execution appeared not only in prominent places throughout Chelmsford, but also in the villages to the east of the town, where the news of the murder had spread like wildfire and had created great interest. Crowds gathered around the notices and planned their day's outing to Chelmsford and its gaol at Springfield on the great day. Wagon loads of folk from the country areas were organised and waggoners made their vehicles available at a very 'reasonable' price per passenger!

NOTICE

Is Given This Day

That on the 27th July 1784

A HANGING

Will take place at Chelmsford Gaol

At ten o'clock in the forenoon

When

The Execution of William Horne

For

The dastardly murder of his wife

To be carried out for all to witness

On the day itself, the open area before the prison was thronged with spectators, food and drink vendors and those who earned a little extra by offering for sale real and imaginary belongings of the condemned person.

"Here you are deary, this here handkerchief were what the poor lady were holding in her hand when she was so foully slain.

There!" pointing at the pig's blood which stained the piece of fabric, "there's her heart's blood what poured out all over it as she died trying to save herself!.... How much? Why only a shilling to you me dear."

As ten o'clock approached, the crowd became more excited and more restless. Amongst the throng were Will's friends. They were there not to take pleasure from his final agonies, but to pray for any release with a swift death. It was not unknown for relatives and friends to hang on the feet of the condemned man, assisting with their weight to hasten his death. Matthew Rowlings stood near the front of the crowd, with head bowed and tears in his eyes as he waited for the moment when his son-in-law, who had killed his daughter, to arrive. He would have liked to have spoken to Will before his execution, to say that he fully understood and that he didn't need to forgive him as none was due, but is wasn't to be. Anything which he might have said, would have been drowned by the cries of the mob, who saw the tumbril with Will in it exit through the open gate of the gaol onto the execution area and took up the chant "HANG HIM – HANG-HIM – MURDERER"!

A few paces away from Matthew stood Old Wilf, with his hand resting lightly on the shoulder of James Towns. Jim was beside himself with grief. He'd not only been too late arriving at *The Black Boy*, where afterwards he felt that he might have prevented the tragedy, but he had lost both the woman who he admired and who had disappeared and the man who had put so much trust in him. Now he was to witness the death of that man for a murder which Jim knew must have been justified.

The cart drew up beneath the gallows and whilst one man held the horse's head, the hangman climbed onto the cart and reaching up drew the noose across and round Will's neck. He had to stretch upwards to be able to place it over the tall man and then having done so, he roughly pulled it tight, drawing shouts of approval from the crowd.

Will gazed out into the crowd and caught the eye of first his brother John, then Matthew and then Jim. To all three, the message which he sent with his look was that all was well and that they should neither mourn, or despair at his going. At that moment at a signal from the hangman, the horse was urged forward and Will was left suspended, kicking on the end of the rope. At first, there was no movement within the crowd, but then out dashed Matthew and John, each grabbing one of Will's legs and pulling him downward for all they were worth. They were joined by Jim, John Laytham and Joshua Roote and within two or three minutes it was all over.

THE BLACK BOY

SUPPLEMENT

After Will's execution his friends took his body down and in accordance with the request that John Horne had made earlier with a large bribe that he had given at the time, they carried him away on one of John's carts.

With the body went Will's brother, John, his father-in-law Matthew Rowlings, his friends James Towns, John Laytham and Joshua Roote. Old Wilf excused himself from joining them in the cart, he preferred to drive his own and took with him several others from Horne Row including Joshua's brother Daniel and David Archer. Other carts and wagons from the area made up a form of funeral procession.

At the alehouse the carts stopped and all but those who travelled with the body, after paying their respects, made their way homeward. Carefully, Will's body was dressed in his best clothes and carried to the end cottage and there, was taken down three steps, through the cellar door to the cellar beneath the house where Will was born, Horne Row, and at the far end, beside a bricked up opening in the outside wall a shallow grave was dug.

"Are you sure about what Will said to you that day?" asked his brother John directing his questions to James Towns, "about Jane?"

"We don't know and probably never will as to where she is, but we all agree that she is dead and by the hand of that crone as was his wife by all accounts. The nearest place as we can put dear Will to be close to Jane and her child, be here in the house where he, like me was born."

"'It is better here than in the alehouse," said Matthew, "who knows what mischief excisemen and the like could get up to in there," he looked at the others, "do we know what happened with the last consignment? Was it all delivered? After Sam were killed, I understood that a lot never went out and I was here helping Jane," Jim said in a hurt voice. "He could have told me. I could have helped like I once offered."

"Don't be harsh on yourself, young Jim, he didn't want you involved in case of he were caught. He thought a lot of you, you know!" Matthew said gently.

"I always believed that Will kept the stuff here in Sam's cellar, but there isn't any sign of it." Said John Horne, looking around him. "So, I don't suppose we'll find it now."

"Let us get this done!" exclaimed John Laytham. "We've got a doorway to brick up after this and we don't want to be here all night."

Gently they had laid Will's body in the grave and his brother had said a few words over him, read from a small prayer book with silver clasps. When finished, he laid the book on Will's chest, beneath his folded hands.

"Do any of you know what happened to Will's ring?" he asked, "just like this one, it was our Pa that gave us one each when we were twenty-one. I remember Will couldn't wait to get his four years after me and thought Pa had forgot! I know that he was wearing it the last time I saw him." All around the grave shrugged and knew nothing of it. "That damned gaol has a lot to answer I reckon." He then removed a ring from his own wedding finger and with difficulty placed it on Will's little finger, which was the only one which it would fit. "There you are brother, noone's going to take it off you now!"

They then filled the grave in and over it Joshua nailed to the wall a simple wooden plaque with the inscription:

> **William Horne**
> **Died 27th July 1784**

When the Revenue Riders came a few days later, as everyone knew they would, they came accompanied by a company of Dragoons. They searched *The Black Boy* from top to bottom. In the cellar they even tried to prise the 'dresser' from the wall, but found that it had been firmly nailed in place and they couldn't shift it. They then searched the stables and dug up the floor in there again drawing a blank.

Then as Sam had predicted so long ago, they turned their attention to the cottages next door. In neither house though, could they find an entrance to a hidden cellar or room; the hatchway of Horne Row being sealed up when Sam had re-floored it to hide its edges and the outside entrance to John Laytham's cellar, bricked up, lime washed and buried!

THE BLACK BOY

PRESENT DAY

MAY 2004

There was little doubt that the climate was changing and we were expecting a very warm summer ahead of us. As it approached Sally Parmenter made the decision to extend her house with a conservatory. She was spending more and more time now out in her garden, which she adored with a passion and would stay out until the light began to fade, she would sit and enjoy dusk as it fell. All very well at this time of the year, she thought, but what if I was able to do the same thing when the days are shorter and cooler? It had been on one such summer's evening that she had thought up the idea of a conservatory.

She had found a cottage, following her divorce from an unsuccessful marriage, and had brought it in 1997 when she had returned to the village of her birth, as far back as she could remember she had always loved this cottage, so she found it fate when it came onto the market. Since then and during the closing years of that recently departed century, she had put her all into her new home and garden. By that May, she had done all that she had originally planned to do both inside and out, and now she was ready for a re-appraisal of her circumstances.

The cottage named 'Cotswold', by a previous owner, was the second of a pair of Queen Anne buildings built around the beginning of the 18th Century on a slope facing the National Trust Common in Danbury, in Essex. It and its semi-detached partner were built in a mellow red and black local brick, in a typical design of the period, with alternate red stretcher and black header bricks, which gave an attractive appearance to the building. At some time in its history, an addition had been added at its rear, probably during the nineteenth century and prior to that an upstairs window in each cottage had been bricked up to avoid the 'window tax' which had been applied by the government in the eighteenth century, to bring in additional revenue.

Both cottages had been renovated by the same builder at much the same time as the one next door, aptly named 'Walnut Tree Cottage', with its magnificent Walnut Tree towering over it in the back garden, was now rented from its owner, who had bought it as an investment, when the building work was completed, by a young couple, Julian and Beck Newton-Smith. Sally, whilst friendly with her neighbours, they often held parties and barbecues where Sally was invited, having very little in common with their 'yuppy' friends, she would often make her excuses and leave for the solitude of 'Cotswold' and sit out on her terrace at the side of the property enjoying the peace of her own little place, albeit, slightly interrupted by the merriment and shrieks from the party-goers next door.

One evening following one of these such events, whilst Sally sat on her patio listening to the noise from next door interrupting her peace and quiet, she started to consider the thought of a conservatory, she began to ponder on how she could still enjoy the 'outside' but blot out the existence of her neighbours. "Now, if this terrace was covered by a conservatory and I was sitting in it, a great deal of the racket from next door would be dead-ened! Not only that but I'd still be sitting in comparative warmth and comfort on what after all is a cool evening." Immediately her mind began to wander to the design possibilities for such an enterprise.

Sally was a talented designer and made a successful, if irregular income from interior design. She also earned from her talents as an actress, with work on film-set as an extra and various bit-parts. The two incomes kept the wolf from the door and suited her lifestyle because of the freedom it gave her. Those who visited her house were constantly full of admiration of her abilities in the way she had decorated, furnished and curtained the place. Now she could extend that talent to an extension of the house.

The permission which Sally sought for the conservatory was granted during the second week in July and with the weather still warm and comparatively dry, she pressed the company to start as soon as possible by digging the footings for the new building and on the 27th of that month, the digger arrived to commence the work.

There were three trenches required for the footings, two dug at ninety degrees to the house wall and the third joining these two to take the outside wall. Firstly, the existing paved area had to be lifted and the slabs laid to one side. They would eventually be re-laid to surround the new structure with the paved walkway. Then the machine began to excavate the first of the footings trenches, starting close to the wall near the front of the cottage. Almost immediately, a foot below the surface of the ground, it's bucket struck brickwork which appeared to run in the precise line of the trench to be excavated, ninety degrees to the house. Four feet from the cottage it ceased and the bucket went down without obstruction to its correct depth. From this point, footings could be dug to it as originally intended.

The digger driver called for the foreman to come over "Here Bill, I think you should see this, looks like we already got a footing coming out from the house, 9" brickwork and solid too, what do you reckon?"

Sally, who had been in the kitchen making coffee for the workmen, now appeared with a tray on which were mugs of coffee and a plate of biscuits. "Here you are boys, time for a coffee break! Where would you like to have your coffee?"

Dave stopped his digger and climbed down to join Bill who was sitting on the low wall which surrounded the paved area and which itself soon to be demolished. "Here would do nicely!" he said imitating the slogan of a certain credit card company. Sally served them their coffee and went over to look into the first footings. She was still peering into it when Bill, his coffee in hand, came over to join her.

"We found that bit of brickwork already there and thought it best to leave it there." He observed. "From the point of view of the footings required for the conservatory, it probably couldn't be better than what we would have put in anyway. It certainly seems to be good and solid, but what it was I don't know."

Sally had stepped down onto the surface of the brickwork and was scratching away at the earth, which was untouched to the side of the bricks. "Bill, do me a favour and fetch me a trowel, or a spade would you please."

"You won't find anymore brickwork to the side there, we have already looked."

"That's not what I'm looking for," Sally replied," at my grandparent's house, there was a cellar with an outside door and the steps down to it had a brick surround. Forget the trowel, if you get Dave to carefully dig out to the side of the end of this brick wall, we might find another wall going off at right-angles to it; that would be the start of the steps. If that's the case then I would expect there to be a doorway right here..." she pointed to the cottage wall below ground and beside the brick wall. "In fact I shall be disappointed if we don't."

Bill shrugged his shoulders and walked over to where Dave still sipped his coffee. "Come on lad, get back on that digger of yours and do as the lady asks, or we'll still be here tomorrow digging these footings."

Dave put down his mug, climbed back on that digger and tracked back to where Sally stood and Bill now directed him. Carefully, he drew his bucket along the side of the exposed brickwork down to its depth from the surface. Almost immediately he hit resistance. He cleared the shallow trench to reveal, as Sally expected, another wall at ninety degrees to the first and by extending his excavation to the side, he exposed more of the same. After 3' he met the third wall, which now returned to the cottage flank wall, forming a rectangular box and further excavation in its centre revealed a flight of three stone steps which terminated at the house wall.

"You were right young lady," said Bill in a somewhat surprised but admiring voice, "whoever would have thought it." He looked at the wall of the house, now exposed. "There isn't a door though," he added almost triumphantly, "so if ever there was a cellar there, it isn't here today!."

"Have you got a yard-broom?" Sally asked.

"Yes, of course we have," said Dave, walking over to where their tools lay heaped beyond the footings area and extracting a bass-broom and handing it to Sally. "Here you are. What are you going to do with this?"

"This," she said taking the broom began vigorously to scrub the surface of the house wall now exposed. The earth which still clung to the bricks fell away and finally, Sally stood back. "There you are!" she declared in triumph. "There was an entrance, you can see the original arch of header bricks over what was the doorway, and you can see that it has been bricked up. Not crudely as one might have expected, but carefully, with each course tied in at the edges. Now why would they have done that I wonder?"

"What do I do now?" asked Dave, "shall I fill it in again?"

"No, leave it please," Sally replied vehemently. "It won't hinder you with the rest of your work and if at a later date I decide to investigate the existence of the cellar, then I shall be able to do so from the inside of the conservatory. All I ask is that you clear away all of the extra soil and leave the steps exposed and clean!"

"Okay, you're the customer, come on Dave lets get on and finish the rest of the digging." Bill did not like interruptions to his carefully prepared plan of work. "And let's hope that we don't find nothing else before we've finished!

THE BLACK BOY

COTSWOLD'S CELLAR

By September, the conservatory was completed.

Sally, whose design for the building evolved around the cellar's entry and exit from the three points, one at each end and one from the house itself and who certainly didn't want to change it, pointed out that a simple hatch over the steps would act exactly the same way as the floor would have done - she had employed a builder to construct a suitable hatch and frame.

When it was finished she had invited her friends around to share a 'conservatory opening' party with her. She also invited her yuppy neighbours. They came of course with crate of champagne.!

Everyone was full of admiration for not only the building, but for the way in which Sally had decorated and furnished it. All of her friends, without exception, were interested in the cellar steps and had to inspect them with the hatch raised. Some lost interest when they saw that there was no cellar door, considering that the effort needed to break through and to discover whether, or, not anything lay beyond the wall, to be hardly worth the effort. After all it was likely to be pretty uninteresting, dusty, dirty, probably damp as well and whoever had sealed it up had thought it to be of little practical use and if that had been then, whenever 'then' might have been, its condition now had to be infinitely worse.

The couple next door showed a smattering of interest, passing comment "how intriguing!" cried Julien, "maybe there's a cellar under ours aswell Becky," then to the others around him, he added "wouldn't that be exciting? But if there is, I don't know how you'd get to it. Mind you, it could have an outside access like this one. We'll have to ask our Landlord – now where's that champers, we've got to toast the lovely lady who party this is!"

One, or two of Sally's close friends showed more interest and offered their assistance, if and when she wanted to break through and find out more.

"I've had a close look at the wall, Sal," said her good friend Tom Warner, taking her aside at one point in the evening. "Whoever filled in that doorway, had every intention of it remaining both closed and hidden. What you brushed off with that broom, and thought was soil, when the contractor first exposed the stairs, was, I think a lime-wash, which had been applied at the time and would then have very effectively hidden the new brickwork. By now it had gone a grey-brown, the colour of the earth against it, hence your assumption. The fact that all courses, either side have been so neatly tied in, makes me believe that whoever did it had something illegal to hide." He saw the look on Sally's face and added hurriedly, "I don't mean necessarily something gruesome, I mean possibly contraband of some type. Let me know when we're going to break in! I'm your man! In the meantime, don't lose sleep over conjecture. What's there has been there for the past, what, two, maybe three hundred years and it isn't going to reveal itself just now is it!" He put a friendly and comforting arm about Sally's shoulders. "Now come on, let's enjoy your party, with or without those frightful people from next door!" He added in a low voice whispered directly into her ear and she laughed.

They moved back to join others who were grouped around a close friend of Sally's, Gordon Braithwaite. Gordon was an amateur historian whose chief interest was the history of Danbury and its surroundings. He had previously completed a small book which traced the history of the village's name, which was derived from it's Danish association with a hill fort settlement, which had probably existed long before the coming Vikings. He had shown its importance as a centre for trade at that time, with its strategic position on the highest point in Essex.

Tonight, he was expounding on the eighteenth century, its buildings, its laws and its taxes. "The window tax for example, was bought in by a government desperate to raise the revenue, which it was losing at the time to "Free Trade", or in other words to smuggling."

"That was why they blocked in the windows to save the tax, wasn't it Gordon?" Someone asked.

"Yes, and you'll notice that these two cottages, each have a bricked in window." Gordon paused as several in his audience, shrugged and shook their heads. "You haven't noticed them, have you?"

"Noticed what?" "The bricked up windows, very cleverly, when these two cottages were renovated, the two blank openings were painted to look like the sash windows of the adjacent window opening. So, cleverly done are they that you need to take a second look to be certain of what you are seeing."

One or two people began to make their way to the door to have a look at the front of the buildings for themselves.

"You'll have to wait until daylight, you won't be able to see them in the dark, try tomorrow….. or, of course, you can take my word for it for now!" He laughed as these people turned and re-entered the conservatory.

Linda, Tom's wife now asked, "I know you of old, Gordon, you haven't started on about the blocked-up windows and window taxes for no purpose, you're leading up to something, aren't you?"

"Yes, as a matter of fact I am. I recently read a definitive description of this tax and it said quote 'the tax was applied to any window or window-like opening.'" He paused and Tom, who now stood with Sally towards the rear of Gordon's audience, said. "I bet I know what the cunning devil's driving at!"

Gordon looked across at his friend, "you've guessed then Tom?"

"Yes, you're going to tell us that the cellar door, which might well have constituted a 'window-like' opening, was blocked in to save taxes, aren't you?"

"Somewhat stealing my thunder Tom, but yes, just that."

Several of the listeners clapped their approval and Julian, having in his opinion taken a back seat long enough, loudly proclaimed that he was coming around bearing yet more 'champers' to fill any empty glass beyond his own.

"I don't agree with you Gordon." Tom said after a few minutes.

"Oh! Why's that?"

"On three counts, really. One, that the doorway could never have constituted as window-like opening. It was in fact below ground, or most of it was anyway. Two, why go to the trouble of bricking it in so carefully when all the other buildings make no effort to disguise the fact that they have been bricked in? And three, why even go to greater trouble to lime-wash the wall to hide it even further?"

Gordon weighed over Tom's reply. "Starting with your last fact, I didn't know about the lime-wash. When did you discover that?"

"Sally had told me that the outline of the doorway wasn't apparent until she scrubbed at the wall with a yard-broom. I realised then that there must have be something to either cause the soil to stick to the wall, or, something very much like soil had been applied to it. I had a look a few days later at the dust, which she had brushed off and realised what it probably was. I've not had it analysed, or anything but I'm willing to bet that's what it is."

"So it would seem that efforts were made to hide the entrance's existence and I suppose you are right, an opening like that could hardly have been considered a window, although, at a time when there were few who would have been able to oppose a ruling which said that it was a window and that a tax should be paid on it, there might have been little argument."

Gordon's job was with a local firm of architects. His interest lay though in history and things historic, and so in the early days he had forever been at loggerheads with partners in the practice whose modernistic ideas were very much against his own ideals. He had realized quite early on that architecture was not something of the past, to be studied in ancient churches and medieval buildings, it was ongoing and although he tried hard to be as forward looking as his subject, he found that it had left him behind. Luckily, the firm he worked for also did large amounts of work for institutions such as English Heritage, the Church and local authorities, who sought advice with regard to listed buildings. Gordon Braithwaite had now become quite well known for his expertise in the renovation of historic buildings in the manner of their original architect, so his place with the company, whilst perhaps isolated from the up and coming youngsters around him, was assured.

The six friends sat discussing the evening.

"Sally darling, that was a lovely evening and everyone thoroughly admired your lovely conservatory. As an architect, I'm not too sure whether is comes under the category of ancient or modern. It has shades of both, which I think meets all tastes, certainly it does mine!" Gordon smiled across to his hostess.

"Thank you Gordon, that's all I want to hear, that everybody liked it and I hope they also enjoyed themselves." Sally could now relax from her duties. "Anyone want another refill, just help yourselves, I don't know if our friends from next door left any of that champagne, did they?"

"No, I think they went when that had gone. God, what a pair of bores!" Linda said quite loudly.

"Sh! Lin! They can hear you next door you know!" Sally hissed at her friend.

"Nonsense, if the wall between here and next door is anything like the one there," Tom pointed at the wall behind him beyond which was the conservatory, "you wouldn't be able to hear a thing!"

"That's just it Tom, it's not. Behind that alcove beside the fireplace the wall is simply lath and plaster on beams. I know because when they've had parties next door, I've been able to hear every sound, every word that's uttered clearly through it." Sally spoke quietly, "so please be careful what you say, I don't want to fall out with them, they really aren't bad neighbours."

"As long as they stay next door!" said Tom with a scathing grin.

"So, what's the general conclusion over there being, or there not being a cellar beneath our feet here?" asked Steve. "I think we ought to have some sort of vote on it, perhaps we could take bets?"

"You would say that" said Jenny.

"Say what?"

"About taking bets. I think you'd gamble on almost anything, wouldn't you Steve?"

"Oh, come on Jen, it's only a bit of fun and yes I like a flutter now and again."

"And again and again…"

"Now that's enough you two, there'll be no squabbling in my house." Sally parted the two of them. "You know Jenny that Steve winds you up, don't you? And you Steve know that she does the same to you. Why, I'd like to know!"

"I don't know, it's something we do to each other at this time of an evening, after a few drinks, silly really, but a sort of ritual!" Steve looked gently at Jenny, smiled and said "Sorry Jen!" She got up went across the room to sit on the arm of his chair, put her arms around his neck and kissed him.

"Right, let's get back to casting the vote." Steve peered out from beneath Jenny's embrace and she with an exasperated expulsion of breath, sat back to allow him to speak.

"So we believe that the cellar still exists? Raise your right hands." Three people's hands rose. Tom, Linda's and Gordon's. "And who believes it does not?" This time only two hands were raised, Steve's and Jenny's.

"What's this Sally? Abstaining, or, can you not yet make up your mind?" Steve asked from across the room.

"I think it's because I don't yet want to make up my mind before I know why the entrance might have been blocked up. I need to get a bit of research done on these cottages before either guessing of the existence of a cellar or what it might have been used for." Sally got up and began to collect up the cups and glasses around the room, Linda got up to help her.

In the kitchen, she said "Sal, you've got two chaps here who are perfectly placed to help you with your research, Tom and Gordon, so call on them for everything they can do." Quietly aside she said "I don't think old Steve's much use here, his interests lie elsewhere."

THE BLACK BOY

RESEARCH

The first person Sally went to see was her father Richard. Dick Parmenter had lived most of his life in the district and had married a local girl, Susan. Between them they knew most of what had gone on in the village, past and present, both fact and rumour, so for Sally, it was an ideal place to start.

She drove down the gravel road known as Horne Row, past the row of Tile Kiln cottages on the site of the old brick and tile works, which had been there two hundred years before and then beyond in the direction of the nature reserve which covered the area which had been clay-pits for the brick-works. At the end of the road was her parent's house.

Sally found her father pottering in his vegetable garden, which was his pride and joy. It had once been much larger, but as he had grown older, it had started to become too much for him and now it was but a quarter of it's original size. The remainder of it had been grassed over and was now, except where the new greenhouse stood, a well kept lawn. The garden was extensive with its borders, lawns, shrubberies and paved areas. It also boasted a large pond in which Dick nurtured both gold fish and koi-carp, some of which had grown to a substantial size. The herons, against which Dick waged a constant war, were kept at bay by an intricate network of lines across the pond, imitation herons and trip wires. As a last resort, although the birds were by now protected by law, Dick would resort to shooting the odd persistent one. Very early on, he had discovered that the imitation birds, which, according to their sales promotion literature, would, by their very presence deter any living bird from landing to fish the same water, in fact had the opposite effect and it hadn't been unusual for Dick to find one, happily sharing the same piece of pond!

Dick's domain in the garden were the vegetables, the greenhouse and the pond. His wife Sue looked after everything else, including the weekly visit by the gardener, who cut lawns and hedges and trimmed edges. Both, in there late sixties, they were content with this arrangement as all the heaviest work was now carried out by the gardener and at last they had time to enjoy the garden which they had created over the years.

Just such a moment to sit and enjoy the garden came when Sally arrived that day. She found Dick weeding leeks, and when she appeared at the end of the row, he looked up and smiled with delight. "Sally, my dear, lovely to see you. Just in time for a coffee I guess. Does you mother know you are here?"

"Hello Daddy, yes I saw her on the way down here and believe it or not she's put the kettle on!"

They kissed one another and Dick put down his hoe and walked up the garden with his daughter. "Where have you been for the last few days? We've not seen you. You're only just up the road, but then I expect you've got lots to keep you busy. Anyway, you're here now, so come and sit down and tell me all your news!"

They walked onto the terrace and sat down at the table there. Sally's mother Sue came out from the house with a tray upon which were a coffee pot, three mugs, milk and sugar.

"Darling, it's lovely to see you. I'm glad you persuaded your father to come and sit down, I never can, he's always got just one more thing to do! Now shall I pour you a coffee?" Sue sat happily down and handed the mugs around. "Now tell us your news. How's that conservatory of yours? We've seen it of course in its various stages but I understand that it's now finished. What did you do with that stairway your builder discovered? Have you filled it in yet?"

"If you were to draw a breath Mummy, I might have a chance to answer your questions!" laughed Sally. "Yes, the conservatory's finished and I hope you'll come up this weekend and see it in all its glory."

"What about the steps? As Mummy said?" Her father asked.

"I haven't decided what to do about them yet Daddy and before I do, I want to know what you know about the area."

"What do you want to know?"

"Well anything really. Who owned the cottages when you were a boy, and who lived there? How old they are? And did anyone know if they had cellars or not?"

"There's not a lot I can tell you about who lived there. The people in the other end I know rented it for years, their name if I recall was Lodge and at least two generations lived there up to the time it became vacant and was renovated. They were certainly there when I was in my teens, but before that I can't be sure. With your house, there was a whole string of different tenants none of whom stayed long. You have to remember that by the end of the war, people were no longer satisfied with a house without plumbing or sanitation of any sort, and your cottage was just that. It had one cold water tap and a bucket and chuck it out the back. Dick stopped, took a sip of his coffee and went on.

"I remember, going there once with a boy from school who lived there, can't remember his name, and being appalled at the conditions in which they were forced to live. That would have been around the end of the war, 1945 '46." He thought for a few minutes. "Honestly Sal, I can't really be more help than that."

"How old do you think they are?"

"That's easier, I don't think there's any doubt that they were built at the turn of the century, the Eighteenth Century that is, 1700, in probably Queen Anne's reign, or the first of the Georges. The style screams that period to me and I remember when they were renovated, thinking how similar their appearance was to your Granny and Grandpa's house, which is definitely 1703. But beyond that I can't really help you."

"Never mind Daddy, I'll go into Chelmsford library and see if I can find anything out there. I'd like to say that I'd look it up on the internet, but I doubt if anything in the area is recorded."

"Just a minute darling, there is something in the area that might get a mention somewhere, although, I've no idea how this internet of yours works." Sue interrupted, and looking across the table at her husband she said, "Dick, you remember telling me about that London Solicitor who bought Blackmore House and modernised it so badly, I remember that you were furious at the time.

"Blackmore House?" Sally shot across the table. "What and where is that?"

"Oh, didn't you know? The house beyond your cottage and your neighbour." Dick answered, "all I know was up to the nineteen-thirties it was public house called '*The Black Boy*', I thought everyone knew that."

"But, that's a modern looking building, I never would have thought of it as being old." Sally was astonished.

"That's because the wretched person who renovated it either knew nothing of the job he was doing, which is probable, or was ripped off by an unscrupulous builder which is even more probable. He removed the lovely old peg tiles from the roof and replaced them with modern concrete ones. He covered the wonderful black and red brick of the eighteenth century with a non-descript modern render and he filled in the cellar there with all the builder's rubbish, to save on skip hire before he concreted it over." Dick frowned at the half-drunk coffee in front of him. "That's what I got so angry about and still do. How dare these nouveau reiche, philistines come into the countryside and ruin a lovely old building like that, just to make a few extra pounds, or because they want the building to look like its modern counterpart in Harlow, or Basildon. It's happening everywhere, that little farm down on the common similar date, similar construction, now you wouldn't know the difference between it and one of your new-town houses." Dick seemed to have a smell under his nose, and both Sally and her mother commented on such, and laughed. "Dick dear, calm down! Don't get on your high-horse again, it's past history now," Sue tried to quieten her husband, fearing that such an upset might not help the angina from which he suffered.

"Yes Daddy, calm down," his daughter seconded her mother. But after a few minutes to allow that to happen, she said excitedly, "so Blackmore House was a pub once and was of similar age to the two cottages. It also, most interestingly had a cellar!"

"I never saw it, but I talked to the builders who were doing the work at the time and they were quite open about the fact that they filled in the cellar and later when I spoke to the Solicitor, a certain Ray Watkins, he in fact confirmed it almost as though it had been his idea. I'm quite certain it wasn't, but he was going along with the builder in order to not look foolish in a world in which he was out of his depth!"

"Did he know that the house had been a pub Daddy?" Sally asked. "And if the old pub had a cellar, do you think that the two cottages had one too?"

"To answer your first question, no, I don't think he did and to answer the second, who knows if they had cellars beneath them, all I know is that *The Black Boy* did, and one assumed that as they were constructed at roughly the same time, in the early days of the Eighteenth century and looking at the way in which they perch above the ground the way they do, yes, I suspect that they all did. Long filled in by now though I bet." Dick let his gaze focus on his daughter who was becoming more and more excited on the other side of the table.

"Now young lady, perhaps you'd tell me why this apparently sudden interest. You know that the steps must have once led down to a cellar, but you seem loathed to break through and investigate. What has caused this hesitation?"

Sally met her father's gaze and replied. "Daddy I think perhaps I'm scared of what I might find. Tom is quite convinced that the existence of the cellar was hidden in such a way as to make it unknown to all and although, he reassures me that it is unlikely to be for any gruesome reason, more likely an illegal one, I'm nervous about breaking in and discovering whatever might be there. That's the truth of the matter!"

"Why does Tom believe that the cellar was hidden?"

"Its all something to do with what the wall was painted with lime to hide up the bricked doorway, also the careful way in which it was done. He thinks that someone had something to hide."

"How exciting," said Sue, "I love a mystery and to have one on our doorstep and in the family too!"

"Steady on darling, I'm not sure that Sally's quite ready for such excitement." Dick frowned at his wife. "You heard what she said, she's nervous about the thing. Now Sal, have you tried the County Library? You might find something there, in the public records office, which mentions the pub, or, alehouse as it might well have been know at the time. You might find that there is some sort of association between it and the cottages.

"OK Daddy, that has to be my next port of call, I'll give it a try tomorrow."

"Right darling, having got the subject of your cellar out of the way, now tell us your news." Sue, who in the main, had listened quietly while her husband and her daughter had discussed the cellar, now wanted to get up to date with family news.

The following day, Sally drove to Chelmsford, parked in the car park behind the records office and entered the reference library. A very helpful assistant listened to her request and then led her to files which were exclusively devoted to local history in the area that she had described.

Of course, it was all done now with post codes, although, when Sally questioned why an enquiry into the Eighteenth century, long before post codes were invented, should have any relevance now, the helpful assistant who was in his early twenties, pointed out that nothing moved nowadays, unless it was directed by a post code. Our lives, our very existence revolved around the use of post codes and whilst old maps, which Sally had suggested might be helpful, they could only be so if associated with the correct code.

Eventually Sally succumbed to his youthful belief that new was good and that methods of the past were so far outdated by computers as to be almost useless, and she left it to his abilities and those of his computer to find what she wanted.

After quite a short while, a map of the area came up on the screen. It was followed by others of varying dates, which revealed several things of interest. Apparently, the area in which her cottage stood, might have once been a small hamlet known as '*Horne Row*'. The gravel road which she knew by this name was simply part of the hamlet. The building now known as '*Blackmore House*' was shown to exist in the early 1800's, but there was no description of what the building was. So, was her father right?

One further thing of interest to Sally was that the cottage next to hers had, until comparatively recent times, been called '*Horne Row*'. Presumably it hadn't taken on its current title until the Walnut Tree had grown to a substantial size and judging its age now to be no more than one hundred years, it meant that until the nineteen twenties, or even the thirties the house would have been called *Horne Row*'. Why? Sally pondered.

"What else can you tell from your records? I know that you can't go any further back with your maps of the area, you've already tried that, but what about the history of the place?" Nothing they had found so far went far enough back. It was the period before 1800 that Sally was particularly intrigued with.

"We can look, but I think one route which you might want to take would be the local newspaper."

Sally looked sharply at the young man to see if he was joking. His serious face told her he wasn't. "How can the paper have records as far back as I'm looking?"

"It won't have everything that far back, but remember it was in existence during the whole of the nineteenth century and part of the previous one, having been established in seventeen something or other, the exact date of it's inception, they'll be only too proud to tell you! If there was anything newsworthy which happened in your area at that time, the paper may well have printed it."

"OK, thanks, you've been a great help. Before I go, is there anywhere else that you would recommend that I try?"

"Depends on how much time you're prepared to spend rummaging. But one other place that springs to mind is the Oaklands Museum at the top of Moulsham Street. They often have bits of historical information tucked away, generally of little interest to most, but could be great interest to some – like you!" The young man walked with Sally to the door, "my name's Gary by the way, I'll keep delving to see what I can come up with, but try the papers and the museum. Give me your phone number in case I come up with anything."

Sally thanked him, scribbled her number onto a page torn from the notebook she carried and went out to her car. She drove immediately to the Museum as it was en route for the newspaper's new offices on an Industrial area outside of town. Up the drive she found the car park and went into the main entrance. At the entrance desk she explained to a slightly disinterested female attendant, what she sought.

"Maps is it?" the woman asked, studying the nails which she had just been filing. "What area did you say?"

"Danbury, or more precisely, Danbury Common."

"Don't know that we've got much about that area except as part of the whole of Essex.... Wait a bit though there was quite a bit going on up there in Napoleon's time wasn't there? We've almost certainly got some maps of them."

Sally remembered what Gary had said about the amount of time she was prepared to spend in research through the museum and wondered if this wasn't what he had meant! "Thank you, possibly they will help, now where do I go?"

The woman directed her up the stairs to the correct department, which she found with surprising ease, when she compared the way she had found it to the lengthy directions that she had been given. "Cartography of Essex" in bold letters on the board on the door, told her that this was her goal and she entered. The room was deserted. Around the walls were maps of all sizes and ages depicting Essex and parts of that county. There were also maps of the whole of the British Isles and of East Anglia. Beneath the wall maps were cabinets of narrow drawers within which Sally discovered by taking a surreptitious glance in one of them, were smaller maps of definitive areas. This was what she sought.

She began going around the room, inspecting the contents labels of each drawer and had just arrived at one which read Danbury 1881, when the door, through which she had come, opened further to admit a very large rotund gentleman, with a shining bald head and a jolly smiling face. "Well, well, well what have we got here? Doing the job for me I see. Before you find yourself searching in entirely the wrong place, young lady, I suggest that we sit down over here at my desk and you tell me precisely what you're looking for! I might even be able to rustle up some tea, how about that?"

Slightly embarrassed Sally sat down; "I'd love and cup of tea and I'm sorry you caught me riffling through your drawers, I think I was getting close to what I sought though."

"Ah, that's as maybe." He said round the mouthpiece of the telephone he had lifted. He now spoke into it, "two teas please Mary, properly presented if you don't mind with sugar in a bowl etc. etc. I'm entertaining today!" Replacing the receiver, he turned to Sally and asked, "now then young lady, what do you seek? If it's here and I have it in my power to do so, we will find it."

Sally liked this man immediately and explained to him her quest. "What I need to know is; do you have maps of the Danbury Common area of Danbury, which are dated between the start of the eighteenth century, Queen Anne's reign to the end of the next century, the end of Victoria's reign.? I need to know about a hamlet called Horne Row, a pub called *The Black Boy* and a Tile Works within the same area?" She paused as the door opened and Mary, who in her smart dark suit could be nothing other than a secretary, came in with a tray of tea, which she set down on the desk.

"Thank you Mary, as always my Florence Nightingale, giving comfort and sustenance whenever I require it." He smiled at her.

"Mr Shepherd, one day you'll perhaps tell your guests, who you so carefully allow to overhear your preposterous statement with regard to the tea I make you, that I've never served your tea in other manner than correctly!" She looked sternly at him and then turned her face away from her boss, to wink at Sally as she went to the end of the room and out of the door.

"Don't mind my secretary young lady," he said, "I love to tease her, but I wouldn't swap her for all the tea in China….. Just one decent cup of it perhaps…!" He ended loudly so Mary could hear.

"She seems to put up with a lot, but I suspect that gives as good as she gets, Mr Shepherd" Sally suggested, laughingly.

"You're right, she does. Now you have the advantage on me, you know my name, but I don't know yours."

"Sally Parmenter, and I only know yours because Mary said it."

"Miss Parmenter is it?"

"It is but please call me Sally."

"Right that's the introductions over, I might have suggested that you used my Christian name too, but my parents had no sense of the damage they were doing when they had me christened and named me Basil!" He looked at Sally who didn't immediately see the problem. "Don't you see my dear, the association of the Shepherd and Ba----sil" he made a sound like a sheep. "During my childhood I was dogged with it, to coin a phrase, so now I avoid it as much as possible."

Sally smiled, "sorry, I'm a bit slow off of the mark. Yes, I see the problem it might have been, but I like Basil, I as bought up with Basil Brush!"

"Well I'll leave it to your judgement and for you to use whatever name you find appropriate. Now let's start looking for some evidence of what you seek!"

Mr Shepherd moved over to a set of drawers and looking quickly down the labels of the contents, he stopped at one marked St Clere's and Heron's Parish, 1540 and drew it open.

"That's a bit early for what I'm looking for, and where is this parish?" Sally looked over his arm as he spread the map on the cabinet top.

"It shows the beating of the bounds, or boundaries of these two parishes which cover the whole of Danbury area in that year. It's the earliest record that we have so it's a good place to start. Now you see here the various tracks and roads that existed then. Do you recognise any of them by their position?"

"Not really, although that area!" Sally pointed to the open central area which had no dwellings in it at all, "looks like the common and these cottages could almost be where my parents live now. But it doesn't exist now, not too surprising really over five hundred years!"

"Of course you're right, but we've established I think that we're in the right location. Now let's try something more up to date, this map of 1761. It doesn't give as much written detail as the last one we looked at, but it does at least show that there were houses in the area at the time and it seems to shoe some sort of business existing at the junction of these roads here. See Sally, beside the group of buildings, some of which look like a row of cottages, faintly is the WORKS. Now it could mean anything, but what do you think? Is that where your Tile Works could have been?"

"Oh yes," Sally cried excitedly, "that track there, which looks quite large on this map, certainly as large as the road above it, which would be the Woodhill Road now, is the top of Horne Row. Where the works are shown, is a row of cottages called Tile Kiln Cottages. It all fits. Now if we follow that along here," she drew her finger along the road towards where she knew her own house to be and was delighted to find drawings of two distinct buildings with a third one of a longer nature beyond. This third building looked as though it was divided into a number of separate cottages and could well have been farm-workers housing.

"Those two, Mr Shepherd, and incidentally, since Mary calls you that, I suspect it is what you prefer to be called, are in fact three." She pointed to two of the houses. "The first, the larger one was, I understand from my father, a pub until the early nineteen hundreds, unconfirmed by the library map and named, again according to my father, '*The Black Boy*'. The other building is in fact two cottages, the second of which is mine and strangely the first of which on the library's map shows it to have been called '*Horne Row*!' Why, I cannot imagine."

"Well, at least now we have a date to go on. They existed in 1761 and since they're still there now, there's little point in delving forward from that date. What we've got to find out however, is, or was this the alehouse." He stabbed is finger on the building in question, "And more importantly, what was it called?" He turned to Sally with an aside, "incidentally very shrewd of you Sally!"

"What is?"

"Oh sorry, my name. Mary had the same enigma thrown at her when she started with me and very quickly solved it. You're quite right!" Sally smiled, "good, so where can we go from here Mr Shepherd?" "You seem to have come a long way in your investigation, before you came here to see my maps. I just said that there was little point in delving forward from that date, but it is possible that a later map might reveal what we seek. It also might confirm that the area was in fact a hamlet known as Horne Row and if so, for how long it existed as such." He patted Sally's shoulder, "you have given me a project Sally, and I shall be delighted to research it, but you can now leave me to it. Come back in a week's time and I'll let you know what progress I have made."

Sally left the museum and went straight to the newspaper's offices of the Essex Chronicle. There she explained her enquiry and after determining the actual dates which she wanted to research, she was given a desk to sit at and a computer which brought up every incident which the paper had reported on during the period of 1700 to 1900. The earlier part of the period gave little of interest; local society weddings, gatherings, functions and the like; the law-court activity mentioning disputes over property and marriage agreements; criminal proceedings against livestock thieves, property thieves, arsonists and smugglers, but nothing which could be associated with Horne Row or Danbury.

Sally was beginning to lose hope that she would find something relevant when her last group of Chronicle Editions from the last part of the eighteenth century, a name sprang out of the page, William Horne.

"On 27th July 1784, the murderer William Horne was hung at Springfield Gaol, for the murder of his wife Annie Horne, who he so brutally did to death at the Alehouse in the hamlet of Horne Row in the county of Essex. This newspaper witnessed the execution and noted that despite angry protests from the crowd there gathered, a number in the throng gladly assisted in the swift dispatch of the condemned man."

Sally read it over and over again. If only the paper had mentioned the name of the Alehouse, but surely there could not have been many in such a small community? And what did it mean about gladly assisting his swift dispatch? Avidly she skipped through the next half of the century of editions which took her over three hours, before she realised that there was nothing more of interest to be found. She thanked the staff at the paper and taking a copy of the August 1784 edition, with its relevant report, she returned home to her cottage, Cotswold.

THE BLACK BOY

THE BREAKTHROUGH

During the week that followed her visits to The Essex Chronicle, the Museum and the Library, Sally waited impatiently for news from one of them. The Newspaper had not been asked for further information and although there had been some interest shown both before and after her study of their records, she expected nothing from that quarter, but after the enthusiasm shown by both Gary at the Library and Mr Shepherd at the Museum, she was disappointed to hear nothing from either of them.

On the Friday, the telephone rang. It was Gary. "Sally Parmenter?" the caller asked, "It's Gary from the Library."

"Gary, I'm delighted to hear from you, I hope you've got something to tell me." Sally could hardly contain her excitement, although she had a feeling that he might well have made this call for social reasons rather than informative ones!

"Yes, I have. I was rummaging through some more old papers of the area, which for some reason or other do not appear to have been transcribed onto our computers yet and I found one which clearly shows the area that you and I were talking about as being a separate community called Horne Row! So, that confirms what we found."

"Oh, Gary that's wonderful, just what I hoped to find!" Sally answered.

"Wait a minute, I have not finished," laughed Gary, "on this map it shows near to the top end, a building beside which is the word 'Alehouse'. Now whether it is the right building or not for your "Black Boy" I don't know, but if you come in and look at it, you can soon tell me."

"You have just made my day, no, my week, Gary. Now listen, I can't get in to town today, but I'll come in on Monday, unless of course you work tomorrow?"

"Wishful thinking Sally! Sorry got the weekend planned, but I'll looked forward to seeing you on Monday."

"Hang on a minute, how about faxing the map through to me, or emailing it, if that's easier?" Sally was anxious to see the map as soon as possible.

"OK, give me your address and I'll email it to you right now."

Sally gave it to him and he rang off. She opened up her computer to await its arrival. After five minutes it told her that the mail had been received and she looked at the incoming documents. Attached to Gary's message was a map just as he had described it, and it clearly showed that the building to the west of the cottages was in fact an Alehouse. It also showed the first cottage named Horne Row, something that Gary hadn't mentioned. Presumably, Sally's thought, he had mistaken the house name for an overprint of the hamlet's name, which appeared lower down on the map. She would have to ask him when next they spoke.

She didn't mention it in her reply, which she sent to Gary thanking him again for the information and making a promise that she would be in touch again next week. Still she didn't have confirmation of the pub's name but on Monday she would go to see Mr Shepherd and see what he had come up with.

That weekend she went through what she had discovered with her friends, Tom, Linda and Gordon. They called in on Saturday morning to see what she had discovered during her enquiries, which they knew her to be making, to find her sitting in the conservatory in front of her computer making notes on her findings. After she had produced coffee for her visitors, she placed the print-out of the map which Gary had sent her, on the table and started to explain what she had discovered so far.

"This whole area, which includes the whole of Horne Row and the lanes that run into it, the common at the top as far as I can make out, including also the Cricketers Arms, which was then a private house and not as it is now, a pub, was a hamlet called Horne Row."

"Hold on Sally, you've not pointed out your cottage, or next door as being part of this hamlet. Was it?" Gordon asked.

"Of course, silly of me, yes it was. As was the building next door, now called Blackmore House, which, if my father is right, was *The Black Boy*, and the row of old cottages beyond that. There were at that time in fact more than just the two that remain there now. One can only assume that they were workers cottages of some sort."

"What about the dates Sally?" asked Tom. "This map is not dated. Did you get any idea of how old the buildings are?"

"We know that they existed in 1761, but there's not much that has been found yet to date them earlier."

"You sound as though you, or is it someone else? Are still searching," Linda chipped in.

"You're right Lin, I've made two friends who are quite keen to carry out a bit of extra research, well one of them is, it's him who sent the email, and I have great faith in the other." Sally said. "And before you say what I can see your raised eyebrows tell me you're about to say, forget it. One is ten years younger than me, or nearly, and the other is old enough to be my Dad, or nearly!"

"I've heard all that decrying of age before Sal, but we'll keep our council for the moment." Gordon looked smugly at the others. "Won't we chaps?" Everyone laughed and nodded. "OK Sally carry on."

"Anything else you've discovered?" Tom enquired.

"As a matter of fact, yes I was saving it until last because it's the most intriguing part of the whole puzzle."

The other three waited with enquiring looks on their faces. "Come on then, spit it out!" demanded Gordon.

"I went to the Essex Chronicle and looked up editions through the whole of the period 1750 to 1850. I discovered that a William Horne had been hung at Chelmsford in 1784 for the murder of his wife in an alehouse in the hamlet of Horne Row!" Sally pulled from beneath the pile of papers on the table, the copy of the newspaper's page, which she had copied at The Chronicle's offices. She handed it to Gordon who read it and passed it onto Tom.

"What does this mean 'a number in the crowd gladly assisted in the swift dispatch of the condemned man'. And what does it mean about angry protest? Were the crowd protesting on behalf of the chap being hung, or vice versa?" Linda's face showed bewilderment as she read it over Tom's shoulder.

"I don't know." Sally said, "I asked the same question myself."

"I think I can answer the first part of the question." Gordon said after a moment, or two. "Hangings in those days particularly in country districts as this was then, were not 'a long drop' resulting in a broken neck and instant death. They were a long drawn out method of strangulation. The person being hung stood, not on a scaffold, but a cart, which was moved away once the rope was fitted around his neck. Sometimes, then the hangman was particularly inefficient, or inexperienced, the rope would be too long and the condemned person ended up with his feet touching the ground, or the rope was too short and he swung straight off the back of the cart and the noose hardly tightened at all. In these circumstances, friends and relatives would hang onto the legs and add their weight to tighten the noose and assist the victim to achieve a swifter death than he would otherwise have had!"

"How dreadful!" said Linda. "You mean that in this case a number of those present were friends, or relatives and they helped hang this chap?"

"In essence yes, but remember it was not out of vindictiveness, but out of mercy." Tom joined in. "I read about this practice many years ago when as a boy, I have a morbid curiosity about the sort of punishments that were used and metered out for quite simple crimes."

"Yes," Gordon agreed, "these people either felt that he was not guilty, or if he was, he didn't deserve the slow lingering death that an inefficient hanging so often created."

"Enough, on that subject I think," Sally said crisply, "I intend on Monday to visit my friend Mr Shepherd at Oaklands Museum and find out what else he had discovered." She sat back and studied her audience. "The next question is, who is going to help me break through into the cellar?"

"I've already told you that I'm your man in that direction and that you've simply to say the word." Tom cut in quickly, "and I know how keen my mate Gordon here is to have a go, so who else do you want?"

"That's what I wanted to hear you say, but aren't you going to ask when?"

"When?" all three including Linda said loudly.

Sally grinned at their solidarity. "Next weekend I think, after I've spoken to Mr Shepherd. So, if you're all here on Saturday morning, a week today, we'll make a start."

On Monday morning Sally drove to Oaklands, but this time, she went straight past the reception desk and up the stairs to the cartography room. Putting her head round the door, she saw that Mr Shepherd was at his desk, in his little side office. She knocked to proclaim her presence and he raised his head, beaming when he saw her and scrambling to his feet and waved her towards him.

"I wondered if, nay I hoped, that you'd come in today. I've got a little more of interest to tell you." He ushered Sally to a chair and sat down himself. From the far side of his desk he pulled forward a buff coloured folder and opened it to reveal a number of papers within. He rifled through them until he found the one he was looking for. "Now this is the first interesting piece I came across. It's a deed issued to a certain John Horne for ownership of a tenement dwelling on the outskirts of Danbury in 1748. Unfortunately, it is unclear as to where it is because there's no plan to go with the title. However, the next document is also of great interest to us in your search Sally!"

"Mr Shepherd, I'm pleased and not a little flattered that you are placing us together in this enquiry!"

"Nonsense, we're in it together! Now this bit of information I came purely by chance. It would appear that the area which we are interested in was in fact a hamlet by the name of Horne Row." He stopped and held his hand in the air when Sally was about to interrupt. "Yes, you may well know that, but I have discovered that it was this John Horne who gave it the name when he founded his Tile and Brick business!"

"Now that is interesting, I wonder what relation he was to William Horne, who was hanged in 1784 for murdering his wife – he was from Horne Row, incidentally."

"Where did you find that out?"

"At the Essex Chronicle, in their archives."

"I don't have any detail of the family history but perhaps, that's the next thing to look for. However, we know that it is probable that the house, which was named Horne Row, was owned by John Horne in 1748, as was the Tile Works and the hamlet named after the man. The only thing that we've yet to discover, is the name of the alehouse. Right?" Mr Shepherd's eyes twinkled in his ruddy face and Sally knew that he was about to deliver his coup-de-gras.

"Go on Mr Shepherd, you're dying to tell me something!"

"That is the problem in having a face like mine, I never could have played poker, however hard I tried to keep a straight face, that's known by the game. Yes I have solved the key question. The name of the Alehouse.

It was indeed *The Black Boy* and as far as I can tell went by that name from somewhere around 1760 until 1920 or thereabouts."

"How did you find that out?"

"Simple really, I looked up a history of Public House names. *The Black Boy*, which is somewhat unusual, was derived from the time of the slave trade and the habit at the time of novel possessions. Black Boys were young negros who were displayed as just a novelty in both the grander houses, where they existed as servants, and the public houses where few white people had seen those with coloured skins. Now, whether or not the alehouse had such a novelty, I'm inclined to disbelieve. Anyway, I digress. A large number of pubs, inns and alehouses had this title and I simply had to look through the endless lists on the internet, to find what I was looking for and there it was… Time and again it appeared between the dates I've mentioned, so it obviously existed throughout the period."

Mr Shepherd sat back with a look of satisfaction on his face.

"So really we've now got the lot." Sally said.

"Not quite," Mr Shepherd reminded her, "we need to know a little bit about the family history and a great deal more about this murder, committed by a possible family member. Looking at the dates, and if the two, John and William were related, they almost certainly had to be of two generations."

"Why do you think that?"

"If John owned the house in 1748, let's assume he was in his thirties. Therefore in 1784 he would have been in his sixties, or even seventies. If William was John's brother, he would have had to be that sort of age. Can you see someone of that age, at the time, when life expectancy was little more than fifty, committing murder?" Mr Shepherd rubbed a hand over his shiny pate. "One other thing if only we could find it, he would be the one who owned *The Black Boy* during this time! Our quest is not yet over, so once again leave me to investigate further."

"How can I thank you for all you've found out for me." Sally said gratefully.

"When you've put it all together, perhaps you'll tell me why the great interest and what has driven you to it."

"Oh, I didn't tell you? It's all because of a bricked in cellar beneath my house! I want to know why it was bricked up and what, if anything, is in there!"

"My dear Sally. The last part of that is simple. Why haven't you got in there yet? Or can I guess? You're wary of what you might find?"

"Basically, yes I am. But next weekend I've organised two or three of my friends to do the job with me. We have the old bricked up doorway and the flight of steps leading down to it so it shouldn't be difficult. I've got two strapping great men to do the hard work for me!"

"Good luck then for next weekend, but come back and see me afterwards, not only to tell me what you discover, but also hopefully to collect from me some sort of family history of the Horne clan."

Back home, the week went slowly for Sally as she made conjecture after conjecture as to what she and her friends might find below her sitting room.

She rang the builder who carried out the renovation work for both her and the owner of Walnut Tree Cottage and asked him why, if there were cellars there, they hadn't been found during the alterations. He pointed out that because the floors were in such good condition, he had lifted only those boards necessary for the installation of electrical wire and central heating pipes. Inspection of the beams which supported the floor boards showed little sign of, either, rot or woodworm and so they had been covered up again. The remainder of the beautiful elm boards of the floor had been left alone.

"Oddly," he said, "one of my men said something about lath and plaster beneath the beams, but, when I looked at what he was pointing to, it looked to me like just the sort of rubbish that you'd expect to find beneath a floor of that age, deep in dust, dirt and old plaster as it was."

"Which cottage was that in?"

"Yours, I think Miss Parmenter."

On Saturday, her workforce arrived early, at eight-thirty when Sally was finishing her morning cup of coffee and cigarette in the conservatory. She found that she was spending so much more time than even she had anticipated there rather than in the house. Her workforce of three had reduced to two with Linda remaining at home with the children. Tom apologised for her absence, "she was so sorry Sal, but she'll come along later to see what, if anything we've found."

"That's OK, we can't all work on that wall at once anyway," Sally smiled, "now chaps, how do we go about it?"

"To start with, we drill a hole through and find out what happens when the bit gets through the wall. We're guessing at the thickness as being probably three bricks or 335mm, or in old money, 13.5", Tom explained. "I've brought with me all the right equipment, borrowed from work!"

"We're lucky that Tom's in that sort of business, otherwise we might have been having to do a lot by hand!" Gordon clapped Tom on the shoulder. "Well done, now let's get on with it."

They set up a portable generator outside of the conservatory and connected up a large hammer drill with an 18" bit and began drilling in the centre of the bricked-up opening. The bit had gone in to a depth of 9" when suddenly and unexpectedly it broke through. There was no further resistance and Tom withdrew the bit. A slightly musty smell came through the hole but it was impossible to see anything through it. He then drilled a second hole to the side of the first and then a third and forth.

"Right Gordon, your turn, use the Kango hammer and break out the brick in the middle of these holes, then break away around that." Tom climbed up the steps and allowed Gordon to descend with the breaker tool.

Within a quarter of an hour, Gordon had opened up an 18" square hole and climbed up into the conservatory to let the dust settle. "There you are Sally, you get the pleasure of the first sight into your cellar which hasn't seen the light of day for perhaps a couple of hundred years. Have you got a torch, or better still a flash light?"

Sally who had been standing at the edge of the steps watching proceedings with ever increasing excitement, went to the settee where she had been sitting when the others arrived and held the powerful flashlight. "I went and bought it yesterday," she said triumphantly.

She descended the steps and directed the light through the opening. What confronted her was nothing particularly out of the ordinary. It was indeed a fairly spacious cellar with an earth floor and brick walls. On one side there were three lines of wooden shelves and in a corner were stacked timbers, some of which were obviously to be used as fire-wood and thrown into a jumbled heap, whilst some more carefully stacked, was there for re-use at some future date. Beyond this, Sally could see very little of interest.

"You chaps had better open up this hole so we can get through and have a good look round." She said as she withdrew her head and the flash-light.

"Let me give you a break on that kanger Gordon," said Tom, I'll give you the pleasure of clearing away the rubbish, although nearly all of it is falling into the cellar."

"Then I'll simply stand and watch!"

Tom picked up the breaker and started to further open the hole. By removing the courses of beneath the hole he was able to work quite quickly and soon had everything removed down to the bottom step. "We were right in assuming the brickwork to be three courses thick. Whoever blocked it in did it in 9" work, after all there would have been little point in a greater thickness for what he was trying to do – hide its existence from the outside."

They could now enter the cellar comfortably and in single file with Tom leading, they went in. There appeared to be little more to be seen than Sally had shone her light upon. Except perhaps for one thing. Between the front wall and the base of the chimney, there was a door. From its position it had to lead into the cellar next door, under Walnut Tree Cottage.

"Now here's a riddle for you Sal," said Gordon. "What do we do now? That door leads into your neighbour's property and legally you have no right to open it. Having said that, it appears that it open towards you, so in practical terms, it is your door. However, what if you find that the cellar next door, unlike this one, has been filled in with loads of loose rubble and so on and your opening the door causes it to slide, creating untold damage to the floor above!"

"Why do you have to be so pessimistic and so practical Gordon?" said Sally angrily, "I prefer to think that nothing will happen and even if it does, it could never be that serious. Surely if we open the door carefully….?"

Gordon looked at Tom, "what do you think?"

"I agree with Sally, I think that having gone this far, we continue. She's right, we can open the door a little at a time and see what happens." Tom like Sally was less cautious than their architect friend.

"OK, then the next trick is opening the door. Have either of you looked at the lock on it?" Gordon took the light and shone it on an old fashioned rim-lock. He peered into the key-way. "Whichever side this door was locked from, the key has been removed, so there's nothing for it but to remove the hinges and open it that way."

"How do we do that carefully?" Tom asked, then as an afterthought, "just a minute, where do you put the key when you leave your house and don't want to carry it with you?"

"But whoever locked this wasn't leaving the house, he went on to seal up the entrance," Gordon replied. "And in doing so, what use would the key be to him in the future?"

"Tom's right, there would have been no point taking key with him, far better to leave it down here," Sally was following Tom's train of thought. "So where would he hide it?"

All three, although with less enthusiasm from Gordon, who really didn't believe that the key would be found so simply, began searching the cellar. Ironically it was Gordon who found it, laid on the highest corbel of the brickwork of the chimney beside the door. The key lay where it had lain undisturbed for all that time. "A good dose of WD40 I think in that lock and we're in business. Now how about a cup of something. Or…." Looking at his watch, "a glass of something? While we let the stuff work. I hope you've got some Sally?"

"Got what, WD40 in my car," said Tom, "lucky isn't it?" he grinned at Gordon.

"OK, with that sorted, how about a beer Sal?" Gordon replied and turning to Tom, "and how did I know that you would have whatever's needed. I think you must spend your days with a crystal ball!" He grinned back at his friend. By this time they were back in the conservatory. "Beer, Sally for two thirsty workers!" But Sally had already left the conservatory and gone into the house, from which she emerged a short while later with four cans of beer. "Are Linda and the children likely to turn up Tom? If so I'll fish out some coke, or lemonade for them. I've put the kettle on for coffee in any case."

"I don't know, she muttered something about doing a bit of shopping and calling in here later, but I don't know what later meant." Said Tom. "I'll just nip out to the car and get the penetrating oil and give the lock a squirt before I have my beer. It'll take half an hour I guess for it to work." Tom got up and went to do what he had announced and Gordon opened a can of IPA.

"What do you think now Gordon? Why was the cellar carefully concealed when it is clearly empty?" Sally sat on the arm of the settee and looked across at Gordon who had seated himself on one of the upright chairs around the small table which stood against the side of the conservatory. Tom entered with the WD40 and disappeared into the cellar.

"I really don't know, it certainly wasn't as I had first assumed, a window tax issue, but neither did we see any evidence of anything illicit being stored there." Gordon's brow furrowed in thought. "Perhaps we should get an extension lead and inspection light down there and have a good search of the floor to see if there might possibly be another hidden cavity beneath it, although, I personally think that doubtful. I wouldn't mind betting that Tom's got one in the car." He chortled as he saw Tom re-appear from the cellar.

"One what!" asked Tom.

"An inspection lamp."

"I've got one at home, but not here." Said Tom.

"That does surprise me!" Gordon then went on more seriously, handing his friend a beer as he spoke. "What do you think Tom, as to why the cellar entrance was hidden as it was?"

"I don't think that it's anything in the first cellar, Sally's, I think it's more likely to be something we'll find next door, but what, I've no idea. I guess in about half an hour we might have an answer!" He held up the key, which he now began to clean with emery paper and a small file. "I've no doubt that this will work, but the lock itself looks really rusty and may take a little while for the oil to penetrate it and that goes for the hinges as well. Give it as long as it takes to finish this beer and we'll have a go."

They left it until Midday and then returned to the cellar. At first, the key, which entered the lock smoothly enough, refused to turn, but further applications of oil and continuous rhythmic twisting of the key, eventually bore results and it turned, drawing back the bolt from the keep. There was no latch or handle so Tom applied more WD40 to the hinges and with a piece of timber stacked for fire wood which he used as a leaver, he began to prize the door open.

Gingerly he peered around the edge of the door to see if Gordon's fears might be fact, only to find that beyond the door was another clear space. Gradually as the penetrating oil began to work on the hinges, the door swung further and further open. Finally, it had moved far enough for the light to be shone into the next door cellar and a clear view of it to be seen.

"Well what can you see, Tom?" asked Sally eagerly.

"Basically, an empty cellar, but there is a flight of steps from the room above, so there must have been access there once upon a time. There are also some bits and pieces of wood against the side here, just like in here and there's something on the wall on either side here, just like it might have some writing on it. We'll have to get in to find out, I can't tell from here." Tom sounded disappointed. He handed the flash-light to Sally. "Here have a look for yourself."

After Sally had looked it was Gordon's turn, and he too seemed disappointed, "I thought at least we'd find a heap of contraband goods, or a miser's hoard or something of the sort. Never mind, it's been an interesting experience if nothing else."

"Hang on you two, don't give up at this stage, lets get the door properly open so we can get in." Sally spoke angrily to her two companions. "Let's find out what that is on the far wall and I don't know if you had noticed, but where it's fixed to the wall, there appears to be yet another brick opening!"

"Yes I saw it," said Gordon, "but I assumed it to be the same external entrance as the one we've just broken through."

Tom applied some more pressure to the door and after a bit of jiggling he had opened it far enough for them to enter through into the next cellar.

"You know that we'll be trespassing once through this doorway?" said Gordon, "Do you want to do that?"

"Don't be silly Gordon, of course we do!" Sally snapped back. "No time now for mamby-pamby attitudes and anyway, who will know?"

"Only warning you that's all. So, come on who's going to lead the way?" He grinned at her and put his arm around her shoulders. "You, I think Sally," and he allowed her to move ahead of him through the door.

THE BLACK BOY

THE GRAVE

With sally leading, the three friends entered Walnut Tree Cottage's cellar. As Tom had said, there didn't appear to be very much of interest. Similar piles of firewood and timber, some loose bricks in a heap against one wall with what looked like a canvas bag, long since eaten away by the lime which it once contained, and a flight of wooden steps, which had once given access to the floor above, but, which was now sealed with solid looking wooden planking. There was also a wooden plaque on the far wall.

Sally approached this, shining the light on it as she went, it was about a foot, or 300mm square with an inscription crudely carved into it's face. It looked as though it had been done yesterday, the lettering was so clean and clear-cut. It simply said.

William Horne
Died 27th July 1784

Sally felt herself go pale and she had to lean against Tom for support. "Whatever's the matter?" he asked worriedly.

"Oh, Tom, its him! The man, who was hanged at Chelmsford. He must have been buried here!"

"Not necessarily," he replied trying to reassure her, "it is probably simply a memorial, either to him, your William Horne, or another of the same name, who may well have lived here, the house being called *'Horne Row'*.

"I agree," joined Gordon, "it's much more likely that it's some sort of commemoration."

"Then if that is so, why is the date the same as for the hanging and what is that?" Sally pointing to the area floor beside the plaque, which was the rough size of a grave and slightly sunken as its centre. "It has to be a grave!"

Close inspection by the other two and they came up with the same conclusion … "I think you're right Sally."

Tom took her arm and led her back the way they had come. "A nice cup of sweet tea, or perhaps something a little stronger is what is called for I think."

When they were seated and Tom had done the honours with a cup of tea for Sally, she had refused brandy, and a beer for him and Gordon, they began to discuss what should be done. "I suppose Steve would be the one to ask," volunteered Sally, "he's the medical man and ought to know about procedures with dead bodies etc."

"We don't actually know that there is a dead body!"

"Well I for one am not digging to find out!" Sally said adamantly, "I'm going to phone Steve right now and see what he thinks we should do."

While she was phoning, Steve and Linda arrived with the two children, their son Shaun and daughter Emma. Immediately, Shaun wanted to go down to the cellar. "What have you found in there Daddy? Buried treasure? Dead bodies?" he added the last with the gruesome relish of a small boy.

"As a matter of fact Shaun, we've found very little and nothing of real interest, have we Gordon?" He asked for Gordon's support.

"Absolutely nothing of any interest so we'll soon be blocking it up again," he said.

"If you are going to do that, then I must look in there before you do." And the boy jumped up and started down the steps.

"Shaun!" his father shouted, "you'll do no such thing until I say you can ….. its dangerous down there," he finished lamely.

"I don't want to go in there Daddy," Emma said, as she watched her brother retreat up the steps and climbing onto her father's knee, said "it'll be full of spiders and all sorts of creepy crawly things." She gave a theatrical shudder and put her arms around his neck. Sally came off the phone at this point and the children ran to her, clamoring for her attention. Sally was their favorite 'aunt'. She went back indoors and got each of them a drink before returning to the conservatory.

"Steve says he'll be here within half an hour, so we'll wait till he gets here," she announced.

"Did he say anything?" asked Tom.

"Mumbled something about notifying the Coroner, but he'll tell us more when he gets here."

"What's this about a Coroner?" Linda asked sounding alarmed.

"Darling, I think it might be better if you take the children home now, I'll explain all this later." Tom said, trying to give a reassuring look without its meaning being misinterpreted. He saw that he wasn't succeeding, so taking Linda by the elbow, he led her outside. The children were now wanting Sally's attention so they made no attempt to follow. Outside Tom said "we think we've found a grave under next door's house. It looks very much like it and it's probably that of William Horne, who possibly once lived there. Steve will be able to tell us the next move, but it wouldn't be a good idea for Shaun and Emma to know about it."

"Oh, my goodness! how dreadful. You do realize that it could well be the poor man who was hanged, he had the same name."

"Yes, Lin darling, we do. Particularly when the date on the plaque down there and the date of the hanging coincide."

They went back inside and Linda made her excuses and taking the children with her, she went home. Shortly afterwards, Steve arrived with Jenny. They came in and peered down the steps at the gaping hole that now led into the cellar.

"Much as I dislike the idea of scambling about in dust and rubble, I suppose the best thing would be for me to take have a look first so I am au-fait with the situation when I report it. So who's going to lead the way?" Steve looked round and both Tom and Gordon offered to do so. "Are you coming Jen?" Steve asked.

"Not likely, that place must be crawling with spiders and you know how I fell about them!" Jenny moved over to sit on one of the comfortable chairs. "I'll stay up here and talk girl-talk with Sally."

The three men disappeared down the steps and into the cellar. After ten minutes or so they re-immerged.

"There's little doubt in my mind that it is a grave, and that of a big man too," said Steve. "Now what we have to do is notify both the police and the Coroner's office. They will have the body exhumed and try to determine when and how the person died. After that a death certificate will have to be produced and then I suspect permission will be sought to re-inter the remains in consecrated ground, which in this case would probably be in the graveyard at Danbury Church."

"One little problem Steve." Gordon said, "the grave and ergo the body, isn't in Sally's property, it belongs to next door - what do we do? Notify the owner that we have trespassed beneath his house in order to discover this macabre object, or simply go ahead letting the authorities do their bit?"

"How the devil can I advise you on that? I'm afraid that's something you'll have to work out for yourselves. I know that sounds unkind and if so I'm sorry, but since I'm going to be involved in this now, I must take a back seat." Steve looked apologetically at the others and shrugged his shoulders. "Having said all that, I will advise and suggest that you contact the owner of Walnut Tree. He might be pleased to know of the cellar's existence! Where does this owner live?"

Sally answered, "I think he lives abroad somewhere, we never ever see him, Julian and Becky pay their rent into an account in Monaco. When they told me that, when I first knew them, they seemed quite proud of the fact that their Landlord had an off-shore account. Somehow they felt that it gave them a social boost!"

Everyone laughed and Jenny commented, "has any of you thought that when you were in the cellar, since I could hear you talking out here, isn't it possible that they have heard you under the floor next door? Bit spooky for them wouldn't you say?"

"If they're in." Sally said. "Most Saturday mornings they're off out shopping somewhere or other. But you're right Jen, we should be careful. Now Steve, when can the Coroner's office be contacted?"

"Not before Monday, and then I don't suppose they'll fall over themselves to dig up a two hundred year old body. No, you'll have to wait till then."

"We've got enough work to do between now and then, Gordon and I have got to finish clearing the brick doorway and fit a new door and frame. If we can find one to suit at one of the local builder's merchants or DIY's open on a Saturday afternoon, we should be able to finish this weekend." Tom looked at Gordon and took a coin from his pocket. "Heads you go for the door, tails I do." He spun the coin and catching it as it fell, deposited it on the back of his other hand. "Heads it is. Better for the architect to find the right equipment than a mere chemist!"

Between them they took the necessary measurements and Gordon set off in his car for Chelmsford, while Tom picked up his tools, started the generator again and using the Kango hammer with a cutting chisel in it, began to open the remainder of the doorway. Steve made various half hearted offers to help him from the comfort of the armchair in which he now sat, but Tom knew of his lack of enthusiasm for anything at all. Gordon returned from the town with a door frame which he had thrust into the back of his Land Rover, Tom had virtually completed the doorway. A few bricks either side, had been broken and needed replacing, but beyond that it was quite a neat job.

Between them they stood the door and frame in the hole and propped it in position until the morning.

Sally did not sleep well that night. So much had happened during the day that she had found quite disturbing. They had found two cellars, where a few weeks ago, they had not even been suspected. They had found a grave, possibly of a murderer, beneath Walnut Tree and now they'd got to involve both the police and the Coroner. She couldn't wait to get the door onto her cellar and the authorities into the clear everything up, particularly the removal of the body. "Strange," she thought to herself, "why do I keep referring to it as the body, after two hundred years it's most likely a skeleton."

The following day, Sunday, Tom and Gordon were as good as their word and fitted the frame and door to the cellar complete with a substantial lock and catch. When Sally was asked to inspect their handiwork, she was not only grateful, but relieved. "I found it difficult to sleep well last night, knowing that the cellar was open, tonight I shall go to bed happy with the thought that nothing is different to the way it was two days ago, all locked up." She laughed at the two men's smiling and sympathetic faces. "I knew you two wouldn't understand!"

On Monday, she phoned Steve early before he left home for his surgery. "Will you contact the necessary people for me Steve? You said you would."

"Of course, as I promised, but I won't do it until after surgery, about 10.30 I guess, unless I have a small number of patients, which would be unusual on a Monday morning! I'll ring you as soon as I've been in touch."

"Ring me on my mobile Steve, I'm going in to Chelmsford now to see Mr Shepherd at Oaklands Museum, I'm hoping that he's got news for me with regard to the Horne Family history." Sally rang off and drove into Chelmsford knowing she would be caught in the morning rush hour. Never mind she thought, I cannot just sit at home and wait for it to disperse, I might as well sit in it. So, this she did for a full hour, arriving at the Museum just after nine.

She again went straight to the Essex Cartography room, but was surprised to find that Mr Shepherd had yet to arrive at his desk. She sat in the chair opposite his and waited for him. At a quarter past nine he arrived and was delighted to see who his visitor was. "Tea Sally?" he asked with raised eyebrows and without waiting for an answer picked up his telephone. "Mary, tea for two is I believe in order right now, Miss Parmenter has called in probably for no other reason than to enjoy a cup of your dreadful brew!"

He faced Sally across the desk. "Now firstly, have you anything to tell me, anything that you have perhaps stumbled across, or unearthed!"

Sally gave a wry grin. "Not quite unearthed yet, but soon to be done," she said.

"This sounds intriguing and almost mysterious, if I might say so." Mr Shepherd leaned forward. "Tell me more!"

So, Sally told him of the breakthrough into the cellar and the discovery of what appeared to be a grave, together with a plaque noting the name of William Horne and the date which coincided with the hanging at Chelmsford's gaol of the man of the same name.

Throughout her narrative, he kept nodding and peering at notes, which he had in a folder on the desk in front of him. When Sally had finished and had explained that a doctor friend was contacting the Coroner's office that morning and that she had to be home before they arrived, he became brisk and business like. Mary came in with the tea and greeted Sally. When there was none of the usual banter from her boss, she looked at him quizzically and with concern asked him, "are you alright Mr Shepherd?"

"As right as ninepence, Mary, but thank you for asking. My friend Sally and I have a great deal to talk about in a comparatively short time, so you must excuse me for seeming a little brusque." He smiled at his secretary and turned to Sally.

"I have been undertaking a little research into old businesses in Essex. It occurred to me that there had to be some record of those who employed others and kept the wheels of industry turning, even if they themselves did not come from 'well to do' beginnings. After all, the mill owners of the nineteenth century very often started from humble backgrounds, but their names are still remembered. So, I began by looking for the name Horne. Almost immediately, I came up with John Horne, who was the founder of a Tile and Brick business on the south side of Danbury. From what I discovered, the business was very successful and covered a large area of the part of the common there. The area itself became known as Horne Row, which appears to have originated from a row of cottages built to house his workers. So, it was John Horne who gave his name to the hamlet of Horne Row."

"You already told me that," exclaimed Sally.

"Oh dear, yes I believe I did, I'm getting forgetful! Anyway to continue, John Horne had two sons, the first, another John, born in 1749 and William, born 1753. The father died in 1775 and the elder son continued with the Tile Works. It is not clear what happened to William between 1775 and 1784, the date when he was, as you have discovered Sally, hung for the murder of his wife Annie. Immediately afterward John Horne's death, an alehouse called *The Black Boy*, became part of the property owned by John Horne. It is strange that the murder itself took place in an unnamed alehouse in Horne Row. There is no record of any other than *The Black Boy*, but what I discovered in my search through Public House names, I think we have to assume that it was the one in which the murder took place and it was the building adjacent to your two cottages, which incidentally, were both owned by John Horne." Mr Shepherd stopped for a sip of tea. Sally's excited face told him to carry on.

"In trying to follow the family's line, I can find nothing connected to William. He and Annie did not appear to have any children, although, there is no proof of that. The records at Danbury, which I've looked at, record only the birth of John's children, five of them, nothing for William."

"What about his marriage to Annie? When was that? Was it recorded?"

"Not at Danbury, but they could have been married elsewhere of course."

"Don't you find it strange Mr Shepherd, that a man with no children, who kills his wife and hung for it, has his body taken down and buried in his old home, if indeed it was his old home. By whom? Relations? There was only one brother and his family. Friends? We don't know who they might have been, but they must have been remarkably loyal friends to do so. And finally, why did they go to such lengths to hide all access to the burial place?" Sally was bemused by the thought that these people had somehow spirited the body of an executed murderer and carefully buried him beneath the house where he was born. Who were they?"

"We may never know, either who they were, or, why they did it, but I think you can be sure of one thing, what they did, they did out of love for the man and not for any other reason. He had obviously, to my mind that is, been highly thought of by his friends and was thought to be either, innocent of the murder, or justified in committing it. They wanted to give him a decent burial and since an executed person could not be buried in consecrated ground in those days, they did their best for him." Mr Shepherd stopped and looked across at Sally, "of course, we don't yet know whose body is in that grave, so we may be quite wrong."

"Oh, I hope not!" Sally said with trepidation in her voice. And he smiled at her and raised his hand with its fingers crossed.

Three representatives from the Coroner's office arrived at Cotswolds at 12.30 that morning, followed shortly afterwards by a police car with sirens blazing. Inside it were two young police officers. The men from the Coroner's office, who by this time were sat comfortably in Sally's conservatory with cups of tea in their hands, looked up as the two young officers came up the path towards where they, together with Sally and Steve sat. Steve had made a point of being there first, in case there were any questions, which needed answering that perhaps Sally might find difficult.

"You do know that this is a very old body don't you?" The leader of the Coroner's men asked as the policemen approached. "This fella's been dead for at least a couple of hundred years and if a crime had been committed, the perpetrator is long dead. Hardly a need for a siren, wouldn't you say?"

"Sorry Sir, force of habit, particularly when you're late like we are." One of the two answered apologetically. "So where is this body then?"

"It's down there," pointing to the cellar door, "but until I've finished this excellent cuppa, it can wait. Have you brought the necessary excavation tools with you?"

"If you mean spades and a pick, yes, as we were instructed, but I thought you chaps were responsible for the digging. I never thought we might need some help!"

"Before you start work, would you two gentlemen like a cup?" Sally asked and receiving affirmative replies, she went into the house, returning with two more cups. "There you are, drink that while I finish telling Mr Williams here about the find we have made."

There wasn't in fact much more to tell, so a short while later, Mr Williams closed his notebook and rose to his feet. "I think we'd better take a look then Miss Parmenter. Dr MacDonald would you like to accompany us as a witness?"

Steve took the key to the new door from Sally, opened it and led the way into the cellar. He carried with him an inspection lamp and an extension lead, which as he unreeled it, he laid out behind him. The door between the cellars was still open and when he reached the far side of the second one, he plugged in the inspection lamp and clipped it to an over-head beam. Sally, who so far had used the flash-light to show the way, now switched it off and pointed to the grave which was clearly visible in this better and stronger light.

Mr Williams inspected the plaque and made careful notes, followed by photographs. He then photographed the grave itself from all angles and then, satisfied, gave instruction for his two colleagues to commence digging.

The grave was very shallow and there was less than eighteen inches of soil covering the body. There was no coffin, so the first thing the diggers unearthed was the remains of a heavy green outdoor coat, which was the outer garment of the buried man. Carefully now, they exposed the skeleton of a man, well over 6' tall, who had been carefully laid in the grave with his hands crossed on his chest, dressed in britches and boots, a linen shirt and cravat and clasped between his hands a small leather bound prayer book with silver clasps. On the little finger of his left hand was a gold ring, bearing the inscription "HORNE."

Throughout the excavation, Mr Williams photographed and took notes of each stage. He knelt down beside the grave and carefully examined the skeleton itself, bending low to inspect the vertebrae of its neck. Finally, he sat back and said, "I know what you have said about your belief that this man was hanged, but he looks unlike any hanged person I've yet to come across. I know that I shouldn't expect to find separated vertebrae as in a modern hanging where the neck is broken by the fall, but, because of the report you read about assistance from the crowd, who must have hung on his legs, I would have expected to find some sort of evidence of that." He stood up. "Of course, in this light and still in the position it is very difficult to be certain. I'll have to wait till we've got him back to the Path Lab and can have a good look at him."

He and his assistants, with the help of the policemen, who until now had little to do, carefully lifted the remains of William Horne from his grave and placing in a body bag ,similar to a carpenter's tool bag, they carried him out to the vehicle supplied for the purpose of taking the body away. With a promise to be in touch as soon as they had any sort of result, Mr Williams and his colleagues together with the police car escort, drove off towards to Chelmsford.

THE BLACK BOY

THE CORONER'S REPORT

During the next few days, Sally was plagued by telephone calls and visits from the press. One of the first of these calls was from a reported at the Chronicle. "Sally Parmenter?" he had said when she answered the phone. "My name is Leon Sankey, from the Essex Chronicle. I understand that something of interest has been found under your house, is that right?"

"Where did you hear that from?"

"Actually, from two sources, a mutual friend, Gary at the Library and from the police. Gary phoned me some time ago to ask if I had any information about Horne Row area of Danbury and apparently he had been making enquiries on your behalf with every possible agency who might have information."

Sally was touched, "how very kind of him," she said.

The reporter saw his opportunity when Sally was in a receptive mood! "May I come and interview you and get a few pictures and that sort of thing?" He asked quickly.

"I don't know." Sally had been warned by her friends that this was likely to happen and she was wary of saying too much. "I don't know how I stand with the police and the Coroner, I don't think I should be splashing the news about until they've given me the all-clear."

"So, there's definitely something been discovered? You mention the Coroner, can I take it from that, that it is a body?"

"I promise that when I've been given the go-ahead, you'll be among the first to interview me and get your story. But for now you'll have to wait."

"Then I guess I'll have to try the Coroner's office and the police again. I'd hate to miss the boat on a story such as this, not much news-worthy happens locally nowadays."

"OK, give me a telephone number where I can contact you and I'll call you just as soon as I can, I promise." Sally wrote down his name and telephone number and replaced the phone. Almost immediately it rang again. This time it was a National paper, to who she said a similar thing. This was followed over the next twenty four hours by further calls and a number of visits from reporters from the tabloid press who arrived unannounced and were accompanied by photographers and intrusive manners. The door to conservatory was firmly locked and Sally answered only her front door to these visitors, refusing to speak to them, but it didn't stop them from photographing both her and the hatch over the cellar steps through the conservatory window.

She ended up almost in a state of siege, but was assisted by both Tom and Gordon who fielded the intruders as fast as they appeared.

It was several days before the report came back from the Coroner's Office. The Path Lab took its time to complete its investigation and it was to be the following week before Sally heard anything and then it was from Steve who had been sent the report.

"Damned cheek," she said when he came round with it. "Whose wretched house is it after all? And whose skeleton?"

"I have to admit I don't know why they sent it to me, the report," said Steve, "except that as the Dr who reported it, if it had been a modern death, then the Dr would probably have been reporting the death of one of his patients." Steve chuckled, "I guess that bureaucracy has directed that I am William Horne's GP."

"So, what does the report say?" asked Sally in an excited voice.

"Very little that you don't already know. I'll precis the important bits of the report. The body is that of a male Caucasian, aged approximately thirty-five, six feet one inch tall. He died as the plaque said, in around 1780 so probably on the date stated 1874 and he died by hanging. There is no evidence of a broken neck, which such a death would normally have produced, but, even though it appears that great strain was placed upon his neck, he was of such a muscular build, that it failed to fracture, probably merely stretching the muscles and ligaments. The evidence is that he almost definitely died of strangulation," Steve stopped reading, "Do you want to hear more?"

"Of course I do," Sally said impatiently, "what else does it say, it has not mentioned his name yet."

"It does, but draws no conclusions, assume only that this was William Horne and that he died on the day stated on the plaque. It goes on to describe the clothing he wore and the personal belongings he carried. There is a prayer book and the ring which we saw, but there was also a pistol and a short cudgel, more like a cosh in fact, in the tail coat pocket. Such a pistol was in those days know as a 'barker' and was carried by most people who travelled the roads on which they might have encountered those who would wish to rob them, highwayman, footpads and the like." Steve stopped deep in thought and then said.

"If he had just been hung, how come he had a weapon, or weapons in his pocket? Surely he would have been relieved of that at the gaol?" He turned a puzzled face to Sally.

She thought for a moment and then said, "I don't believe he went to prison in those clothes. I believe that he was dressed in his finest clothes after he had been hung and before he was buried. If the pistol was already in the coat pocket, then that would explain it. Otherwise, it could have been a proud procession and that I don't believe."

"Why not? It could have been." Steve said.

"No, if it was, it would have been laid in his hands like the book, not tucked away in a pocket. No, I think that it was already in his coat together with the cosh when they dressed him in it."

"Yes, Sally, I believe you're right. It certainly makes sense." Steve leaned back in his chair and gazed up at the ceiling. "I wonder how long he was kept in gaol before he was hung. Prisons in those days were pretty disgusting places, no sanitation, no washing facilities and nothing but straw on the floor to sleep on. Decent clothes would have been at a premium in a place like that. If our man went dressed as we found him, his clothes wouldn't have lasted long, either from the wear and tear they'd get or from the thieves from all around him, clamouring for his clothing and after all what he had he got to lose, he was going to be hanged anyway, so he might well have sold at least his coat!"

"I don't think there's any doubt that he was dressed for his burial," Sally said, "And I think it goes to show that William Horne was a decent man, well respected and loved by his friends. So what happens now Steve?"

"What do you mean?"

"What happens to William's body? Does it get re-buried and if so where?"

"I think we will have to claim the remains and arrange for the burial. I'll do what I can with regard to the vicar, but it should be OK. However, I don't think we should be too emphatic about the manner of William's death. I know times have changed, but murderers are still frowned upon by the church and their burial in consecrated ground is still taboo. I think we should play on the fact that the Coroner's office is less than committed as to the manner of his passing and the fact that his body was so lovingly interred points to a good and possibly innocent man."

"I don't know how we can keep that much a secret Steve. If I was able to find the record of his hanging as easily as I did, how long do you think before the press have uncovered everything about him?" Sally was now very concerned about the fate of the poor man who had been secretly buried beneath the house.

"Leave it to me in the first place to talk to the vicar. In the second place, give away no information to the press, public interest in stories like this are short lived and the papers know it. They won't pursue it for too long. I wonder if we can somehow avoid his name getting out. After all, the Coroner is not sure, so perhaps his office will be content with 'unknown person'. If they are then all of our problems are solved for us. I'll have words with them and see what they are going to release to the press, who by now must be sniffing at their door." Steve rose and handed the report to Sally. "Now I must go, I'll leave the report with you, I've taken a copy for my file, but I must get back to my rounds." He kissed Sally on the cheek and left.

Soon after he had gone, there came a tap at the window of the back door, where Sally was in the kitchen preparing her elevenses. Julian and Becky waved through the glass and let themselves in.

"Sorry to burst in on you like this Sally but we have some news for you, which really couldn't wait." Julian said excitedly.

"I'm sure it can wait until I've made a cup of coffee and we can sit down and drink it – Yes?"

"Of course, delighted, where shall we sit? In here or in your new conservatory?"

"Yes out there, although it's not quite so new now! Go on through and I'll be with you in a moment."

Sally carried the tray through and placed it on the table in the conservatory. She was a bit annoyed at this intrusion when she wanted to re-read the report and think about what might happen next. Cheerily though she said "whatever finds you both at home on a weekday? Obviously something to do with the important news. You're not pregnant are you Becky?"

Becky shrieked with laughter, "good heavens no, God forbid! It's much more exciting than that!"

Sally bit her tongue to avoid making the sort of reply which sprang to her lips. Whatever could be more exciting than a baby on the way she thought. This girl was so shallow. "So what is the news then?"

Julian spoke first, "let me tell her Becky, after all it's my job that started it." Becky made a little moue but kept silent. Julian went on. "I think you know that we both work for the same Banking group. It's where Becky and I met, Becky joining the bank soon after me, in a slightly different capacity you'll understand," he had to add pompously, "and we've been with them for five years now, last week I was offered promotion to manage their investment business in Shanghai. This is really big stuff, billions of dollars-worth, so of course I've accepted the challenge! We are hoping that Becky will be able to join the wage-roll as soon as we get there, but as my wife, she gets free travel and accommodation in any event. Believe me Sally, the salary and bonuses being offered me are such that I can't possibly turn it down – we're talking mega bucks here!" He looked at Sally and grinned.

For the first time Sally wondered how long these two would remain together, Julian was clearly single tracked in his goal for money and position and Becky having to take a back seat but occasionally thrusting herself into the fore as his wife and equal partner. For once she felt sorry for Becky. How would she fare amongst the people she'd meet in Shanghai? To Julian Sally said, "so this is truly exciting news for both of you, when do you go?"

"I go next week and Becky joins me in a fortnight's time, as long as she's managed to tidy up our affairs here before then."

"So you're not going together? That's a bit unfair on Becky isn't it Julian?"

"Thank you Sally," replied Becky. "Kind of you to think like that, but it's alright really, I don't mind and Julian has to get there as soon as he can to get things 'up and running' as he says." She gave a brave little smile and Sally's dislike of Becky's husband intensified beyond that of her earlier disinterest in the days when he had bored her at parties.

"What about your tenancy agreement here? How long has it got to run and will your Landlord release you from it?" she asked.

"I've contacted him at his address in Antibes where he lives and as long as I pay him the three months still to run, he'll release my deposit and call it square."

"You wouldn't like to give me his name and his address would you Julian, just in case an alternative tenant comes along. It would be such an advantage to vet any new tenant beforehand to ensure such good neighbours as you have been to me." Sally could hardly believe hearing herself say those words, but an idea had come to her like a bolt from the blue. By some means or other, she had to have access to their cellar. It was clear that despite all the goings on, the Newton-Smiths knew nothing of either it, or the discovery of the body.

"Of course, good idea, I'll pop round with it later. I've also got the chap's phone number if you want it?"

Julian was as good as his word and came round a short while later with the name, address and telephone number of his Landlord.

That evening Tom and Linda came round to dinner as previously arranged and prior to the mean, they were most interested in the Coroner's report on William Horne. Sally brought them up to date with detail of the conversation she had had with Steve, both with regard to the clothes on the body and the possible problems regarding re-burial. She also told them of her neighbour's imminent move to Shanghai.

Linda's immediate reaction to the latter was "Good riddance," but when Sally pointed out her feelings of sympathy for Julian's wife, she capitulated and said "OK, they weren't that bad and I suppose it was him who was the biggest pain in the neck what with his loud ways and brash talk, perhaps you're right, Becky was only trying to keep up with him."

"Whatever will happen next then when new tenants arrive to be told, which they will have to be, that there is a cellar beneath?" Tom offered. "I presume Sally that you will tell him that the skeleton of a man has been found beneath his house and that man had been murdered. What do you think his reaction might be?"

"I think the first thing he'd ask is how was it discovered, precisely where and by whom." Said Tom. "The second thing he might ask himself

is, 'however am I going to find a tenant for a house with such a history.'"
Yes Sally, as long as you can suitably dodge the first question I think you
might be onto a winner with the second. But I have to ask, what are you
trying to win? An empty house next door?"

"You are partly there Tom, but not quite, I'm going to try to
persuade the owner, Mr Phillips to sell the house!"

"Sally! What are you saying? Can you afford it? It'll be dreadfully
expensive, just look how house prices have accelerated in this area recently."
Linda was incredulous.

"I'm hoping for two things Linda, firstly that Mr Phillips might be
only too pleased to make a small profit on his original investment, which
incidentally because I did my own house at about the same time, I know
roughly what his costs must have been. Secondly, I'm hoping that Daddy
will either buy it himself or loan me the money to do it."

"Would he do that, and why are you so keen to own the house
Sally?" Asked Tom. "It's not I know for any commercial reason, so what
is it?"

"Silly really, but I want to preserve the sanctity which those who
buried him wanted for him and if any reason it should be necessary, I
want to have the ability to bury him again where they laid him."

By this time the mean was over and they sat around the table
drinking coffee. For a few minuted the three of them sat in silence. Tom
was the first to break it.

"Well good luck Sally dear, I hope it goes well for you. Keep us
posted on whatever you do and of course it goes without saying, that if
we can be of any help, you've only to call."

"I know that Tom and thanks to you both."

The following day was busy for Sally, firstly she telephoned Mr
Phillips at his home in Antibes and was quite surprised that he was the
one to answer the telephone. She had expected a whole array of minions
to protect him from possible unwanted calls, but instead of that a friendly,
affable voice answered her, "Henry Phillips, hello." She hesitated a moment.
"Mr Phillips, my name is Sally Parmenter and I live in the cottage next to
Walnut Tree Cottage which I believe you own in Danbury."

"Yes I know your name and I did once see you from a distance, but
now, hello, how nice to talk to you, what can I do for you?"

"I don't know exactly how to put this but I suppose honesty is the best policy." Sally started.

"Yes I agree, it's always the best way." Mr Phillips replied.

"I was planning to tell you that a skeleton of a murderer who himself had in effect been murdered, has been found beneath Walnut Tree Cottage. I was then going to ask you what I've phoned to ask, will you sell the cottage to me?" The words tumbled out and Sally realized that from the onset she had handled it badly. "Oh God, that sounds awful doesn't it?"

"Not that bad really. Is this why my tenants, the Newton-Smiths have given notice?"

"No they don't even know about it, they're leaving because he's got some sort of promotion to a high flying job in China."

"How come they don't know about this skeleton when you do?"

"This sounds even worse Mr Phillips, but it was because of the investigation and discovery of my own cellar, that we discovered the body." Sally then went onto describe everything that had happened ever since she had the conservatory built. "So you see, our neighbour's knew nothing of it and still don't. I am just keen to safeguard the burial place and protect the memory of this poor man."

"Either that, or you have some ghoulish plan to exploit this situation. Have you Miss Parmenter?"

"Oh no! What I've said is the truth. Whoever went and buried this poor man two centuries ago did so out of kindness and it is for this reason that I like to preserve his resting place." Sally was almost in tears and the break in her voice was obvious down the phone.

There was a silence from the other end for a few moments and then; "Miss Parmenter, may I please call you Sally?" and receiving an affirmative from Sally, he continued. "I am astounded that in this modern day and age that someone could show such caring for someone she doesn't know, particularly when he died two hundred years ago! The answer to your question is, yes I probably will sell you Walnut Tree Cottage, but only after I have met you face to face. Can we do that? I am coming to the UK on the 1st December for a week, give me a phone number and I'll contact you when I arrive."

Sally gave him her mobile number, rang off and immediately went to see her father. She explained the situation and what had been said during her phone call with Mr Phillips.

Her father was as usual, sceptical. "Why should he be so kean suddenly to sell? He's a businessman after all. Has he mentioned a price?" and when Sally admitted that price had never been discussed her father said, "I thought as much, he can see how keen you are and he's going to milk you for every penny! Tell me, did you actually cry over the phone?"

"Yes a bit."

"Then that settles it in my mind. He'll pop over, exploit the situation and persuade you to pay an exorbitant price for the cottage."

"Daddy, I think you've got him wrong, but we'll have to wait and see won't we?"

"All I say now is that yes, if the price is sensible and I'm not likely to lose on the deal, then I'll lend you the money to buy the cottage." Dick Parmenter was still suspicious of the owner's intentions. "I hope on your irregular income from acting and design you can afford it Sally. I repeat though I think it may be a non-starter when your Mr Phillips comes up with his price!"

Over the next two weeks, press interest in the discovery seemed to fade. Sally gave the interviews, which she had promised, but on each one she had, whilst mentioning the cellars and the grave, made no mention of who was buried there. At the end of that period, Becky finally moved out and the last of the couple's belongings were loaded onto a removal van. Most of their furniture had been taken to a sale room in Chelmsford the week before, so now the house was empty. Sally saw Becky off and admired her stoicism towards the move, which although she had shown excitement for it up to a point, it now clearly filled her with trepidation. Sally gave her a hug and a smile before waving her goodbye in her taxi, feeling sad for her but not wishing to undermine the brave face which Becky had put on.

A week later on the 1st December Sally's phone rang. It was Henry Phillips. He was at Stansted airport and he asked if on his way to London, he might call to see her. He would be with her by two pm he thought. When he had rung off, Sally dashed around the house tidying here and there and then pouring herself and gin and tonic she sat in the conservatory to drink it. She really was on tenterhooks regarding the forthcoming meeting. Was her father right? Had she been silly to believe that Mr Phillips would be generous in his price? Above all what was he truly like? He had seemed so kind and affable on the phone, but as Daddy had said, he was a businessman and he didn't get to living in the South of France without being successful and with a certain amount of ruthlessness!

An hour later and from where she sat she saw a large silver car draw up outside. Out stepped a chauffeur who opened the rear door for its occupant who stepped out and looked up at the two cottages. He was a tall man, with a slightly receding hair line, greying at the temples with an athletic figure. His face was unlined apart from the laughter lines around his mouth and eyes. He was in fact exactly as Sally had originally imagined him to be, except that he appeared to be younger, early fifties, or even late forties. He said something to the driver who got back into the driver's seat of the car and opened a newspaper. Mr Phillips came through the gate and up to the path to where Sally sat in the conservatory. She got up to greet him at the door.

"Hello Sally," he said with a beaming smile and outstretched hand, "Henry Phillips."

She shook his hand and invited him in. "Coffee?" she asked, "or something else."

"Coffee would be lovely, black please, no sugar."

Sally directed him to a seat while she went to make the coffee. She was back in a couple of minutes to find him peering down the cellar steps, the hatch over which he had raised. "Hope you don't mind, purely my inquisitiveness." He said, "incidentally, you have had this!" indicating with outstretched arms, "the conservatory built since last I was here and a wonderful job it is too. I love the way you have had it fitted out and furnished, or did you do it?"

"Yes it's what I do, interior design, in between bit-parts acting." Sally was pleased that he liked her work and although there were plenty of people who praised her for it, somehow, coming from him it seemed important.

"So, this was how you discovered your cellar? The entrance is just as you described it to me over the phone and that leads through to the one next door does it?" Henry Phillips sipped his coffee and looked at Sally. "Do you want to see down there Mr Phillips?" she asked, "I'll get the key…."

"No, Sally I don't, I might get to thinking, what does the addition of a cellar add to the value of a house? And then where would we be?" He laughed and Sally saw the cause of all the laughter lines on his face. He was a contented man with a sense of humour. "Don't worry Sally, before

I leave, you and I will have agreed a price which will suit both of us……
and by the way please call me Henry, or, if you've mind to it, Hal as my
friends do."

"OK Hal, where do we start, with the pricing that is?" Sally was
trying to be brisk and business-like before this elegant, handsome tycoon,
whose greatest charm was his smile, which she found irresistible and
which she found herself replying to his every sentence.

"There are two ways to go about it Sally, the first is for me to tell
you shat I want for it and the second for you to tell me what you feel
comfortable paying. Somewhere along the way, we should come to a
mutually agreeable figure. So shall I start?"

Sally nodded, unable to do more as she had suddenly become
extremely nervous.

"I bought the house when you did in 1997 and I think you know
what I paid for it then. I had renovated in much the same way as you, by
the same builder I recall. If I then add the inflationary figure of say 3%
per annum and then a small profit at the end of say 5% we have a figure
to commence on. Lets say 130K shall we?"

Henry Phillips looked at Sally and smiled again. "Right Sally, now
your turn."

"Whatever can I say? If you're serious I really shouldn't mention
what, in your words, I might have been comfortable paying. I think you
are being not only extremely generous, but very kind as well!" Sally looked
hard at him to make sure that he wasn't playing some sort of a game with
her, not that she for one moment suspected that, and discovered that by
looking into his eyes, he definitely wasn't.

"So, shall we settled on one hundred and thirty thou?"

"Oh Hal, only if you are sure that you will be happy with that, you
see I know what a house like Walnut Tree Cottage would fetch in this
area right now."

"My dear Sally, don't think for one moment that I don't know as
well, but I said to you over the phone, I'm astounded that your sole
reason for wishing to buy the house is to safeguard that which the friends
of your skeleton, what was his name…?" and when Sally reminded him,
"Oh yes…. William Horne, wanted to preserve for him, I found the
whole thing very touching and your personal commitment to it particularly
endearing! You were honest with me on the phone about all that and

how foolish I was to misinterpret your motives as being ghoulish!" Hal looked at Sally almost with affection, certainly with admiration. "For that reason I shall be very pleased for you to buy the cottage. I will add that whilst I'm happy yo sign whatever agreement you are happy with, I'll not press for an early completion unless it suits you. How's that?!"

Sally was so excited that she could hardly contain herself and in a moment of exhilaration she leapt up and leaning over Henry where he sat, she kissed him. If he was surprised, he didn't show it. "Thank you, Sally, that was nice, sealed with a kiss they say."

Sally drew back and returned to her chair, "Sorry about that, I got a bit carried away," she said.

"Never ever apologise for such a lovely gesture," Henry said. "Now if I go and call my driver, he'll bring us a document already drawn up for you to sign as long as you agree to it of course." He stood up, "OK?", he asked.

"You've had it all worked out and drawn up before we even met! How did you know that I'd agree?" Sally was incredulous.

"Simple really, it didn't matter too much what you agreed to we'd have filled it in to suit the moment!" Again, Henry gave her that wonderful magical smile of his and Sally's heart melted.

He went to the door and signalled his driver, who seemed to have been awaiting his summons because he immediately leapt out of the car carrying a briefcase which he carried up the path to where his employer stood and handed it over.

"Thanks Tony," Henry said, "I shan't be long now, I'd be grateful if you'd wait a moment to witness a couple of signatures. Come on in. "He led the driver back inside and drew a folder from the briefcase and laid it on the table. "There you are Sally, I'll simply fill in the figure as agreed £130,000 and we each sign, here and here, as vendor and purchaser and the job's done!" He leaned over the document and entered the sum and then signed as the vendor. "Now all you've got to do is sign as purchaser here?" Sally did as he directed and signed her name. "Now all we need to is a witness and who better than Tony here, my driver, who has been with me for so long that I can't remember."

"Since 1984 Sir, however long that is"

"Surely, you're not counting Tony?" Henry laughed.

"Oh dear me, no Sir, I've enjoyed every minute!"

"Alright, enough flattery, just stick your moniker beside our two signatures and then we can get off to London."

Tony signed and then excused himself to go back to the car. Henry was left with Sally who didn't know what to say next.

"Left a bit of void hasn't it?" Henry said "Never mind by the next time we meet I'm sure that it will be filled. The next time, incidentally, will I hope be when you allow me to take you to dinner."

"That would be lovely," Sally answered quickly, afraid that the offer might go away.

"As I said, I'm here for only a week this time and I'm on a very tight schedule so it'll have to be next time. I have your phone number. I'll call you when I know I'm coming over." Henry looked at Sally and said "when I make a commitment it is total and dinner with you is just such a commitment, remember this." And he kissed her on the lips.

THE BLACK BOY

WALNUT TREE COTTAGE

The day following Henry Phillip's visit, Sally went to see her father and mother. He saw her coming as she walked down the path towards the vegetable garden where he was working, spreading compost on the ground which was shortly to be dug and he leaned on his fork as she approached.

"Don't tell me he's come up with a figure already." He said and then seeing her smiling face. "If he has, you don't seem too unhappy about it, or has something else happened. I know, you've won the lottery Sal!"

"Wrong Daddy, although in a way I feel that's exactly what I've done."

"Perhaps you 'd like to explain that Sal, some one, we'll go up to the house and Mummy can here what you've got to say." He took her arm and led her into the kitchen, where they found Sue preparing lunch. Once they had sat down around the kitchen table, Sally told them of her meeting with Henry Phillips. She started off by saying what a delightful and charming man he was, to which her father said, full of scepticism, "I bet he was when he was selling you the cottage."

"I told you before that you were wrong about Henry, Daddy."

"It's Henry then is it! Christian name terms! You obviously got on well together; was that before, or after he came up with a price?" Dick continued to be scathing.

"If you don't stop this Daddy, I'll go away and won't tell you any more. I'll come back another day." Sally began to get up and her mother leapt into the gap. "Dick you are incorrigible. For heaven's sake, let Sally tell us just what has been said and swallow your belief that everyone is out for what they can get. Now Sally darling, sit down again, ignore your father and tell me all that was said."

"Sorry Sal, just me and my silly attitude. Let's hear it all please." He father looked apologetically at his daughter, who sat down again and related the whole of her meeting with Henry Phillips. When she came to the figure that he had suggested and they had agreed upon, her father who until that moment remained silent, couldn't contain himself any longer.

"How much?" he said.

"One hundred and thirty thousand, Daddy. I've got the sale document here to prove it, all signed and witnessed legally, I think you ought to be delighted with that and proud of me to boot!"

Sue stepped in first. "Darling, your father and I are delighted for you. I know how much Daddy was expecting to have to lend you and it was a lot more than that, wasn't it Dick?"

"It certainly was. You have done quite remarkably well, but that other side of me is always looking for a catch! What else is this chap after?"

"Oh Daddy I wish you weren't such a Doubting-Thomas !" Sally laughed, "I've told you, he admired why I wanted to buy Walnut Tree and he is both wealthy and generous and so could see a way of helping me." She looked across the table at her parents. "By the way he's coming over to take me out to dinner soon!"

"Darling, that sounds wonderful, what especially? All the way from the South of France?" Sue was really excited, "could this mean something serious!"

"I'll let you know." Sally said with a laugh. "Now Daddy are you still happy to lend me the money?"

"I have to admit that I'd be happier to buy it, sell it and make a handsome profit." He replied with a grin. "Yes Sal, I'll be delighted to lend it to you, you'd better let me know when you need it."

Christmas was fast approaching and ten days beforehand Sally received a phone call from Henry to say that he had not forgotten his promise and that he would be back in England for Christmas and the New Year. He would, he said be very pleased if she would join him for dinner on the 22nd December and he named an exclusive local restaurant, one which Sally had been to once before, but only the once, because with its prices, she didn't think she would be likely to go again! Neither she, nor her friends could run to that sort of expenditure very often! She accepted with delight and Henry collected her in his car three days before Christmas Eve. At the restaurant Sally and Henry were dropped at the door and Tony, who had driven them there, left discreetly to find somewhere to park until his employer called him.

They had a wonderful evening. The table had been especially prepared before they arrived with a centre decoration of red roses and later in the evening, the head waiter appeared carrying a colossal bouquet of flowers which he presented to Sally. Attached to it was a card which read "to a very special lady whose heart is as soft as her face is beautiful."

She was overwhelmed and tears came to her eyes and started to run down her cheeks. She dabbed them away with her napkin. "Oh Hal, they are the most lovely words, definitely unfounded, but thank you for them and of course for the flowers."

Henry reached across the table and took her hand. "I have to tell you Sally, that ever since I first spoke to you that day on the phone and then when we met at your charming home, I've not been able to get you out of my thoughts. I'm a bit long in the tooth to be saying this to someone of your age, but I've had to say it. It's been a wonderful evening, you have been wonderful company and I believe that I'm the envy of every man in this room! So even if we never repeat it, it has been worth every minute!"

He went to withdraw his hand from Sally's but she clasped it tightly. "Hal I don't think I have ever been happier and I do so hope we'll repeat it more than once! And you're not long in the tooth as you describe yourself."

"I was fifty two this year, which compared with your tender age, must be described thus, and in all these years, never have I felt before as I do now about you, who in fact, an outsider might say, I hardly know. But that wouldn't be true. I feel that I have known you for ever and everything I have discovered about you I like …. No, more than that I love!" Henry continued to allow Sally's hand to grasp his and returned her grip.

They left the restaurant after midnight and Tony drove them back to Horne Row. Henry walked with her up the path, but he declined her invitation for a cup of coffee. "No I won't this time Sally, but I hope the invitation might be repeated in the future. I'll be in touch in the morning when you've given this evening and what I've said some thought and decided whether or not on the cold light of day you would like to repeat it. For now, though goodnight and thank you for a lovely evening." He leant forward, put his arms around her and kissed her.

"You told me to remember that last kiss you gave me. I'll remember this one aswell. And I don't think that I need either, a night's contemplation, or the cold light of day to tell you that I can't wait until the next time." Sally looked up into his face and smiled at him.

"Until next time then." Hal said.

"Until next time and thanks for everything." Then as he was walking away down the path she called after him. "You still haven't seen the cellar. I'd love you to have a look at them sometime and for me to show you William's plaque and grave. Perhaps next time?"

"How could I refuse such a charming invitation, 'come and see the two hundred year old grave of someone who's buried in my cellar' – charming, I'd love to." With that he walked laughing to the gate, turned, gave a cheery wave and got into the car, which drove off in the direction of Chelmsford and London.

The following day, Henry phoned her, to say that with only two days to go until Christmas it was unlikely that he would get to see her again until after the holiday. He had a sister in Sussex who he had promised to spend the festive season with. Sally got the impression that it was more for the sake of Henry's nephew and niece that for that of his sister.

Sally who spent Christmas with her parents and her sister and her family, was disappointed that she wouldn't be seeing Henry during the holiday period, but is saved complications. She would prefer her family to meet him once or twice before inviting him to spend any length of time with them. Anyway, it wasn't fair on either of them, or him to drop them in together on what was, after all, one of the few family reunions during the course of the year.

Her sister and her husband lived in Scotland, his job being something to do with oil, Sally was never sure what it was he did, although he tried to explain on several occasions, something to do with the analysis of core samples, or something, and they came down south to Danbury only three, or four times a year. These occasions had to coincide with school holidays and were the only times that Dick and Sue had a chance to see their grandchildren, who were now just into their teens.

It wasn't to be until New Year's Eve that Sally was to see Henry again. He as before collected her and swept her off to dinner and a New

Year's Eve Ball in a London Hotel, after which she was driven home. This time he came in for coffee but stayed no longer than the time it took to drink it! Explaining that he would like his poor chauffeur to get some rest, it was now three am and they yet had to drive back to their hotel. Over the course of the next few weeks, Henry was a constant caller and although he had to make the occasional trip to France, he was extremely attentive.

On St Valentine's Day Henry asked Sally to marry him. He arrived at Cotswolds as usual driven by Tony, and came up the path carrying a single red rose. She was in her kitchen preparing a meal for the two of them as they had previously arranged and was aware of his presence only when he kissed her on the back of the neck as she bent over the onions which she was slicing for the steak and onion pie which she was preparing.

"Hal! You made me jump I might have cut myself, or worse, I might have taken you as a rapist or stalker, or something and defended myself with a horrible result for you!" She lifted her face to his and kissed him. "I won't touch you with my hands like this, covered in steak and onion and flour." She saw that Henry was holding something behind his back. "Is this a bottle of wine you've got there?"

"No!" He answered.

"I'm so glad, for ages I've been wanting to be really extravagant and so I lashed out a little while ago and got hold of bottle of Gevrey Chambertaine 1998, I think it is, I do hope it will be to your liking Sir!" she added with an elaborate curtsey.

"It will be lovely I know and I'm sorry that my supplying the wine cramped your style. You should have said. I do however, have a little present for you, this…." And he brought from behind his back a single red rose.

"Oh Hal that's lovely, thank you….."

"I haven't quite finished yet Sally." Henry went down on one knee, took her hand in his and said, "Darling will you marry me?"

Sally lifted him gently to his feet again. "Yes, my darling I most certainly will." She said with tears of joy in her eyes.

Henry took out a small jewellery box from his pocket and opening it took from it a solitaire diamond ring and placed it on Sally's finger. It fitted perfectly.

"How did you know the size darling?" she asked.

"By subterfuge and help from your friend Linda!"

THE BLACK BOY

THE TUNNEL

Sally was in favour of a summer wedding and so she and Henry had settled on a date in June. Her friends had been over the moon when she told them her news. They had, by that time, all met Henry and without exception liked him.

"All that match-making we've tried to do over the past three or four years and you manage to come up with your own perfect man all by yourself Sal!" said Linda, "don't know how you managed it without our help!"

"But you did help I hear Lin, you told Hal the ring size!" She smiled at her friend. "To tell you the truth, I didn't have much to do with it, Hal swept me off my feet from the word go," Sally said happily.

She, together with Graham, Steve and Jenny were at Tom and Linda's for supper. The children had been tucked up in bed and now the adults sat around the table sipping coffee and finishing the wine, a delicious Australian cabernet sauvignon from Yara Glen. It had been sent by Henry with apologies for his absence that evening due to a business commitment in Nice where he currently was.

"Knows his wines does your Henry," observed Gordon as he sipped from his glass. "This is truly gorgeous, I must remember it next time I'm down Tesco's!" he laughed, knowing that Sally was about to tell him he'd have to look elsewhere than on a supermarket shelf. "Only teasing you Sal."

"On a serious note, Sal," Tom began, "I'd like to talk about something else. Over the past few weeks, ever since we discovered old William's grave, I've been wondering about that blocked up doorway in Walnut Tree's cellar. Has any of you given any thought to it?"

"That's all it is Tom, another bricked in doorway like the one into Sally's, surely we agreed on that," Steve said.

"We may have agreed that it was the most likely explanation but look at the facts." Tom looked around the table and saw that he had everyone's attention. "Sally's doorway was filled in from the outside to make it invisible. The brick courses were tied in and pointed up on the outside to achieve this. No attempt was made to do the same inside, yet in Walnut Tree it was and painstakingly too."

"Perhaps the outside of that one had been filled in earlier and what was done from the inside of the cellar was merely finishing it off." Suggested Linda.

"I don't think so for a couple of reasons." Tom stopped and to Gordon he said, "what do you think Mr Architect?"

"I'd not given it much thought, but I see what Tom's driving at. If the doorway had first been bricked in from the outside, it would have been done in nine inch work as yours was Sal. That being the case any completion on the inside would have been a single skin only, assuming of course that both cellars had thirteen and half inch brick walls around them."

"I'm sorry, I don't follow, would you like to explain that Gordon?" Linda said.

"Certainly, the wall on Sally's side was three bricks thick. Each brick is four and half inches, so the overall thickness of the wall is thirteen and a half inches, OK so far?"

Linda nodded, but mumbled something about Gordon being patronising.

"Seriously Lin, I wasn't being that, I just want you to understand the argument that Tom is raising. Now you'll remember that when we broke through into the cellar on Sally's side, the doorway had been filled with nine-inch brickwork and that the outside had been made to match the remainder of the wall. If it had been done with one thickness only it could not have matched unless the builder had gone to the trouble of cutting every header brick instead of laying in a whole one as he could with every nine-inch work. Still with me everyone?"

They nodded in agreement and now Tom took over from Gordon. "My argument is that if an external cellar door had been filled in earlier or even at the same time, it would have been done in the same way was Sally's, with two skins of brickwork only laid from the outside to camouflage the original entrance. They wouldn't have bothered to fill in the inside with that additional skin!"

"So, what do you deduce from all that?" asked Steve. "That the entrance to Walnut Trees's cellar was filled in perhaps earlier, from inside and not out, and the steps down to it were perhaps filled in with soil and rubble long ago?"

"It's possible Steve, but one other thing that I've not mentioned and no-one has here either, and that is the existence of the stairs from the room above." Tom paused and those around him gave small sounds of appreciation.

"If there was access to the cellar from above, there would be no need for an external door, would there? And there are no steps in my cellar, whereas there definitely is an outside door." Said Sally with understanding dawning on her face. "So, what we're seeing as a bricked up outside entrance could in fact be something entirely different."

Tom beamed all over his face. "In a nutshell Sal, in a nutshell!"

"So what do you think is behind that brickwork then Tom?" Jenny spoke for the first time. "Something exciting, more bodies?!"

"That could be exciting in itself couldn't it?" said Steve with something like glee, he had enjoyed the diversion from the humdrum round of everyday doctoring to involvement with the Coroner over the body of William Horne.

"No it wouldn't, one body and such a sad one as William's is quite enough!" declared Sally vehemently.

Tom raised his hand to quieten the table down. "I certainly wouldn't expect to find anything of the sort, but I'm intrigued by why the infilling was done and what lies behind it. It may be nothing of course, and in anycase it's Sal's decision as to what to do next, but I hope it will be that, we have to look through the wall!" All eyes turned to Sally.

"Whatever can I say? Yes, like you say Tom, it's intriguing, but I'm going to ask you eager beavers to wait until Hal's here so he can be part of it. After all if it wasn't for him, we wouldn't even be thinking of it." She grinned and added "Except maybe clandestinely one dark night!"

"OK, that's fine, of course we agree to wait for him. When did you say he was back?"

"This weekend. He flies into Stansted at two o'clock on Friday, that's the day after tomorrow and he's stopping at Cotswold for the weekend, so if you'd like to have a go at the wall on Saturday I'm sure that I can persuade Hal to join you. You might all be surprised just how practical and able he is and his enthusiasm for this sort of activity is boundless – You'll see!" Sally said proudly.

On Friday afternoon at a little after two-thirty, the Bentley arrived at Cotswolds. Tony opened the car door for his employer and then collected his bag from the car's boot and followed him up the path, where Henry was greeted by an exuberant Sally who threw her arms around her fiance's neck and hugged him to her.

"My goodness, what a welcome! Darling, I hope you never stop greeting me with such enthusiasm, because the day you do I'll start to worry!"

"Theres no chance of your ever needing to worry then is there?" she said. "Now come on in, I've cooked us a special meal tonight, " - Sally then saw Tony behind Henry's shoulder. "Oh Tony, I'm sorry, can I offer you something? A drink of some sort?"

"No, thank you ma'am," said Tony and Henry helped him out.

"I'm afraid poor Tony has a little way to go yet and the last thing he would that you for would be something alcoholic to drink, which I think is what you might have been offering. He also has, I understand, a date with a young lady later this evening and will be collecting her and taking her to both dinner and the theatre. So I think he might want to be away as soon as he can. Am I right Tony?"

Tony gave a courteous little bow and said "One hundred percent Sir."

"Right, off you go then and don't forget, I want collecting here on Tuesday morning at eight thirty."

When Tony had left, Sally asked Henry "have you lent Tony the car for the evening? He must be thrilled with that."

"Tony and I have a perfect arrangement Sal. He chauffers me wherever I want to go and at whatever time, but when I don't want the car, he is at liberty to use it at his will. Trust is a two-way thing!"

"Oh Hal I know that and I think you are one of the most thoughtful and kind people I have ever known."

"That's enough of that, now lead to this wonderful food, I've luckily brought with me a bottle of Chablis, which should go quite well with it.

I also brought a red with me in case you were going to produce steak and kidney pie, I know it is one of your favourites."

They went through to the dining room and there everything was laid out to perfection. "Oh Sal, this looks both charming and romantic, you've gone to such trouble, thank you," Henry took her in his arms and kissed her passionately.

Sally pushed away from his and at last drew breath. "I think that can wait until after we've eaten don't you my darling?" she said coyly. "I want you to appreciate my cooking first."

Over supper, Sally told Henry about her friend's conclusion over the bricked up door in the cellar. She explained the theory which both Tom and Gordon held and that tomorrow, they planned to open the doorway and discover what lay beyond. Hal was both excited by the prospect and enthusiastic as to what they might find. "I do hope that they'll allow me to take part in their investigation," he said. "I'd find that sort of thing most exciting."

"Hal, they are expecting you to be here tomorrow, probably leading the way, so come on, let's go to bed now and leave the washing up until tomorrow, I can do it while you're down there bashing holes in the wall next door!" arm in arm they walked up the stairs to the bedroom.

The following morning, Sally and Henry woke in good time. Sally went down to make the tea, bringing it up to the bedroom where the two of them drank it in leisurely style. "You realise that in a month's time, we shall be doing this quite legitimately don't you darling?" Hal said, "We'll be man and wife as they say!"

"I can't wait," said Sally, "my only fear is that I will be leaving my lovely house for long periods of time to follow you around the world and that might make me quite sad."

"I have news for you my love." Said Henry sipping his tea, "I am retiring from business and intend to spend all of the time that I have with you. I shall of course retain the house in Antibes, where I hope you will come on occasions, it is wonderful place for a holiday as you know when you came over last month. I shall allow my investments to, how shall we say it, 'blossom,' but apart from that I am all yours and if you wish for us to spend the rest of our days here at Cotswolds, then that is what will happen."

Sally snuggled up to him. "I cannot believe how my life has turned around in a little over six months. I didn't know that such happiness existed except in fairy stories."

"Maybe, that's what this is, a fairy story!" Hal laughed and jumped out of bed. "You're Snowwhite and I am one of the dwarfs, Hi-ho-Hi-ho and off to work we go……" he sung as he pranced around the room with an imaginary pick over his shoulder, "If your friends are coming to do what they've got to do this morning, I'd better get down there if I'm going to join them."

"Darling, you don't know how ridiculous you look, dancing around like that without a stitch of clothing on, I'm sure that's not how the dwarfs did it! Incidentally, which one of the seven do you want to liken yourself to? Dopey, Grumpy, Dozey or WHO?"

He leaned onto the bed, kissed Sally and said "Simple, I'm Happy!"

Half an hour later he was downstairs dressed in the old work clothes which he kept at the cottage to wear when helping Sally in the garden. She followed him down and they sat in the conservatory with a cup of coffee and a bowl of cereal, awaiting the arrival of the others.

Tom was first to arrive on his own. "Linda not with you Tom?" asked Henry.

"No, she'll be along later when she's sorted out the kids and got the house straight and so on." Said Tom. "Great to see you Hal, Sally told us that you'd be here this weekend and that you're keen as mustard to see what we might uncover down there."

"Rather like the opening of Tutankhamen's tomb, I feel like either Howard Carter or Lord Canarvern must have felt on the brink of a great discovery."

"I don't think that it's likely to be that monumental a discovery, but we'll see."

Gordon now arrived and soon after came Steve and Jenny. "Come on in and have a cup of tea before you start." Sally offered, "Tea or coffee?"

"Tea for me Sal," said Jenny, but all of the others shook their heads. "We'd rather get on if you don't mind Sal," said Gordon. "We'll have something later on in the morning if that's OK with you."

"No problem," Sally answered. "Hal's got the key to the cellar so off you go."

Henry unlocked the cellar door and led the way in. Some time ago, Tom had connected up to the electric circuit and fitted lights in both cellars, so there was no need for a flashlight and the four men made their way through to the far cellar under Walnut Tree. The grave where the body of William Horne had lain for two centuries was now empty, his body still being retained by the Coroner's office, awaiting a decision as to where it could be reburied.

On the wall behind was the plaque recording William Horne's death. Behind was the filled in doorway.

"First, we need to set up the generator and the drill and we'll do what we did to enter Sally's cellar. We can guess again that the wall is a maximum of thirteen and half inches thick but more likely nine, so we'll go carefully from nine inches on." Tom had taken charge. "So if you Steve, get the generator going out there and you Gordon bring the extension lead and drill down here, we can make a start."

"You haven't given me a task Tom." Said Henry with a twinkle in his eye, "don't for one minute think that because I've got many years on you, or because of my seemingly sedentary lifestyle I am incapable of any form of strenuous work. On both counts you'd be wrong, so what do you want me to do?"

Tom grinned at him. "You're going to have the pleasure of drilling through the wall Henry! We've been saving it for you. As Sal says, if it wasn't for you, we wouldn't be doing this anyway!"

Hal replied "Thanks, but it's a bit like laying a foundation stone isn't it? Whatever happens afterwards is incidental and not truly ones responsibility."

"Not that I am in any way used to laying foundation stones, I don't think that this is at all similar Hal. What we find, if anything, will be totally your discovery, so let's get on with it shall we?" and with that Tom handed the hammer drill which was now connected to the generator to Henry, who placed the drill bit on the centre of the wall and pressing the trigger, began to drill.

The bit passed easily through the soft red bricks and at a depth of nine inches, suddenly broke through. Almost immediately it came up against another obstacle but one which felt entirely different in nature to the brickwork. Henry immediately withdrew the drill and looked enquiringly at both Tom and Gordon, who were watching with bated breath.

"Well what now?" he said. "A very short distance beyond the bricks, the drill came up against something else. My guess it is wood of some sort, but I could be wrong."

"We were a least right in our assumption of the wall's thickness, which means the infilling was done from this side. The first thing to do now is to get a torch and see if we can see anything through the hole you've drilled Hal. We couldn't see anything like that with Sally's when we did it, but that was because there was nothing to be seen, only the void in the cellar. Here we have something very close to the wall so we should be able to see what it is. Failing that, our next move will be to break the brickwork out further." Gordon was trying to peer in the hole but could see nothing.

They called to Steve, who was sitting drinking a beer in the conservatory with Sally and Jenny, asking him to bring a flashlight down to them, Sally found the light and brought it down herself.

"So what have you found so far?" she asked.

"Where's Steve, I thought he was going to be involved down here?" Tom sounded a little irritated.

"He's enjoying a beer and a chat with Jenny and unless you find another grave, I think that's where he'll stay!" Sally laughed. "Not the most adventuress is our Steve. I repeat what have you found?"……

"I'll let you know as soon as I've shone that light you're carrying through the hole that Hal has made." Tom held out his hand, took the light and held it up to the hole. For a little while he moved it around trying to get a view of what lay beyond the wall. Finally he gave up, "It looks like the side of a barrel, or something like that, but I really can't be sure. It's certainly wooden, but we need to enlarge the hole to be able to see properly. It could simply be material used to fill the hole from the other side."

"Let me drill a few more holes, Tom," suggested Henry, "and we'll break out a few bricks and see what's beyond. If we don't make it too big a hole, we can easily block it up again if needs be."

"OK, go ahead but be careful not to let the bit get away from you on the other side!" Tom said warningly.

"Tom, you should know that I was doing work like this, with tools like these when you were still in school. My property business started with places like this. I'm sorry if that sounds in any way pompous, I don't mean it to be, but I'd just like you to know that you don't have to worry, OK?" Henry said quietly.

Tom grinned at him, "Sorry Hal, I get carried away sometimes and never think that others know as much, or more than I do. Please carry on."

Henry drilled four more holes, each one penetrating beyond nine inches and then with the spade and chisel attached to the Kango hammer, he broke out the centre of the bricks. The hole now cleared was about nine inches square and gave, with the use of the torch, a clear view of what lay on the other side. Henry was of course the first to get a clear look, but then each in turn followed. What they saw appeared to be the bottom of two wooden barrels. Above and below these two there appeared to be more, but beyond, they couldn't see, but it appeared that there were similar stacks in front.

"You appreciate that what you've discovered here my friends." Said Henry, "is a store of contraband goods, of that I have no doubt. However, there is a small danger that these barrels could contain something other than strong drink, they could bed filled with gun-powder!"

"What?" came a chorus of voices from the others?

"I don't think it's likely, but I'm simply warning you all that we should be careful."

"OK, you're quite right Hal, let's expect the worst and avoid anything which is likely to be hazardous." Said Tom. "If you are happy to carry on Hal, I suggest that we break out the remainder of the opening and see the extent of what we've found."

"Hal darling, do be careful. If that's what you think, surely anything can set if off." Sally stood close to her fiancé and held his arm.

"Even if it were filled with gunpowder, it would need a naked flame to set the stuff off and we're not using rush lights, nor candles, or oil lamps to see, we're using electric light, so there really is no danger. Even a spark would be unlikely to penetrate a barrel, and in any case I'm convinced that these barrels contain liquids rather than powder." Hal squeezed Sally's hand and picking up the breaker again, commenced enlarging the hole.

An hour later after careful excavation, the doorway was clear exposing the bases of numerous wooden barrells laid on their sides and stacked on top of one another. It appeared that beyond these were more barrels stacked in a similar way. There was nothing for it but to remove the first stack of barrels in order to see further into what appeared to be a tunnel shaped addition to the cellar. Carefully, they lifted out the barrels and stacked them in Walnut Tree's cellar in a similar way to that in which they had been found. They then removed the next stack and then the next. To this point they had removed thirty six barrels and still had no idea of what they contained.

"Have you noticed," said Steve who together with Jenny had by this time joined the others in the cellar. "That the barrels are of different weights? Some are quite heavy while others are quite light. Why do you think that is?"

Henry answered Steve. "Almost certainly the light ones are so due to evaporation. I don't think any of them are full, but I do think it's time to open one or two of them and find out what they contain. After two hundred years, nothing drinkable I'll be bound. Tom, how would you like to do the honours?"

Tom went out to his car and returned with a bag of tools. He took out a screwdriver and prized out the wooden bung in the centre of the side of one of the lighter barrels. Rolling it over to one side, what came out eventually was a viscous material, not unlike molasses. It might have smelt of a spirit, but it was a long time since it had been one. The next barrel, appeared more promising, when the liquid which flowed from it appeared to be a tawny colour and smelt of brandy. "Now that's more like it," Gordon proclaimed as he dipped his finger in the liquid and tasted it. "I'm no connoisseur of brandy, but there's no doubt that it what this is and not too bad either."

Henry was next to taste it and agreed that it wasn't bad, he wouldn't want to offer it to guests after dinner though! Everyone now had a little taste if only for the novelty. After all how many can say that they've tasted a two hundred year old brandy?

"So, what do we do now?" asked Gordon. "Do we have to report this finding of a hoard of illicit spirits etc.? I hope it won't mean a huge bill of duty evaded with compounded interest over two centuries!" Everybody laughed. "Not after Customs and Excise have tasted it!" said Henry.

"I think what we've got to discover is the extent of this new cellar." Said Sally. "At present we can't even see how long it is, or what else is in it."

"It looks to me rather like a tunnel than a cellar." Said Tom. "Look at the arched roof."

They all agreed, but it was Jenny who said, "correct me if my sense of direction is wrong, Steve always says that I can't read a map or a plan, but that direction," and as she pointed towards the opening which had been made, "is straight towards Blackmore House, or as Sally has discovered *The Black Boy!*"

"Jen sweetheart, you're right! This has to be a tunnel connecting the two! Now we're getting somewhere in this investigation!" Steve hugged his girlfriend.

"So, let's clear the tunnel and find out what's at the other end." Exclaimed Tom.

Sally said, "I hope you won't be too disappointed Tom. According to my father, this London Solicitor had the cellar there filled in back in the 1970's, so I don't think that we will find very much by way of access that end!"

"Let's find out then shall we? Come on everyone, lend a hand and we'll bring everything in there out here," said an enthusiastic Tom, indicating the cellar in which they stood.

The four men formed a line and began removing barrel after barrel until they had a total of over seventy stacked in Walnut Tree's cellar. Then came some bales of what might have been tobacco stalks and leaves. These were so flimsy and brittle, that they began to collapse as they tried move them, and so had to be pushed to one side in the space now made by the removal of the barrels.

At the far end of the tunnel was a stout wooden door, firmly locked from the other side.

"I think we know where that once led to, so there's little point in trying to open it, but it is there Sal?" said Tom. "The only thing I'd question is, if that is all that's between us and *The Black Boy*'s cellar, why ever did the chap fill it in without taking a look in here first? A mystery, which no doubt won't be solved now."

Henry meanwhile had been inspecting the area to the side of the door. Here hadn't been a stack of contraband, it was almost as though the area had been cleared. Leaning against the wall in the corner was an ancient long handled shovel, the shaft of which had been turned to powder with woodworm, which had been dining on it. A shallow hollow in the ground indicated that something had been buried there and at the head of this hollow lay a pewter tankard, which might once have held some sort of plant or plants. There were strands of material inside and around it and on the ground a scattering of seeds.

He called the attention of the others, who were grouped around the door, to what he was looking at in the corner. "I fear that we have stumble upon another grave Sally," he said almost apologetically to his fiancé, "smaller than the one next door, but a grave nonetheless." Hal put his arm around Sally's shoulders. "I know that this is the last thing you've wanted to find, so the sooner we get the proper authorities into sort it out the better, I suggest that for today, we call it a day and go back into the daylight and all have a good stiff drink of something other than that two hundred year old brandy!"

THE BLACK BOY

LOVERS REUNITED

No more work was done in the cellar that weekend and first thing on Monday morning, Henry persuaded Steve to contact the Coroner's office. "So much better coming from Steve after the last time, they'll already have you on their files as the GP of every skeleton found around here!"

"Thanks very much Hal, before you know it I'll have patients calling me Shipton!"

This time the Coroner was quicker off the mark and that afternoon, the same Mr Williams arrived with his two assistants and accompanied by the police car and two constables.

After he had been introduced to Henry, Mr Williams asked, "So what have you found this time Miss Parmenter? Another possible body I understand. Have you unearthed it yet?"

"No, definitely not, we leave that job to you chaps. Of course, it might not be a body at all." She replied.

"Shall I lead the way down there Mr Williams?" offered Henry. "I'm afraid our Doctor friend Dr McDonald hasn't arrived yet, but he was awaiting our phone call so he may be a little while as he's out on his rounds."

Sally, seeing that the men all seemed to be waiting for the cup of coffee which they had enjoyed last time, said "coffee for everyone? I'll have it ready for you when you've finished in the cellar, but I'd like to be present this time when you uncover whatever it is that's there."

In the cellar, everyone was both amazed and excited to see the extraordinary pile of contraband that Sally and her friends had unearthed. Briefly, Henry told them how to hoard had been discovered and he led them into the tunnel where it had been found.

"This is fascinating," said Mr Williams, inspecting the vaulted ceiling, "I wonder when this was built, beautiful bit of brickwork. And this was full, as you say of those barrels."

Henry nodded, "yes, from the floor to the ceiling at this end, the end we came in. There were also several of those," he pointed to the remains of the tobacco which now lay in what looked like heaps of autumn leaves, where they had been pushed against the side of the walls. "That is, or was I suspect, tobacco. However, at this other end, we found this." He walked to the far end and pointed to the shallow depression and to the pewter mug. "I believe, before you start with your excavation and make your own assessment, that the tankard once contained flowers, and that they were placed at the head of the grave by whoever dug it and did the burying. Now Miss Parmenter and I will watch you if we may, while you carry out your investigation." Henry took Sally's arm and stepped back out of the way to watch.

After taking the preliminary photographs, Mr Williams carefully removed the tankard and set it to one side and moved out of the way to let his two assistants start digging. This grave was even shallower than the one next door had been. Little more than a few inches of soil lay over the remains. Once the earth was removed, the contents of the grave was revealed. Lying there was the skeleton of a young woman, in whose arms lay that of a child – a newly born baby it would have been as to the size of it. They lay on and had been covered by what appears to have been a coarsely woven mat. The left hand of the woman held that of the baby and a ring, several sizes too large for her small hand, was on her wedding finger. Across the face of the ring was engraved the one word HORNE.

The Coroner's report followed a few days later, again sent to Steve who had not actually been present at the exhumation, although he had arrived later when they were carrying out the bodies. It stated that there were cut marks to the tender bones of the baby, consistent with having been stabbed viciously and further cut marks on the lower spine and pelvis of the woman were of a similar nature. The conclusion was drawn that the baby had probably been stabbed whilst still in the womb, although it was soon to be born, having reached the age of full gestation. The woman had been around seventeen or eighteen years of age when she died. Regarding the belongings found in the grave, there was very little. The clothing was that of a working girl of the eighteenth century, although much of it was unrecognizable. The coroner found a ring of interest, when it so closely resembled the one found in William Horne's grave. There is nothing else.

Identification was impossible, but the report assumed that as the rings in the two graves were similar, then the bodies were probably related. A DNA test had been ordered but the result was a yet unavailable.

Henry had been back in France on Friday of that week and that evening, he and Sally sat in the conservatory enjoying the last rays of the evening sun. "Hal I've not stopped thinking about the two, no three bodies. It is plain as a pikestaff that they are somehow related, but before we hear the DNA result, try this;" She sat back comfortably and gazed through the glass at the few stars which were beginning to appear in the May heavens.

"Carry on Darling, I've got all night and I can see by your position that this may take that long." Hal also took a reclining position on the settee.

Sally ignored him. "First of all we find William. He is a big man who has been buried by his friends. On his finger, his little finger, we find a ring with HORNE on it. We know that he was hung for murdering his wife. Why did he kill her?" She stopped for a moment, gathering her thoughts. "Next we find the body of a young woman and baby, both apparently brutally murdered, by WHOM? On the wedding finger of the unfortunate young woman we find another ring also with HORNE on it. This time, the ring is far too large for the woman's finger, more like that worn by someone with a big hand." She dropped her gaze from the stars to Hal's face. "So what do you conclude from that?" She asked him.

"That somehow the rings were swapped?"

"How and why should they have been?"

"Alright, so perhaps someone by the name of Horne, put his and I say his because of the size of the ring, on the dead girl's finger."

"OK, so how come the smaller ring is on William's hand?"

Henry paused for a moment. "Another family member of his family must have put it there when he was buried? I really can't think of any other explanation. Perhaps all the family members had one of these rings?"

"I don't know about the last bit Hal, but you're brilliant, that's exactly what I came up with. I believe that she was William's woman and the baby his. She couldn't have been his wife on two counts. One; if he was hung for murdering her, how come her body was not found for proof; and two; more importantly, why was the girl laid so carefully in her grave with her new born dead baby - I think that who ever buried William was as you say, a relation."

It was to be another week and only two before Sally and Henry's wedding, that the DNA report came through. The child was undoubtedly that of William Horne. A request from Sally for the release of all three bodies for re-burial in Danbury Churchyard was approved by the Coroner's Office and the internment agreed with the vicar. He had initially been undecided with the Coroners over William, who might or might not have been guilty of murder, but following the eloquent arguments raised by Henry and then by Sally, he capitulated.

"Who are we to judge so long after an event and everything you have told me points to a very poignant love story. Yes, I shall be happy to bury these poor souls. The thing is when?"

"It's got to be within the next two weeks, because as you know you're reading our banns at the moment, we are to be married here in a fortnight's time!" Sally said.

On the following Monday, a vehicle from the Coroner's office arrived at the Church. Inside was a coffin within which were the bones of all three bodies. Before being carried to the grave, which had already been dug, Sally asked to see inside the coffin. The lid was raised and she saw that her request with Mr Williams had been granted. On the fingers of the left hands of the two adults was a ring with HORNE engraved on them.

CUTTING FROM THE ESSEX CHRONICLE
10th June 2005

'200 YEAR OLD BODIES FOUND BURIED
IN DANBURY'

Three bodies that had been discovered buried beneath a cottage in Danbury were re-interred in the graveyard at Danbury on Monday last.

The Eighteenth Century skeletons of a man, woman and a baby were discovered in a cellar by the owner of the house Miss Sally Parmenter, whilst making alterations on her home.

The identity of the bodies is likely to remain a mystery, although the name Horne seems to have been associated with at least one of the bodies. However, since the area within which they were discovered, was originally known as Horne Row, there appears to be some confusion.

When interviewed Miss Parmenter, who is to be married next week to Property Tycoon, Henry Phillips; said that a suitable memorial would eventually be erected at the grave, but would not be committed to names. DNA results show that at least two of the bodies were related.

LOVERS REUNITED